Joan Jonker was born and bred in Liverpool. She is a tireless campaigner for the charity-run organisation Victims of Violence, and she lives in Southport with her husband and son. She has two sons and two grandsons.

Joan Jonker is that author of *Victims of Violence*, and two further novels, *Man Of The House* and *Home Is Where The Heart Is*, which continue the story of this engaging group of Liverpool friends. Her affectionate and humorous tales have already won her many fans in her hometown and they are sure to delight readers everywhere.

When One Door Closes

Joan Jonker

HEADLINE

First published in paperback in 1991
by Print Origination (NW) Ltd

First published in hardback in 1994
by HEADLINE BOOK PUBLISHING

Reprinted in this edition in 1994
by HEADLINE BOOK PUBLISHING

20 19 18 17 16 15 14

ISBN 0 7472 4551 7

Typeset by Keyboard Services, Luton

Printed and bound in Great Britain by
Clays Ltd, St Ives plc

HEADLINE BOOK PUBLISHING
A division of Hodder Headline PLC
338 Euston Road
London NW1 3BH

To my dear husband for his understanding during my writing, also to Mary Johnson whose wonderful help and patience helped me to put commas and full stops in the right places.

Chapter One

Mary bent her head against the wind and wrapped her edge to edge coat more closely round her slim body. It was more like winter than spring, and her feet moved faster as she thought of the hot cup of tea waiting for her at home. And with a bit of luck her mam might have scrounged enough coal together to have a fire lit. How she hated this two to ten shift. Life was all bed and work.

It was pitch dark as Mary hurried along the maze of streets with their two-up-two-down houses, and her high heels tapping the paving stones were the only sound breaking the stillness. In rhythm with her feet her long blonde curls bounced up and down on her shoulders. A gust of wind blew strands of hair across her face and as Mary brushed it aside the strap of her gas mask fell from her shoulder. Blasted gas mask, she muttered, pulling it back. I wish me mam wouldn't make me take it everywhere with me.

There were no street lights burning, nor were there any chinks of light through the drawn curtains of the houses. But Mary knew these streets like the back of her hand and could have walked home from the bus stop blindfolded. It was May 1941, and by now everyone was used to the blackout, the rationing and the wail of the air-raid siren. That was the one thing Mary dreaded most . . . the wail of the air-raid warning. Liverpool had been getting a hammering from the German bombers every night for weeks, but thank God none of the bombs had dropped near where she lived.

I hope there's no raid tonight, Mary thought, as her long slim legs covered the ground quickly. I'm so tired I don't think I'd even hear the siren. A smile tugged the corners of her mouth. Not that me mam would let me sleep through it. She'd drag me out of bed if she had to.

Reaching the small terraced house, Mary let herself into the tiny hall. She was closing the door behind her when a frown creased her forehead and her head cocked to one side. Voices? No, everywhere was quiet. It must have been next door's wireless she heard.

Walking in from the darkness, Mary was blinded for a few seconds until her eyes became accustomed to the glare from the electric light. Then she smiled when she saw her mother sitting in her armchair at the side of the grate where a fire burned brightly. 'Oh, Mam, that fire looks lovely! It's so cold . . .' Mary had turned to close the door when she saw the soldier sitting on the opposite side of the hearth. Her mouth gaped. 'Bob! When did you get home?'

'A few hours ago.' Bob's grin was wide. 'You should see your face! You look as though you've seen a ghost!'

Without taking her eyes from him, Mary slipped out of her coat and threw it over the back of a chair. 'Why didn't you let me know you were coming?' Bob's eyes held hers briefly, then looked away. 'How about making that cup of tea, Mrs B? I don't half miss your tea when I'm away.'

'Never mind the tea!' Mary frowned. 'Why didn't you let me know you were coming home?'

'I'll put the kettle on.' Martha Bradshaw rose, smoothing down the front of her floral pinny. She smiled at her daughter. 'You must be dying for a drink.' With her snow-white hair, Martha looked much older than her forty-six years. The deep lines etched on her forehead and the sadness in her faded blue eyes told their story of suffering and heartache. It was hard to believe that only eight years ago Martha Bradshaw's hair had been the same golden blonde as Mary's. That the eyes had been the same vivid blue, and her pretty face had never been far from a smile. Her world had been so happy then, with a husband she adored and a daughter they both idolised. When George had come home from work one day saying he didn't feel well, Martha had no idea it was the beginning of the end of her perfect world. She had nursed him for twelve desperate, nightmare months, before he died of TB at the age of thirty-eight. Within weeks Martha's hair had turned white. During those first weeks all she had wanted to do was die herself. But it was Mary who made her carry on, and who kept her sane. Mary, who at fourteen couldn't understand why her dad had been taken from them, needed all the love Martha could give. They had clung to one another then, and the strong bond between mother and daughter had never weakened.

On her way to the kitchen Martha laid her hand on Bob's

shoulder. 'I'm making some toast, son, d'you want some?'

'What do you think, Mrs B? Have you ever known me to refuse anything except blows?'

As soon as the kitchen door closed, Mary knelt in front of Bob. 'What's going on? I know there's something up by me mam's face.'

Bob West stared down at his clasped hands. 'I'm on a twenty-four-hour pass, love, and I couldn't let you know because I didn't know meself until the very last minute.' He rubbed his thumb gently over her slim fingers. 'I've got to go back on the six o'clock train from Lime Street.'

'But it's time to go back before you get here!'

'Our unit's on stand-by,' Bob said softly. 'We're being shipped out soon.'

'Shipped out!' Mary's voice rose. 'Shipped out where?'

'I don't know, love! They don't tell us anything.' There was no mirth in Bob's laugh. 'Being a poor private, I'm not in on the secret.'

Mary shivered. 'You're not going where the fighting is, are you?'

Bob stroked her face. 'You look pale tonight.'

'You mean I look a sight!' Mary suddenly grinned. 'If I'd known you were going to be here, I'd have combed me hair and put some lippy on.'

Bob fingered the golden hair before cupping her face between his hands and kissing her gently on the forehead. Seeing them together for the first time a stranger could easily take them for brother and sister. Their hair was the same blond colour and their eyes the same vivid blue. But while Bob's face was square and rugged, Mary's was heart

4

shaped. She wasn't just pretty, she was beautiful. Her wide eyes were fringed with thick black lashes beneath perfectly arched eyebrows that needed no help from tweezers or eyebrow pencils. Her skin was flawless, and when she smiled she revealed a set of small, white, even teeth. While Bob was tall, over six foot, and thick set, Mary was five foot four and slim. She had a tiny waist that Bob could span with his hands, and a firm full bust. Every time he looked at her, Bob told himself he was the luckiest bloke alive that she'd chosen him when she could have had her pick of any of the lads in the neighbourhood.

Mary drew his hands from her face and held them tight. 'They can't just give you twenty-four hours embarkation leave . . . it's not fair!'

'Nothing is fair in war, love.' Bob sighed. 'All I know is there's a lot of activity at the camp, and over the last few days several units have been shipped out.'

'And when the war started everyone said it wouldn't last long.' Mary dropped her gaze. She felt frightened inside. What would she do if anything happened to Bob? She couldn't imagine life without him because he'd been part of it for so long. His family only lived a few streets away and they'd played together as kids. They'd started school the same day, and left the same day to take up jobs locally. Mary had gone to work behind the counter in a sweet shop, while Bob started as an apprentice with a furniture manufacturer. They'd each had their own friends but would meet at dances at Barlows Lane or the Aintree Institute. One night Bob had asked her for the last waltz and as they were dancing he'd asked if he could walk her home. As they stood outside her house he'd suddenly bent forward and kissed her on the cheek before hurrying away, red faced with embarrassment. He'd been shy the next time they'd met, but when Mary treated him as she'd always done, he became bold and asked if he could take her home. That night his lips had brushed past her cheeks and landed, for a second, on her lips. Neither had spoken, but, as Bob walked away and Mary opened her front door, they both knew their relationship had changed. And a week later they started to date without their friends.

The kitchen door was pushed open and Martha bustled in. 'I've made enough toast for both of you, so eat it before it gets cold.' She smiled at Bob as she set the tray down. 'No sugar I'm afraid, son! We've used all our ration till next week.' Stifling a yawn with the back of her hand, she looked at Mary. 'I'm off to bed, I'm dead beat.'

'It's not that late, Mam!' Mary jumped up. 'Have a cup of tea first.'

'No, I really am tired.' After patting her daughter's arm, Martha turned to Bob. 'I won't see you before you leave, then?'

'Afraid not, Mrs B, I've got to be on that six o'clock train.' Seeing the concern on the face of the woman who was like a second mother to him, Bob joked. 'Can't have them thinking I've gone AWOL, can we?'

Martha ruffled his hair. 'Look after yourself.' She gave a last smile before closing the door and mounting the narrow stairs. Twenty-two years of age and being sent off to war . . . it just wasn't right! By God, that Hitler had a lot to answer for! She stopped on the top stair to catch her breath and sighed deeply. Surely there was enough sadness in the world without people fighting each other.

Mary stacked the dishes on the wooden draining board. Any other night she would have rinsed them through, but every second she could spend with Bob was precious. He was sitting on the floor in front of the fire when she ran back in the room, his back leaning against the couch. 'Put the light out, love. It's nice sitting in the firelight.' He waited till Mary was nestled beside him then slipped an arm across her shoulders. 'Now, let's have all your news.'

'Oh, I lead a very exciting life, and I don't think!' Mary pulled a face. 'Unless you call sitting in next door's air-raid shelter every night exciting.' She snuggled closer. 'Tell me what you do with yourself.'

'Go for a pint with me mates. There's quite a few lads from Liverpool in our unit, and we have a good laugh.' Bob squeezed her shoulder. 'That Spud Murphy from the Dingle is a real case; he's always playing jokes on people and there's never a dull moment when he's around.'

'You've got a flamin' cheek, Bob West!' Mary dug him in the ribs. 'Going out every night and getting blotto, while I'm stuck in work or in next door's shelter!'

It was cosy sitting in front of the fire holding hands, but as the minutes ticked by Mary could feel the nerves in her tummy tightening. 'I wonder when we'll be able to take the ferry across the Mersey again? Remember when we used to go to Seacombe and walk from there to New Brighton? We had some good times, didn't we?' There was a sob in Mary's voice. 'Are you sure you're being sent overseas? Perhaps you're just moving to another camp.'

'No such luck, love! This is one of the camps where units are shipped out from. I knew as soon as we were sent there that it wouldn't be long before we were on the move.' Bob was silent for a few seconds. 'You can understand all the secrecy though, because if they told us where and when we were going, they might just as well tell the Germans and they could have their subs ready and waiting to pick us off.' He felt Mary's shiver. 'Don't you worry about me, Mary Bradshaw! You won't get rid of me that easy. I'll be home before you know it, and I intend marrying you quick, before someone else snaps you up.'

'You better had!' Mary was running her fingers through his thick, coarse hair. 'I've started me bottom drawer already. I went to Paddy's market with Eileen last week and bought a tea set and some towels.' Giving his hair a gentle pull, she laughed. 'You should see the spivs down there. They look like gangsters with their trilby hats and long overcoats. I don't know where they get the stuff from, but you can get anything from them if you've got the money. They're making a packet out of the war.'

Bob took his arm from her shoulders to light a cigarette and Mary stared at the dying coals in the grate. He'll be going soon, she thought, and God knows when I'll see him again. When he'd first been called up he'd been stationed at Speke, which was only a few miles away, and he'd been able to get home a few times a week. Even when he was sent down South he'd been home every few weeks on leave. But now he was going overseas the war took on a new meaning to Mary. She'd seen pictures of the fighting on the Pathe News at the pictures, and the thought of Bob being in the thick of it terrified her.

Overwhelmed with emotion, Mary pulled Bob's face down to hers and rained kisses on it. Suddenly they were locked in each other's arms, straining to get as close as they could. 'I love you, Mary Bradshaw,' Bob whispered as he flicked his cigarette into the grate before easing her backwards until she was lying on the floor wrapped in his arms. He caressed her face and neck, and when his hand brushed accidentally against her breast a tingle, almost like an electric shock, ran through his body and passion raged high within him. What would he do if she met someone else while he was away? He looked down at the lovely face, the thick dark eyelashes fanning her cheeks, and his love for her overpowered him. His lips came down hard on hers as he moved sideways to tear at the buttons on his trousers. The coarse material of his uniform and his awkward position made it difficult and he pulled frantically, almost ripping the buttons off. It was as the last button gave way that a bomb seemed to explode in his head, clearing his mind. 'What the hell am I doing?' he whispered. He thought of her mother asleep upstairs, trusting him not to do anything to harm her daughter, and shame flooded his body. He mustn't betray that trust. He bent to kiss Mary gently, but the second their lips met his love and his need surged like a tidal wave, and Martha was forgotten.

Bob's hand up her dress sent warning signals to Mary's brain. 'No!' Quickly her arm moved from his neck to push his hand away. 'You mustn't.' But Bob was past the point of reason. All he could think of was going away and leaving her. It might be years before he held her in his arms again ... if ever! 'Please, Mary?' His voice was thick with emotion. 'I love you so much.' Mary screwed her eyes up. What he wanted to do was a sin and against everything she'd ever been taught. But she loved him so much she couldn't bear to refuse him. Sighing deeply, her arms went round his neck and she held him tight.

The fire had died down, sparing Bob the embarrassment of meeting Mary's eyes. His hands trembling, he fumbled for his packet of Capstan and struck a match. As he drew hard on the cigarette he recalled snatches of conversation he'd heard between blokes in the barracks. He'd learned that some women didn't like sex, and that was why a few of the men went with other women. Bob started to tremble inside. After what he'd just done, would Mary's feeling towards him have changed? He forced himself to turn and ask, 'All right, love?'

Racked with guilt and shame, Mary slipped an arm through his. 'Me mam would kill me if she knew.'

'It's my fault, love. I shouldn't have let it happen.' Bob reached for her hand. 'I wish we'd got married last time I was on leave.'

Mary's laugh was shaky. 'You'll have to marry me now to make an honest woman of me.' Her voice was wistful. 'I wish you were back in civvie street.'

'Me too! But if everyone felt the same way then Hitler would walk through this country as easily as he's walked through the rest of Europe.'

'I know, but I'm frightened of anything happening to you.'

'Nothing's going to happen to me!' Bob pulled playfully on her hair. 'With you to come back to, I'll outrun every German bullet there is. Anyway, what about yourself? It's not exactly safe around here with bombs dropping every night. Gerry's after the docks and the munitions factory, and this is not far from either of them. I know Spud Murphy's worried to death about his family because they live near the docks at the South End. So, while I'm busy looking after meself, will you promise to go to the shelter every time there's a raid?'

'I don't have much option with me mam around.' Mary's brow creased. 'I've just realised, this is the first night we haven't had a raid for weeks!'

Bob chuckled. 'I gave orders that I didn't want me leave spoilt.' He moved his arm from her shoulder and struck a match. 'Oh, lord, it's nearly four o'clock! I'll have to make tracks or I'll miss the train.'

'Just stay for a few more minutes.' Mary clung to his arm. 'We've only had a couple of hours and it might be ages before I see you again.'

'I wouldn't need much persuading, love, so don't coax me, please!' Bob prised his arm free. 'By the time I get cleaned up and have a few minutes with me mam and dad, I'm going to be hard pushed. There's a tram leaves Fazakerly terminus at five o'clock and it gets here at twenty past. I'll have to be on that to get to Lime Street station for six.'

'Let me come to the station with you.' Mary pleaded. 'At

11

least we'd have a bit more time together.'

'I'm not saying goodbye to you on a crowded station platform.' Bob stood up and switched the light on. He held her at arm's length. 'I don't want anyone around when I tell you I love you more than anything in the world, and I'll be counting the days until I'm home again and we can get married.'

'You better had marry me, or I'll tell me mam and she'll come after you with a shot gun.' Mary gazed into the features she knew as well as she knew her own. The thick bushy eyebrows she was always kidding him were long enough to put in curlers. The blue eyes that crinkled up when he laughed or shone with tenderness when he looked at her. He was smiling now, showing the gap where a kick during a football game had robbed him of one of his teeth. Her heart swelled with love as she stood on tiptoe to kiss him. 'I love you, Bob West.'

'I'd better go! You're very tempting, Mary Bradshaw,' Bob reached for the door, 'and I'm crazy about you.'

Trained to be careful of the black-out, Mary switched off the light before opening the front door. Standing on the top step, she went to put her arms around Bob's neck but he gripped her shoulders and held her from him. 'Don't forget to go to the shelter when there's a raid on, d'you hear? Otherwise I'll be worried to death every time I hear there's been a raid on Liverpool.' He bent his head, kissed her briefly, and whispered 'I love you', before hurrying away.

Mary watched till he reached the end of the block, and when he turned and blew her a kiss she blew one in return. Then he was out of sight. Mary stood for a few seconds staring down the deserted street then walked slowly back into the house. Inside, she leaned against the door and closed her eyes. The tears came slowly at first, trickling down her cheeks. Then they were gushing from her eyes as great sobs racked her body. Afraid of waking her mother, she tried to stifle the sound by putting a hand across her mouth. But she felt the beating of her heart was louder than her tears, and she had no control over her heart.

Chapter Two

Eileen Gillmoss was joining the end of the bus queue when she saw the familiar figure of Mary in the distance. 'Blimey! She's feelin' energetic!' Ignoring the curious glances coming her way, she set off after her friend. Puffing and panting she urged her eighteen-stone body forward, but Mary was walking faster and the distance between them grew. 'She'll be at the bloody Black Bull before I catch her up.' Then Mary stopped to look in a shop window and Eileen breathed a sigh of relief. Cupping her hands round her mouth, she bellowed, 'Hey, kid! Hold yer horses, will yer!'

Mary turned. She could see Eileen's face red with exertion as her huge body waddled from side to side. 'You walking, too?'

Small rivers of sweat trickled down Eileen's face as she panted, 'I didn't intend bloody walkin' till I saw you. Yer can't half move, kid! Yer like a bloody whippet!' She grinned and linked her arm through Mary's. 'Yer can help carry some of me weight.'

Mary's eyes slid sideways. Over the last eighteen months Eileen had been a very good friend to her. She lived in the same street as Bob, but Mary had only really got to know her when she started work in the munitions factory and had been put on the same machine as Eileen. That first day had been terrible. The huge conveyor belt looked like a monster and the noise on the shop floor was deafening. It was so different to working behind a shop counter, Mary thought she'd never get used to it. And she wouldn't have done if Eileen, fifteen years her senior, hadn't taken her in hand and shown her the ropes.

'What made yer decide to walk to the Bull, kid?' Eileen always looked untidy, as though she'd dashed out of the house without even running a comb through her mousey coloured, straggly hair. The hem on her shabby, grey swagger coat had come undone in places and was hanging down. And her black, flat heeled shoes looked as if they'd fall to pieces if they saw a duster or polish. 'Won't yer get enough standin' on yer feet in work?'

'I felt like some fresh air.' Mary looked straight ahead. 'Bob was home and I was late getting to bed.'

'Home on leave, is he?'

'He had to go back this morning. He only had a twenty-four pass.'

'Bloody hell! Wasn't worth coming home for.' Eileen noticed Mary's pale face. 'Course it was worth it! When yer in love, ten minutes is worth it.'

'It was embarkation leave. He's expecting to be sent overseas.'

'Poor bugger! The sooner this bloody war's over, an' all our lads are home, the better.'

They were passing Woolworths on Walton Vale and

Eileen pulled Mary to a halt. 'Cissie Nolan's on the sweet counter 'ere. I'll see if I can cadge some Liquorice Allsorts off her.'

'Our bus is in,' Mary protested. 'You won't have time.'

Eileen pulled free. 'Two shakes of a lamb's tail, kid!'

Mary kept her eye on the factory bus standing outside the Black Bull pub. If it went without them they'd be late clocking in. But within seconds Eileen reappeared, grumbling, 'Just my bloody luck! She's at her break!'

'I'll go ahead,' Mary was already running. 'I'll keep the bus till you get there.' She was waiting on the platform when Eileen came along, gasping for breath. Pulling herself aboard by the hand rail, Eileen waved Mary ahead of her. 'You go first, kid, and I'll sit on the outside so me backside can hang over the seat.'

Mary was turning sideways in the seat to give her friend more room, when she felt a dig in the ribs. Her eyes followed Eileen's finger pointing to a couple passing the bus window. The man was an American soldier and the woman clinging to his arm was laughing up into his face. 'Look at that brazen bitch!' Eileen's voice carried the full length of the bus and the loud chattering stopped as all eyes focused on the target of Eileen's temper. 'Her feller's out there fightin' for his country and she's knockin' it up to anyone in trousers.' Eileen lowered her voice. 'She deserves a bloody good hidin', and she'll get it if her feller finds out what she's been up to.'

Mary eyed the big woman with genuine affection. God knows, Eileen had more than her share of worry, but she never complained. Her husband, Bill, had been taken

17

prisoner in the fighting in Crete, and all Eileen had been told by the War Office was that he was in a prisoner of war camp. 'Don't you ever get fed-up, Eileen? If I had three kids to look after, and come out to work, I'd never stop moaning.'

Eileen ran her fingers through her hair, making it stand on end. 'Moaning wouldn't get me anywhere, kid. Anyroad, I've got me mam to help with the kids, so we manage all right.'

They showed their passes to the security guards at the gates of the Kirkby factory, and Eileen linked her arm through Mary's. 'There'll be a lot of poor sods in for a shock when this war's over, I can tell yer! There's a woman livin' next door to me auntie, and guess what? She had a baby last week, and her feller's been away for fourteen months.' Eileen whipped her clock card from the rack and punched it in the machine. 'I'd like to be a fly on their wall when she tries to talk her way out of that!'

The noise in the cloakroom was deafening, with thirty women all talking at once. Mary hung her coat under a sign CARELESS TALK COSTS LIVES, and grinned when Eileen's voice rose above the din. 'Bloody hell! It's like walkin' into a chicken coop with all the cacklin' going on.'

'Hark at her!' Maisie Phillips had been talking to her friend, Ethel Hignet, when she heard Eileen's words. Maisie was small and thin, with bleached blonde hair, a heavily powdered and rouged face, and bright orange Tangee lipstick on her thick, full lips. It was difficult to guess Maisie's age, but according to Eileen she'd been thirty-nine for ten years. Her friend Ethel was a foot taller, thin as a bean pole, with overpermed, frizzy black hair. Her face was devoid of colour and her ill-fitting false teeth clicked every time she spoke. 'If we sound like chickens, Ethel,' Maisie asked, 'what would you say she sounded like?'

'Cock of the North.' Ethel's teeth left her gums, then clicked back into place.

Eileen's figure wasn't so noticeable in her loose coat, but without it her huge body seemed to be fighting to get out of the too tight dress. 'Don't mention cocks, Ethel; it brings back too many memories.' Laughing at her own joke, Eileen held her tummy while her whole body shook and her eyes disappeared behind the folds of flesh on her cheeks.

'What does her bust remind you of, Maisie?' Ethel's head was tilted. 'It reminds me of two barrage balloons floating in the wind.'

'Oh yeh!' Maisie giggled as she eyed the bouncing mounds. 'I wondered where I'd seen them before.'

'Yer only jealous, Maisie Phillips.' Eileen wheezed. ''Cos yours are as flat as pancakes.'

Maisie shrugged. 'Aye, I could do with a bit of your bust. Even Mae West would look flat chested next to you.'

The women had formed a circle around the three who were guaranteed to give them a laugh and put them in a happy frame of mind for the eight-hour shift ahead. Mary stood outside the circle ... too shy to join in. But she enjoyed the exchange and when she walked with Eileen on to the shop floor she was feeling much more cheerful.

The women on morning shift left and Mary and Eileen took up their positions on each side of the long conveyor

19

belt. Their job was to pick out any faulty shells as they passed down the conveyor. It was a monotonous job, but you needed to be alert all the time. Letting a faulty shell go through could cost the life of a soldier. Sometimes the women wrote messages on the shells to let the 'lads' know everyone at home was thinking about them. Eileen's messages and crude drawings were always rude and they made Mary blush, but they were guaranteed to bring a smile to the face of a homesick soldier. Everyone working in the munitions factory was conscious of how important their job was. You couldn't fight a war without ammunition, so working overtime was part of the war effort and no-one complained.

Mary was thinking about Bob as she watched the shells go by. He'd be back at camp now, and if he wrote right away she'd get a letter the day after tomorrow. On the other side of the machine Eileen was taking the mickey out of one of the labourers who was replacing the full trolley of faulty shells with an empty one. 'How d'yer manage yer love life on this shift, Willy?'

Willy Turnley was thirty-nine years of age and would never be called up because of his asthma. He was a small, thin, sickly looking man, with beady brown eyes and large, yellow coloured teeth. He'd lost all the hair from the top of his head, so he let the sides grow long and combed them over in an attempt to hide the baldness. He thought he was God's gift to women, and Eileen liked nothing better than to pull his leg. One of the wheels on the trolley had a mind of its own, wanting to go in a different direction to the others, and Willy bent to fix it before answering. 'I don't do so bad! If I get away handy I can get to Barlows Lane before the last waltz.' He pushed down the packet of five Woodbines sticking out of the breast pocket of his overalls and showed his yellow teeth in a grin. 'It's the last waltz that's important, yer see.'

'Always get a click, do yer, Willy?' Eileen's eyes slid from the conveyor. 'I bet the girls queue up for yer to take them home.'

'I can't complain.' He smirked. The war was the best thing that had ever happened to Willy. With the shortage of men, even he could 'cop off'.

As she turned back to the conveyor, Eileen saw their supervisor walking towards Mary. She leaned forward and bawled, 'Ay out! Here comes lover boy.' Mary glared, but didn't have time to answer before Harry Sedgemoor was standing beside her. She'd known Harry all her life because they lived only a few doors away from each other. But he was five years older, so had never been one of their gang. She knew he'd tried to join the Army but had been turned down because of perforated ear drums. He was a tall handsome man, with jet black hair, deep brown eyes, a strong jaw, white teeth and a dimple in his chin. Unmarried, he was the target for every female in the inspection department ... even the married ones. They fell over themselves to flirt with him, but although he was pleasant with everyone, as far as Mary knew he had never been out with any of the women he worked with.

Harry checked every conveyor twice during each shift, and if he stayed longer by Mary's machine she put it down to their being neighbours. But Eileen had noticed the hungry look in his eyes when he was near Mary and she pulled her friend's leg about it.

'Hello, Harry.' Mary glanced at him briefly. 'Everything all right?'

Harry nodded. 'How are things with you?' Someone had told him they'd seen Bob yesterday, and he waited now to see if Mary would tell him. But when she walked down the conveyor, saying over her shoulder, 'I'm fine!' he had little option but to carry on to the next machine.

As soon as he was out of earshot, Eileen clapped her hands to attract Mary's attention. 'He doesn't half fancy you, yer know! Yer better watch out!'

Mary shook her head vigorously. 'Knock it off, will you, Eileen! It's not like that at all! I've known him all me life and he's like a big brother.'

Eileen whooped. 'There's nowt brotherly about his feelings for you, my girl! He wouldn't need much encouragement to push Bob's nose out of joint.'

'Fat chance!' Mary huffed. 'He'd be wasting his time.'

'Time is something he's got plenty of.' Eileen's voice never seemed to lose its volume, no matter how long she shouted. 'He's not a bad catch, yer know. There's plenty of women would give their eye teeth for him to look at them the way he looks at you. He's handsome, got a good job, and, more important, he's here!'

Mary tapped a finger on the side of her head to indicate she thought Eileen was barmy for thinking Harry Sedgemoor could hold a candle to her Bob.

After their half hour dinner break the rest of the shift flew over and it seemed no time at all before they were stepping off the bus and Eileen was walking to the bottom of Mary's street with her. 'One more shift then I'm off for two glorious days. Ain't that a lovely thought?!' Her voice loud enough to wake the dead, she yelled. 'Ta-ra, kid! See yer tomorrow!' The words were no sooner out of her mouth than the air-raid siren started. 'Oh, Christ, the buggers are at it again! I better get a move on and help me mam get the kids to the shelter.'

Mary was already running up the street. Doors were opening and families pouring out to go to the safety of the Corporation shelter in the park. Children too small to hurry were being swooped up into arms, while the older ones were urged to move more quickly. Searchlights lit up the sky and as Mary neared her home she saw her mother standing on the doorstep.

'Come on, lass; let's get next door before Gerry starts.' Martha was pushing Mary ahead of her through the house. 'I've made a flask of tea so you can have a drink in the shelter.'

Mary laughed as she picked up the big bag standing by the kitchen door. 'Ready for any emergency, aren't you, Mam?'

'Better sure than sorry, lass.' Martha switched the light off and pushed Mary out of the back door. 'They're early tonight. Let's hope it doesn't last long.' They made their way through the temporary gate between the two houses and stumbled down the crude steps into their neighbours' shelter. Fred Smith had had half his back yard dug up, about five feet down into the earth. The walls of the shelter were corrugated iron outside and lined with wood inside. A piece of corrugated iron also served as a roof. It was a home-made affair, and Mary felt they would be just as safe in their own house under the stairs.

Fred and Elsie Smith were already in the shelter with their two sons. Tommy was twelve and Dennis ten. They were huddled on two of the three benches that ran round the walls, and the two boys sounded half asleep, as though they'd just been dragged out of bed. The smell of the damp earth invaded Mary's nostrils and she shivered with the cold. How Mr Smith could stand it she'd never know. He was a chronic asthmatic and sometimes could hardly breathe in the claustrophobic atmosphere. When it was quiet in the shelter you could hear him gasping for air, and Mary was more frightened of him stopping breathing than she was of the German planes.

'They're at it again, Martha.' Elsie Smith's whining voice matched the rest of her. In all the years they'd been neighbours, Mary had never heard Elsie Smith give a hearty laugh. It was too dark in the shelter to see her, but Mary could picture how she'd look. Her sparse grey hair would be snatched back from her face and tied in a bun. And her pinched face would be sunken because she'd have left her false teeth in a cup at the side of the bed. She was a miserable woman was Elsie Smith. Old before her time.

'Let's hope it's a false alarm.' Martha reached for the blanket Mary had taken from the bag. 'Give it here, lass, and sit down and have a drink to warm you up.'

Mary wrapped the blanket over her knees. 'D'you want a drink, Mam?'

'No, thanks, lass. What about you, Elsie? Any of yours want a drink?'

'No, ta, Martha.' Elsie felt Tommy stir and said quickly. 'Oh, no you don't! You'll be wanting to go to the lavvy, and you're not moving till the all-clear goes.'

The hot steam wafted up into Mary's face. She gauged the cup to be half full then balanced it on her knee while she screwed the top back on the flask. Warming her hands round the cup she sighed in appreciation. 'I can feel the warmth go right through me body.' She had the cup half way to her lips when the ack-ack guns started and a second later a terrific explosion shook the earth all around them.

'My God, that was close,' Fred croaked. 'Too close for comfort.'

Mary had jumped with fright, and now she could feel the hot tea trickling down her legs and into her shoes. She bent to put the cup on the ground but froze when there came the whistling sound of a bomb coming down. It seemed like an eternity, but it was only seconds before the explosion shook the tiny shelter. The drone of planes overhead became louder until it seemed the sky must be full of them. Mary put her hands to her ears to blot out the sound of bombs as they dived towards their target, but she couldn't blot out the sound of them exploding or the ground shaking beneath their feet. When the sound of the planes died away and the ack-ack guns stopped firing, they could hear the crashing of buildings and the shouts of people shouting and screaming.

'This is the worst night we've had.' Fred's breathing was laboured. 'There must have been hundreds of planes out there, and there'll be plenty poor buggers without a roof over their head after this night. And for all we know, we might be among them.'

Mary's tummy was knotted with fear. Would Bob's mam and dad be all right? And what about Eileen and the kids? Please God, let them be safe, she prayed.

'Is it over now, Dad?'

Mary hadn't realised it had gone quiet until she heard Tommy's high, tearful voice. Poor kid, she thought. I'm frightened, so how must he feel?

'It won't be long before the all-clear goes, son. And it mightn't be as bad as we think. Things always seem worse when you don't know what's going on.'

'What time is it, Mr Smith?' Fred always brought a torch with him, and now Mary could see the tiny glow.

'It's twelve o'clock, lass. It might be over, but if I were you I'd wait till the all-clear goes, just to be sure.'

'Oh, we're not going!' It was Martha who answered. She heard Mary's weary sigh and put an arm across her shoulders. 'You're dead beat, lass. Put your head on my shoulder and if you fall asleep I'll wake you as soon as the all-clear goes.'

Mary nestled into her mother's neck where it was safe and warm, and she felt herself drifting away from the sound of Elsie Smith's voice.

Chapter Three

Eileen broke into a run after leaving Mary. The wail of the siren was urging her on but the exertion of forcing her heavy body to move quickly was causing her heartbeat to race and she had a pain in her chest. Beads of sweat ran down her neck and into the valley between her breasts. How the hell I keep so fat I'll never understand, she muttered to herself. It's not as though I sit on me backside all day doing nothing. I'm on me feet from the time I get up in the morning till the time I go to bed. In fact, if it wasn't for me mam, I wouldn't get to bed at all!

When Eileen's dad had died eleven years ago, just after her and Bill got married, she'd asked her mam to come and live with them to save being on her own. And what a Godsend she'd been since the war started and Bill had been called up. If it wasn't for her helping with the kids, Eileen wouldn't be able to go out to work and she'd have to struggle along on Bill's Army pay. At least now they could afford a few luxuries.

People were walking in the opposite direction and Eileen scanned their faces looking for her mam and the kids. But she was at the corner of their street before she saw them.

The two girls had hold of their nanna's hands and all three were looking over their shoulder. There was impatience in her mother's voice as she called, 'Come on, Billy! Hurry up!'

'OK, kids; what's goin' on?' Eileen's voice made them jump, then the two girls started to talk at once. 'Our Billy wouldn't get out of bed, Mam!' This was from the baby of the family, Edna, who was six. 'He gave me nanna cheek, too!' said Joan, who was eight.

Billy, the object of their complaints, hung behind. He was ten years of age and full of fun and mischief. Although she wouldn't admit it, even to herself, he was the apple of Eileen's eye. Every time she looked at him she could see Bill. Young Billy had the same jet black hair as his dad, and the same deep brown eyes. But he was more stubborn than his dad, and would have the last word even if it meant getting a clip round the ear for it.

'OK, kids! Let's get our backsides down to the shelter before Gerry starts his shenanigans.'

'Ah, ray, Mam!' Billy wailed. 'Why can't we stay in our own 'ouse? Robbie Watson sleeps under the stairs in their 'ouse, so why can't we?'

''Cos I say so, bugger lugs!' Eileen grabbed him by the scruff of his neck and marched him in front of her. 'Been playin' yer up, has he, Mam?'

'He's no different to the others; none of them do as they're told.' Maggie Henderson tried to keep the weariness out of her voice. At sixty-five she was finding it a handful looking after three lively children. But not for a big clock would she tell Eileen. Her daughter had enough on her plate with working and worrying about Bill. Anyway, Maggie felt sorry for the kids. They missed their dad.

Walking behind Eileen, Maggie noticed the weary sag of her body. She could see her shoes digging into the fat hanging over them, and knew each step must be agony. Maggie sighed. Where she gets her size from I don't know. She was as thin as me until she started having the children. Then she'd piled the weight on, and had never lost it since. Maggie's eyes went down to the two girls holding on tightly to her hands. They were the image of Eileen at their age. She used to be like them; small, with thin spindly arms and legs. They had her mousey coloured hair, too; and it was cut in a fringe just like hers used to be.

They turned in the park gates and when they reached the long, sloping concrete path that led down into the shelter, they could hear singing.

'Sounds like a full house, Mam,' Eileen laughed over her shoulder. 'Yer wouldn't think there was a war on, would yer?'

'That's the only good thing about the war,' Maggie answered. 'Everybody's more friendly. Pity it takes a war to bring people together, though.'

When the shelter was built, just before the war started, nobody ever thought it would be used. They certainly didn't think they'd be getting out of their beds every night to come to it. And they didn't, until the blitz started a few weeks ago. Now it was full every night.

Eileen pushed her way good-naturedly through the noisy crowd, with Maggie and the kids following. Their neighbours smiled when they saw the small procession. Eileen was well liked in their street because you could always go to her if you were skint in the middle of the week and didn't have anything for the pawn shop. Never see you stuck for a couple of bob, would Eileen, and she had a smile for everyone.

'Sit yerselves down there!' Eileen pointed to an empty space by the wall. 'And for Christ's sake, don't start fightin' like yez did the other night or yer'll get a clip round the ears.'

'Well tell our Billy not to keep pinchin' us when you're not lookin'.' Joan glared at her brother who stuck his tongue out at her. 'He's always kickin' or pinchin' us.'

'Then pinch him back where it hurts! But for cryin' out loud, sit down and shut yer gobs.' Eileen turned to smile at a little woman standing near. She was about seventy-five, and was wrapped in a blanket with a scarf over her head. 'Hello, Nellie! Where's your feller tonight? Out with that young blonde again, is he?'

The lines in Nellie's face deepened as she grinned. 'It's his night for fire watching. He was out with the blonde last night.'

'Oh, aye! Playin' with fire both nights, eh?' Eileen laughed. 'He'll be comin' home one of these nights and tellin' yer he's got a girl in the family way! Yer can't trust these men, yer know.'

'Oh, my feller's fire burned out a long time ago.' Nellie was enjoying the joke. 'There's not even a flicker left now.'

'He's no good to me, then! I'm lookin' for a man with fire in his belly! Mind you,' Eileen grimaced, 'it's so long since I had a man I wouldn't know what to do with one now.'

A small, thin woman, whose dark hair was heavily tinged with grey, touched Eileen's arm. 'Getting to be a regular thing now, isn't it?'

'Hello, Mrs West! Where's yer husband?'

'Fire duty,' Bob's mam answered. 'D'you know if Mary would have had time to get to a shelter?'

'Yeh. She'd be home before me, so don't worry.'

'Come on, let's have a song,' a young sailor shouted. 'Any requests?'

'Roll Out The Barrel!' a voice from the crowd called. 'You start, and we'll all join in.'

Everyone started to sing with gusto, and they were halfway through the song when an almighty explosion shook the shelter. The voices stopped as one, and all eyes turned upwards, expecting the roof to cave in on them. There was a shocked silence for a few seconds then women started screaming and there was a mad scramble for the exit as another explosion shook the earth beneath and around the shelter.

The kids had jumped up crying, and they clung to Eileen's waist. She glanced from her mother to Mrs West and saw stark fear in their eyes. Then she was aware that the movement of the crowd had stopped, and she heard a voice telling people to calm down. It was an Army corporal, and with two other soldiers he was trying to stop people leaving the shelter. 'You're safer here than outside,' he told them. 'These shelters will stand up to anything, so calm down and wait till the all-clear goes.' What the corporal didn't tell them was that he'd been on the slope outside when the last two bombs landed. They'd been very

31

close, and the corporal knew that the homes of some of the people he was trying to calm down would be in ruins.

There was a shuffling of feet but no one made any move to leave the shelter. Complete silence reigned until the ack-ack guns started again, and they could hear the drone of planes. Eileen gathered the children to her ample breast and rocked gently to and fro. 'It's all right,' she crooned softly. 'I won't let anything happen to yez.' But the children screamed as the ground trembled beneath their feet. 'I'm frightened, Mam,' little Edna sobbed. 'When can we go 'ome?'

'Soon, baby, soon.'

The corporal pushed his way to where the young sailor was standing and whispered in his ear. The sailor nodded, then in a loud voice, called, 'One more song, folks, then I promise it'll all be over.' No one was in the mood now for singing and they turned their backs. He looked at the corporal and shrugged his shoulders. 'Go on!' mouthed the corporal, and after another shrug the sailor opened his mouth and his clear voice rang out.

'Land of hope and Glory, Mother of the free,
How can we extol thee, who are born of thee.'

The servicemen in the crowd joined in, then a few people half-heartedly spoke the words. Gradually more voices joined, softly at first, then stronger as the words gave them courage, determination and pride.

'Sod the Germans.' Eileen wiped a tear away and her voice rose to join the chorus. Each time the song ended the sailor would begin again, and they were halfway through the fourth rendition when a voice shouted, 'The all-clear's going.' Immediately there was a stampede towards the entrance and Eileen held her children close in case they were trampled underfoot. The corporal and two of his friends formed a barrier across the entrance, and it was the note of authority in his voice that halted the surge. 'Just hang on a minute! It's pretty bad out there, so don't anyone go home on their own. Stay with friends and keep away from the fires.'

Eileen held the children back. 'Let's wait till the crush is over. You wait with us, Mrs West, and we'll all walk home together.'

Ten minutes later the front of the shelter still hadn't cleared, and Eileen whispered in her mother's ear. 'There's somethin' wrong, Mam! Keep your eyes on the kids while I go and see what's up.'

Elbowing her way through the crowd she reached the slope which was jam packed with people who were standing like statues. She didn't have to ask why. 'Bloody hell!' she gasped. The whole sky was like a bright orange ball, and Eileen felt her heart turn over in fear. 'Would yez all start movin' please? No one can get out while you're blockin' the entrance, an' we'd all like to get home.' Her loud voice brought the people out of their trance, and slowly the mass started to move. Her face grey, Eileen fought her way back to the family. 'I don't know how far away it is, but it looks bloody awful out there.'

'What is it?' Lily West's face was anxious. 'What did you see?'

'From the colour of the sky, I'd say half of Liverpool was on fire.'

'Oh, dear! I hope Bob's all right.' Lily was shaking with nerves. 'He's on duty, and he'll be in the thick of it.'

'Don't start worrying till yer know what's happened.' Eileen winked over the heads of the children in a warning not to frighten them. 'The fire might be miles away for all we know.'

It was ten minutes before the shelter cleared and Eileen was able to move her family out. She heard Lily's cry of horror as they reached the end of the path and could see the flames licking the sky and heard the sound of crashing buildings.

'Mam, will our 'ouse be all right?' Tough little Billy wasn't feeling so tough now. He was frightened.

'We'll have to hope for the best, won't we, son?' In her heart Eileen was crying. Oh, God, Bill, where are yer? Me and the kids need yer! For the first time in her life she was afraid. 'Stay with us, Mrs West! We'll walk yer home.'

'I'll run on and see if Bob's all right.' Lily was impatient. The children were slowing her down. 'I'll be fine; don't you worry!'

'Mrs West, wait! Those fires are near our street, an' I think we should stick together.'

But Lily ran on, and Eileen had to force the children into a trot to keep up. They were three streets from their home when Lily screamed. 'It's our street that's on fire; I know it is!' Then her feet seemed to leave the ground as she spurted forward. Eileen dropped the girls' hands and took off after her, shouting over her shoulder 'See to the kids will yer, Mam?'

Fear must have given wings to Lily's feet because she was

out of sight in no time. Gasping for breath Eileen turned the corner, then leaned against the wall. Her eyes widened in horror as she took in the scene further down the narrow street. It seemed as though the whole bottom of the street was on fire. In the light from the flames Eileen could see men shading their faces with their hands, against the heat. Others were stooping down throwing bricks into the middle of the road.

When her breathing had eased Eileen walked down slowly to where Lily West was being restrained by two men. 'I want to get to my house!' she was screaming. 'Leave go of me! It's my house, and I want to get me things.'

One of the men holding her spoke softly. 'You can't go any nearer, love! The whole place could go up any minute.'

His words caused Lily to struggle more violently. 'Me husband might be in there! Let go of me!'

'Your husband will be here soon, love! He's all right, and we've sent for him.'

'You're lying!' Lily spat. 'He's in there, and I want to go to him.' She was nearly demented as she wriggled to free herself. 'Take your hands off me!'

Eileen moved forward. 'Let me talk to her.'

The man moved aside and Eileen took hold of Lily's arm. 'Yer husband's all right, Mrs West, honest! He'll be here soon!' She put her arms round the shaking woman and held her close. Patting her back as she would a baby, she soothed, 'That's it; have a good cry.'

The two men watched for a few seconds, then seeing Lily was in good hands they went back to work on the fire that was destroying her home.

Then Bob West was standing in front of them and Eileen turned Lily round. 'Here's yer husband.'

Bob didn't speak. He just held out his arms and his wife rushed into them. 'Thank God, you're safe.' Sobbing uncontrollably, she cried, 'Our house has gone, Bob! We've got no home, now.'

'There now, lass, don't cry! We're safe, and that's the main thing.' He held her close till her sobbing eased, then he looked over her head to Eileen. 'Stay with her, lass, till I run for her niece. Lily can stay with her until I can get something sorted out. Then I'll have to get back to the depot, because they need every pair of hands they can get.'

Eileen couldn't trust herself to speak. Putting her arms round Lily, she drew her from Bob's arms and nodded.

Maggie was standing at the front door, a worried expression on her face. 'I'm afraid you're coming into a right mess, love!'

'Mam, if the four walls are standin' I'll consider meself very lucky.' Eileen waved her arm down the street. 'The Wests have lost their home; it's been gutted! And when yer think, it could just have easily been this end of the street that caught that lot!'

'I've put the kids to bed; they were falling asleep on their feet.' Maggie followed her daughter down the hall and watched the expression on her face as she surveyed the mess in the living room. 'I haven't had a good look upstairs, but it doesn't seem too bad. There's a few broken windows, and some of the ceiling's down in your room, but nothing that can't be put right.' Eileen stepped over the broken mirror and ornaments strewn across the soot-covered floor. She was about to sit down when Maggie said sharply, 'Don't sit down! Everything's filthy!'

Sitting down heavily, Eileen closed her eyes. 'Mam, I really couldn't give a shit!'

'There's no need for language like that.' Maggie tutted. 'I don't know where you get it from. You never heard me or your dad use that sort of language.'

'I know, I know! Neither does me posh sister, Rene!' Eileen sounded weary. 'I'm the black sheep of the family, and I'm no lady! But yer know what they say, Mam; yer can't make a silk purse out of a sow's ear.'

'Don't talk stupid! You're as much of a lady as our Rene, except that she puts on airs and graces.' Maggie grinned, 'Anyway, there's more of you than there is of her!'

'Yeah! About ten stone; give or take a stone or two.' Eileen suddenly started laughing. 'We've certainly picked a fine time to have a heart to heart talk, Mam! This place is like a midden, and we're discussin' whether I'm a lady or a big, fat, loud-mouthed cow!'

Although they were alike in looks, except that Eileen was fatter than her mother had ever been, Maggie wasn't as outgoing, or as outspoken as her daughter. She looked at her now and pursed her lips. 'I don't know what's come over you lately. You've changed since Bill went away. When he was here you never used to swear, and you always kept yourself neat and tidy! Now you don't seem to care how you look.'

'What's the good, Mam? With Bill not here, who is there for me to dress up for?' Eileen's body sagged, as though all the fight had gone out of her. 'I don't half miss him, Mam! I wouldn't mind so much if I knew he was all right, but I don't! Sometimes I think I'll never see him again.'

'Of course you will!' Maggie had never heard Eileen sound so defeated. 'What's the matter with you tonight? I've never heard you talk like this before.'

'No! I'm the big, tough Eileen, who wouldn't worry if her backside was on fire! That's what everybody thinks, isn't it, Mam?' Eileen's voice was bitter. 'Well there's times when I get fed-up tryin' to put a brave front on, and tonight's one of them. I'm tired, Mam! Tired of goin' to work every day, and tired of tryin' to be both Mother and Father to the kids.'

'Shall I make us a cuppa?' Maggie didn't know how to take Eileen in this mood. 'That's if we've got any cups left.'

'No, thanks, Mam! I'm goin' to bed.' Eileen put her hands on the side of the chair to lever herself up. 'Yer've had all me moans tonight, but don't worry, I'll be back to normal tomorrow.'

'You might be back to normal, but this room certainly won't!'

'Well, I've got two days off after tomorrow's shift, so I'll get stuck in. A dollop of elbow grease an' we'll soon have it straight.' Eileen reached the door, and when she turned there was a grin stretching from ear to ear. 'If I got a telegram tomorrow, saying Bill was on his way home, you wouldn't see me heels for dust! I'd be down at the hairdressers getting me hair permed, then on to TJs to buy meself some glamorous clothes. I'd even buy meself a pair of them french knickers!'

'Go on with you!' Maggie laughed. 'French knickers indeed!'

Eileen had her foot on the first stair, then turned back and popped her head round the door. 'On second thoughts, I won't bother with the french knickers! They're very expensive, an' it would be a waste of money because Bill would probably tear them off in his haste to get to me body!'

Chapter Four

'Come on, lass, the all-clear's gone.' Martha shook Mary's shoulder. 'Fold the blankets and let's go home.'

Mary bent her head as she stood up, careful not to bang it on the low roof. She bundled the blankets into the bag and opened the door. The sight that met her caused her to gape in horror and brought cries from the others. The whole sky was a bright orange glow from the fires they could see raging above the roofs of their houses. They could feel the heat on their faces, even inside the shelter, and were rooted to the spot, unable to take in what they were seeing. The smell and crackle of burning wood was mixed with the roar of the flames, the crashing buildings and the screams.

'Oh, my God!' Martha's voice was hoarse. 'I wonder how far away that is?'

'Very near, I should say,' Fred whispered. 'I think we've been very lucky.'

'We don't know till we've looked,' Elsie cried. 'Our house might be damaged.'

'You're alive, aren't you?' Fred spoke sharply. 'From the looks of things, I'd say there's plenty out there would change places with us, so just thank God we're all right!' He put an arm round each of the boys' shoulders when they started to cry. Tonight they'd found out war wasn't pretend, and nothing like Cowboys and Indians.

'I'll go in, Mam, and see if everything's all right,' Mary said. 'You stay here till I get back.'

'Oh, no, you don't!' Martha pushed her out of the way. 'I'm coming with you.'

'Can we leave our things, Mr Smith?' Mary asked. 'I'll get them later.'

'Yes, love. We'll sort things out later. Goodnight and God Bless.'

Something in the tone of Fred's voice turned Mary round. In the light from the fires raging round them and the searchlights still zig-zagging across the sky in search of any German stragglers, Fred looked more stooped and more filled with despair than Mary had ever seen him. He's such a nice man, she thought, and God knows he deserved more in life than a moaning wife who was draining all the spirit from him. The only sunshine in his life were the two sons he doted on. Impulsively, Mary touched his arm. 'Thanks for everything, Mr Smith! Goodnight and God Bless.'

'It seems all right, Mam.' Mary had her head poked round the kitchen door.

'Well get in and let's have a look.' Martha gave her a gentle push. 'If the ceiling was going to come down it would have done it before now.'

Mary's foot came into contact with something that

42

skidded across the floor, and her heart leapt until she heard the tinkling of broken crockery. 'Ooh, I got the fright of me life, then! I thought it was a mouse.'

'If you put the light on, we might be able to see what we're saying.' Martha gave her another push, then grimaced when she heard the sound of splintering glass. And when the light flooded the kitchen she shook her head in dismay. 'Dear lord, it looks as though every dish in the house is broken.'

It was impossible to see the colour of the oilcloth with the things covering it. Everything that had been hanging on the walls or on the shelves had been thrown to the floor, and if it was breakable then it had broken. The small kitchen table was lying on its side, and the two sauce bottles which had been standing on it smashed to smithereens. The red and brown contents from the Daddie's Sauce bottles were trickling over pieces of crockery, and the smell from the broken bottle of Aunt Sally liquid soap filled the air. Martha stepped gingerly over to the small floor cabinet. 'Thank God! Most of the stuff in here is all right, so at least we've got some crockery left.'

'Mam!' Mary's nose was twitching. 'There's a terrible smell of soot.' She opened the living room door and her gasp of horror brought Martha to peer over her shoulder. The heavy fall of soot, inches deep, had spilled over the firegrate and covered the carpet in front. Everything in the room, including walls and ceiling, was covered in a thick coat of the black coal dust. The air was filled with small particles of it, and Martha put a hand over her nose and mouth as she moved forward to retrieve a framed photograph that was lying amongst the ornaments on the floor. The glass in the frame was intact, and Martha wiped the dust from it with the back of her hand. It was a wedding photograph of her and George, and in the few seconds she gazed down at their smiling faces it ran through her mind that while she was growing old, George never would. To her he would always be a young man. Standing the photograph back on the sideboard, Martha turned to her daughter. 'We can't do much in here tonight, lass! I'll open the windows and see if we can get rid of any of this soot, then we'll see what we can do in the kitchen.'

'I'll do the kitchen, Mam! I'll be quicker on me own. You go and see if everything's all right upstairs.' Half an hour later, when Mary opened the door to say she'd cleaned the kitchen as much as she could, she grinned when she saw her mother covered from head to toe in soot. 'Mam, you look like little orphan Annie!'

'Have you seen yourself? It's like the pot calling the kettle black.' Martha managed a tired smile. 'I think we deserve a cup of tea.'

'Not for me! I want to go out and see what's happening.' Mary saw the surprised look and went on quickly. 'You needn't come, Mam, but I want to go and see if Bob's mam and dad are all right.'

'I'm not staying here on me own.' Martha looked down at herself. 'Are we all right to go out like this?'

'With what's going on out there, who the heck's going to worry what we look like?'

Outside, they linked arms as people ran past. Some were shouting, others screaming hysterically. One woman was being supported by two men, and Mary heard her pleading, 'Have you seen our Billy?'

The air-raid warden helping her sounded weary. 'I haven't, Missus. But he was probably in the big shelter, or at a friend's.'

'Mam, I'll have to try and get to Bob's house. I couldn't go to bed without knowing if they're all right. Bob would expect me to look out for them.'

'You won't get through!' Martha's voice rose. 'There's all them fires between here and their street.'

'I've got to try, Mam!'

Hearing the determination in her daughter's voice, Martha gave in. 'I'll come with you to the bottom of the street, and if we can get through I'll come with you to the Wests'.'

As they walked to the end of their block of terrace houses, they could feel the heat from the fires on their faces, and sparks and soot were shooting in the air like fireworks. The noise was deafening, with the sound of exploding gas mains, crumbling buildings and the screech of fire engines.

'We'll never make it.' Martha stopped walking. 'We'd be crazy to try.'

'I've got to try! Bob's not here to help, so I've got to.' For reassurance, Mary added, 'They're probably safe and sound, because Mrs West always goes to the park shelter when there's a raid.'

Just then one of their neighbours came hurrying past, and Mary grabbed his arm. 'Mr Fellows, can you tell us which streets have been hit?'

Jim Fellows, like most men who were too old for the Army, did so many nights a week fire watching. He'd just dashed home to make sure his own family were safe. Sighing now, he answered. 'I'm sorry, Mary, but until the fires die down it's impossible to say what the damage is. There's been a few direct hits, but where they are I just couldn't tell you.' Jim Fellows, usually a very mild tempered man, sounded angry. 'They just dropped their bombs at random, not worrying about hitting houses and killing innocent civilians.'

'Has anyone been killed?' Mary waited fearfully for the answer.

'I don't know yet.' He wiped his eyes with the backs of his hands in an action of despair. 'Why the hell people haven't got the sense to go to a shelter when a raid starts I just don't know! We've found some injured, but I think we'll find a lot more when we can get the fires out.'

'D'you know if Bray Street was hit? That's where Bob's mam and dad live.'

'Mary, I've told you, I don't know anything for certain yet! We only cover a certain area, and Bray Street isn't part of our patrol.'

'D'you think we could get down there?' Martha asked.

'If you want my advice, Martha, you'll go home and stay there until things settle down a bit. You'd only get in the way, and I don't think you'd get through, anyway.' Mary was still holding on to his arm, and Jim now pulled it free. 'I'll have to go! There's too much to do to stand talking. Take my advice and go home.'

Martha took Mary's arm. 'You heard what he said. Let's go home and try in the morning.'

Mary refused to move. 'I'm going to try and get to the air-raid shelter. Someone may know if the Wests were in there, and if they were I'll come home. But I can't go to bed unless I know they're safe.'

Martha sighed. 'Let's see if we can work our way round the fires, then.'

They'd reached the bottom of their street when two men in special police uniforms blocked their way. 'Where are you two ladies going?'

'Bray Street, or the park shelter,' Mary told him. 'We want to find out if our friends are all right.'

'You won't be finding out tonight! I can't let you past this point.' The man's abrupt tone softened. 'Is it someone special?'

'Me boyfriend's parents. He's in the Army, and I'm worried about them.'

'Well, I'm sorry, love, but I daren't let you go any further. There's unexploded bombs in there.' He waved his arm in the direction of the fires. 'There's also the risk of explosions from leaking gas mains.'

'Why do they bomb houses?' Martha asked, bitterly. 'What good does it do? How can they go home and sleep with a clear conscience after what they've done?'

'It isn't only houses they've bombed, Missus. We've heard the docks at Seaforth got a real hammering! We asked for reinforcements, but soldiers and volunteers have been sent down there. One of the ammunition ships was hit, and you know what that means.' The officer shook his head. 'All hell's been let loose tonight, and for those men working to put the fires out, it must seem like hell.'

Two women made to run past them but were pulled up short by the officer who so far hadn't spoken. Pressing them back to where Mary and her mother stood, he said, 'Please go home! We can't let you through because it's dangerous. There's no one to answer questions at the depot because every available man is out helping. They've got enough on their plates without people wandering around buildings that are likely to explode any minute, so go home!'

Mary didn't resist when her mother led her back up the street. Neither of them spoke until they were sitting in the kitchen drinking tea. Her hands round the steaming cup, Martha shook her head sadly. 'It's hard to believe what's happening. Never in me whole life did I think I'd ever see scenes like them out there. I wonder if the pilots have families of their own, and how they'd like it if their houses were bombed.' Suddenly her cup clattered to the saucer, and covering her face with her hands she started to cry.

Mary stared at the bowed head. She couldn't remember seeing her mam cry since the day her dad was buried. 'Don't cry, Mam.' She reached across the table and pulled Martha's hands from her face. 'At least we're all right, and our house is safe. Things mightn't be as bad as we think. Most people will have been in the shelter, you'll see! I know it's terrible that people have lost their homes, but you can build a new home. You can't bring people back to life.'

'I'm sorry, lass.' Martha wiped her eyes on the corner of her pinny. 'It's just that it all seems so hopeless and unnecessary! What they've done won't bring the war to an end any quicker, so why?'

'Perhaps they're getting desperate. They say our lads are beginning to fight back now, so the Germans are throwing everything they've got at us.'

Martha looked thoughtful. 'What do you do if there's a raid when you're at work?'

'I've told you dozens of times, we go to an underground shelter! And it's a damn sight safer than going next door.'

Martha stood and stretched her back. 'Let's get to bed! I don't know how we'll sleep with all the noise but we can't sit looking at each other all night. Besides you need some sleep if you're going to work.'

'I want to get round to the Wests' early, Mam.' Mary nodded her head towards the closed living room door. 'Would you mind if I left you with all the mess? I'll try and get back in time to give you a hand.'

'I wish we had one of those vacuum cleaners. I believe they get rid of the dirt in no time.'

'When me and Bob are married, we'll buy you one.'

'I've managed with a stiff brush all me life, so it won't kill me.' Martha looked at her daughter with deep affection. She knew Mary would give her the world if she could. 'What time d'you want me to call you?'

'Eight o'clock, if you're awake.'

Martha groaned as they went through the living room. 'Fancy having to come down to that! Still, we're lucky compared to some poor souls.'

Mary climbed the stairs behind her mother. 'Aren't you glad you stood in a queue for that fish today? Otherwise we'd be having conny-onny butties for our dinner.'

Holding on to the bannister, Martha turned. 'There's plenty would be glad of conny-onny butties! When I was a girl, condensed milk was considered a luxury.'

'You won't forget to wake me, will you, Mam?'

Martha faced her across the landing, 'Will you stop worrying! I'll wake you in plenty of time.'

As she slipped between the sheets, Mary had so much on her mind she didn't think she'd sleep. But sheer exhaustion took over, and within seconds of laying her head on the pillow she fell into a deep, dreamless sleep.

Chapter Five

Martha stood looking down on the sleeping form of her daughter. The sheet was pulled over Mary's face and all that could be seen was the blonde hair spread across the pillow. Her breathing was deep and even, and Martha was reluctant to wake her. But she'd promised to call her at eight o'clock and it was nine now. 'Come on, lass! It's time to wake up.'

Mary shot up in bed, her eyes blinking rapidly. 'What time is it?'

'Nine o'clock! I came up at eight, but you were in such a good sleep I didn't have the heart to wake you.'

'But I never get up till nine when I'm on afternoons.' Her eyes full of sleep, Mary peered at her mother. 'What have you got that old mob cap on for?' She leaned closer. 'Your face is all black!'

'I've been dragging the carpet out into the yard to try and shake some of the soot out of it.' Seeing Mary's puzzled expression, Martha reminded her. 'You wanted to go and see if the Wests are all right.'

Mary's eyes widened as the full horror of last night came flooding back. 'Oh, my God, I must have been dead to the world!' She threw the bedclothes back and leapt out of bed. 'Have you been up long, Mam?'

'I couldn't sleep with all the noise, so I got up about five. I thought I might as well be doing something as lying in bed. I went out to the front to talk to some of the neighbours, but they haven't heard anything. Their houses are all like ours, but at least they're in one piece.'

Mary threw a dress on the bed. 'Will you be an angel, Mam, and make us some toast while I have a swill and get dressed?' Ten minutes later when she walked through the living room she was surprised to see most of the soot cleared from the floor. 'You haven't half been busy!'

Martha's face looked drawn under the streaks of dirt. Dragging the carpet out to the yard had taken all the strength from her. 'It'll take weeks to get rid of the soot from the couch and chairs. And I can't do anything about the walls and ceiling! I tried brushing it off, but I only made matters worse. The whole room will have to be stripped and decorated.'

'I think you've done wonders! At least we won't be breathing and eating the stuff all the time.'

'How you slept through the noise I'll never know.' Martha hadn't closed her eyes. 'They must have been pulling houses down, and every time one collapsed the whole foundation of this shook and I expected it to come down on me.'

Seeing the tiredness, Mary tried to cheer her up. 'Mam, you look like Granny Grunt in that mob cap! You look as though you've been up the chimney.'

'I didn't need to!' The smile was weak, but it was there. 'There was more soot in this room than up the chimney! We won't need the sweep for a long time.'

Mary struggled into her coat. 'I'll be as quick as I can, then I can give you a hand. Unless you want to come with me?'

'No thanks! I'll have something ready for your dinner when you get back. But be careful, lass! They say there's unexploded bombs around.'

'OK, Mrs Mop! I'll be careful.'

Mary closed the door behind her and stepped into the street. Small groups of neighbours were standing talking, and their serious faces made Mary's heart beat rapidly. Please God, she prayed, let the Wests be safe. And Eileen and the kids.

Their next door neighbour, Vera Jackson, was standing at the door and she gave Mary a thin smile. 'Some night, wasn't it?'

'You're not joking!' Mary walked up to her sighing. 'I'm going to see if the Wests are all right. You haven't heard anything have you, Vera?'

'I haven't, love! I spent most of the night trying to clear away some of the soot.'

'So has me mam.' Mary swung the gas mask over her shoulder. 'I'd better get going, 'cos I've got to go to work this afternoon.'

Mary waved to some of the people as she ran down the street but didn't stop to talk. She kept up the pace until she reached the building which used to be a small Mission hall, but since the war started had been used as headquarters for the Home Guard. Breathless, she pushed the door open and stepped inside. The room was crowded and noisy. Women with children clinging to their skirts were crying loudly, while others looked frightened and bewildered. Mary recognised Annie Callaghan, who lived next door to Bob, and she was crying on her husband's shoulder. Oh, God, if they were in trouble, then so were the Wests!

In the far corner of the room a man was sitting behind a desk talking to a group of people, and Mary pushed her way towards him. Impatiently moving from one foot to the other, she waited for the people to move away then stood in front of the desk. The man was in khaki uniform, and when he looked up Mary could see tiredness and despair on his face.

'Can I help you, Miss?'

'I'm trying to find out about Mr and Mrs West, from Bray Street. The streets are cordoned off and I can't get through.'

For the first time that morning the man had something to smile about. He had a pretty girl standing in front of him and good news to give for a change.

'Oh, Bob West's all right! In fact he's here now, in the back room. I'll give him a shout.'

Mary blew out a sigh of relief as she watched the man open a side door and yell, 'Bob! There's a young lady to see you!'

Bob's dad came through the door looking drawn and weary. His face was covered in black streaks and his clothes were crumpled and dirty. He was a lot smaller than his son, but in features they were very much alike. He smiled when he saw Mary and she rushed to throw her arms around him. 'Oh, am I glad to see you! We've been worried to death because we thought your street had been bombed.'

'It was, lass!' Bob West let out a long drawn out sigh. 'Our house got a direct hit. It's been completely gutted.' Tears came to his eyes and he wiped them away with the back of his hand. 'I was on fire duty, and Mam, thank God, had gone down to the shelter. It's a blessing she did, because she'd have been killed for sure if she'd been in the house.'

Mary was stunned. Her voice a whisper, she asked, 'Where is she now? Why didn't she come to us?'

'She's at her niece's.' He looked ready to drop from exhaustion.

'I've got to wait till the fires die down before I can get near enough to see if there's anything to salvage. But from what I've seen there won't be anything to save! Funny, isn't it, lass, but we've lost everything, and all Mam's worried about are the photographs we've had in the family for years, and our insurance policies. I don't think what's happened has sunk in yet.'

'Have you tried to let Bob know?'

'I contacted the Army base early this morning and asked if he could come home on compassionate leave. I hope to God he can, because his mam needs him now.'

'He'll get home!' Mary tried to sound confident. 'They can't have shipped him out yet.' She released her hold on him. 'D'you know if Eileen's all right?'

'They were all with Lily in the shelter, thank God! Their house is intact too, because it was our end that caught it.

Our house got the direct hit, but the ones either side had to be pulled down because they were dangerous. The next street got it worse than ours, and the men are still sifting through the ruins. It's a terrible job because the fires are still smouldering, and there's a danger of gas explosions.'

'I'll be going to work at one o'clock, but you know if you and Mrs West want to come to our house you'll be more than welcome.'

'I know that, love! But I think Mam is better at Joyce's. She's in a terrible state, and I can't think properly meself at the moment.' He shook his head. 'I haven't said anything to her, but where are we going to find somewhere to live? And even if we got a house, what would we use for furniture? We've lost everything we had!'

Mary didn't answer. If she opened her mouth she knew she'd start to cry. She watched Bob's dad wipe a hand across his face, spreading the streaks already there. 'It's hard to take in, love, that the home you've had for thirty years is gone in a matter of seconds. All the things we've gathered together over those thirty years, wiped out in a flash. I just hope our Bob gets home, otherwise I don't think the wife will be able to cope.'

Mary swallowed to move the lump in her throat. 'The main thing is you and Mrs West are safe.'

'I keep telling meself that, but it doesn't help.' He put his hand on Mary's arm. 'I'll have to go, love! There's not enough men as it is, because they've all been sent down to the docks. I only came in for a cup of tea, and I'll have to get back to let one of the other lads have a break.'

'Will you let me know what's happening?' Mary begged.

'If Bob comes home he won't know where you are.'

'I'll let your mam know, I promise.'

Mary gave him a quick kiss before weaving her way through the crowded room. Some of the people she brushed against wouldn't be leaving the building as relieved as she was. It was terrible that the Wests had lost their home, but at least they were alive!

'D'you think Bob will get home?' Martha toyed with the fish on her plate. Her appetite had gone since hearing about the Wests.

'I hope so! They can't have shipped him out already.' Mary didn't feel hungry either, but she wasn't going to waste the fish after her mam had stood in a queue to get it. 'Surely they can't refuse compassionate leave under the circumstances!'

'Why don't you take the day off?' Martha asked. 'You've never taken one day's unofficial leave since you've been there.'

'I'll wait and see if Bob gets home. If he does, I'll take a few days off so I can go round to Joyce's. He won't be able to come here much, because his mam will want him with her.'

'I should think she would! She must be in a right state!' Martha started to stack the dishes. 'You'd better get a move on if you don't want to be late.'

As Mary reached for her coat, Martha added, 'Hurry home tonight, in case Gerry starts.'

'OK, boss! I'll run all the way like little Red Riding Hood.'

* * *

Walking past the streets that were cordoned off, Mary could see people standing in front of empty spaces where only yesterday houses had stood. Some were crying, while others just stared as though they couldn't believe what had happened. Mary had been walking slowly, now she reminded herself that if she didn't hurry she'd miss the bus. She quickened her pace but as she neared the Black Bull she saw the bus pulling away and had to wait fifteen minutes for the next. There were only a few travelling on the late bus so Mary had a seat to herself for the twenty-minute journey. Looking out of the window she was surprised that the further away from Aintree they travelled the more normal everything seemed. Even when she reached the factory it looked just like any other day, with latecomers like herself rushing to clock in on time. It didn't seem real that everything here looked exactly the same as it had yesterday, when only a few miles away there was such devastation.

It was only when Mary pushed open the cloakroom door that she realised things were far from normal. There weren't nearly as many women there as usual, and those that were there were clustered around Maisie Phillips who was sobbing her heart out. Her face was red and blotchy and her make-up wiped away by the sodden handkerchief she held to her eyes. Ethel Hignet had an arm round her friend's shoulder and her own face bore signs of recent tears. 'They're bastards!' she spat the words out.

'Yer can say that again!' Eileen's voice rang out. 'If I had my way I'd shoot the bloody lot of them!' She caught sight of Mary standing just inside the door and came towards her. 'Yer all right, kid? When yer weren't on the bus, I got worried.'

'I missed our bus and had to wait for the next.' Mary nodded towards Maisie. 'What's wrong?'

'Her sister's 'usband got killed last night.' Eileen ran her fingers through her hair in an action that said she was lost for words. 'He was at Spellow Lane when a bomb dropped.'

'Oh, my God!' Mary whispered. 'Isn't that terrible!'

'He 'ad two kids, too.' Eileen snorted. 'It's gettin' to be as dangerous for civilians as it is for soldiers now.'

'Why didn't Maisie stay off?'

'The two kids were evacuated to Wales, and someone's gone down to bring them back. After tonight, Maisie's takin' a week off to help Florrie.'

Harry Sedgemoor's head appeared round the cloakroom door. 'I'm sorry, girls, but it's time to be by your machines. The morning shift are waiting to go home.' He held the door open as the women filed past, then watched as Mary tied the turban round her hair. As she and Eileen walked past him, he let the door swing after them. 'You and your mam all right, Mary?'

'Yes, thanks, Harry,' Mary answered briefly then turned to Eileen. 'You were with Mrs West last night, weren't you?'

'Don't remind me, kid! I've never been so frightened in all me life! I really thought we were all goners in that shelter. And poor Mrs West . . . I felt so sorry for her. She was like a raving lunatic!'

'Who wouldn't be if they'd lost everything like she has?'

'I know, kid! It's enough to drive yer insane!'

They were sitting in the canteen and Eileen was speaking through a mouthful of bread. 'No one knows what's in store for them, an' I suppose it's just as well we don't. Otherwise we'd be putting a shilling in the gas meter and stickin' our heads in the oven.'

Mary pushed a stray curl under her turban. 'It seemed like the whole of Liverpool got it last night.'

'They reckon it's the worst night we've had! London got it the worst, but from what I've heard Liverpool got a real pasting too! They say a lot of the big shops in town were hit, and Paradise Street's in ruins.'

Mary sighed as she scraped her chair back. 'Come on, back to the grind for another four hours.'

Eileen heaved her body from the too small canteen chair. 'Thank God I've got me two days off to look forward to! Two glorious, bloody days!'

'Mr West came, lass, but there's no word of Bob.' Martha watched her daughter's shoulders slump and she tutted impatiently. 'I think you forget he's in the Army! He can't just pack his bags when he wants to.' She bustled towards the kitchen. 'There's only powdered egg for supper because I was afraid to go out in case I missed Mr West.'

After supper they sat on the couch with their cups of tea. There was no fire lit tonight because the weather was warm, but Mary missed the cheerful glow.

'Did you listen to ITMA?'

Martha pulled a face. 'I don't know whether it was me not being in the mood, but it didn't seem as funny tonight. It was probably looking at the state of these walls.'

'Eileen said her house is in a right mess, too!' Mary grinned. 'At least that's what she meant, but she didn't use the word "mess". Anyway, she's got two days off now, so it'll give her time to clean up.'

'She's certainly got her hands full! I don't know how she manages to be so cheerful all the time.'

'She's a marvel, Mam! Honest, she's always . . .' The wail of the siren cut off Mary's words as mother and daughter jumped with fright. The cup on Martha's saucer was rattling as she groaned, 'Oh, no, not again! I don't think I could stand another night like last night.'

Watching her mother's face drain of colour, Mary stood up and took the cup from her. 'Come on! Back to the hole in the ground! That place is beginning to feel like home.'

'It must be a false alarm!' Fred Smith shone the torch on his wrist. 'It's twelve o'clock!'

'No such luck! They're around somewhere.' Elsie sounded as pessimistic as she always looked. 'Any minute now and they'll be here, mark my words.'

She'd no sooner finished speaking than the ack-ack guns started up, and they could hear the drone of planes. 'Why didn't you keep your mouth shut?' Fred growled. 'Proper bloody Jonah, you are!'

'Let's have a song.' Mary slipped her arm across her mother's shoulders. 'Eileen said they sing every night in the big shelter, and it helps pass the time.'

61

'Yeah!' Tommy's voice piped up. 'What shall we sing, Mary?'

The whistling of a falling bomb stopped Mary from answering. She sat with bated breath waiting for the bomb to reach its target, and heard her mother give out a long shuddering sigh just before the explosion shook the shelter.

'That wasn't too close.' Fred always spoke in a whisper, as though he was afraid the German pilots could hear him. 'I'd say that was a few miles away.'

Mary suddenly felt the full weight of her mother's body leaning against her, then it slumped forward and fell across her knee. 'What's the matter, Mam? Have you dropped something?' When there was no answer Mary started to panic. 'Mr Smith, there's something wrong with me mam! She's not moving!'

Fred threw his blanket aside and pulled the torch from his pocket. 'Hold this torch, Mary, till I have a look. Likely she's just fainted.' He thrust the torch into Mary's hand. 'Shine it down here! How the hell can I see what I'm doing if you're pointing the thing in the air?!' Mary felt her mother's weight being lifted from her, then heard the urgency in Fred's voice. 'Get up, Mary!' She moved away as he ordered his wife, 'Fold a blanket for Martha's head.'

'What's wrong with Mrs Bradshaw, Dad?' Little Denis sounded scared. 'She's not dead, is she?' The band of pain in Mary's chest grew tighter, and even Fred's assurances that Mrs Bradshaw just didn't feel well did nothing to ease the pain.

'It's bloody freezing in here!' Fred barked. 'Give us another blanket!' When Mary made no move he snatched it from her hand and draped it over Martha. He was usually such a civil man, always softly spoken, and hearing his tone now Mary knew he was worried. It took all her willpower to turn her eyes to where her mother lay, her face lit up by the torch. Her eyes were open and her mouth moving as though she wanted to say something but no sound would come. A cry escaping her lips, Mary knelt at the side of the bench. 'Don't worry, Mam! You're going to be all right, isn't she, Mr Smith?'

'Course she is, love! I'll run down to the depot and see if there's a doctor on duty.'

A loud wail left Elsie's lips. 'You're not going out while the planes are still around.'

'I'll go, Mr Smith! I can run faster than you.' Mary gave her mother's arm a squeeze. 'I'll only be five minutes.'

Fred followed Mary through the house and as she made to run off down the street he caught her arm. 'I don't want to worry you, love, but I think your mam's had a stroke.'

'No!' Mary cried. 'She was just frightened by the bombs! She'll be fine when I get her home.'

'I hope you're right! Anyway, run like hell, but if the planes come back take cover, quick!'

Mary nodded, then started to run faster than she'd ever run in her life. Tears blurred her vision but she made no effort to wipe them away. Round the corner she dashed, colliding with a man. 'I'm sorry,' she mumbled, and went to race on. But a hand pulled her up short. 'Mary! What the hell are you doing out? Why aren't you in the shelter?'

It was Bob's voice and Mary threw herself into his arms. 'Bob! Thank God!'

'What's wrong? Where are you running to?'

Mary was sobbing into his shoulder. 'It's me mam! Mr Smith thinks she's had a stroke.'

'Oh, no!' Bob sounded weary. 'First me mam and dad, now this!' When Mary pulled away, saying, 'I've got to get a doctor!' he took her hand in a vicelike grip and started to run, pulling her along. 'Let's move then.'

Apart from the searchlights zig-zagging across the sky in their search for enemy planes, there was no sound or movement as they raced through the streets. They were out of breath when they reached the depot and Mary couldn't get her words out to the man in charge. Between tears and breathlessness, she couldn't make herself coherent. It was Bob who had to coax every word out of her until the man in charge of the station understood why she was so distressed. 'I think you're in luck, dear.' His voice was gentle. 'The duty doctor's here now, and I'm sure he'll come and see your mother.' He disappeared through a side door, and a few seconds later when the door opened again Mary gave a cry of relief. 'Oh, I'm glad it's you, Doctor! Me mam's taken ill, and Mr Smith said she's had a stroke.'

John Greenfield looked too young to be a doctor. He was thirty-seven, but with his short, slim, boyish figure, baby-fine blond hair that refused to stay combed back, and a delicate complexion, he looked ten years younger. He was the Bradshaws' family doctor, and although he didn't see much of them, he knew the history of the family well. His pale blue eyes searched Mary's face. 'Calm down, Mary, and start at the beginning.' When she'd finished, he said quietly, 'I'll get my bag and run you back in my car.'

* * *

Fred met them outside the shelter. 'Your mam's just the same, Mary! We'd better stay out here while the doctor examines her.'

Bob put his arm round Mary when the doctor, head bent, disappeared into the shelter. 'Don't worry, sweetheart, your mam's going to be fine.' He didn't have time to say more before John Greenfield reappeared. 'I couldn't examine Mrs Bradshaw in those conditions.' He looked across at Bob. 'Will you help me carry her into the house? And you, Mary, be a good girl and nip in and get the couch ready.'

Nervously wringing her hands, Mary ran into the house. 'Get the couch ready,' she spoke to the empty room. 'How do I do that?' She put two cushions at the end of the couch then dashed upstairs for a blanket. She was spreading it out when the door was kicked open and the doctor and Bob came in carrying her mother between them. Martha's clothes were riding high on her hips and Mary rushed to pull them down, trying to speak lightly, 'You're too old to be showing your legs to strange men.'

'You two, out in the kitchen while I examine the patient.' John was looking at Bob. 'You could put the kettle on because I think we could all do with a drink.'

'Come on, love.' Bob's arm went round Mary's waist. 'Do as you're told.' It was Bob who filled the kettle and lit the gas ring. For a few seconds he watched the flames lick the bottom of the kettle, then, squaring his shoulders, he faced Mary. 'The doctor's right; a cup of tea will make us all feel better.'

'Even me mam?' Mary flashed back. 'Will a cup of tea make me mam feel better?'

'Don't bite me head off, love! And carrying on like that won't help anyone . . . particularly your mam!' He lowered his eyes. 'Your mam has had a stroke, but the doctor doesn't know how bad, yet, and he's asked me to have a word with you. He doesn't want your mam to see you upset or she'll think she's worse than she is.'

'But I can't pretend there's nothing wrong with her, can I?'

'Nobody's asking you to pretend there's nothing wrong! Just try not to upset her, that's all!'

The kettle started to whistle and Mary automatically brewed the tea. She picked up a knitted tea cosy, and as she held it in her hands she had a mental picture of her mother sitting in her favourite armchair by the side of the fire, needles clicking away as she knitted the cosy from odd bits of wool. Sighing, she slipped the cosy over the spout of the pot. 'Everything seems to be going wrong.'

There was a tap on the door before the doctor walked in. He sat on the edge of the small kitchen table, and before Mary could fire the questions he could see in her eyes, held his hand up. 'I may be needed down at the depot, so I'll have to make this quick. Your mother's stroke has affected her down the right side of her body, and her speech.' When Mary's head dropped, he went on quickly. 'That doesn't mean she's always going to be like that. It's too early to say for sure, but if your mother has got the spirit and the determination to get better, then I think the chances of her regaining some use of her limbs are pretty good. I'm even more optimistic about her regaining her speech, but it might take time.' He stood up. 'I'll ring the hospital from the depot, but I don't think I'll be able to get her in right away because we've had so many casualties.'

'Can't I look after her at home?'

'You might have to for a while! It depends upon whether there's an empty bed.'

'You couldn't manage your mam on your own.' Bob had been silent till now. 'You'd never be able to lift her.'

'I can try,' Mary said stubbornly.

'Let's see if we can get her into hospital first,' John cut in. 'If I can't, I'll get a nurse in twice a day to wash and change her. Then you'd only have to lift her when she wanted to go to the lavatory.' A smile crossed his boyish face when he saw Mary blush. 'You'll get used to that, my girl! Everyone needs to go to the lavatory . . . I've even been known to go myself on occasion.' His smile faded. 'We'd better go in or Mrs Bradshaw will wonder what's going on. Before we do, I must warn you you'll see a difference in her appearance. The right side of her face has been affected and her mouth is lopsided. But that could be back to normal in a few days. The main thing is not to let her see you're upset, and keep all stress and worry away from her. Say nothing about the war unless it's good news.'

It was three o'clock before Mary and Bob sat facing each other across the kitchen table. Both were dead tired, but felt a sense of achievement. They'd managed to carry Martha's big, iron bed down the stairs, and while Bob had gone to ask the Smiths if they could borrow the commode they had, Mary had been able to undress her mam and get her into bed.

'I think you've done wonders!' Bob reached across for her hand. 'I don't know how you managed to undress her on your own.'

'Me mam did most of the work! I was frightened of hurting her at first, but she can use her left arm and leg and we soon got the hang of it.' Mary looked down at their joined hands. 'D'you think we're being paid for committing a sin?'

Bob flushed. 'I've thought of nothing else since I heard about our house being bombed! I keep telling meself that ours wasn't the only house to go and there's fellows being killed every day at the front. They can't all have committed a sin.'

Mary started to cry softly. 'We shouldn't have done it! I'll always blame meself for what's happened to me mam. It's God's way of paying us back.'

'What can I say, love?' Bob shook his head. 'Except I'm sorry!'

'It wasn't your fault. I've got a mind of me own, and I should have known better.' Mary sniffled. 'You'd better go, because the doctor's coming at nine o'clock and I want to have the room cleaned up before then.'

'Where are you sleeping?'

'On the couch. I couldn't go upstairs and leave me mam on her own.'

'I'll be off then, and let you get some sleep. I'll be back early to give you a hand.'

'Leave it until dinner time, love. There's a nurse coming

and you'd only be in the way.' Mary suddenly put a hand across her mouth and her wide eyes stared into his. For the first time since she'd dashed round that corner and bumped into him, she remembered why he was home. 'I haven't even asked about your mam and dad! Oh, Bob, I'm sorry! Everything went out of me mind, worrying about me mam.'

'We'll talk later.' Bob kissed her gently. 'You've had enough for one day.'

Chapter Six

The couch was hard and unyielding and Mary tossed and turned. So much had happened her mind was in a whirl. Finally, telling herself she'd have to get some sleep or she'd be no good to anyone, she punched the pillow into a more comfortable position and did what her dad had taught her when she was a little girl and couldn't get to sleep. She started to count. After a while her body became light and she felt the lovely sensation of floating on air as she drifted into a deep sleep. It was the sound of bells that woke her, and she sat up with a start. Everywhere was quiet, and telling herself she must have been dreaming she went to settle down again. It was only then she realised she'd been sleeping on the couch, and the memories came rushing back. Peering through the darkness she put her hand out and felt for the wooden headboard. 'Oh, my God! What time is it?' Flinging the bedding aside she crossed the room and drew the heavy curtains back, filling the room with light. Turning to the bed, she met her mother's eyes. 'I'm sorry, Mam, I must have been out for the count, and . . .' A look of panic crossed her face as the knock came. Glancing down in dismay at her nightdress, her eyes then travelled the room, taking in the rumpled bedding in a heap on the couch and her clothes strewn across the backs of chairs. 'Who the heck can this be, so early? I'll die if it's the doctor, and this place in such a mess.'

Her dressing gown was upstairs, so Mary reached for the coat hanging over the nearest chair. As she did so, she caught sight of her mother's face. 'Don't worry, Mam.' She shivered as her arms came into contact with the cold lining of the coat. 'I won't let anyone in unless it's Doctor Greenfield. I can hardly ask him to come back later.'

Stifling a yawn with the back of her hand, Mary wrapped the coat around her before opening the door. The last person in the world she expected to see standing on the step was Harry Sedgemoor, and her brows drew together in a frown.

'I'm sorry if I woke you.' Harry looked awkward. 'Fred told us what happened and I'm just calling to ask how your mam is.'

'Harry!' Mary couldn't keep the impatience out of her voice. 'It's a good job you did wake me, 'cos the doctor's coming at nine and the place is a right mess.'

'Can I do anything to help?' Even with her eyes full of sleep, her hair all over the place, and wrapped in an old coat, she still looks beautiful, Harry thought. 'Is there anything at all I can do?'

'No, thanks! Bob helped me bring me mam's bed downstairs.' Feeling mean, she added, 'We'll be all right, but thanks for asking.'

'Bob got compassionate leave then?'

Mary started to close the door as she nodded. 'I'll have to go! I've got so much to do before the doctor comes.'

'I'll let them know in work, so don't worry.' Harry was reluctant to move. 'You just look after your mam.'

Mary stepped further back into the hall. 'I'll have to go! I'm not even dressed yet.'

Before the door closed on him, Harry said, 'If you ever want me, Mary, you know where I am.'

'It was only Harry Sedgemoor, asking about you.' Mary stood at the side of the bed. 'I've got twenty minutes to get you, meself, and this room sorted out, so I'd better get me skates on.' She forced a smile as she looked straight into her mother's face. She wanted to fling her arms around her and tell her what she'd never put into words before. That she loved her very much. But this wasn't the time. 'I'll get cracking!'

'Whew! I never thought I'd make it!' Mary surveyed the room. It was as good as she'd ever get it, with the walls and ceiling covered in black streaks, and the big bed taking up half the room. The bedding from the couch had been whipped upstairs, a duster run over the furniture, and a fire was just beginning to crackle in the grate. 'I'll just make meself a bit presentable.'

John Greenfield stood on the step with a nurse by his side. The Bradshaws had been on his mind a lot over the last few hours, and he was expecting to find Mary tearful and quite unable to cope. He was amazed when she opened the door with a big smile on her face and a cheery 'Good morning' on her lips. He was even more amazed when he saw Martha propped up in bed looking very comfortable, the room neat and tidy, and even a fire glowing in the grate. 'Well, well! It seems I've been worrying myself for nothing!' He indicated the nurse by his side. 'This is Nurse Nolan, and she'll be coming in twice a day to freshen you up.'

Rose Nolan was middle aged with a round, plump body, and a rosy, cherubic face. The hair showing beneath her nurse's hat was steel grey, and neatly curled. When she smiled her whole face lit up, and Martha knew right away she was going to like Nurse Nolan.

'No luck with the hospital,' John told Mary, 'it may be a few weeks before they have an empty bed. Can you manage till then?' When Mary nodded, he looked at Martha. 'While your daughter's getting the water ready for the nurse, I'll give you a good examination.'

'You get the towels while I see to the water.' The nurse beamed at Mary who was standing by the sink. 'You've managed very well, but I'll be coming twice a day till your mum goes into hospital, so that will make things easier for you.' She threw a towel over her arm before lifting the bowl. 'I'll stay for a while after the doctor goes, to show you how to lift your mum without straining yourself.' When Mary rushed to open the door for her, she asked 'Where's her clean clothes?'

Mary closed her eyes. 'I never thought about clean clothes.'

The beaming smile took the sting out of the words. 'Not much good getting her all nice and clean, then putting dirty clothes on her, now is it?'

Mary blessed her mother for being so fussy when she

found everything she wanted, all neat and tidy and in the right place.

Mary saw Bob passing the window and the door was opened before he had time to knock. 'How's it going, love?' He lifted her off her feet and held her tight. 'I haven't slept a wink, thinking about you.' Lowering his voice, he whispered, 'I love you, Mary Bradshaw!'

'I love you, too!' Mary gave him a hug. 'Now, come in and see me mam.'

There was welcome in Martha's eyes as Bob bent to kiss her. 'You certainly gave us a fright, last night! Now you look better than either of us! I hope you feel as well as you look.'

A low sound came from Martha's mouth, and Bob's eyes flew to Mary. But she wasn't looking at him. Her brows were drawn together as she stared at her mother. 'Did you say something, Mam?'

Martha's mouth moved slowly and agonisingly. Then, softly, like the rustle of a leaf, came 'Eth.'

Mary ran to the side of the bed. 'Say it again, Mam!' She watched with Bob as Martha's distorted mouth moved. 'Eth.'

Bob's laugh filled the room. 'That's the best sound I've ever heard in me whole life!'

Mary was laughing and crying as she kept asking her mother to repeat the magical word. In the end Martha was tired out and waved her hand in the direction of the kitchen to indicate she wanted them to leave her in peace.

Bob removed his tunic coat and draped it over the back

of one of the kitchen chairs. 'Sit down and tell me everything that's happened.'

Mary's face was aglow. She had Bob sitting opposite to her and her mother had said her first word. 'Well! Where to start?! The doctor and nurse were here at nine o'clock, and it's been all go since then. They can't get Mam in hospital yet, but I don't mind because with the nurse coming twice a day I'll manage fine. She's lovely, the nurse, and we had a good laugh when she was showing me how to lift me mam without strangling her.' The happy smile dimmed a little. 'Trying to feed me mam was the worst. With the right side of her face, and her tongue, being paralysed, she can't swallow and I had to try and get soup into the back of her throat and let it slide down. As quick as I was spooning it into her mouth it was trickling out again. She looked so helpless, and sort of ashamed, that I'd have burst out crying if the nurse hadn't been there.'

'What does Doctor Greenfield think of your mam's chances?'

'He said he can't say much until she goes into hospital. You know what doctors are, they won't commit themselves. But he did say her face and speech should return to normal.'

'That's good news then, isn't it.' Bob pulled at one of her curls and watched it spring back into place. 'I've got some news of me own.' When he saw Mary's eyes cloud over he caught her hand. 'It's not bad news, so don't start getting all het up! It's just that me mam and dad are going to live in Preston for a while, at me auntie's. They can't stay at our Joyce's because she's only got two bedrooms and she's got the two kids. Me Auntie Nancy's got a big house, and there's only her and Uncle Dick so there's plenty of room for Mam and Dad. It's only till they can get fixed up round here.'

'How is your mam?'

'In a state of shock.' Bob's head shook in despair. 'That's why Dad wants to get her away from here. She keeps going back to our house . . . or what was our house . . . and while she keeps doing that she'll never get better. I feel sorry for me dad! He wants to get her away from here but it means him packing his job in.'

Mary sought for words to comfort him. 'There's plenty of people moving away from here since the bombing, so they might get somewhere pretty quick. And your dad will easy find another job.'

'Anyway, they're going to Preston tomorrow and I'm going with them. I'll stay two days to see them settled, then I'll come back for the last two days of me leave. I can sleep at Joyce's, and spend the days round here.' He looked appealingly at Mary. 'Any chance of getting someone to sit with your mam so we can go out?'

There were lines on his face Mary had never seen before, and she reached out to touch them. 'Elsie Smith would sit with her, but she's so miserable she'd make Mam miserable.' Running her fingers lightly over his lips, she thought she'd never seen him look so unhappy. 'I know! I'll ask Vera Jackson from next door! I know she'll come!'

'Isn't that the woman with the little mongol girl?'

'Little Carol! Me mam loves her! She'd be made up if Vera brought Carol to sit with her. I'll slip in later and ask her.' The tinkling of a bell brought Mary's brows together. 'What the heck was that?'

Going into the living room she saw the small ornamental bell in her mother's hand. She remembered giving it to her last night and telling her to ring it if she wanted anything. She remembered something else, too. 'Did you ring that bell this morning, Mam?'

'Eth.' Martha nodded.

'I thought I'd been dreaming! Were you telling me there was a knock on the door when Harry Sedgemoor called?'

'Eth.'

'And has there been a knock now?' Mary was being too slow for Martha and she became impatient. 'Eth, eth, eth!'

'OK, keep your hair on!' Mary laughingly made her way to the door. Let her get as bad tempered as she likes, she thought, it means she's still full of spirit.

'Hello, kid!' Eileen stood on the step holding out a paper bag. 'I met Mrs Sedgemoor in the queue at the bread shop, and she told me about yer mam. I thought she might just fancy these.' Her eyes disappeared as she grinned. 'I just 'appened to be there when they fell off the back of a lorry.'

'Aren't you coming in?'

'Yer mam won't feel like visitors. How is she?'

'Don't be daft and come on in!' As Mary pressed back against the wall to let Eileen pass, she whispered, 'You'll see a difference in me mam's face, but don't let on.'

'Well, now, will yez look at this! Here's me feelin' all sorry for yer 'cos I thought yer were sick.' Eileen's voice boomed out and suddenly the room was bright and cheerful. 'I even tried to get grapes for yer, and the man in the shop asked me if I knew there was a war on!' She sat on the edge of the bed and the springs groaned under her weight. 'I think you're just havin' us on! Yer look bloody healthy to me!'

Bob's head appeared round the kitchen door. 'I thought it was your musical tones I could hear.'

'Oh, you're 'ere, are yer, General West!'

'Now, Eileen! No sarcasm if you don't mind. I may be only a private now, but you never know, I could end up being a general before the war's over.'

'Then all I can say is, God help us all! We'll never win the bloody war!' The bed springs groaned again as she stood up. 'I only called to see how me mate is.' She smiled fondly at Martha. 'I'm in the middle of strippin' the walls, but I couldn't rest till I came to see yer for meself. I'd have had the walls stripped by now if it wasn't for those kids of mine. They won't leave me alone to get on with the job. Me mam, God bless her, tries to keep them out of the way but they take no notice of her. The trouble is, she's too soft with them. Where I'd slap their backsides, she just pats them on the head.' The laughter rumbled in Eileen's tummy before it left her mouth. 'She pats them on the head so often they've got square heads!'

'Stay for a while,' Mary begged.

'No! I've got me two days off, an' if I don't get the rooms done now I never will.' She handed Mary the bag. 'Be careful with this; it's got a couple of newlaid eggs in, a tin of Spam and a box of saccharins.' She wrinkled her nose. 'Bloody awful things they are, but handy when yer run out of sugar.'

'We can't take these . . .' Mary's words were cut off as Eileen pressed the bag into her hand.

'Get hold of them and shut yer gob! And for God's sake be careful of the eggs or the poor chicken's gone to a lot of trouble for nothin'.' Turning to Martha, Eileen gripped her hand. 'Look after yerself, me old mate. I'll be back to see yer in a couple of days, an' I want to see yer out of that bed! D'yer 'ear?'

'So yer don't know how long yer'll be off?' Eileen had to look up to Mary who was standing on the step.

'It depends when they can get me mam into hospital. It could be a few days or a few weeks. Harry said not to worry though, he'd tell them in work.'

'Mmm! Yer've seen Harry, then?'

'Yes, he called this morning.' Mary could have bitten her tongue out when she saw the knowing look on her friend's face. 'Oh, go on, you! He only called to see how Mam was!'

Eileen spread her hands in mock innocence. 'I never opened me mouth!'

'You don't need to; your face is enough!'

Eileen became serious. 'Is it true the Wests are going to Preston?'

'Bob's taking them tomorrow. He's staying two days then coming back for the last two days of his leave.'

'This bloody war's not half upsettin' people's lives! I never thought when it started it was goin' to be this bad.'

'I wish Bob wasn't going away.' Mary shivered. 'Another four days and he might be sent into the thick of it.'

'If yez want to go out when he's home, yer only have to

ask, yer know, kid! I'll come and sit with yer mam.'

'But you're on nights next week! You have to leave for work at nine.'

'So, are we going to lose the war because I go in late for two nights?' Eileen grinned. 'Anyway, what's more important . . . the war or your love life?'

Mary didn't need much persuading. 'I was going to ask one of the neighbours, but I'd much rather you came, and I know me mam would.'

'It's a date then, kiddo! I'll come about six on Wednesday and Thursday, an' yez can toddle off an' enjoy yerselves.' Eileen couldn't resist the temptation to add, 'Don't do anything I wouldn't do, though!'

Guilt brought a blush to Mary's face. 'Is there anything you wouldn't do?'

'No, kid, not much!' Her playful push nearly sent Mary flying, and her cheeky face grinned as she gave an exaggerated wink. 'The trouble is, nobody asks me!'

'She's a case, that Eileen!' Mary was closing the living room door after seeing her friend out, when she heard the rat-tat of the knocker. 'We're certainly having our visitors today!'

The colour drained from her face when she saw who their visitor was. 'Father Murphy!'

'Hello, Mary! I was told at Mass this morning about your mother.'

'Come in, Father.'

'Well, now, Mrs Bradshaw, and what's this I'm after hearing about you?' The young priest's soft Irish voice had a lilt to it, and his blue eyes held a twinkle. He was the

youngest priest in the parish, and in the three years he'd
been there he'd become very well liked and respected. The
pews in the church outside Father Murphy's confessional
box were always full. He was understanding and compassionate for one so young, and more people preferred to
confide in him than the older priest, Father Younger,
whose sermons were full of hell-fire and brimstone, and his
penance for sinning was always twice as many Hail Marys
as Father Murphy's.

'And how are you managing, Mary?' The priest's
attention turned from Martha.

'Fine, Father.' Mary bent her head to straighten the
bedspread, convinced her face would give away her guilty
secret. 'I'll be getting plenty of help.'

'Well now, I'm glad to hear that!' The blue eyes turned to
Bob. ''Tis a terrible thing that's happened to your family,
Bob! I've just been to see your parents, and they tell me
they're going away.'

'Yes, Father! It'll be better for me mam to get away from
here for a while.'

'What a wicked evil world we live in! We can only pray to
the good Lord that it will all be over soon.' Father Murphy
sighed as he turned back to Martha. 'You'll not be able to
get to church, Mrs Bradshaw, so I'll have to bring the
church to you. When were you last at confession?'

Martha's eyes went to Mary for help. 'She can't speak,
Father, but I know she was at confession on Wednesday.'

'Then I'll bring you communion tomorrow.' The rosy
cheeks creased into lines as he smiled. 'I've got a young
couple coming to see me about putting the banns up for

their wedding, but we'll say a little prayer for your speedy recovery before I go.'

Mary made the sign of the Cross and repeated the words of the prayer as her mind branded her a hypocrite.

'I'll see you out, Father.'

'Will you be at Mass tomorrow, Mary? We're having special prayers for all those who have suffered, and all our young men overseas.'

'I'll try and get to confession tonight, Father, and if I can leave me mam for an hour in the morning I'll be at Mass.'

'Good girl.'

Later, Mary asked Bob if he'd sit with her mam while she went to confession. 'I won't be very long.' But she was gone an hour and a half, and when they were alone in the kitchen, Mary admitted she'd been too frightened to go to their own church and had gone to one in the next parish. 'I was too ashamed to go to Father Murphy, and if I'd gone to Father Younger he'd have wiped the floor with me.' But her heart felt lighter ... as though she'd been carrying a heavy burden around for a long time and someone had just lifted it from her shoulders.

Chapter Seven

On her way home from Mary's, Eileen was passing the corner shop when she remembered they needed potatoes. Might as well get them now, she thought, and I can pay me bill while I'm at it. Squeezing through the narrow doorway, she shouted, 'I don't suppose yer've got a leg of mutton under the counter, have yer, Milly? If yer have, I'll have five pound of spuds to go with it.'

'Ay, the only legs under this counter belong to me! And I'll have you know they ain't mutton, either!' Milly Knight was the same age as Eileen, and almost as big. She kept herself tidier though, and her dark hair was always neatly waved, and her round, happy face was never without make-up. No matter what time you went in the shop you'd always get a smile from Milly; even though she opened at six in the morning and didn't close till ten at night, seven days a week. You could buy anything from Knight's corner shop. The smell of paraffin mixed with the smells of cakes and greengrocery, and whether you wanted a gas mantle or a reel of cotton, Milly could always produce it. She once said the only thing they didn't sell was arsenic. Her husband, Les, had been called up a few months ago and she had her work cut out trying to run the shop without him. With all the young women either in the forces or on munitions, the only help she could get were two older women who came in to help when she was busy. Like Eileen, Milly would moan that she didn't know how she kept so fat, but then she would grin and admit she couldn't pass the bottle of Dolly Mixtures without stuffing a handful into her mouth.

'Come 'ed, Claire, darling.' Milly was patiently waiting to serve a little girl who was standing on tiptoe to see over the counter. But Claire shook her head. Biting a precious ha'penny between her tiny, pearl-like teeth, her eyes moved from the brightly coloured gob-stoppers to the black sticks of liquorice. It was a big decision and Claire wasn't going to be rushed. 'Claire's one of me best customers, aren't you, sunshine?' Milly winked at Eileen. 'So I'm going to do her a big favour and let her have a gob-stopper and two sticks of liquorice, all for her ha'penny.'

Claire's angel face broke into a huge smile until she saw Milly pick up a pink gob-stopper. 'Can I 'ave a green one, please?'

The shop filled with Eileen's laughter, and as Milly went to change the offending sweet she said. 'Give 'er them both, an' another two sticks of that black stuff! She can have them on me . . . she deserves them!'

Little Claire ran out of the shop with the sweets clutched in her hot little hands. She couldn't get away quick enough in case the big woman changed her mind. 'I haven't see her round here before.'

'Yes, you have! It's Irene Thompson's little girl. Claire was evacuated to Wales last year, but she was fretting that much they had to bring her home! I didn't know her meself at first 'cos she seems to have shot up.'

'I often wish I'd let mine go when all the others went. Especially now with all the bombin',' Eileen said. 'But it was bad enough Bill goin' away without losing me kids as well.' A glint came in her eyes. 'Mind you, our Billy would have been in his element if he'd been evacuated to a farm in Wales. Can yer imagine 'im muckin' out the pig sties?'

'Speak of the devil!' Milly nodded to the window. 'Here he comes!'

Billy ran into the shop breathless. 'Me nan said can yer let 'er 'ave a packet of biscuits, Mrs Knight?' His eyes caught sight of Eileen and the words poured from his mouth. 'Where've yer been, Mam? I've been lookin' all over for yer. Me Auntie Rene's in our 'ouse!'

'Oh, gawd, that's all I need!' Eileen groaned. 'Her house is like a show place, an' she has to come when ours looks like a muck midden!'

'She's been cryin', Mam, an' me nan's been cryin' too!'

Eileen, who'd been leaning her elbows on the counter, straightened up. 'Give us five pounds of spuds, Milly, and a packet of firelighters.' She looked down on Billy. 'Run 'ome and tell yer nan I'm on me way.'

'What about the biscuits for me nan?'

'Have yer got any biscuits, Milly?' Eileen opened her purse. 'Here's a thru'penny joey. Get some sweets, but mind yer share them with Joan and Edna.'

'I haven't got much selection in biscuits, Eileen.' Milly stood in front of a row of tins. 'Only Marie or Arrowroot ... the others are all broken.'

'Give us some of each, will yer?' Eileen waited till Billy had the biscuits and sweets, then told him, 'Straight home, d'yer hear? An' no pinchin' any, or I'll strangle yer!' When he'd gone she pulled a face. 'Sounds like I'm going home to a happy house, doesn't it, Milly? Anyway, I'll pay yer for these, an' I got some tick off yer through the week, so I'll settle up now.'

Eileen was thoughtful as she plodded her way down the street. I wonder what's up with our Rene? She might have waited till I'd got the room papered. She turns her nose up at it even when it's tidy, so God knows what she'll think of it now, with half the walls stripped.

Her sister was five years younger than Eileen, and they'd always got along together until Rene had started courting Alan. He had a good job in an insurance office and his family were comfortably off. It was then the two sisters started to quarrel, with Rene being ashamed of her home and the way her family spoke. If ever Alan had been coming to pick her up – which wasn't often because Rene kept him away as much as possible – their dad was warned not to wear his cap in the house, and Eileen told to watch her language and not tell rude jokes. When Rene and Alan had their big posh wedding, it was Rene who bought her mother's and Eileen's dresses, so they wouldn't show her up in front of her new in-laws. And they'd gone straight from the wedding into the new house they were buying at the Old Roan, which had a garden back and front. From then on Rene had become such a snob Eileen hated her coming to visit them.

The funny thing was, Eileen got on well with Alan who wasn't toffee-nosed at all! He'd joined the Army at the start of the war and was a captain now, serving under General Auckinleck in the Middle East.

The front door was open and as she walked down the hall Eileen heard her mother say, 'It's no good getting upset until you know what's happened!' Rene was sitting on a chair that had been rescued from the pile, and Maggie was standing over her. They looked round when Eileen walked in and the sight of her sister brought forth a fresh flow of tears from Rene, who was wiping her eyes with a sodden handkerchief. The two sisters were so different in looks it was hard to believe they came from the same set of parents. Eileen with her huge body and clothes that looked as though they'd come off the cart of a rag and bone man, and Rene with her tall, slim figure, dark hair that always looked immaculate and fashionable clothes she wore like a mannequin. She was an attractive woman, with a clear complexion and unusual green eyes.

'What's wrong, our kid?' Eileen asked as she dumped the shopping on the sideboard.

'Alan's been wounded.' Rene's face was red with crying, and her eyes bloodshot.

Eileen spun round. 'How d'yer know?'

Maggie started to speak but Eileen silenced her with a frown. 'Let her tell me, Mam!'

'I had a letter from the War Office saying he'd been

wounded,' Rene was gasping for breath, 'and they'd keep me informed.'

Eileen looked at the bowed head and memories came flooding back of when they were kids. Rene had always been the timid one, with Eileen, the big sister, fighting her battles for her. It was Eileen who took her to school and brought her home again because Mam said she was the oldest and had to look after her little sister. Many's the clout Eileen got because she wouldn't let Rene play with her and her mates. The other kids used to laugh at her because she always had to drag her kid sister with her everywhere she went. But she hadn't been a bad kid, Eileen thought now. She'd never been a cry baby or a clat tale, and she'd always been generous with sharing sweets and toys. And when Eileen was being told off for giving cheek, Rene would always stand by her side and stick up for her.

'How long will it be before yer hear anything, did it say?'

'I rang the office this morning to tell them I wouldn't be going in, and I spoke to Mr Crowley.' Rene had gone to work in the insurance office where Alan had worked. 'He's going to ring London today, and if he can get any information he'll ring me.'

'How the hell can he ring yer when yer not at home?!' Eileen looked up at the ceiling. 'For Christ's sake, our kid, why didn't yer wait for him to call?'

'Because I couldn't stay in that house another minute on my own.' Rene's voice was low. 'I'd go out of me mind just sitting there looking at the four walls all day.'

You wouldn't be on your own if you hadn't decided you didn't want any babies, Eileen thought. But for once she didn't voice her thoughts. Instead of the sister who insulted them every time she came by wiping the chair before she sat down, she was seeing the kid who used to run down the street after her, shouting, 'Ah, go on, our Eileen! Let's play with yer.' 'If yer like, I'll ask Milly Knight if yer can use her phone, and yer can ring this Mr Crowley. Milly won't mind.'

'Will you come with me?'

For the first time, Maggie spoke. 'Of course she will!'

Eileen looked at the half-stripped walls and shrugged. 'I'm never goin' to get this room done! Still, come 'ed, our kid.'

Maggie stood on the step and watched her two daughters walk down the street – one so big and ungainly, the other slim and elegant. But she loved them both, and it did her heart good to see them walking together. That's the way sisters should be, and not always at each other's throats. Mind you, she could understand Eileen getting in a temper sometimes because Rene could be a right little madam with her airs and graces.

'Yer don't mind, do yer, Milly? I wouldn't ask yer if it wasn't important.' Seeing Rene's red, swollen face, Milly was dying to ask what was wrong, but the look on Eileen's face warned her not to. 'Course I don't mind!' She lifted the hinged part of the counter top. 'The phone's out here.'

Eileen pushed her sister forward. 'I'll wait for yer here.' She heard the tinkle as the phone was lifted, then Milly came back in the shop, curiosity written all over her face. 'What's happened?' When Eileen quickly explained she shook her head. 'What a life!'

'You ain't kiddin'! The world's full of troubles and I seem to get the bloody lot!'

Rene came back and slipped through the counter. Shyly she pushed a sixpenny piece across to Milly. 'Thanks very much.'

Milly pushed the coin back. 'Don't be daft!'

'No, you've been very kind, please . . .'

'For cryin' out loud, kid,' Eileen cut her short, 'how did yer get on?'

'He couldn't find anything out.' Rene's lip started to tremble and Eileen knew she was near to tears. Cupping an elbow, she steered her sister towards the door. 'Ta, Milly! I'll see yer tomorrow!'

Neither spoke till they were in the house where an anxious Maggie waited. 'Well?'

Eileen pointed to the chair. 'Sit down, our kid.' She lifted down another two chairs that were piled on the table. 'Be an angel, Mam, and make a cuppa.'

Unbuttoning her coat, Eileen threw it on the couch which was covered with bits of plaster that had come away from the walls when she was scraping. 'I'll just give me mam a hand. Won't be a tick!'

Maggie turned from the stove when Eileen reached across to take down three cups that were hanging on hooks. 'Did she find out anything?'

'Not as far as I know! She was ready to start howling in the middle of the shop, so I got her out, quick.'

'It's a shame, though.' Maggie took a deep breath. 'It must be terrible for her not knowing what's happened to Alan, and being on her own.'

'For Christ's sake, Mam, don't start sympathisin' with her or yer'll make it worse! Don't forget my feller's a prisoner of war and I've got to get on with it like thousands of others.'

'But she hasn't got your strength . . . she never had!'

'Ah, come off it, Mam! Because I don't bawl me 'ead off every time something goes wrong, yer think I'm bloody Tarzan!'

Maggie put a finger to her lips. 'Sshh, she'll hear you!'

'Too bloody bad!' Eileen banged the cups down. 'You make the tea an' I'll go and hold her hand.'

Rene was sitting with her head bowed, nervously clasping her fingers. She jumped when Eileen asked, 'D'yer want to stay and have some tea with us? It's only bangers and mash, though!'

'Can I sleep here tonight?'

'Sleep here?!' Eileen's voice rose as she imagined her sister wrinkling her nose at the state of the bedrooms. 'There's nowhere for yer to sleep!'

'I could sleep on the couch! I wouldn't mind!'

Maggie bustled in with the tray. 'You'd get no sleep on that couch, love; it's got more humps than a camel's back.' Handing Eileen a cup, her nostrils flared and her eyes glinted. 'She can sleep with you! You've got a big double bed all to yourself.'

'With my size, I need it!' Eileen knew it was no good fighting. Her mother would harp till she got her own way.

'Well, when I've kicked yer out of bed in the middle of the night, our kid, don't say yer weren't warned!'

In the street, Billy was sharing the sweets with his sisters. 'Me Auntie Rene's in our 'ouse, an' there must be summat up 'cos she's been cryin'.' He tried to put an extra sweet on his pile while imparting the news, but Edna was too quick for him. 'I'll tell me mam on yer! Yer a cheat, our Billy!' So Billy counted the sweets again, happily thinking of the two bull's eyes he'd hidden in his trouser pocket.

Their mouths black-rimmed from the black jacks, Edna and Joan ran home filled with curiosity. They were in awe of their auntie who spoke posh and didn't ever have much to say to them except ask how they were getting on in school. But she always gave them a penny for sweets and this was in their minds as they barged through the front door. They were out of luck though as Eileen met them half way down the hall and turned them back.

'I'll give yez a shout when the tea's ready.' Lowering her voice, she hissed, 'And behave yerselves or I'll tan the backsides off yer. No wipin' yer nose on the back of yer sleeves, d'yer 'ear?'

Eileen had to stretch the food out to cover an extra plate, but was rewarded when Rene wiped her plate clean and said, 'I enjoyed that!' If the oilcloth covering the table caused her to think of her own highly polished table, with its snow-white damask cloth, she didn't let it show. She knew she was the reason for the kids being so quiet and tried to draw them out. 'What's your favourite game, Billy?'

Billy's face flamed. 'I dunno!'

'Yes you do, our Billy!' young Edna piped up. 'It's Cowboys and Indians.'

'No, it's not!' Billy kicked her under the table and she let out a shriek.

''E kicked me, Mam.'

'I thought it was too good to be true.' Eileen started to collect the dishes. 'Any more, and yer'll all go to bed.'

'Ah, ay, Mam! Can't we play out?' Billy glared at his sister who was rubbing the ankle he'd kicked. 'Go on, Mam! We'll only play in the street.'

Three pairs of eyes fastened on Eileen as Joan coaxed, 'Honest, Mam, we'll stay near the 'ouse.'

The thought of them playing out was far more attractive than having them in the house shouting and squabbling. 'OK; but in by seven, mind!'

The dishes washed, the three women sat at the table with their second cup of tea. 'Are yer goin' in to work tomorrow, sis?'

'I may as well, or I'd go nuts in that house all day on my own.'

'You may hear something in a day or two,' Maggie offered. 'They're bound to let you know what's happening.'

'Mr Crowley said Alan may be in a field hospital.' Rene bit her lips to stop them trembling. 'He said if Alan's not fit for active duty they'll send him home.'

'Kid, it's time to start worrying when yer've got something to worry about!' Eileen's eyes travelled round the half-stripped walls. 'You two mightn't have anything better to do, but I've got to get crackin' on these walls! I've only got tonight and tomorrow to get them finished.' She glanced sideways at Maggie. 'Why don't you an' our kid go to the pictures? It'll take yer mind off things, and give me a chance to get some work done.'

'No!' Rene answered quickly. 'I'm not going to the pictures! I'll give you a hand with the scraping.'

Eileen looked at the smart navy blue dress with its neat white collar and burst out laughing. 'Dressed like that?'

'You can lend me an overall, can't you? And I'm quite capable of scraping walls.'

Ten minutes later Eileen and Maggie were doubled up with laughter as Rene stood before them in one of Eileen's overalls. 'Yer look like little orphan Annie.' Eileen was convulsed. 'Me mam could get in there with yer.'

Rene looked down at herself. 'I could fit in one of the sleeves!' Her green eyes were shining and Eileen could see the sister she used to know. She hasn't changed that much, she thought. Not deep down she hasn't.

After tying a belt round her waist, which had the effect of making the overall look like a tent, Rene rolled her sleeves up. 'What are you standing around for? Let's get crackin'!'

'You hold the ladder while I reach up to the top.' Eileen had her foot on the bottom rung when Rene burst out, 'Not ruddy likely!' She was standing with her hands on her hips surveying the rickety ladder. 'If you think I'm going to hold this with you on top, you've got another think coming! If you fell I'd be crushed to death!' She shook her head vigorously, 'Oh, no! You hold the ladder and I'll do the scraping. Then, if I fall, I'll have a nice soft cushion to fall on!'

'The flamin' cheek of you!' Eileen winked at Maggie.

'D'yer hear that, Mam? I'm gettin' insulted in me own 'ouse!'

Unhindered by too much weight, Rene worked quickly. By ten o'clock the walls had all been stripped, the floor brushed, the old paper crammed into a cardboard box and the ladder back in the outside lavvy. 'I'm glad yer came, our kid!' Eileen grinned. 'Yer'd make a good labourer!'

'Now who's got a flamin' cheek?!' Rene folded the overall. 'I did all the flamin' work!'

That's more like it; Eileen exchanged knowing glances with her mother. She's beginning to sound like our Rene now!

Eileen lay on her back in the bed. 'Yer'll let us know as soon as yer hear anythin', won't yer?'

'I'll come straight up, I promise.'

'Well, I'm dead beat so I'll say goodnight, our kid.' Eileen turned on her side, as near to the edge of the bed as she could get to give her sister more room. 'God bless!' She felt an arm come round her ample waist, 'Night and God bless, Eileen, and thanks.'

We used to sleep like this as kids, Eileen remembered. She could feel a lump come into her throat and tutted to herself. This cryin' lark must be catchin'! They've got me at it now!

Chapter Eight

'Your hair looks lovely, Mam.' Mary touched the snow-white hair washed earlier by Nurse Nolan. 'I'm glad I put those curlers in.' She sat down then bounced up again. 'It's no good, I can't settle! Where's he got to!? I'm going to see if there's any sign of him.' She opened the door to see Vera Jackson from next door hurrying past, her three-year-old daughter clasped in her arms. 'Off to the shops, Vera?'

'No, I'm nipping to the doctor's to see if he can give me anything for Carol's cold.' Vera transferred the child to her other arm. 'God, she's not half a weight to carry round.'

Mary smiled at the little mongol girl and the moon-like face with its unblinking eyes smiled back. 'Are you coming in to see Nanna Bradshaw?'

'Your mam won't want to be bothered with us,' Vera answered.

'What d'you mean, Vera, she won't be bothered? You know she dotes on Carol!' Mary shot a glance at the woman who, when she was a teenager, Mary wanted to grow up to be like. Vera had been very attractive then. She used to walk down the street, tall and slim in her three-inch heels, her thick auburn hair worn in a long page-boy bob, her face carefully made-up and wearing what Mary thought was the very latest fashion in clothes. She was so full of life and always happy. Then Carol was born and the change in Vera was dramatic. Flat heels replaced the fashion shoes, she ceased to wear make-up, her beautiful hair was combed back from her face and tied with a piece of string and the clothes she wore were dowdy.

'Come in for a few minutes.' Mary walked back into the house leaving Vera to follow. 'Look who's come to see you, Mam.' Mary took Carol from Vera's arms and stood her in front of Martha. The child tried to struggle free and Mary's grip tightened. 'You're only little but you've got the strength of a horse.'

'You can say that again!' Vera sighed. She loved her daughter dearly but was worn out by her constant demands for attention. It wouldn't be so bad if she was the only child, but there were the two boys to look after as well. And nobody ever knocked on her door and asked if they could mind the baby, like they did at other houses. In fact some of the kids made fun of Carol when they saw her, and this caused fights between them and Colin, who was twelve, and Peter who was nine.

Vera watched Mary lift Carol carefully on to Martha's knee, and as soon as Martha had her safely in the crook of her arm she snuggled her to her breast. Carol was gurgling with contentment and Vera thought how much love her daughter needed. But apart from these two, and myself, she doesn't get it. The boys were kind to her in their own way, but she embarrassed them, and Vera couldn't blame them when people said their sister wasn't 'right' in the head. Even Carol's own father, Danny, was ashamed of having sired a mongol. He'd never admit it, but it was the truth. Never once, since the day she was born, had he held her in his arms or kissed her.

'Come on, love, time to go.' Vera swept Carol up, bringing forth a howl of protest. 'I know, you're nice and comfortable, but we've got to get to the doctor's and back before your dad comes in for his tea.'

Pity he can't make his own tea for a change, Mary felt like saying, but she held her tongue. Vera never complained but they knew what the situation was next door. They'd heard Danny bawling if ever Vera asked if she could go to the pictures for a break. 'I've been working all day an' I'm too tired to be mindin' a whinging brat while you go off and enjoy yourself.' So Vera would stay in, and when they heard the door slam later, Mary would say: 'He's not too tired to go for his pint.'

Mary walked to the door behind Vera. 'I'm expecting Bob any minute. You know his parents have gone to live in Preston, don't you?'

'Elsie Smith told me.'

Mary laughed. 'You don't need to buy the *Echo* with her around! She knows everyone's business, and what she doesn't know she makes up.'

Back in the living room, Mary stood in front of her mother's chair. 'I feel awful sorry for Vera. She doesn't get much out of life with that lazy husband of hers.' Then came the sound she'd waited for all day. 'He's here, Mam!'

Martha heard Mary's cry of pleasure, then Bob's deep

laugh. 'Hey, watch it! You're nearly strangling me!'

They came through the door arm in arm, their faces shining with the joy of being together. And when Bob saw Martha sitting in her chair, his mouth gaped. 'Well, I'll be blowed!'

'Doesn't she look great? Nurse sat her out yesterday while we changed the bed and Mam wouldn't go back. So Nurse said she could sit out each day until she comes in the afternoon to wash her.'

Mary pulled at Bob's coat sleeve. 'Take your coat off and look as though you're staying!'

'I was hoping to catch an earlier train, but when the news came on the wireless me dad couldn't stop talking about it and I didn't like just walking out.'

Mary's eyes clouded. 'What news?'

'You mean you haven't heard? Hitler's declared war on Russia!'

'We haven't had the wireless on.' Mary frowned. 'What does that mean?'

'It means that Hitler threw everything he could at us during the blitz, hoping to put us out of action so he could have a go at Russia without us being able to do anything about it. But he's picked on the wrong ones with the Russians. They won't let him walk all over them like the rest of Europe has.'

Martha's eyes moved from one to the other as Mary asked, 'Is that good news for us?'

'I think so! He'll be fighting on more fronts now, and God only knows where he's getting all the troops from. He's got to keep armies in all the countries he's occupied because of the underground movements there.'

Mary folded his coat over her arm. 'Will the war be over quicker?'

'Well, I think Hitler's crazy; but crazy or not he's lifting his two fingers up to the rest of the world. Look at the fool he made of Chamberlain! Peace for our time, Chamberlain said when he came back with that piece of paper, and the ink wasn't even dry on it when Hitler's troops invaded Czechoslovakia.'

Mary's hand flew to her mouth. 'Here's the nurse! Let her in will you, love, while I get the water ready.'

Rose Nolan gave Bob a cheerful smile. 'So you're the boyfriend Mary never stops talking about?'

Bob laughed as he followed her into the room. 'I hope it's all good.'

'According to Mary, you're going to stop the war single-handed when you get over there.' She beamed at Martha before adding, 'Listening to her, you're Cary Grant, James Stewart, and Gary Cooper, all rolled into one.' She took the bowl from Mary and nodded towards the kitchen. 'Vamoose, while I get on with my work.'

Mary pulled Bob's arm. 'Let's go before she gives us all a bed bath.'

As soon as the kitchen door closed behind them, Bob took Mary in his arms. 'How's it been?'

Mary's head went back and she smiled into his face. 'When the nurse said it would be as easy as falling off a bike once I got the hang of it, I didn't believe her. But she was right, and I can manage fine, now.'

'You're going to make a smashing wife.' Bob nibbled her

ear. 'Slippers waiting by the fire when I get home from work, and a cushion for me back.'

'Some hope you've got, Bob West! If you think I'm going to wait on you hand and foot you've got another think coming.'

'I wish we were married.' Bob fingered her hair. 'Then I wouldn't have to go to our Joyce's tonight to sleep.'

'How's your mam and dad? I didn't want to ask in front of me mam in case she got upset. D'you think they'll settle down there?'

'Me dad might, but I don't think me mam will. She's walking round in a dream and even I couldn't get through to her. They got some emergency clothing coupons and I took her round the shops thinking it would pull her out of herself, but she wasn't interested. The only time she showed any emotion was when it was time for me to leave, and it nearly broke my heart to walk away from her.'

They broke apart as the door was pushed open and Nurse Nolan grinned at their blushes. 'Caught you in the act, did I?' She looked over her shoulder at Bob as she tipped the water into the sink. 'What d'you think about Adolf starting on Russia?'

'He must be mad if he thinks he can get away with it.'

'He's got away with it so far! He collects countries like other people collect stamps.'

'Wait till I get over there.' Bob grinned. 'I'll sort him out!'

Eileen's nose twitched. 'Got yer Evening in Paris on, kid? Yer smell like a rose garden.'

Mary flushed as three pairs of eyes fastened on her. 'Where d'you want to go, Bob? Margaret Lockwood on the Vale, or Abbott and Costello on the Atlas?'

'It's up to you, love! I don't care where we go.'

Eileen's push sent Bob reeling. 'Yer'll get more than a laugh if yez go to the Atlas! They don't call it the flea pit for nothing! Yez go in there in a blouse and come out with a jumper!'

Mary was smiling as she kissed her mother. 'We won't be late.'

'Don't hurry on my account,' Eileen told them. 'Just enjoy yerselves.' When they passed the window, their arms around each other, she grinned at Martha. 'Love's young dream! What it is to be young, eh?'

Martha gave her lopsided grin. 'Eth.'

Eileen tilted her head. 'Yer know, Mrs B, if yer can say that, yer can say other things.' When Martha shook her head, pointing to the side of her face, Eileen tutted. 'Yer don't need to move yer lips! A bloody ventriloquist doesn't move his lips, does he? Just watch me!' She pressed her lips together hard before half opening her mouth, and from the back of her throat came a deep mumble. 'Can yer hear me, Mother?'

Martha nodded, her eyes full of laughter at Eileen's comical face. 'Never mind how bloody daft I look, just try it!'

Over and over Martha tried. She would have given up but Eileen wouldn't let her. 'Yer know what they say . . . cruel to be kind! Have another go.'

When the first recognisable word came it was supposed

to be 'Mary', but came out ''Ary'. Eileen was so excited she nearly hit the ceiling. 'See, I told yer, didn't I?' Her eyes roamed the room picking on items. 'Come on, have a go!' Mirror came out as ''irrer', and couch as ''oush', but Eileen was delighted. 'Keep that up, Mrs B, an' yer'll be talking proper in no time.'

Martha's faded blue eyes were bright with pleasure and hope. What a blessing it would be if she could talk!

'Practise when yer on yer own,' Eileen advised. 'And don't give up or I'll have yer guts for garters if yer let me down.'

They heard the key in the lock and Eileen's eyebrows shot up. 'They're early!' She put a finger to her lips. 'Not a word to Mary! It's our secret till yer can surprise her. And don't do it when I'm not here, 'cos I want to see her face when yer start talkin' to her.' When Mary came through the door, Eileen asked, 'Yez didn't come home early because of me, did yer?' Mary shook her head. 'We came out before the second house started. We'd seen most of the big picture anyway, so we knew how it ended.'

'Don't believe her!' Bob chuckled. 'She'd have sat through it all again if I'd let her. Of all the pictures to take me to, she picked one she could sit and cry all the way through.'

'Margaret Lockwood, eh?' Eileen grinned. 'Yer big soft nellie!'

'Stewart Granger was in it, and it was lovely.'

Bob raised his eyes to the ceiling. 'If it was so lovely, why did you cry all the way through? I can't understand you women . . . never happier than when you're crying.'

'Yer should have stayed at home,' Eileen told them. 'We've had a fine time, haven't we, Mrs B? Pulling everyone to pieces.'

'Take no notice of him,' Mary said. 'I haven't cried all night . . . only part of it! We came home early so you can get to work on time tonight, in case we're late tomorrow. Bob's taking me somewhere tomorrow night and he won't tell me where.'

Eileen smiled at Martha as she reached for her coat. 'Try and think of someone we haven't pulled to pieces, an' we can have a go at them.' She brushed aside Mary's thanks. 'I'll see yez tomorrow . . . ta-ra.'

Mary had her coat on ready when Eileen came the next night. Bob had been at the house since early morning and had been restless all day. But when Mary questioned him about where they were going, all he would say was 'wait and see'.

'Has he told yer where yez are going, yet?' Eileen asked.

'No!' Mary pouted. 'He says it's a surprise.'

'I 'ope it's a pleasant one!'

Bob tapped a finger on his nose. 'You know what curiosity did to the cat!' He pulled on Mary's arm. 'Let's go before she wheedles it out of me.'

Mary turned at the door and winked at her mother. 'Don't let Eileen teach you any bad habits, Mam!'

Eileen feigned amazement. 'Bad habits! Me! Me mind's as pure as the driven snow.'

'Aye! When you're asleep!' Bob ducked as Eileen raised her arm. 'Come 'ed, Mary, before she floors me!'

As they turned into the main road Mary grabbed Bob's arm. 'Quick, there's a bus coming.'

Bob pulled her back. 'Let's wait for the tram. This is my night, remember, and I'd rather go on one of the old rib ticklers.' As the bus pulled away they heard the familiar trundle of a tram car. 'See, we didn't have to wait long.' Bob pinched Mary's bottom as she ran up the stairs. 'Sit in the front.'

'Buses are much more comfortable,' Mary grumbled as she sat on the hard wooden seat. 'You get corns on your bottom from these hard seats.'

'Buses may be more comfortable but there's no magic to them. Give me the old trams any day. They remind me of when we were kids and could go anywhere for a penny.'

Mary grinned as fond memories flooded back. 'A bottle of water, a ha'porth of lemonade powder, a jam buttie, and a penny for the tram! We could spend a whole day at one of the parks for three ha'pence.'

Bob slipped his arm across the back of the wooden seat. 'Even when I was only ten, I wanted to marry you! You were the prettiest girl in school, and every playtime I used to stand with me face pressed between the railings watching you playing hop-scotch. All me mates used to make fun of me because I fancied you.' The tram was travelling towards Scotland Road and Bob leaned forward to point out the bombed buildings. 'They've had it pretty bad around here.'

Mary's voice was sad. 'The poor old Rotunda. That corner won't look the same without it.'

'There's going to be a lot of building up to do after the war.'

'I don't care what they do after the war, as long as you're home.'

'It might be over sooner than we think, now the Russians are in it. I think Hitler's got too much on his plate. He was better equipped than we were because he's been preparing for years, but we're starting to fight back. All we had in the beginning were a few planes and some very brave fighter pilots. If it hadn't been for them we'd have been done for.' Bob envied the bravery of those pilots who risked their lives daily to keep the skies over Britain clear. He wished he was that brave, the thought of being sent overseas frightened the life out of him, and he knew he wasn't the only one. The lads in his unit joked about killing Germans, but Bob knew that deep down they were as afraid as he was. Perhaps everyone was afraid when faced with danger . . . even the fighter pilots. Perhaps it was only when it was a case of kill or be killed, that a person found the courage to fight back. He leaned forward and rubbed the sleeve of his jacket across the steamed-up window.

'Come on, this is our stop.'

The tram lurched on its way leaving Mary and Bob standing outside St George's Hall in Lime Street. 'We should have got off in London Road.' Mary looked up into Bob's face. 'Aren't we going to Sampson and Barlows?'

Bob shook his head and pointed across the road to the Grand Western Hotel which fronted Lime Street Station. 'That's where we're going.'

'We can't go in there!' Mary started to laugh. 'You're pulling me leg.'

'I am not pulling your leg! That's where we're going!'

109

'I can't go in there looking like this.' Mary looked down at her coat, made out of a blanket to save coupons. 'That's where all the posh people go.'

'If you wore rags you'd still look lovely. And, Mary, I've been saving up for something special, so let's blow it on one good night out.'

Mary's eyes widened when they entered the foyer of the large Victorian hotel. Her first instinct was to turn tail and run when she took in the rich velvet curtains, ornate chandeliers, carved wooden doors and deep soft carpets. 'Let's go,' she whispered. 'I'm not staying here.'

'Too late,' Bob whispered back as a waiter in black suit and bow tie appeared and beckoned them to follow him into the dining room. At every table they passed sat servicemen with pips or heavy gold braid on their uniforms. Mary's heart pounded as she wished the floor would open and swallow her up. After showing them to a table the waiter left to fetch a menu, and Bob smiled encouragement as he reached across the table to take hold of her hand. 'It rather looks as though I'm the only private here, but my girl outshines all their gold braid.' He glanced around. 'Some of them are probably catching trains tonight back to their base.'

Mary shuddered. 'Don't let's talk about the war tonight.'

The waiter was clearing away their plates, and Bob ordered another drink. 'Bang goes me ciggie money, but what the hell! It's been worth it.'

The two glasses of sherry were having an effect on Mary. Her face was lit up with happiness and her shyness gone.

The people around her were forgotten as she looked across the table. 'Can Eileen be me maid of honour when we get married? She is my very best friend.' Bob thought he'd never seen her looking so lovely as he nodded in agreement. 'And can we get a parlour house so me mam can have her own room?'

'Mary, you can have the world if you want it,' Bob teased. 'And now, how about telling me why you want to marry me?'

'Because I love you so much it hurts.'

'Let's go.' Bob beckoned the waiter. 'I think it might cause a stir if I kiss you here.'

The waiter brought the change from the £5 note on a small silver tray and Bob picked up the £1 note, leaving the loose change as a tip. He waited till they were on the street outside before throwing back his head and laughing. 'The tip was almost a week's army pay!'

When they got home Eileen was bursting with curiosity but Mary wouldn't let Bob tell her where they'd been. 'I want to tell you, and it would take too long. Wait till you come next time and you've got more time.'

Eileen's eyes disappeared in a grin. 'OK, kid! I'll call tomorrow and yer can thrill me with excitement.'

'I'll see Eileen out.' Bob moved to the door after her. 'We don't want an audience for our farewell kiss.'

'A man at last!' Eileen winked at Martha. 'See yer tomorrow, Mrs B. Ta-ra.'

Bob looked down from the top step. 'Thanks for letting us have some time on our own, Eileen. And will you do me another favour and keep your eye on Mary for us, while I'm away?'

'Course I will! She's me best mate, isn't she?' Eileen wrapped her coat over her ample bosom. 'Now, how about that kiss? It's such a long time since a man kissed me I've forgotten what it feels like.' She lifted her head for Bob's peck on the cheek then walked away shouting over her shoulder, 'I hope my feller does better than that when he gets home! Proper bloody tame, that was! Ta-ra, Bob . . . look after yourself.'

'What was Eileen shouting about?' Mary was perched on the side of the bed. 'She's got a voice like a foghorn.'

'She was complaining that my kiss wasn't passionate enough for her.'

'Cheeky beggar! I've got no complaints.' Mary's light-hearted chatter didn't fool Martha. She knew it was put on for her sake. And later, when Bob was leaving and he bent to kiss her, saying he'd probably be home again in a few weeks, she tried not to let her sadness show. It was all pretence, but she went along with it.

'What will happen if there's a raid, with your mam the way she is?' Bob whispered in Mary's ear as he held her tight. They were standing in the tiny hall and in a few minutes he'd have to be on his way.

'I've been thinking about that meself,' Mary whispered back. 'The only thing is a Morrison shelter, but I don't think we'd get one in the room with the bed in as well.'

'What's a Morrison shelter?' Bob asked. 'I've never heard of them.'

'There's a family down the road got one. They're like a big steel table with wire mesh round the sides.' Mary managed a weak smile. 'They're like a monkey's cage, but they reckon they'll stand up to a house falling on them. I wouldn't like to put it to the test meself, though.' She heard Bob sigh and knew the longer they put off saying goodbye the worse it would be. She was steeling herself not to cry because she didn't want to upset her mother, but the lump in her throat was growing. 'Don't forget to wipe the lippy off your face before you get to your Joyce's. There's more on your face than there is on my lips.' There was a catch in her voice as she hugged him one last time. 'I'll say a prayer to St Anthony every night to watch over you.'

Chapter Nine

'Shall I take Madam's coat?' Mary stood in the middle of the room and with raised eyebrows, bowed from the waist. She folded an imaginary coat over her arm and walked towards the door with her nose in the air and her back as stiff as a poker. Then, bending double she shook with laughter. 'Honest, I nearly died of embarrassment when he walked down that posh room with me blanket over his arm.'

Even the floorboards trembled as Eileen's laugh boomed out. 'Can yer imagine 'is face if I'd handed him this Paris model?' She looked down at her old faded coat, and with a finger indicated the various coloured stains, the frayed cuffs and the missing buttons. 'I'd have been thrown out on me arse, that's for sure!' She winked at Martha whose eyes were wet with tears of laughter. 'I think your daughter needs taking down a peg or two, don't you, Mrs B? How about her makin' us a cuppa?' A sly grin on her face, she reached into her shopping bag and produced a packet of tea and a pound of sugar. 'Don't ask me where I got them. If yer ask no questions yer'll be told no lies.'

'We can't keep taking things off you! Every time you come you bring us something.'

'You don't have time to go to the shops and stand in a queue, so shut yer gob an' take them.' Eileen shoved the packets in Mary's hand. 'And don't worry about us going short at home, 'cos we're not!' A wicked grin crossed her face. 'There's only one thing I'm goin' short of, and I won't be gettin' any of that till my Bill gets home. Unless, of course, I can find meself a bit on the side.'

'You're past the post, you are!' The sound of the door knocker brought a frown to Mary's face. 'I wonder who this can be?' She dropped the precious tea and sugar on to Eileen's lap. 'Shove these in the kitchen for us, will you? It might be Elsie Smith, and the least she knows the better.'

Instead of the small figure of Elsie Smith on the step, it was a tall, slim girl dressed in a WRNS uniform. Mary's mouth gaped. 'Barbara!'

Barbara Wilson grinned as she twirled round. 'How do I look?'

'Fabulous! When did you join up?'

'Three months ago. I did call round to tell you, but there was no one in.'

'I'm standing here gawping like someone soft. Come in and tell us all your news.' As Mary stepped aside to let her friend pass, she whispered, 'Have you heard about Mam?' When Barbara nodded, Mary flung the living room door open. 'Wait till you see what the wind's blown in, Mam!'

Barbara stood in front of Martha and drew herself up to her full height. 'Do I look like the pig's ear, Mrs B?'

Martha nodded, her eyes bright with pleasure. She was

very fond of the girl who had been Mary's friend since they started school. At one time she'd never been away from the Bradshaws' house, till Bob came on the scene. Martha was used to seeing her with her dark hair down to her shoulders, but now it was cut in a short bob, and the style suited the white uniform hat she was wearing at a jaunty angle. Her brown eyes and white teeth flashed as she grinned. 'It was like this, you see, Mrs B! All the lads were getting called up, so I thought if I was ever going to get a feller I'd better join up too!'

'This is Eileen, a friend from work.' Mary made the introductions as she pushed Barbara down on the couch. 'I'm dying to know what made you join the Wrens, and where you're stationed?'

Barbara rolled her expressive eyes. 'My dear, I look positively ghastly in khaki. Doesn't suit my complexion, don't you know!' Her put-on posh accent sent Eileen into gales of laughter and Mary into a fit of the giggles. 'No, seriously,' Barbara went on, 'I never even considered anything but the Wrens. I'm stationed at Plymouth, but before you ask what everybody else asks, the answer is "No", I haven't even been on a ship yet!'

'Never mind the ships,' Eileen said, 'have yer got a feller?'

'You've heard about sailors having girls in every port, well I've got a feller on every ship. The trouble is, they're never in port long enough to get to know them.'

Mary was hanging on to every word. 'How long are you home for?'

'I go back next Thursday.'

Mary looked at her friend's neat uniform, the black stockings, and her flat-heeled highly polished shoes. 'You look dead smart in the uniform.'

'I've got another surprise for you. I met Jean Graves at the shops this morning, and she's joined the Land Army!'

'Go way?' Mary shook her head. 'I haven't seen Jean for ages.'

'I'm meeting her tomorrow – we're going to Reeces' tea dance.' Barbara's eyes lit up. 'Why don't you come with us? It would be like old times, the three of us together again.'

'I couldn't!' Mary's refusal came quickly. 'I couldn't leave me mam, and I'm not in the mood anyway.' She saw the query in Barbara's eyes. 'Bob only went back off embarkation leave this morning, so I'm a bit down in the dumps.'

'Don't be so bloody daft!' Eileen snorted. 'Yer not going to bury yerself till Bob comes home, are yer?' She saw Mary's eyes flash, and hurried on. 'I can sit with yer mam, so yer've no excuse.'

'You're on nights tonight, so you won't feel like coming here tomorrow afternoon.'

'I can have a few hours' kip in the morning, and I can sleep all tomorrow night 'cos I start mornings on Sunday.' Eileen clicked her teeth. 'For cryin' out loud, kid, what do we have to do to get you to go out and enjoy yerself?'

'Come on, Mary,' Barbara wheedled. 'Let's give Jean a surprise. I'm meeting her outside Reeces, so we could go down on the bus together.'

It was the look on her mother's face that decided Mary. 'OK! I know when I'm licked.'

Barbara wasn't convinced. 'You won't change your mind?'

'No chance!' It was Eileen who answered. 'You call for her at two tomorrow and I'll see she goes. Even if I have to carry her there.'

When Eileen waved Mary off at two o'clock the next afternoon she didn't expect her back till after six o'clock. So there was surprise on her face when Mary let herself in just after five. 'You're home early! Wasn't it any good?'

'Yeah, it was all right!' Mary stood at the bottom of the bed and smiled at her mother. 'Barbara and Jean got off with two naval officers and I felt like a gooseberry, so I came home early. They're staying in town and going out with them tonight.'

'What about you?' Eileen asked. 'Didn't you get any dances? I can't see the other two copping off, and not you! Unless all the fellers needed their eyes testing.'

'I had a few dances.' Mary kept her eyes averted. 'Harry Sedgemoor was there and he got me up a few times.'

'Well, fancy that!' The astonishment on Eileen's face was genuine. She'd told Harry that Mary was going to Reeces, but she didn't expect him to turn up there. 'He gets around, doesn't he?'

'It was crowded! You could hardly move on the dance floor. It looked like the League of Nations with British, French, Dutch and American uniforms.' Mary's face became serious. 'I got a shock when I saw what the bombing had done to Blacklers. To think I was in there only two weeks ago getting knickers for me mam, and now it's in ruins.' Suddenly remembering she wasn't to give her mother any bad news, she forced a smile. 'Anyway, what have you two been up to?'

'While you've been out flyin' yer kite, it's been like Casey's court in here! First Father Younger called to see how yer mam was, an' he ended up giving me five rounds of the kitchen for not going to Mass on Sunday. Said I was settin' a bad example to the kids.' Eileen rolled her eyes upwards. 'I told him I was doing me bit for the war effort by working on Sundays, but he said it was no excuse. If I couldn't get to church in the morning I could always go at night to the seven o'clock service.'

'Who else called?'

'Doctor Greenfield! Yer mam's goin' in the 'ossie tomorrow. They've got a bed for her in Walton 'ospital.'

'That was quick.' Mary didn't know whether to laugh or cry. She knew her mother would be better off in hospital, but she didn't want her to go. 'I'll have to get your things ready.'

'Nine o'clock the ambulance will be here.' Eileen managed to heave herself off the couch after the third push. 'I may as well get home and get some washing on the line while there's a bit of dry out. It's been in steep all night so I've only got to put it through the mangle.'

'Thanks for coming, Eileen! You're a pal!'

'Think nothin' of it, kid! I'll call in tomorrow an' see if me mate here,' Eileen winked at Martha, 'gets settled in the 'ospital all right.' She got to the door and turned. 'I'm glad for your sake yer going in 'ospital Mrs B 'cos they'll get yer better. But I'm glad for me own sake too, because tatty head here can come back to work now.'

'Why?' Mary looked puzzled. 'Who've you been working with?'

'Bloody Jean Simpson, that's who!' Eileen walked back into the centre of the room. 'Honest to God, if I have to work with that stupid cow much longer I won't be able to keep me 'ands off her.' Eileen looked from Mary to Martha. 'All day long her mouth's goin', chewin' bloody chewing gum! It never stops, even when we're havin' our break she's blowin' bubbles with the bloody stuff.'

While Mary's shoulders shook with laughter, and Martha held her hand over her distorted mouth, Eileen got into her stride. Between roars of laughter she did an impression of Jean Simpson and the offending mouth. 'Can yer imagine lookin' across the machine all day, an' seein' this peroxide blonde with about two inches of black root showin', and a mouth that's doin' bloody contortions?! I know I should be pitying her instead of makin' fun, but I can't help it! She's shaved all her eyebrows off, an' she's got this thick black pencil line where her eyebrows should be. She looks like a clown, but thinks she's the pig's ear 'cos she's goin' out with a Yank. The poor sod's even talkin' like a Yank now!' Eileen held her hand up for silence. 'If yez can stop laughing for a minute, I'll tell yez something that'll really knock yez out!' She waited for Mary to control her giggles before putting on a solemn face. 'She calls me "honey"!'

'Will you shut up!' Mary had her arms folded across her tummy. 'I've got a pain now with laughing.'

'Yer wouldn't be laughing if yer had to put up with it!' Eileen saw the smile leave Martha's face. 'What is it, Mrs B?'

Martha held her hand up, her head cocked, listening. Mary had stopped laughing now and she too was straining to hear the raised voices coming from next door. 'How many times do I have to tell yer to keep her from under me bloody feet? Get her out of here . . . quick!' Danny's angry voice filled the now silent room, and Eileen jerked her head towards the wall. 'What's goin' on?'

'Big, brave Danny Jackson, picking on a woman and a little girl.' Mary's face was white as she shushed. 'Listen!'

Once again Danny's voice invaded the room. 'Keep on like that an' you'll get another belt!'

'The bastard!' Eileen stood up. 'He'll not hit a woman or a baby while I'm around.'

'Don't interfere, Eileen.' Mary laid a restraining hand on her arm. 'If you go round he'd kill Vera after you'd left.'

'Yer mean we sit here and do nowt?! Let him get away with it?'

'Me mam had words with Danny once, and it ended up with Vera getting a black eye.' Mary gave out a long shuddering sigh. 'He often gives her a belt.'

'Bloody hell! What he needs is a man to sort him out!' Eileen was roaring like a bull. 'I'd better go before I burst a blood vessel.' She crossed to the bed. 'I'll be in to see yer in 'ospital, Mrs B. You do as they tell yer an' yer'll be up and about in no time.'

Mary's face was dark with anger as she stood by the door. 'If he's upset me mam, I'll go in there and kill him meself!

She's always said he'd do Carol an injury one of these days.'

Eileen had never seen Mary so angry before. 'We'd soon sort him out, wouldn't we, kid? I'll hold him, while you thump him!'

Mary's face relaxed into a smile as the picture of Eileen holding Danny in an arm lock flashed through her mind. 'Lovely thought, isn't it?'

'It sure is, kiddo! But this isn't gettin' me washing done, so I'll toddle off and see yer tomorrow. Tar-ra, kid.'

Mary went straight upstairs to get the suitcase to put her mam's things in ready for the hospital. It was an old and battered case, but it was the only one they had so it would have to do.

Eileen trudged up the side streets on her way home. Two things were blighting her usual happy nature. One was Danny Jackson ... the bullying bastard! ... and the other was the agony she felt as her shoes dug into her swollen ankles. When she'd got the washing out she'd have to put her feet up for an hour. She turned into her street and when she saw Joan and Edna playing skipping rope further down, she waved in greeting.

'You're late!' Maggie was leaning against the front door, her arms folded. 'I was beginning to wonder where you'd got to.'

'Yer knew I was callin' to Mary's!' Eileen pushed back the turban which was sliding down her forehead. 'You're blockin' the doorway, Missus! Can I come in?'

In the living room, Maggie watched her daughter throw her coat over the back of a chair before delving into her apron pocket and pulling out a crumpled letter. 'This came after you'd left.'

Something in the tone of her mother's voice sent a shiver down Eileen's spine as she stared at the letter, but she made no move to take it. She was afraid of the disappointment she'd feel if it wasn't from the one person in the whole wide world she wanted it to be from.

'Take it, lass!' Maggie spoke softly. 'It's from Bill.'

'Oh, dear sweet Jesus!' Eileen snatched the letter and stared at the handwriting. 'I never thought I'd hear from him again.'

Maggie fussed. 'I'll make the tea while you read it in peace.'

'Do us a favour, Mam? Take some of the clothes out of the tub and rinse them for us. I want to get them on the line while there's some dry out.'

'Forget the clothes!' Maggie huffed. 'Fancy worrying about clothes at a time like this!'

'I'm not worryin', Mam.' A faint smile crossed Eileen's white face. 'It's our Billy who'll be worryin' if he's got no kecks for school tomorrow.'

Maggie closed the door behind her. It was the first letter Eileen had received from Bill since he'd been taken prisoner, and it wasn't before time something nice happened to the daughter who helped other people in trouble but never complained about her own. She lifted some of the clothes out of the tub where they'd been steeping all night and wrung them out as well as she could before throwing them in the sink and turning the tap on. She was deep in thought, watching the cold water begin to cover the clothes, when the door was nearly burst off its hinges and Eileen stormed in, waving the letter. 'I don't believe it! I don't bloody believe it!'

Maggie turned the tap off. 'Keep your voice down! The whole street can hear you.'

'I don't care if the whole of bloody Liverpool can hear me!' Eileen raved. 'Look at it, Mam! There's only about ten words that haven't been censored!' Maggie took the letter being pushed in her face. One look at the page told her why Eileen was so mad. The letter started. 'My dear Eileen. I am in a prisoner of war camp in . . .' The rest of the sentence and every word on the page had been lined through with heavy blue ink, making it impossible to read what had been written underneath. Maggie turned the page over to see the censor had been busy again. Only the last four lines had been left untouched. 'Give my love to our Billy, Joan, Edna and your mam. Tell our Billy he's the man of the house now, till I get back. I wish I could give you your kiss in person, but it'll have to wait until I get back. I love you. Bill.'

Maggie handed the letter back without a word. She watched Eileen walk back into the living room, her shoulders slumped in utter dejection. Wiping her hands on a bit of towel, Maggie followed. 'At least you know he's safe.'

'All these months I've waited and worried, without a word, and that's all I get.' Eileen's voice was soft. 'I know I'm lucky compared to the thousands of women who'll never hear from their husbands again, but I still don't know where he is, or if he's all right.'

'All letters are censored, love, not just yours.'

Eileen jumped up. 'To hell with censors, and to hell with this bloody war! I'm goin' to get me washing done.'

'For God's sake sit down,' Maggie pleaded. 'I'll see to the washing.'

'No, thanks, Mam! You've got enough to do looking after the kids all day.' Eileen sniffed back the tears. 'I'll take me temper out on the mangle.'

Eileen opened a drawer and took out some pegs. With a nightie of Joan's in her hand, and a couple of pegs in her mouth, she went into the yard. Shaking the nightie by the shoulders she held it up to peg on the line before realising the line wasn't there. 'That's all I need,' she growled as she walked over to the wooden post that one end of the line was tied to. There was only a short piece of rope dangling from the post, and when Eileen looked across the yard to where the other end should have been tied, there was nothing there at all.

'Where's the clothes line, Mam?' Eileen tried to stay calm, but it had been a hard day.

Maggie thought Eileen was pulling her leg at first, then decided that today was not a day for leg pulling. 'In the back yard of course, where else would it be?'

'I know that, Mam, and you know that. The trouble is, the bloody clothes line doesn't know it!' Eileen's facial muscles were twitching. 'It's gone!'

'Gone! Don't be so daft! How can it be—' Maggie's eyes widened and her hand went to her mouth. 'Oh, no! I saw

Billy with a knife in his hand before, and I took it off him. But he wouldn't do a thing like that, would he?'

The picture of Joan and Edna skipping flashed through Eileen's mind, and for a woman of her size she was out of the room like a flash.

'Joan, Edna, get down here, fast!' her voice thundered.

'But we're playin', Mam!' Joan protested.

'I said get down here, quick!' The girls knew better than to argue with that tone of voice, and they ran as fast as their thin legs would carry them.

'Where did yez get that skipping rope?'

'Off our Billy.' Joan knew trouble when she saw it and her mouth started to tremble. 'Our Edna was cryin' because Vera Steadman wouldn't let us play with her, so our Billy said he'd get a skipping rope for us.'

Eileen pointed ominously to the front door. 'Inside, both of yez!' She pushed them before her down the hallway. 'Where's our Billy?'

'I dunno, Mam! Last time we seen him he was playin' with his mates.'

There was no sign of the culprit in the street so Eileen marched back through the house to the entry. Not a soul was in sight as she walked down the narrow cobbled entry, until a small figure appeared round the corner of a side alley. Dressed like an Indian, he was creeping stealthily, body bent, eyes looking back over his shoulder, alert for an ambush from behind. He'll be in for it when his mam sees him, Eileen thought. The boy's face and legs were blackened with soot, and on his face, over the soot, he'd painted blue and white chalk stripes. A piece of string was tied around his forehead and stuck into the string was a chicken feather. A home-made bow hung over his shoulder, and the sticks of wood in his hand were make-believe arrows. 'Have you seen Billy Gillmoss?' The boy jumped at the sound of Eileen's voice, and when he looked up her mouth dropped in horror. 'You little bugger! Look at the state of yer!' Eileen grabbed the now terrified Billy by the scruff of the neck and raised her arm to belt him one. Her hand was in mid-air when, cowering, young Billy looked up and she found herself looking into his dad's eyes. Her hand dropped to her side ... all the anger dying away. Billy cringed, waiting for the clout he knew he deserved. When it didn't come he ventured a squint through half-closed eyes. His mam had a funny look on her face and Billy was quick to take advantage of the situation. He tried to squirm free of the hand holding him tightly by the scruff of the neck. 'Ah, ray, Mam, leggo! Yer not half hurtin' me.'

Eileen dropped her hand. 'Get in the house, right now! And don't you dare go in the living room until I've had a scrubbing brush to yer.'

The three children sat on the couch watching their mam and nanna through the window, trying to knot the clothes line together. 'It's all your fault, our Billy!' Joan gave her brother a kick on his shin. 'Yer didn't tell us it was me mam's clothes line, did yer?!'

Young Edna joined her sister in raining blows on any part of Billy's body they could reach. 'Yer always gettin' us into trouble, you are!'

Trying to deflect the blows coming at him from all

directions, Billy grunted. 'Yer were cryin' 'cos yez didn't have a skippin' rope, weren't yer?' There was disgust in his voice as he gave his opinion. 'Girls are just like babies. Yer should be suckin' dummies.'

A shadow crossed the window and in a flash all three were sitting quietly. Eileen stood in front of them, her hands resting on her wide hips. 'Well? What have yez got to say for yerselves?'

'It was our Billy's fault, Mam!' Joan piped. 'It was all his fault!' echoed Edna.

Billy glared at his sisters, vowing he'd never do anything for them again. 'I was going to put it back, Mam. I thought I'd have it back before yer came home.'

'Aye, well yer know what thought did, don't yer? He followed a muck cart and thought it was a wedding.' Eileen glared when Joan started to titter. 'Yez are all as bad as one another, so don't come the little innocents with me.' Looking at the cause of all the trouble, his head buried deep on his chest, it took Eileen all her time to keep her face straight. 'As for you, Big Chief Sitting Bull, if yer do anything like that again I'll tan yer backside so hard yer won't be holding no pow-wows for a long time, 'cos yer won't be able to sit down.' Looking at his bowed head, a wave of tenderness swept over her. Poor little bugger, she thought. Does his sisters a favour and gets into trouble for it.

'The end of a perfect day, eh, Mam?' Eileen looked over the rim of her cup. The kids were in bed and the house quiet. 'Who'd have kids?'

'I used to think that about you and our Rene.' Maggie grinned. 'You were no angels!'

'Did yer see the look on our Billy's face when he read what his dad said about him being the man of the house? His chest nearly burst out of his shirt. He'll give the girls a dog's life now.'

'He might try, but he won't get very far,' Maggie said dryly. 'They're as cute as a boxload of monkeys.'

'He's ruined his kecks and his jersey.' Eileen burst out laughing. 'Here was me feelin' all sorry for his mam 'cos I didn't recognise him!' She rocked back and forth with laughter. 'An' when he saw me, the poor little bugger must have nearly done it in his kecks with fright!'

Maggie stretched her arms and yawned. 'I'm going up; I'm dead beat.'

Eileen eyed the lines on her mother's face and the hair that was growing whiter each day. 'The kids are too much for yer, aren't they? I should pack in work and give you a break.'

'You'll do no such thing! We'd never manage on your Army allowance and my few bob.'

'I could get a cleaning job for a few mornings a week. We'd get by.'

Maggie shook her head as she made for the door. 'Leave things be.'

'OK, boss! I'll just iron a few of the kids' clothes, then I'll be up meself. Goodnight and God Bless.'

As Eileen listened to her mother's footsteps on the stairs, her eyes swept the room. Clothes were flung over the backs of chairs, shoes scattered across the floor and the sideboard piled high with more clothes. 'I'd get the length of Bill's tongue if he could see this place.' Eileen spoke to the empty room. Her Bill was a quiet bloke and everybody thought she was the boss in the house. But they were very wrong. He didn't say much, but when he did, everybody took notice. He didn't have to bawl his head off at the kids like she did. All it needed was a wag of his finger and they knew better than to answer back. He was strict with her, too! Wouldn't let her get anything on the never-never, which was just as well or she'd have them up to their necks in debt.

Eileen lumbered to her feet and walked through to the kitchen. There was a smile on her face as she put the flat iron on the gas ring ready for Billy's trousers. 'A lot of things would be different if my Bill was home! I wouldn't be standin' here talking to meself like someone doodle-allie, for a kick off! And I wouldn't be walking up those bloody stairs on me own every night, either!'

Chapter Ten

Mary lay in the darkness listening to her mother's gentle breathing. The illuminated fingers on the alarm clock told her it was half past six. Too early to get up yet. Through the stillness she heard the faint click of the letter box, followed by the plop of a letter as it landed on the lino in the hall. She threw the bedclothes back and felt her way round the furniture to the door which she closed quietly behind her. The envelope lay face upwards and the sight of the familiar handwriting sent Mary's heart racing. She picked the letter up and was tearing it open as she took the stairs two at a time.

My darling Mary,

I've just got back to camp and it's bedlam. Everyone's rushing round like mad because we're moving out tonight or first thing in the morning. No one is allowed out of camp so one of the women from the NAAFI has promised to post this letter if I can get it to her before she goes off duty. I don't know when I'll be able to write to you again, but you can keep writing to the usual address and the letters will be sent on to me.

I'll be thinking about you all the time, and I'll keep your photo next to my heart. Remember me to your mam and tell her I hope she'll soon be better.
I love you, my darling, with all my heart.
Yours till hell freezes over.
Bob.

Mary read the letter through again then hunched forward on the side of the bed. He'd be on a ship now, miles away! She suddenly had a clear vision of Bob standing on the deck of a ship surrounded by hundreds of soldiers. They all had heavy kit bags on their shoulders and were carrying rifles. The picture was so clear in her mind she could even see Bob laughing as he talked to the soldiers standing near him. Then the sound of a bell ringing transported her from the deck of the ship back to her bedroom. Folding Bob's letter she placed it on the tallboy and called, 'I'm coming, Mam!'

The room flooded with light when Mary drew the heavy black-out curtains and she turned from the window to see her mother struggling to raise herself on her left elbow. 'Hang on a minute, Mam! I'll lift you!'

Carefully avoiding the eyes that could read her like a book, Mary propped her mother up on the pillows. 'It's not worth lighting the fire this morning, but I'll clean the grate out before I see to something to eat.' Taking the poker from its hook on the companion set, she started to rake the ashes out, her mind on the letter upstairs telling her Bob had gone. Tears threatened but she willed them away. She mustn't upset her mam. Martha watched her daughter rattle the poker between the bars of the grate and something about the set of her daughter's shoulders told her all was not well. She thought of her promise to Eileen, then brushed the thought aside. She had to know what was wrong.

'You . . . awight?'

The poking stopped and Mary turned her head slowly. Her eyes travelled the room before coming to rest on her mother's face. 'Did you hear anything?'

'You . . . awight?'

Mary's eyes never left her mother's face as she stood up. Then she blinked several times before whispering, 'Mam?'

'Eth . . . Mary?'

The poker went flying as Mary dashed across the room. Flinging her arms round Martha's neck, she sobbed, 'Oh, Mam! Mam!'

'Now . . . now.' Martha could feel the tears on her neck. 'No . . . need . . . to . . . cry.'

'I'm crying with happiness,' Mary gulped. 'I can't believe it!'

'Not . . . good . . . yet.' Martha's words were slow and slurred, but clear enough to be understood. 'Get . . . better . . . soon.'

'Not good! You're brilliant!' Mary took her arms away and wiped her eyes with the back of her hand. 'But I don't understand how you can talk all of a sudden?'

'Eileen . . . help . . . me. We . . . want . . . surprise . . . you.'

'You've done that all right!' Mary was laughing and

crying. 'Just wait till I see that Eileen! Fancy not letting on!'

'I ... let ... cat ... out ... of ... bag.' Martha's throat was sore but she carried on. 'You ... looked ... sad.'

'I'm not sad,' Mary lied. 'I heard the postman and I didn't want to disturb you so I took the letter upstairs to read. It was from Bob.'

'Bob ... awight?'

'He's fine!' Mary jumped from the side of the bed. She couldn't face her mother and tell lies. 'I'll have to shift if we want to be ready when the ambulance gets here.'

There was a bus pulling up at the stop outside the hospital and Mary ran to catch it, cursing the old suitcase banging against her legs. It was only a couple of stops to Walton Vale and Martin's cake shop. There was a line of people outside, and as Mary joined the end of the queue it struck her that this was what her mother had had to do every day to make sure there was something on the table for her dinner.

The queue moved quickly and soon there was only one woman in front of her.

'Six pies, please.' Mary heard the woman ask, then the assistant telling her, 'Only two pies and a small loaf to each customer.'

'Fat lot of good that is for a family of six.'

'I'm sorry.' For the umpteenth time that morning the fed-up assistant tried to explain. 'If we gave everyone what they asked for, we'd be sold out in five minutes. So we try to be fair and ration them out.'

When Mary left the shop she was carrying two piping hot

pies and a small crusty loaf. Martin's were noted for their pies, which were baked on the premises and served straight from the ovens with gravy oozing out of the holes cut in the top. She could feel the gravy running down her wrist and her steps quickened. She'd forgotten how hungry she was until the smell of freshly baked bread had wafted up her nostrils.

Mary could feel the loaf under her arm starting to slip so she stopped and put the case down so she could swap hands. Then she noticed she was outside Allen's, the fish shop. There was no queue outside, nor was there any fish on display in the window. But feeling brave after her success at Martin's, Mary walked in. The shop was empty of customers and staff and Mary was about to leave when a man came out of the side door. 'Can I help you, love?'

'It doesn't look like it.' Mary smiled. 'You seem to be sold out.'

The man had a roving eye for pretty girls, and he stretched his five foot seven frame to its full height as he stroked his Clark Gable moustache. 'You're in luck as it happens.' He rubbed his hands together. 'I've got a nice piece of cod under the counter that I was saving for me own tea. But who could refuse a pretty girl like you.'

'I wouldn't dream of taking the bite out of your mouth.' Two red spots appeared on Mary's cheeks. She hated men who fawned over women. And this one looked a right Casanova, with his hair plastered down with brilliantine. 'I'll come back another day.'

'I was only joking! I always keep a bit of fish back for me regulars.'

Forget your pride, an inner voice whispered. If you don't take it then someone else will. 'Thanks, that's very nice of you.'

The man wrapped the fish in newspaper and as he handed it to Mary he caught hold of her hand. 'Shall I save you a piece tomorrow?'

Mary's smile was tight as she withdrew her hand. 'I'd be grateful if you could keep me a piece on Friday . . . fish day!' She took the one and threepence out of her purse to pay for the cod. 'Will that be all right?'

'I'll look out for you.' The false teeth flashed. 'There'll be a nice fillet of plaice under the counter, just for you.'

Once outside the shop, Mary grinned. All that for a piece of flamin' fish!

Mary's appetite vanished as soon as she stepped into the empty, silent house. It didn't seem like home without her mam. And the pies she'd been looking forward to didn't taste the same, either. She dropped her plate into the kitchen sink and lifted her face to stare at her reflection in the small mirror. You're twenty-two years of age, Mary Bradshaw, and it's about time you grew up. Self pity won't get you anywhere. All your life your mam's done everything for you. But she's not here now, so you'll just have to get on with it. There's other people far worse off than you. Look at Eileen and all the trouble she's got! And look at Vera Jackson next door, with that beast of a husband of hers! No, Mary Bradshaw, you don't know how lucky you are.

Mary turned and walked through to the living room. I

wonder how Vera got on last night? There hadn't been a sound from there after Eileen had left. On impulse, Mary grabbed her purse with the front door keys in and headed for the Jacksons'. Three times she rapped on the knocker, and was about to walk away when the door was opened slowly. 'Oh, my God!' Mary gasped when she saw the angry red and black bruises on Vera's face. 'He did that?!'

The door was opened fully. 'Come in.'

Carol was sitting in the middle of the floor surrounded by coloured bricks and her arms went out when she saw who their visitor was. 'Hello, sunshine!' Mary swept her up and held her tight. 'Give us a big kiss.' She sat on the couch with Carol on her knee and looked up at Vera. 'How d'you put up with it?'

There was despair and hopelessness in Vera's eyes. 'If he didn't have me to lash out at, he'd take it out on her.' She nodded to Carol who was stroking Mary's long hair. 'I can take it, she couldn't.'

'Why don't you leave him? I couldn't live with a man who hit me.'

'If you only knew how many times I've promised meself I'd leave the next day. But where would I go? Who'd have me with three kids; especially with her being the way she is? And what would I live on?'

'But it's not fair to you or the kids!'

'He's not bad with the boys.' Vera sighed. 'It's always her he picks on. He's ashamed of her and doesn't want to look at her.'

'It's not your fault Carol's the way she is.' Mary hugged the little girl, wondering how anyone could hurt her.

'Oh, but according to Danny it is my fault! He throws it up every time I dare answer back.'

'He wouldn't hurt her, would he?'

'If he ever laid a finger on her, I'd swing for him.' Vera's voice was like cold steel. 'I may be weak for letting him treat me the way he does, but if he ever hurt her, I'd kill him.'

'What do Colin and Peter think about their dad?'

'How would you feel, Mary, if your twelve-year-old son said, "He won't hit you when I'm big, Mam, because I won't let him"?' There was a catch in Vera's voice. 'They're both frightened when he starts, and the baby's terrified.'

Sensing something was wrong, Carol stretched her arms out. 'Mama.'

'Here's your mama, sunshine!' Mary placed her in Vera's arms. 'Your mama loves you, doesn't she? And Auntie Mary loves you!'

'Thanks for coming, Mary.' Vera held her daughter tight. 'It's nice to have someone to talk to, and I feel better now.'

'If he kicks off again, knock on the wall and I'll come in.'

'He'd be as nice as pie with you. But the minute your back was turned I'd end up getting another one of these.' Vera winced as she touched her bruised face. 'You see, Mary, my husband's a coward.'

Mary banged her leg on the end of the bed in her haste to open the door for Eileen. 'Boy, am I glad to see you! The house is as quiet as a graveyard!'

'I can't stay long.' Eileen was out of breath. 'I've only

called to ask how yer mam got on, an' to tell yer me news.'

'Me mam was fine! The ambulance men put her in a wheelchair and she waved to Elsie Smith like she was the Queen.' Mary lowered her head. 'It was me that was crying, not me mam! Anyway, what's your news?'

'I've had a letter from Bill!'

Mary's mouth puckered in surprise. 'Isn't that great! Where is he?'

Eileen lowered herself down on the couch and in graphic detail explained all about the letter. It didn't take long for her to go from the letter to the clothes line and Billy's Red Indian outfit. A natural story teller, she soon had Mary in stitches as she described, in colourful language, every little detail. She couldn't talk without using her hands and they were waving about all over the place, adding humour to the story. She was shaking with laughter herself by the time she came to the end of the tale, and the springs in the couch were groaning. 'Every time I think of meself feeling sorry for this kid's poor mother, I nearly wet meself laughin'.'

Mary was rocking to and fro, her arms wrapped round her tummy. 'I've got a stitch in me side with laughing! I'll have to run to the toilet.'

Still laughing when she flew in from the yard, Mary was closing the door behind her when she heard Eileen's voice. 'You can get locked up for talking to yourself . . .' The words died on Mary's lips when she saw Harry Sedgemoor leaning against the sideboard, smiling at her. 'Hi, Mary!'

When Mary didn't answer, Eileen asked, 'Cat got yer tongue, kid?'

'No! It was just a surprise, that's all.'

'I couldn't keep 'im standing on the step while you were on the lavvy, could I?'

To cover Mary's embarrassment, Harry said, 'I just called to ask how your mam was, and to see when you'll be coming back to work.'

'I'll go and see them in the office in the morning.'

Harry straightened his back. 'No need! I'll fix it with them in the office. D'you want to start tomorrow?'

'She better 'ad!' Eileen made a fist and shook it at Mary.

Harry grinned. 'I wouldn't have come if I'd known she was here.'

'Oh, yer wanted to get Mary on her own, did yer? Mmmmm!'

'Knock it off, Eileen!' Mary met Harry's eyes. 'Take no notice of her, she's round the twist.'

Eileen held on to the arm of the couch as she fell on her knees in front of Mary. Holding her arms aloft, she cried, 'Come back to work, please?!'

'Get up, you daft thing!' Mary grinned. 'I don't know about Jean Simpson driving you crazy, I think it's the other way round.'

'Seein' as she's crazy already, I'd have a job.' Eileen banged her elbow on the bed as she was struggling to her feet. 'The sooner yer get this bloody thing out of the way the better!'

'I know,' Mary agreed. 'I'll have to do something about it.'

'Yer can't do it on yer own! We'll do it for yer, won't we, Harry?'

'Yeah! We could do it now.' Harry moved as though he

142

intended to do it there and then. 'It'll only take ten minutes.'

'Not now!' Mary reacted quickly. 'I've got to go to the hospital.'

'Tomorrow then?' Harry raised his brows at Eileen. 'After work?'

'Suits me! I was going into town to get our Billy a new pair of kecks, but another day showin' his backside to the world won't kill him.'

'See you in work tomorrow then?' Harry waited for Mary's reluctant nod, then added, 'We'll come home on the same bus, and get this bed moved.'

Mary looked at the conveyor belt the next morning and felt as though she'd never been away from the place. On the other side of the machine Eileen was grinning from ear to ear, happy now her mate was back. Mary returned the grin then let her eyes fall to the passing shells. Shutting off the noise from the shop floor, her thoughts wandered. How long would it be before she heard from Bob again? She'd have to try and write to him tonight. Then her mind went to her mother, and how nicely she'd settled into the hospital. She looked well, too! Her speech was coming on in leaps and bounds, and her face was nearly back to normal.

Mary sensed someone standing beside her and turned to see Harry watching her. 'I was miles away! Did you want something, Harry?'

'I just wanted to say it's nice to see you back. That machine hasn't looked the same without you standing beside it.' When Harry's eyes moved across the machine,

Mary's followed. Eileen was waving her arms about and bawling. 'Don't forget about the bed!'

'I won't forget.' Harry winked at Mary. 'See you on the bus, eh?'

Mary slipped the key out of the lock and pushed the door open. 'I'm sorry the place is in a mess, but I didn't have time to tidy up.'

'Don't worry.' Harry smiled. 'Men don't notice things like women do.' This wasn't true. His mother would never have a thing out of place. But she was lucky because she didn't have to go out to work. She had two wage packets coming in every week.

'Put the kettle on while we get crackin'.' Eileen struggled out of her coat. 'And don't forget I like me tea like me men ... strong!'

'Before you disappear, Mary, have you got the spanner for the bed?' When Harry saw the puzzlement in Mary's eyes, he explained. 'They're special spanners, and you must have had one when you brought the bed down.'

'Bob dismantled the bed. I don't remember what he used.'

'Never mind, we've got a set at home. I'll slip along and get them.'

As soon as his back was turned Mary rushed round like a mad woman. The bedding was scooped up from the couch with her pyjamas and she rushed upstairs to throw them on her bed. Then her breakfast dishes were cleared away and a *True Confessions* magazine pushed under a chair cushion. Eileen watched the activity with amusement. 'I don't know what yer runnin' round like a blue-arsed fly for! Yer can tidy up when we've gone.'

'I felt ashamed letting him see the place in such a mess.' Mary whipped a pair of stockings off the sideboard. 'I bet his house is like a palace.'

'So it should be! His mam's got nowt else to do!' Eileen gave one of her famous snorts. 'If I didn't have to go out to work my place would be like a palace, too!'

Harry came back with a set of spanners wrapped in a piece of sacking. He was checking the size he needed when he glanced round the room. 'You've been busy, haven't you?'

'I can move when I want to.' Mary pulled a face. 'The trouble is, no matter what I do the room doesn't look any better.'

'It looks like mine did when the bomb dropped.' Eileen looked at the black streaks on the walls and ceiling as she held the end of the bed while Harry unscrewed the bolts. 'If you strip the walls, kid, I'll paper it for yer.'

'I don't fancy you on the top of a ladder.' Mary's eyes twinkled. 'I'd hate to see you end up in the next bed to me mam.'

'Don't be so funny, young lady! I'll 'ave you know I do all the decoratin' in our house, an' I can swing on a ladder as good as Johnny Weismuller.'

Harry lifted the bedstead free of the headboard and nodded to Eileen to tip it sideways. 'To save any argument, I'll paper the room.'

Mary's smile faded. 'The room can stay as it is for a while.'

'Wouldn't it be nice for yer mam, though, if she came out of 'ossie to a nice room?' Eileen spoke over her shoulder as she helped manipulate the iron frame through the narrow door. 'Tell yer what, kid! If it didn't need decoratin' before, it will when us two are finished.' The dimples in the fat on her elbows deepened as she strained to push the bed towards Harry who was standing on the bottom stair. 'Move yer bugger, move!'

Mary put the kettle on then came to stand at the bottom of the stairs. She could hear Eileen and Harry laughing as they tried to bolt the bed together again. 'Get hold of it, will you!' Harry's voice floated down.

'You cheeky bugger! I hardly know yer, an' yer asking me to get hold of it! Fast bloody worker, aren't yer!?'

Mary felt herself blushing. It's a good job I'm not up there with them or I'd die of embarrassment! A slow grin crossed her face. It's a good job Father Younger's not up there, either!

Harry came down first. 'I'll get myself a proper labourer next time.'

'You wouldn't enjoy it half as much.' Eileen was the full width of the staircase as she plodded down behind him. 'What's the good of livin' if yer not going to enjoy yerself?'

They moved the furniture back into place before sitting down for a cup of tea. 'That's more like it.' Eileen surveyed the room. 'Yer'd be able to swing a cat round now, if yer had one.'

'I was thinking of sleeping upstairs tonight.' Mary looked doubtful. 'But I think I'd be too frightened in the house on me own.'

Eileen winked at Harry over the rim of her cup. 'Now there's an invitation for yer!'

'You've got a one-track mind,' Harry told her. 'Don't you ever think of anything else?'

'What else is there?'

Mary quickly changed the subject. 'I got a shock when I saw Blacklers. Have you seen it since it was bombed?'

'The Gerries did a lot of damage in the city on those two nights,' Harry said. 'Particularly down Paradise Street.'

Mary shivered as she remembered what those two nights had cost. She held her hand out for Harry's cup. 'Another cup?'

'If there's one in the pot.'

'None for me, ta, or I'll be spending pennies all night.' Eileen handed her cup over. 'Anyway, I'll have to get going.'

'Half a cup won't hurt.' Mary had no intention of being left alone with Harry. 'And it'll only take you five minutes to drink it.'

Harry sipped his tea slowly. He'd never been so close to Mary before and God knows if he'd ever get the chance again. If she knew how he felt about her she'd run a mile. While these thoughts ran through his head, he studied the changing expressions on her face as she listened to Eileen. She was smiling now and her blue eyes were shining. When she moved her head her long blonde hair swung across her face, and Harry felt the urge to reach out and touch it. She was so beautiful he would have been content to sit and look at her all day.

'Ay, tatty head!' Eileen stood in front of him. 'Come 'ed!

Me mam'll think I've run off with the coal man.'

Harry picked up the spanners, wishing he had the nerve to ask about papering the room. But his courage failed, and he was following Eileen to the door when there was a knock. Eileen moved aside to let Mary pass, muttering, 'A few more people an' we can have a bloody party!'

'Hello, Harry!' Barbara came into the room first, followed by Jean. 'Nice to see you again.'

'Oh, yeh, I forgot!' Eileen gave Harry a knowing look. 'Yer went to Reeces, didn't yer? And yer never told me!'

Mary introduced Jean to Eileen, before saying, 'You're in civvies again! You promised to let me see you in your uniform!'

'I look like a ruddy farmer in it!' Jean was a tall girl with broad shoulders, wide hips and fiery red hair. At first glance her face appeared plain, with a too large nose, square chin, and thick eyebrows that met in the middle. But when she smiled her face was transformed. Large hazel eyes twinkled with humour, and her mouth parted to reveal a set of strong, white perfect teeth. 'We're meeting the boys in town, but we thought we'd call and bring you up to date with our news.'

Eileen put her bag down. 'I'm not missin' this!'

'What a time we've had!' Barbara trilled. 'It's been great, hasn't it, Jean?'

Mary was only half listening to Jean's answer as she watched the way Barbara was preening herself in front of Harry. She hadn't sat down, but was standing near the sideboard where he was leaning. Mary had once heard Eileen saying that a woman in work had 'real come-to-bed eyes'; well the description seemed to fit the way Barbara was flirting with her eyes.

'I thought we'd have seen you at Reeces yesterday.' Barbara's lashes did a little dance. 'I kept my eyes open for you.'

Jean's mouth dropped in surprise. 'Well, you could have fooled me! You've never taken your eyes off Cliff for the last few days.'

Barbara shot Harry a glance. 'They're nice fellows, but there's nothing serious in it.'

Mary looked at Harry. Why didn't he go? Surely a man wasn't interested in girl talk! But Harry seemed to be enjoying himself and showed no signs of leaving.

'Come on, now,' Eileen coaxed. 'Yez must have a bit of juicy gossip to tell us.'

Jean grinned. 'We don't tell tales out of school, do we, Barbara? You'll have to use your imagination.'

'And Eileen's got plenty of that!' Mary said. 'Tell her half a story and she'll make the rest up herself.'

'Well, if there's no scandal, I'm going.' Eileen flicked an imaginary speck off her faded coat then nodded to Harry. 'Come on, let's go.'

Harry laughed as he followed her into the hall. 'Yes, boss!'

'You don't need to go because of us.' Barbara put a hand on his arm. 'We'll be going soon.'

Mary practically pushed Harry into the street after Eileen. 'I'll see you tomorrow.'

Eileen stood outside Harry's front door. The glint in her

eyes warned him she was going to say something out-
rageous, and he was grinning before she spoke. 'Yer could
have got yer leg over there, yer know! That Barbara was
handin' it to yer on a plate. She was like a bitch on heat, an'
I thought she was goin' to drag yer down on the floor an'
have her wicked way with yer.'

'Oh, aye; and what d'you think I'd be doing?' Amusement showed on Harry's face as he waited for her answer.

'Enjoyin' yerself, if yer've got any sense!' The fat on
Eileen's cheeks moved upwards as she winked. 'Or could it
be yer eyes are on someone else?'

'You know the answer to that without me telling you.
Not that it will ever do me any good because she doesn't
even know I exist! Still, no one can stop me dreaming.'

'No they can't, kiddo! You keep right on dreamin', 'cos
life has a funny way of working things out.'

Chapter Eleven

'You're leaving early, aren't you?' Maggie watched her daughter struggle into the coat that had fitted her five years ago but was now straining at the seams. 'That coat's seen better days; isn't it about time you gave it to the rag man?'

'It'll do me a turn yet!'

'In the name of God!' Maggie was exasperated. Eileen used to be so pretty, but since Bill went away she'd let herself go to the dogs. 'Anyway, why are you leaving so early?'

'I want to call in to Mary's. I'm dead worried about her, Mam! She's changed so much you wouldn't think she was the same girl. Yer can't get a smile out of her, and she bites yer head off if yer ask her what's up. If she carries on like this she'll end up having a nervous breakdown.'

Maggie huffed as she followed Eileen down the hall. 'I'd have thought you had enough troubles of your own without taking anyone else's on.'

'She's got no one else, Mam! We don't get a chance to talk in work with all the women around, so I'll catch her at home.'

'She's heard from Bob, hasn't she?'

'Yeah! He's in the Middle East with the Eighth Army. I know she's worried about him, but I don't think it's that that's makin' her the way she is. And her mam's coming on well in hospital, so it can't be that, either!' Eileen put her hand out to open the front door at the same time as the flap on the letter box started to rattle. 'Strewth! Frightened the life out of me!' She was the full width of the hall and Maggie had to stand on tiptoe to see who was standing on the step. When she spied the top of Rene's head, she cried, 'Where've you been? We've been worried to death about you!'

'I didn't have anything to tell you.' Rene looked as smart as usual in a mulberry-coloured skirt and jacket, over a cream tie-neck blouse. But her face showed signs of strain and sleepless nights. 'I only got word myself this morning.'

Maggie tugged on Eileen's arm. 'Will you let the girl in!'

Eileen waddled back down the hall leaving Rene to close the door. 'Have yer heard from Alan?'

'He's coming home.'

'Yer mean home to your house?'

'No, to a hospital.' Rene's lip trembled. 'The letter said they'd notify me which hospital as soon as they could.'

'Did they tell yer what's wrong with him?'

'Only that he's been wounded in his right arm.' Rene blew into a wisp of a handkerchief. 'It must be bad though, for them to be sending him home.'

Maggie was fussing round the chair, wringing her hands. 'You don't know that, love! Perhaps he's just got shrapnel in his arm.'

Rene shook her head, tears near the surface. 'If it wasn't bad they'd have fixed him up in the field hospital.'

Eileen and Maggie exchanged glances. Everyone knew they didn't send soldiers home unless they were no longer fit for active duty. 'It mightn't be that bad, our kid! And at least he'll be out of the war, and yer'll have him home. I'd be glad to have Bill home no matter what was wrong with him.'

'Have you told Alan's mam and dad, yet?' Maggie asked. 'They'll be worried.'

'Not yet! I've come here in my lunchtime, but I'll call there on the way home and tell them.' Rene looked up at Eileen who was standing in front of her. 'When I find out which hospital he's in, will you come with me to see him? I'd be too frightened to go on my own.'

'Of course I will! But for Christ's sake, don't go thinking the worst till yer know for sure. Yer might be worrying yerself to death for nothing.'

'I hope you're right, but I've got this horrible feeling, here.' Rene sniffed as she put a hand to her heart. 'I'll be all right once I've seen him, but I'll be glad if you'll come with me the first time.'

'I'll come,' Eileen promised. 'It'll be a good excuse for a day off work.'

Rene stood up. 'I'd better go or I'll be late. I only get an hour for dinner.'

'I was on me way out, so I'll walk down the road with yer.'

Rene walked quickly, and by the time they reached the corner where they would part company, Eileen was puffing and blowing. 'I'll have to lose some of this weight! I'm built like a bloody battleship!'

'You're all right, our kid!' There was humour in Rene's eyes. 'Big and cuddly you are, just like a teddy bear.'

'Go on with yer, Sis! You look like a fashion model an' I look like a tramp.' Eileen's face reddened with embarrassment. 'Get goin' or yer'll be gettin' the sack.'

Rene's thoughts were as fleet as her footsteps as she walked to the bus stop. So, I look like a fashion model! She lowered her eyes to take in the suit and blouse. They were both four years old, and sharper eyes than Eileen's would have noticed the frayed collar and cuffs. She was careful with her clothes though, and with a bit of care, and needlework, she'd get another year out of this suit.

It wasn't that Alan had kept her short of money when he was in civvie street, but they'd both agreed, when they got married, to be careful with money. They'd planned to pay cash for everything for the house, so they wouldn't have hire purchase payments to make on top of the mortgage. They'd been so full of plans when they'd got married. They wouldn't start a family until they had everything they needed for the house, so that when children came along they'd be able to give them the best of everything. The trouble was, it hadn't worked out that way. They'd been married for two years and the house was just the way they wanted it, when they tried for a baby. When the first month passed and Rene hadn't conceived, they hadn't been worried. But when the fifth and sixth month passed, Alan had stopped coming home with a look of hopeful expectancy on his face when Rene's monthly period was due. For a year they'd pretended it didn't matter, but deep inside both were deeply disappointed. In the end, thinking there might be something wrong with her, Rene had gone to the hospital for an examination. She was given the all-clear, and the doctor at the hospital suggested her husband should come for a test. Rene could still remember the day Alan came home after hearing the results of the test. With a wide smile on his face, he'd told her there was nothing wrong with him. She could even remember the words he'd used. 'The doctor said we're probably trying too hard! Relax, forget about babies, and in no time at all your wife will be pregnant.' It hadn't worked though, and a year later Alan had joined the Army.

Rene sighed. Our Eileen thinks I've got everything I want. But what's the good of a nice house if there's no family to live in it? No children's toys on the floor and no childish laughter to make it sound like a real home. No; me and Alan would swap everything to have what our Eileen's got.

As she passed the window, Eileen rapped loudly on one of the panes, then stood muttering as she waited for Mary to open the door. 'I'll find out what's wrong, even if I have to drag it out of her.' But when she saw Mary's pale, drawn face, her resolve wavered.

'What's up?' Mary stepped back to let her pass. 'It's too early for work.'

'I had to go on a message an' it wasn't worth going home again, so I thought I'd come and have a cuppa with yer. We can go to work together.' Eileen followed Mary through to the kitchen and settled on one of the wooden chairs while Mary filled the kettle. 'Had yer dinner yet, kid?'

'I've had cheese on toast.' Mary eyed her friend suspiciously. 'I thought you said you'd been on a message .. where's your bag?'

'That was a lie!' To hell with it, Eileen thought. What's the good of messing around. 'I came early so we could have a natter. We don't seem to get a chance in work.' She pointed to the chair opposite. 'Sit down, kid, yer making me nervous.'

The kettle started to whistle and Mary filled the pot. 'I'll let it brew for a while, otherwise you'll be moaning about it being too weak.'

'Then for Christ's sake sit down while yer waitin', instead of hopping round like a cat on hot bricks.'

Mary sat down, nervously biting on her bottom lip. Her eyes fixed on a spot on the wall behind Eileen's head and her fingers picked at the skin around her nails. Her whole body was as taut as a violin string, her eyes refusing to meet her friend's.

'What is it, kid?' Eileen reached across to touch her arm. 'Yer look worried to death.'

'How should I look?' Mary's laugh was high pitched. 'Me mam's in hospital and me boyfriend's thousands of miles away! You don't expect me to go round laughing and singing, do you?'

'Yer know I don't mean it like that, so there's no need to be sarcastic.'

Eileen's voice was soft. 'I know yer've had a lousy time over the last few months, but there seems to be something else worryin' yer. I thought yer might need a friend to talk to . . . and we are friends, aren't we, kid?'

When Mary screwed her eyes up tight, Eileen could see a tear glisten on the long black lashes. 'What is it, kid? Tell your Auntie Eileen.'

The sympathy in her friend's voice was all Mary needed to burst out crying. 'I don't know what to do, Eileen! I'm going to have a baby!'

'Jesus Christ!' Eileen's mouth gaped. 'Are yer sure?'

'I should have started me period last week, and I haven't come on.'

Eileen's chest heaved in relief. 'That's nothing to worry about! I'm often a few days late!'

'But it's the second month I've missed. And I know I am because me whole body feels different.'

Lost for words, Eileen could only shake her head. 'What yer goin' to do?'

'What can I do? Bob's not here to marry me, and I can't tell me mam 'cos it would kill her.' There was bitterness in Mary's voice. 'You're not going to believe it, nobody is, but it only happened the once. That was when Bob came home on those twenty-four-hours' embarkation leave.'

'I don't know what to say, kid.' Not for a second had Eileen guessed this could be what was worrying Mary.

'It's me mam I'm worried about. I won't be able to look her in the face.'

'Don't say anything to her until yer've seen the doctor. Yer might not be pregnant after all.'

Mary drew back, a look of fear on her face. 'I couldn't tell the doctor! I'd be too ashamed!'

'If yer are pregnant, there's a lot of things yer'll have to do that yer won't like! Having a baby isn't something yer can keep to yerself.'

'I can't sleep for thinking about it.' Mary covered her face with her hands, muffling the sound of her voice. 'The shock will kill me mam!'

'Have you written and told Bob?'

'No! I can't give him this worry when he's out there fighting! I feel like running away and hiding meself from everyone, I'm that ashamed.' Mary's eyes begged. 'What can I do, Eileen? I'm so frightened.'

'It's no good telling yer not to worry, kid, 'cos that would be daft. But at least I know now, and I can help yer. The first thing is to see the doctor and find out for sure.' When Mary shook her head, Eileen said. 'Just hang on a minute, will yer? I'll see the doctor and tell him what's going on, and I'll make an appointment for yer to go for an examination. You aren't the first girl to get herself in the family way, an' yer won't be the last.' She stood up and put her arms round Mary's shoulders. 'The scandal-mongers will have a fine time, kid, but it'll only be a nine days' wonder. An' I'll see yer come to no harm.'

'Have you mentioned the decorating to Mary yet?'

Eileen's eyes slid sideways to see Harry with a sheepish grin on his face. What a mess, she thought. Here's a good bloke, crazy about Mary, and trying to win her over. I should tell him the truth, but it's not up to me to interfere in people's lives. He'd be finding out soon enough, anyway. 'Why don't you ask her yerself?'

'She's more likely to agree if you ask her.'

The short sleeves on Eileen's overall strained against the expanding muscles as she lifted a faulty shell from the conveyor and transferred it to the trolley. Tucking a wayward strand of hair back into her turban she looked into brown eyes that were pleading. 'Please, Eileen?'

'Bloody hell, Harry! I'm trying to work! I've said I'll ask her, an' I will when I get the chance. But I can't twist her flippin' arm!'

'I'm only askin' you to try.' Harry walked away leaving Eileen thoughtful. He was a nice bloke and she wished she could help him. But he'd never really stood much chance with Mary, and the way things were now, he stood even less.

John Greenfield looked across his desk at Mary's bowed head. He could almost feel the tension as her hands clasped and unclasped on her knee. 'Are you going to tell me about it, Mary?'

Her head shot up. 'Eileen said she'd told you!'

'Eileen told me you think you're pregnant. I want you to tell me why you think this. Have you seen a doctor?'

Mary shook her head. She'd never discussed her periods with her mother, never mind with a man. Her face flooded with colour and John said softly, 'I am a doctor, Mary, and used to these things.'

'I feel so embarrassed.'

Looking at the beautiful, sad face, John was put in mind of a gentle, frightened fawn. Eileen had told him, in her own outspoken way, that Mary had been caught the only time she'd had intercourse with her boyfriend. They weren't Eileen's exact words, and John had to hold back a smile as he remembered how the big woman had sat where Mary was sitting now. 'Bob was on embarkation leave, an' the silly sods got carried away. They'd never done it before ... in fact she's that bloody innocent I'm surprised she knew what it was for!'

John sighed. It was going to come as a shock to Mrs Bradshaw, and he wondered whether she was strong enough to stand the shock, and the shame that went with it. 'You won't know for certain whether you're expecting a baby until you've been examined. So, behind those screens, and take some of your clothes off. I'll send Mrs Cooper in to help you.'

When Mary was lying on the couch, naked from the waist down except for a half blanket Mrs Cooper had given her, John walked over. 'Relax, Mary! You're far too tense!' His hands moved over her tummy, pressing gently. 'Open your legs, there's a good girl, and draw them up to your chest.'

Mary turned her head to the wall, sick with humiliation. She had no idea that this was what an internal meant.

'Right! You can get dressed now.'

Mary shot from the couch with the blanket held tightly around her. And when she came back from behind the screens, John was sitting at his desk going through some papers. She sat down, her eyes fastened on an ink stain on the wooden top of the desk, and she didn't look up till John spoke. 'You are pregnant, Mary.'

A sob left Mary's throat. 'What about me mam?'

John gazed thoughtfully at the nib on his fountain pen

before answering. 'We're going to have to consider very carefully how we do this. Your mother is responding quite well to treatment, but I don't know how a shock like this will affect her.' He could see the pain in Mary's eyes and wished he had a magic wand to make the pain disappear. But being a mere mortal, he had no magic wand. 'I think we'll leave it for a week before doing anything. After all, a week's not going to make any difference. I'll have a word with the hospital, then we can talk about it.' He came from behind the desk. 'In the meantime, look after yourself and remember you're eating for two.' He rushed to open the door for her. 'I'll see you the same time next week.'

Mary made herself a cup of tea and spread some Marmite on a round of bread. She carried them through to sit on her mother's chair and rocked slowly to and fro as she forced herself to eat the bread which tasted like sawdust. Her mind was in turmoil. She felt she was being swept along on a tidal wave and had no control over her life. Over the last two weeks her mind had been too numbed with worry to face what the future held in store. All she'd been able to think about was having to face her mother. Now she thought of all the other people she'd have to face. The neighbours who had known her since the day she was born.

The chair stopped rocking as a loud cry left Mary's lips. Oh, dear God! How was she going to face Father Younger and Father Murphy?

It was a long time before Mary could bring herself to move from the chair. If only Bob was here to share the trouble with her. But then there wouldn't be any troubles if he was home because they'd be married.

* * *

Eileen kept her eyes on her daughters as she dumped her bag on the floor. They were huddled together on the couch and young Edna's face was blotchy from crying. 'OK, let's have it! What have yez been up to?'

Maggie was hovering in the background nervously clutching her pinny. 'They got sent home from school.'

'Oh, aye! What for?' Eileen put a hand under each of the girls' chins and lifted their faces. 'Come on, out with it!'

'I didn't do nothin', Mam!' Joan moved away from her sister, disassociating herself from trouble. 'Teacher made me bring our Edna home.'

'What did yer do, Edna?'

'It wasn't my fault, Mam! I 'ad me hand up, but teacher took no notice of me.' The words spilled from Edna's trembling mouth. 'By the time she said I could go to the WC it was too late ... I'd wet me knickers.'

'What?' Eileen exploded. 'Six years of age, and yer wet yer knickers!'

'It wasn't my fault! I had me hand up for ages and Miss Devereux took no notice of me.' Tears spilled out at the injustice of it. 'She made me stand in front of the class and say, ten times over, "I'm six years of age but I'm like a little baby who can't ask if she can go to the WC."' Memories of the humiliation brought forth loud sobs as Edna wiped her running nose on the back of her hand. 'Then she sent for our Joan and told her to take the baby home.'

She'd make a good actress, this one, Eileen thought, as she struggled to keep a smile at bay. 'It's over now, so stop crying. But in future don't leave it till the last minute, like yer always do! Hopping up and down on one leg instead of goin' to the lavvy when yer need to. Anyway, yer've learned yer lesson now, so off out to play.'

As the two girls pushed each other out of the way in their scramble for the door, Eileen grabbed Edna's arm. 'Have yer changed yer knickers?'

It was Maggie who took pity on the big, sad eyes. 'I changed everything she had on.' She waited till she heard the footsteps running into the street, then turned to Eileen. 'Poor kid! Fancy having to stand in front of all the class, then come home and face you! She went green when she heard you coming in; thought she was in for a hiding.' Maggie's features softened. 'She's the spitting image of you, you know. She looked just like you did the day you were sent home from school for wetting your knickers.'

Eileen gasped. 'I never did no such thing!'

'Oh, yes you did!' Maggie's head bobbed up and down. 'Twice!'

'And you're goin' to give the game away on me, are yer, Mam?'

'Not on your life! I won't tell them about the times you put a ball through windows, either! You were more trouble than the three of them put together!'

Eileen grinned. 'Anyway, there's a bloody war on, and more important things to worry about than our Edna wettin' her knickers.' A look of resignation crossed her face at the sound of the knocker. 'What is it now?'

At first she didn't recognise the man standing on the step, and when she did her mouth gaped in shock. It was only two months since she'd seen Mr West, but the man standing in front of her had aged ten years. He'd changed so much she hardly recognised him. His clothes were hanging loosely from his stooped shoulders and his face was grey and haggard. 'Hello, Mr West!' Eileen was so taken back by his appearance it took her all her time to smile. 'Come in.'

Bob West stood in the middle of the room nervously twisting his cap in his hand, 'Hello, Maggie.'

'Bob!' Maggie took in the sunken eyes and the deathly pallor. Something was very wrong here. 'Sit down, Bob! I didn't expect to see you round here so soon.'

'I've got bad news, Maggie.' Bob's adam's apple moved up and down as he tried to control his emotions. 'I called here before going to Mary's.'

Eileen had gone into the kitchen, but now she rushed back. 'Has something happened to Mrs West?'

Bob shook his head slowly, in a movement of despair. 'It's our Bob! He's dead!' Unable to say more, he slumped in a chair and buried his head in his hands.

'Oh, dear God!' Maggie cried. 'And here's Mary . . .' A heavy push almost sent her sprawling as Eileen guessed what her next words were going to be. This was no time to tell him Mary was pregnant, and it wasn't their place to tell him, anyway. After a warning glance at her mother, who was wringing her hands as she stared at the broken man before her, Eileen asked, 'How d'yer know?'

'We got a telegram yesterday from the War Office, saying he'd been killed in action.' Bob lifted his head and the pain in his eyes told of his suffering. 'Lily answered the door to the postman and she opened the telegram. Me and Nancy heard this thud, and when we dashed into the hall there was Lily on the floor with the telegram clutched in her hands. I thought she was dead, too! If it hadn't been for our Nancy, I don't know what I'd have done.'

'So Mary doesn't know yet?' Eileen asked quietly.

'No! With her mam being the way she is, I thought I'd come here first and see what you think.'

'Her mam's been in 'ospital for nearly two months.' Eileen chewed on her bottom lip. 'Are yer going to Mary's now?'

Bob nodded. 'I'm dreading it. You know how it was with her and our Bob. They'd been sweethearts since they left school.'

'I'll tell her.' The words left Eileen's mouth before she could stop them.

'I couldn't let you do that! Mary would go mad if she thought I'd been here and didn't have the guts to tell her myself.'

Little do you know what this is going to mean to Mary, Eileen thought. She's not only lost her sweetheart, she's lost the father of the baby she's carrying. 'You've got enough on yer plate with Mrs West. I'll tell Mary, and yer can come and see her in a few weeks when Mrs West is feeling better.' His face buried in his hands, Bob West cried. 'The times me and Lily have talked about when they'd be married and the grandchildren we'd have. Now we'll never see our son again, and we'll never have grandchildren.'

Maggie looked at Eileen to see if she was going to tell him there would be a grandchild, but Eileen shook her head. 'You're in no fit state to tell Mary, Mr West! Honest, it would be better for both of yer if I did it.'

Maggie stretched out and touched Bob's arm. Friends and neighbours they'd been for over thirty years and her heart went out to him. 'I've got me two daughters and me grandchildren, and I love them dearly. But I lost me partner in life, Bob, and I miss him terrible. You and Lily have got each other, and that's a lot to be thankful for. When you get home, you tell Lily I said that.'

Maggie was waiting when Eileen came back after seeing Bob West out, her face wearing a worried expression. 'You must be mad!'

'Tell me what else I could have done with Mary expectin' a baby?! Can yer imagine what the two of them would have been like?'

'Her life's in a right mess,' Maggie agreed. 'And she's such a nice girl.'

'I'll go and see the doctor and ask his advice. I can't just barge in an' tell her Bob's dead. The way she is now, the shock will kill her.'

'She's got to be told, though!'

'I know that, but I'm not going till I've had a word with the doctor.' A loud sob left Eileen's mouth before her shoulders started to shake and tears ran down her cheeks. 'Poor Bob! A lovely young feller like that to be killed. It's downright wicked! And poor Mary! First her mam, then findin' out she's pregnant, and now this! She'll never be able to cope with it all.'

'It always happens to good girls. The bad ones get away with it.'

'I thought I had troubles but they're nothing compared to

Mary's.' Eileen sniffed. 'I just hope she can take it.' She turned to the door, a weary droop to her shoulders. 'I'll get to the surgery and see what Doctor Greenfield says. He's very understanding. He'll know what's best to do.'

Mary came back from the hospital feeling drained. For the first time she'd been glad to hear the bell that announced the end of visiting time. Trying to smile and make conversation when her heart was breaking was too much. Her mother had commented on how tired she looked, and Mary had put it down to working seven days a week. She was tired, too! Mentally and physically. So when the door knocker sounded ten minutes after she got home, Mary groaned. She didn't feel up to talking to anyone. Unless it was Eileen. With Eileen she didn't have to tell lies or pretend.

'Doctor Greenfield! Eileen!' Mary's thoughts went at once to her mother. But she'd only just left her, so it couldn't be that. 'Come in.'

Eileen sat on the couch while the doctor stood facing Mary. 'I'm sorry, Mary, but we've got some bad news for you.'

'But I've just left me mam, and she was all right!'

'It's not your mother, Mary.' John was used to telling patients that someone they loved was dead, but Mary had had so much to contend with it seemed cruel to add to it. But putting it off wasn't going to change things in the long run. 'It's Bob.'

'Bob!' Her eyes went from John to Eileen. 'What's happened to Bob?'

John pointed to the couch. 'Sit down, Mary.'

'No! I want to know what's happened!'

'I wish there was a way to say it that would make it easier, but there isn't. Bob is dead, Mary! He was killed in action.'

Mary stared unblinking into his face, then she turned to Eileen. Her eyes pleaded with her friend to say that what she was hearing wasn't true. 'No! For God's sake, Eileen, tell me it's not true!'

'I'm sorry, kid!'

Mary's eyes darted round the room like those of a trapped animal looking for a way of escape. Her face had lost every trace of colour and she seemed to have stopped breathing. 'No! No!' her cries filled the room then ceased suddenly as she fell to the floor in a dead faint.

When Mary opened her eyes everything was hazy. The light in the ceiling was spinning round and she couldn't focus. She felt her head being lifted, and a voice which sounded as though it was coming through a long tunnel, said, 'Drink this, Mary.' She spluttered as the liquid touched her throat and tried to turn her head away, but someone was holding it in a tight grip and forcing the liquid into her mouth.

'Sit up, kid.' Eileen eased Mary's legs over the side of the couch then slipped her arm round her friend's shoulders and raised her up. Their eyes met, and at the despair in Mary's, Eileen had to turn her head away. 'I'm sorry, kid.'

Mary's face crumpled and a cry left Eileen's mouth as she took her in her arms. The tears flowed and sobs racked Mary's body as Eileen stroked the long blonde hair, crooning words of sympathy as she felt her dress being soaked by the tears that seemed never ending. She looked up into the compassionate eyes of John Greenfield, her own eyes begging him to do something to help her friend.

'Mary, will you drink this for me? It will make you feel better.'

Mary looked up quickly. She'd forgotten he was there. 'I don't want anything, doctor.' She was gasping for breath as fresh sobs shook her body. She turned away from the cup being held out to her, but Eileen forced her head round. 'Drink it, kid.'

Like a child, Mary did as she was told, then asked, 'How d'you know?'

'Mr West came to our 'ouse. He wanted to come and tell yer himself, but I wouldn't let him.' Eileen fought to keep back her own tears. 'Yer see, I didn't know whether to tell him about the baby or not. It wasn't my place to do that, was it? So I went to see the doctor, an' he said he'd come with me to tell yer about Bob.'

Mary was looking at John. 'I wish I was dead meself.'

'Life has certainly dealt you a raw deal, Mary, but you're only young and time has a way of healing.' John opened his black case. 'I'll leave you some tablets to make you sleep, and I'll come back in the morning and we can have a good talk.' His eyes questioned Eileen. 'It would be better if Mary wasn't left alone tonight. Are there any relatives she could go to?'

'We've no relatives.' Mary's voice was choked. 'There's only me mam's sister in Wales, and we only hear from her at Christmas.'

'I'll stay here tonight.' Eileen eased Mary back against the couch. 'Will you stay here a few minutes, doctor, while I find someone to go and tell me mam?'

Seconds later she was banging on the Sedgemoors' door. 'Is Harry in?' Lizzie Sedgemoor's eyes widened in surprise when she saw the distressed state of Eileen. 'Yes, he's upstairs . . . is anything wrong?'

'Call him down, will yer, Lizzie? I'll tell yer both together.'

A smile lit Harry's face when he saw Eileen but it quickly disappeared when he heard why she'd called. 'I'm stayin' the night with her, 'cos the state she's in she's likely to do anything! Would you run round and tell me mam for us, Harry? Ask her to see to the kids for us.' A thought suddenly crossed Eileen's mind. Oh, dear God, what if me mam mentions about Mary being pregnant? 'Tell her not to tell a soul anything, will yer? The last thing Mary wants is people knockin' on her door.'

Harry was reaching for his coat on the hallstand. 'You won't be in work tomorrow, then?'

'I'll see how things are,' Eileen told him. 'If she's not fit to be left, then I won't leave her.'

Harry was already on his way up the street. 'If you're not in tomorrow, I'll call in to Mary's after work.'

The doctor had gone and Mary was sitting next to Eileen on the couch, her face ravaged by tears. 'I can't believe I'm never going to see Bob again, Eileen! I don't know what to do! I feel like doing away with meself.'

'Yer can cut that sort of talk out for a start!' Eileen had

grown so fond of this beautiful, gentle girl, she felt torn apart looking into the grief-stricken face. 'There's thousands of people suffering in this war, kid, don't forget.'

'D'you know anybody else whose mother is in hospital and might never walk again? And who's expecting a baby by a man who's just been killed? I'm expecting an illegitimate baby, Eileen, and the shock will probably kill me mam.'

'I think yer mam loves yer enough, and is strong enough, to get over it, kid! And you're only young . . . yer've got yer whole life in front of yer.'

'I don't want a life without Bob.'

'That's how yer feel now, but believe me, the pain gets easier as time goes on.' Eileen picked up the box of tablets the doctor had left. 'Two of these now, my girl, and off yer go to bed.'

'Can we both sleep in me mam's double bed? I don't want to be left on me own.'

When Harry called the next afternoon Eileen's face was grim. 'She's in a terrible state! I can't leave her here on her own, so when I've been in the 'ossie with her tonight, I'm taking her home with me for a few days.'

'Can I come in and see her?'

'She doesn't want to see anybody, Harry! God knows what she's going to do when she sees her mam! I only hope she doesn't break down.'

'She's not going to tell Mrs Bradshaw then?'

Eileen shook her head. She had to keep reminding herself that he didn't know about the baby. 'The doctor came to give Mary something to calm her down, an' he said not to tell Mrs B yet.'

'She's having a hard time of it, isn't she?'

'Yer can say that again! She's 'ad the bloody book thrown at her!'

'Only half the book, Eileen. The other half hasn't been written yet.' Harry sighed. 'Will you be in work tomorrow?'

'Yeah. I can't afford to take any more time off. Me mam will keep her eye on Mary.'

Chapter Twelve

Martha's face broke into a smile when Eileen waddled through the ward door with Mary. Funny how just the sight of the big woman brought a smile even when you were down in the dumps.

'You've got the pleasure of my company tonight, so behave yourself.' Eileen's voice boomed round the ward as she pulled a chair closer to the bed. 'An' how's me old mate doing?'

Martha's patience and practice had paid dividends, and her speech was almost back to normal. 'Fine! How are you and the children?'

'I could do with swapping places with you for a week! Laying back lookin' all pale and interestin' and wallowing in sympathy! It would suit me down to the ground. What d'you think, Mary?'

Her face thickened with powder to hide the tear stains, Mary swallowed hard. 'I certainly can't see you looking all pale and interesting. You wouldn't get any sympathy from me!'

'There's a friend for yer! Me fingers are worked to the bone, I'm as thin as a rake, but even me best mate doesn't feel sorry for me.' Eileen had never felt less like laughing in all her life. All night she'd lain next to Mary, feeling the shudders as her friend cried into the pillow. And all day she'd watched as the grief and worry etched deeper on her face. And Eileen suffered because she couldn't share the burden. But there was something she could do now to help. She could distract Martha's attention away from the tell-tale signs on her daughter's face. 'Imagine me in 'ossie! It would take six nurses to lift me on to a bed pan, and givin' me a bed bath would be like exploring unknown territory because I've got bigger mounds on me body than Mount Everest.'

Martha could hear the visitors at the next bed tittering. 'You should have been a comedienne.'

'Now, begorra,' Eileen adopted a thick Irish accent. 'An' I would have been! But wasn't someone after tellin' me dear old mother that she shouldn't be putting her daughter on the stage, Mrs Worthington.'

While her mother was laughing, Mary's eyes were on Eileen. She'd never get through this visit without breaking down if it wasn't for her. Big fat Eileen. Always looking untidy and talking like a barrow woman, but she was the kindest, most gentle person in the world.

Eileen stopped laughing suddenly and looked gob-smacked. 'Well, be gosh and begorra! If it isn't Mr Harry Sedgemoor himself, the darlin' man!'

Harry nodded to Eileen then held his hand out to Martha. 'How are you, Mrs Bradshaw?'

Martha's smile was genuine. 'I'm fine, Harry! This is a nice surprise.'

'I was visiting a friend in the men's ward, and me mam asked me to call in and give you her regards.'

He's a better bloody liar than I am, Eileen thought. I bet if I asked him which ward his friend's in, he'd die of fright.

Harry looked across the bed. 'You're a glutton for punishment, aren't you, Mary? I'd have thought you'd have had enough of Eileen in work.'

'Mary's very quiet.' Martha looked closely at her daughter. 'Are you all right, lass?'

'Yes! I only seem quiet because I can't get a word in edgeways.'

Eileen moved in quickly. 'That's right, put the blame on me! Everybody picks on me 'cos I'm too shy to stick up for meself.'

'You shy!? That's the best joke I've heard in years!' Harry's heartbeat was returning to normal. It had taken all his courage to come here tonight, but the thought of seeing Mary had drawn him like a magnet. May God forgive him, but when Eileen had told him Bob had been killed his first thought was that he might now stand a chance with Mary. He'd tried to push the thought out of his head, telling himself a good bloke was dead and he should be ashamed of himself. But he couldn't help it. For as long as he could remember, he'd loved Mary Bradshaw. Even when he'd been too young to know what love was, he knew there was something special about the little girl with blonde curls and big blue eyes who lived a few doors away. And now, as he looked across the hospital bed, he knew he'd love her all his life.

The ting-a-ling told them it was time for visitors to leave, and Martha's face fell. The days dragged but the half hour visit flew over.

'I'll be in tomorrow, Mam.' Mary bent to kiss her mother. 'And I'll try and drag Eileen along to cheer you up.'

Harry moved to Martha's side. 'Can I tell me mam you're getting better?'

Martha shot a glance at Mary before answering. 'I'll get better, please God.'

'I'll be in again to see me friend, so I'll pop in and see you.'

Eileen nudged him. 'What ward did yer say your friend's in?'

'Oh, I didn't say!' Harry returned her look calmly. 'You don't think I'm that daft, do you? You'd be up there before I could say "snap".'

'Miserable bugger!' Eileen grinned, giving him top marks for quick thinking.

'No, I won't come home with you, Eileen, if you don't mind.' They were standing at the bus stop. 'I'd rather be in me own house.'

'Don't argue . . . yer comin' home with me!' Eileen spoke sharply, then softened her tone. 'I don't like to think of yer in that house all on yer own.'

'I'll be all right, honest! I'll sleep better in me own bed.'

The bus came and Harry sat in the seat in front of them. 'Can me mam do anything for you? Shopping, perhaps?'

'No thanks, Harry. Eileen got some things for me today, so I'll manage for a few days.'

When Mary stood up to get off, Eileen squeezed her arm. 'I'll stay on till the next stop to save me legs, seein' as yer've got Harry to walk yer home. Try and get some sleep, an' I'll call in on me way home from work tomorrow.'

Not a word was spoken as they covered the ground. Harry couldn't think of anything to say and Mary just wanted to get home. They reached the door and without turning round she said, softly, 'Thanks for going to see me mam, Harry. Goodnight.'

'I'm sorry about Bob, Mary.'

There was no answer as the door closed in his face.

Mary drew the curtains, switched the light on, and sank into her mother's chair. For the first time since John Greenfield had told her Bob was dead, she was alone with her grief. Eileen meant well when she said she didn't want to leave her on her own, but she didn't understand that having people around you didn't make the pain and grief go away. It only put off the time when you could give way to your emotions.

The tears started and Mary could feel the warmth as they trickled down her cheeks. Then she doubled up and rested her forehead on her knees as her sobs filled the room. Her thoughts were distorted by the gushing sound in her ears as she slowly rocked to and fro, her arms wrapped around her waist. Dark patches of damp appeared on her dress as the tears flowed unchecked, but she didn't see them as she swallowed hard to clear the lump in her throat that was threatening to cut off her breathing. All the emotions she'd had to keep at bay poured out with her tears, until at last they were spent and the pain in her head eased.

Mary reached for her handbag at the side of the chair and opened it to take out some photographs. Bob's face looking back at her from the top photograph was like a knife turning in her heart. They'd loved each other so much, had so many plans for the future, and now he was gone. Never again would she see his blue eyes crinkle at the corners when he laughed, or hear him say, 'I love you, Mary Bradshaw'.

Mary rubbed a hand across her eyes and picked up another photograph. She was leaning against the rail of the Seacombe ferry boat, and Bob's arms were around her. He was smiling down at her, and Mary remembered that just after the photograph had been taken, he'd bent down and kissed her. She raised the photograph to her lips and whispered, 'I'll always love you, Bob West.'

Eileen searched Mary's face as she squeezed past her in the small hall.

'I've been that worried about yer, I couldn't keep me mind on me work. How've yer been, kid?'

'I took a couple of the sleeping pills and slept on and off for a few hours.' Mary's face was swollen and her hair a tangled mass. 'If I'd had the guts, I'd have taken the lot and got it over with. But I'm too much of a coward to even do that.'

'Not a coward, kid.' Eileen held her arms wide and Mary walked into them. 'Just a very frightened girl who's had more trouble in the last few months than most people get in a lifetime.' She held the shuddering body close. 'That's it, kid; cry it all away.'

'I can't stop thinking about me mam! I did wrong and deserve to be punished, but me mam's never done anyone any harm. She doesn't deserve to suffer.'

'There now,' Eileen crooned as she stroked the tousled hair. 'I know things look black now, but it'll all work out, I promise.' She waited till the sobbing eased then gently pressed Mary on to the couch. 'Sit down, kid, and let's talk it over. It's no good me sayin' I know how yer feel, 'cos I don't! Only you knows how much hurt and pain there is inside yer. And if I say things that upset yer, I'm only being cruel to be kind.' Eileen leaned forward and took one of Mary's hands. 'Live one day at a time, kid, and worry about tomorrow when it comes. If yer want my advice, I say the best thing yer can do is get back to work. Mix with people, so yer don't have time to think. Sittin' here all day on yer own won't do yer no good.'

'I'm not going back to work!' Fear showed in Mary's eyes. 'I couldn't face the women.'

'The women don't know yet! And even if they did, what's it got to do with them? They're not going to keep yer!'

'But when I start showing, they'd all be talking behind me back and I couldn't bear it.'

'Everyone is going to find out sooner or later, so yer better start getting used to the idea. Havin' a baby isn't something yer can keep a secret.' Eileen let out a deep sigh. 'Look, kid, I'm not going to say everything in the garden's going to be rosy, 'cos it would only be a pack of lies an' yer wouldn't thank me for it in the end. Life is hard, an' people can be cruel, so the sooner yer learn to stand up to it, the better. Whether yer like the idea of going back to work or not, yer really don't have much option, do yer?'

Mary shivered, 'I wouldn't be able to hold me head up.'

'OK; so don't go back to work! Where will the money come from to live on? What about all the things yer'll need for the baby? The only way to get money is to earn it, 'cos nobody's goin' to hand it to yer on a plate.' Eileen screwed her eyes up as she squeezed Mary's hand. 'Look, kid! The people you've got to worry about are not the people in work, but yer mam and the baby. They'll both be dependent on you, but without money yer won't be able to help them.'

There was a long silence before Mary whispered, 'I'm due at the doctor's on Friday, but I could go Thursday instead and turn in to work on Friday.'

'That's my girl! Like I've said, kid, take life one day at a time.'

Eileen gave Mary's hand one last pat before standing up. 'I'll get home and do some work before it's time for us to go to the 'ossie.' As she walked to the door her eyes travelled round the soot-streaked walls. 'This room is enough to give anyone the bloody willies! Why don't yer let me an' Harry paper it for yer? We're on afternoons next week and we could have it done in two mornings.'

'I don't want the room doing, Eileen! Forget it, will you, please!?'

'OK! Don't bite me head off!'

Eileen had only been gone five minutes when there was a rattle on the letter box, and Mary opened the door thinking her friend had forgotten something. 'I've just met Eileen, and she told me about Bob.' Elsie Smith was wringing her hands, her pinched face trying hard to look tragic. 'I got an awful shock when she told me.' Her eyes darted past the half open door, hoping Mary would take the hint and invite her in. When she didn't, the whining voice continued. 'You're having more than your share of bad luck, aren't you? And Bob's poor mam and dad must be out of their minds! Losing their home, and now their only son!'

Mary felt hysterical. She wanted to slam the door and shut out the sight and sound of the woman who revelled in other people's suffering. Bob's death would keep her in gossip for the next few weeks, or until some other unfortunate person caught her evil eye. Eileen always said she would make a 'bloody good professional mourner', and she was right. Just being near Elsie Smith made your skin crawl.

'Let's know if there's anything I can do.' The voice brought Mary back to life. Aye, she thought ... let you know, and it would be all over the neighbourhood within hours. 'Thanks, Mrs Smith, but I'll manage.'

'Does your mam know about Bob?'

'No! Not until the doctor says she's fit enough to be told.'

Elsie's eyes narrowed. 'Funny you being so friendly with Eileen Gillmoss. She's so tough and common, she doesn't seem your type.'

Mary's nostrils flared. 'Eileen Gillmoss is a smashing woman, and she's my best friend! At least she tells you to your face what she thinks about you; she doesn't go behind your back!' With that parting shot, Mary slammed the door leaving Elsie Smith standing with her mouth open.

When Mary walked into the cloakroom on Friday morning, all heads turned towards her. No one said a word, but the women conveyed their sympathy in the patting and squeezing of her arm as they walked past. Mary knew they'd been warned, and she was grateful to Eileen. It would only take one word to break down her fragile defences.

Even Harry kept out of her way until it was time for his routine check. And when Mary just nodded in reply when he asked if everything was all right, he rounded the machine to where Eileen stood. 'How is she?'

'Well she's here, and that's a start.'

'Have you mentioned decorating the room yet?'

'Bloody hell, Harry! That room's coming between me and me sleep!' Eileen's eyes swivelled sideways. 'Why haven't yer got yerself a girlfriend? I'd have thought a man of your age would need a woman.'

'Needing and wanting are two different things, Eileen!'

'My God, the man's going all poetic!' Eileen grunted. 'Hidden talents, eh?'

'I can be very determined, too!' Harry's smile didn't reach his eyes. 'All I need is a little help from a friend.'

Eileen turned away. She should put him straight about Mary, but that would mean betraying a confidence. 'Oh, go and find yerself a girlfriend! There must be plenty around.'

When Harry stood silent, his eyes questioning, Eileen sucked her breath in.

'OK! But don't ever say I didn't warn yer.'

* * *

They were sitting in the canteen and eight pairs of eyes were watching, fascinated, as Eileen piled chips on to a full round of bread and then squashed them down with another round. Her fat hands gripped the enormous sandwich and lifted it to her mouth where her lips were parted in readiness to receive it.

'My God!' Maisie Phillips shook her head. 'You couldn't take her anywhere, could you? She'd make a holy show of you!'

Eileen gave her a disdainful look, and crooking her little finger into what she thought was an elegant pose, said haughtily. 'Hi'll have you know, my good woman, that Hi've heaten with the best!'

The women laughed goodnaturedly as they stood up. 'Aye! The best down and outs in Liverpool!'

Left alone with Mary, Eileen rubbed a hand across her greasy chin. 'How did it go at the doctor's?'

'He said to leave it for another week and see how me mam is.' Mary gave a quick glance around. 'I asked him about going into Oxford Street to have the baby.'

'What a hope! Yer need a letter from Our Lord to get in there! They only take complicated cases in, unless yer live round there.'

'He told me that, but I'd still like to try. He's going to give me a letter next week, to take down. So I'll keep me fingers crossed.'

'Yer'll need to keep more than yer fingers crossed, kid!' Eileen held on to the table while she scraped her chair back, then she linked her arm through Mary's and they made their way back to the shop floor. 'Don't bite me head off, kid, but I've been thinkin'. Don't yer think it's a bit selfish of yer to let yer mam come home to that filthy room?'

'But me mam's not coming home yet.'

'How d'yer know? Once the 'ospital say they can't do any more for her, she'll be sent home. And fancy havin' to lay all day looking at those bloody walls.'

Mary bit on her lip. 'I wouldn't mind you doing it, but I don't like the thought of Harry Sedgemoor being in our house.'

'I don't know what yer've got against him! He's a smashing bloke!'

'I've got nothing against him,' Mary insisted. 'But how d'you think I'm going to feel when he knows I'm pregnant?'

'You're going to need friends, kid, and Harry could be a good friend.' They were nearing their machine and Eileen turned to face Mary. 'Shall I ask him to give me a hand with the room next week, then?'

The hesitation was brief. 'Yes, please. I'll start stripping the walls. And thanks, Eileen. I know I don't sound grateful, but I am.'

Harry couldn't sleep on the Sunday night. He tossed and turned, telling himself he was acting like a kid going to see a cowboy picture instead of a grown man going to decorate a room. He was meeting Eileen at Mary's at nine, but by seven he couldn't stand it any longer and went downstairs to make himself a drink. When his mother came down at her usual time of seven thirty, her eyes full of sleep, she stared in surprise. 'Couldn't you sleep?'

'I woke up early and couldn't drop off again. So I came down and made meself a drink.'

'Is there any left in the pot? I'll have a quick cuppa before I make your dad's breakfast.' Over the rim of her cup, Lizzie noted her son's restlessness and wondered if it had anything to do with Mary Bradshaw. 'What time will you be home for dinner?'

Harry stood up to comb his hair in front of the mirror over the fireplace. 'I won't be coming home.' Their eyes locked through the mirror. 'Me and Eileen want to get as much done as we can, so we're going to have a bite at Mary's and go straight to work.'

He was putting the comb back in his pocket when the door opened and his dad came in. 'What's up with you two this morning?' George Sedgemoor looked at his son. 'I thought you were on afternoons?'

'I am.' Harry could feel his face redden. 'I'm giving Eileen Gillmoss a hand to paper the Bradshaws' living room, so it'll be nice when Mrs B comes out of hospital.'

'Aye, young Mary could do with a hand.' George nudged his wife who was still sitting at the table. 'Come on, Lizzie! I haven't got all day.'

His dad had gone to work and his mam was tidying up when Harry came down with his overalls over his arm. 'I'll see you tonight, then, Mam.'

Lizzie nodded. She liked Mary, but if her son had any ideas in that direction he'd best be forgetting them. It would be a long time before Mary was ready to look at another man.

185

* * *

Mary was alone when Harry arrived, and although he'd rehearsed what he would talk about, when the time came he was tongue-tied. Mary didn't help much, either! She handed him the bucket when he asked for it, then left him alone in the kitchen. He half filled the bucket with cold water and slowly stirred the contents of a bag of flour into it. He'd scrounged two bags of flour off the local baker and hoped it was enough to do the whole room. He was stirring the mixture with a piece of wood when he heard Eileen arrive, and as soon as she walked through the door the atmosphere changed and the house became alive. It wasn't only the house that became alive, either, because Mary was like a different person as she greeted her friend. 'And where d'you think you've been to, lazy bones?'

'The flamin' cheek of you! For your information, Miss Bradshaw, I've got three kids off to school, made the beds, dusted, and left the dinner ready for me mam.' Eileen reverted to the posh accent she loved so much. 'Hi haven't been sitting on my harse, you know.' She saw Harry lounging in the doorway and beamed. 'I hope yer in the mood for work, Mr Sedgemoor.' Without waiting for a reply, Eileen eyed the bare walls. 'Yer've done a good job there, kid! Now, if yer get the scissors we'll start trimmin' the paper. It takes longer to trim the bloody paper than it does to put it up.'

Mary looked at the larger than life woman and asked herself, yet again, what she'd do without her. 'I'll make us a pot of tea.'

Harry wagged the piece of wood at Eileen. 'If my

labourer is late again I'm going to dock her pay.'

'Oh, no!' Eileen clutched her heart. 'I've got a mother and three kids to support! Take pity on me, please, sir? It won't happen again, I promise.' She delved into her shopping bag. 'While you two have been lazin' around, I've been standing in a queue to get some pies to feed yer faces!' She thrust the bag into Mary's hand before slipping her coat off. When she saw Mary eyeing the three safety pins holding the hem up, she threw the coat over Mary's shoulder. 'Never mind laughin'! Just you put this Paris model on an 'anger.' She waited till Mary was in the hall then bawled, 'If you 'aven't got an 'anger, throw it on the floor.'

'Any chance of getting some paper trimmed?' Harry asked. 'It'll be time to go to work before we start.'

Eileen picked up the scissors. 'Hi'll have a glass of champagne with me meal, please! Oh, and do make sure it's a good year.'

Harry kept stirring the paste while the women trimmed, and when Mary had finished a roll he measured the wall and started to cut the paper to size. He was listening to Eileen telling Mary about one of her neighbours coming to complain about Billy playing football outside her house, and he grinned when Eileen said, 'Miserable old cow!'

'Give me a hand with the paper, Eileen, while Mary carries on trimming.'

Harry came through from the kitchen with a strip of pasted paper over his arm, and Eileen held the bottom of the paper while he climbed the ladder. Mary became more relaxed as they worked and talked to Harry as though it was an everyday thing for him to be in her house. His pleasure showed on his face, and Eileen, whose eyes didn't miss a thing, wondered whether she'd done the right thing in letting him get so involved. She should have kept her big mouth shut!

At eleven o'clock they stopped for a break and sat on hard chairs in the middle of the room. One wall was finished, and Mary, her hands curled round her cup, said. 'The room looks brighter already! The paper's nice, Harry; you've got good taste. Just wait till me mam sees it, she'll be thrilled.'

'I think the ceiling's going to spoil it.' Harry cast a critical eye over the sooty ceiling, 'I asked you to let me do it before we started putting the paper up.'

'Oh, sod off, Harry!' Eileen clicked her teeth. 'Yer've harped on about that bloody ceiling since we started!' She heaved herself up. 'Yer'll have to hang on a minute 'cos if I don't go to the lavvy I'll burst.'

Mary looked at Harry. 'While you're waiting for Eileen, I'll pass you one of the strips up.'

Carefully folding the pasted strip, she carried it through to where Harry was standing on a middle rung of the ladder. He turned sideways to take the paper from her, and was so intent on keeping his balance he didn't see Mary sway before she fell limply to the floor. He looked down in horror, half the paper in his hand, the other half wrapped round Mary's body. He came down the ladder and carefully stepped over her. Beads of sweat ran down his face as he stared helplessly at her still form. He bent to lift her, then straightened up and ran to the kitchen door calling Eileen.

* * *

Eileen was holding a damp cloth to Mary's forehead when she came round. Still dazed, she could remember nothing but the blackness and the feeling of falling into space. 'Come on, kid, yer all right now.' Mary opened her eyes at the sound of Eileen's voice, but it was Harry she saw, standing at the end of the couch. She sat bolt upright, straightening her skirt over her knees. 'I'm OK,' she whispered. 'I went giddy for a minute when I handed the paper up to Harry, but I'm all right now.' She jumped up. 'Come on, I've held the job up long enough.'

'Stay where you are,' Harry said sharply. 'Me and Eileen can manage.'

'No, I'm fine! I never could stand heights, that's all.' On legs that felt like jelly, Mary walked through to the kitchen and stayed there until it was one o'clock and time to have their dinner before going to work. Two of the walls were finished and Mary forced herself to look as pleased as Eileen and Harry when they gave one last look before walking out of the door.

The next morning Eileen was at Mary's when Harry arrived and they started work right away. Mary felt terrible, and tried to hide the fact by being more talkative than usual. She made them a cup of tea at eleven and was rinsing their cups out afterwards when, without warning, she started to vomit. She turned the tap full on as her head bent over the sink, hoping to cover the sound. But Eileen heard, and when she saw the puzzled expression on Harry's face she guessed the thoughts running through his head. 'What's wrong with Mary?' Harry ran his fingers down the blades of the scissors to wipe the paste off. Then he looked deep into Eileen's eyes. 'What's wrong?'

'She's probably not been eating properly, I suppose.' Eileen turned from his questioning eyes. 'I'll get another piece of paper.'

'You'd have a job!' Harry sounded bad tempered. 'There's none pasted!'

'All right!' Eileen stuck her tongue out. 'Don't get off yer bike! Get some pasted!'

Mary was opening the oven door when Harry asked. 'OK, Mary?'

'Fine!' Oh God, I hope they didn't hear, Mary prayed. 'I'm just warming the pies up.'

'We're on the last three strips now, so we won't be long.'

They were eating their pies and Eileen broke the heavy silence. 'Yer'd think we were at a bloody wake! Just look at the gobs on you two!'

Harry forced a smile. 'We don't all lead exciting lives, like you.'

'Pooh! Me lead an exciting life! Yer must be joking! The only excitement I get is when our Edna wets her knickers, or our Billy puts a ball through somebody's window.' Demolishing half the pie in one mouthful, Eileen looked at Mary. 'Remember me goin' into town a few weeks ago to get our Billy a new pair of kecks?' She waited for Mary's nod. 'Well, I was walkin' home the other day and there was me bold laddo lyin' full stretch in the gutter. He had his hand down the grid pokin' around in all the muck, an' him with his best kecks on! Him and his mate had pulled the grid top off, an' his mate was holding his legs while he fished around in all the muck! I was so flamin' mad, I grabbed him by the scruff of the neck and dragged him home while he screamed blue murder! All I could hear was that his "bobby dazzler" had rolled down the grid an' he wanted to get it 'cos he'd swapped three of his ollies for it. The racket he was kickin' up, yer'd have thought he'd lost a pound.'

Harry's white teeth gleamed as he roared with laughter. 'I know how he felt! I had a "bobby dazzler" once, and it was me pride and joy! Many's the scrap I had over that "bobby dazzler".'

'I bet your mam wasn't daft enough to fish it out of the grid for yer, though, was she?' When Harry's mouth gaped, Eileen smirked. 'That's what yours truly did! I lay down in the gutter and put me hand in all that muck to get it out for him!'

Mary gasped. 'You didn't!'

'I bloody did!' Eileen's dimples appeared at the same time her eyes disappeared. 'Can yez imagine it? Me lyin' in the gutter, with me backside stickin' up and showing everything I've got? Must have been a sight for sore eyes! But it was worth it to see his face when I handed him his "bobby dazzler". I was filthy, his new kecks were filthy, an' he couldn't have cared less. He ran in to wash it under the tap, then he polished it on his sleeve till it was shinin'.'

'It's lovely!' Mary's gaze swept the room. 'I don't know how to thank you.'

Eileen gave her a gentle push. 'Just remember us in yer will.'

'It's a pity I didn't have time to put the border up.' Harry looked disappointed. 'And I still say the ceiling spoils it! One thing's laughing at another.'

'Oh, God, here he goes again,' Eileen groaned. 'It's too late now, so just forget it!'

Harry ignored her. 'I'm on days on Saturday and Sunday, so I could put the border up and see what I can do with the ceiling.'

'No!' Mary flashed. 'I'll be going in to see me mam.'

'That doesn't matter! I can do it while you're out!'

'For Christ's sake, stop arguing.' Eileen pushed between them and made for the door, muttering, 'I bet they don't have as much trouble decoratin' the bloody Adelphi!'

Chapter Thirteen

It was half past six when Mary opened the door to Harry on the Saturday night. She had her coat on, and after telling him she'd mixed the paste ready for him to put the border up, said she'd have to go or she'd be late at the hospital. 'I'll be back about eight o'clock.'

'I'll have the border up by then.'

'OK!' Mary slammed the front door shut at exactly the same time as Danny Jackson came out of his house. His face broke into a smile as he fell into step beside her. 'Hello, Mary! How...' his words petered out as Mary took to her heels and fled down the street as though the devil was chasing her. 'What the hell's up with her?' Danny asked aloud, as he watched Mary fly round the corner. 'Stuck-up little bitch!' He kept on walking, still muttering to himself, till he reached the pub where he spent most evenings. He was early tonight because he had to go back to work to finish loading the ship he was working on, which was due to sail with the early tide.

Not that Danny felt like going back to work, but the extra money would come in handy. The fifty shillings a week he gave to Vera didn't leave enough for his ciggies and beer money. He never gave her any extra when he worked overtime, because he figured that if he did the work he was entitled to keep the money.

'A pint of bitter, Sid!' Danny lit a Woodbine and leaned both elbows on the bar counter. Into his mind flashed the picture of Mary running away from him, and a frown crossed his swarthy features. He hadn't been bad looking when he was younger, but the years of heavy drinking and smoking had taken their toll. His face was bloated, his once white teeth were yellow with nicotine and lack of cleaning, and he had a beer belly.

Gulping down his first pint fast, Danny pushed the glass across the counter. 'Same again, Sid!' It was too early for any of his cronies and having no one to talk to, the second pint was downed as quickly as the first. 'Fill her up!' Danny's big mouth didn't make him one of Sid's favourite customers, and he pulled the pint and served it without saying a word. He then walked to the other end of the bar to continue his conversation with an elderly man who came in every night for his two glasses of stout and a chat about the progress of the war. There were only a few customers in the pub, and Sid was taking it easy before the crowd came in and he'd be rushed off his feet.

Left on his own, chain smoking and drinking pint after pint, Danny started to get moody. The target of his dark thoughts was Mary Bradshaw. Who the hell did she think she was, snubbing him like that? Miss High and Mighty needed taking down a peg or two! By the time he left the pub he'd drunk six pints of beer and his bad temper was smouldering. All it needed to reach boiling point was to see

Carol sitting on the floor tearing up pieces of old newspapers. 'Get 'er up to bed, where she should be,' he growled.

'She's not doing any harm!' Vera could see the rage on his face and thought, wearily, Oh, God he's going to start again and I don't think I can take any more.

'I'm not 'aving her under me feet,' Danny thundered. 'I'm goin' to work soon, an' I'm not sittin' lookin' at her gormless face.'

'I'll take her to bed with me when you go out. You know she's frightened in the dark.' Although Vera was frightened herself, she loved her daughter more than she feared her husband. 'She's doing no harm.'

'Aren't you listening to me? Get her upstairs before I give 'er a belt!'

Vera scooped Carol up from the floor in case Danny lashed out with his feet. Her fear turned to anger. 'What's up with you? Was the beer off?'

'Don't start gettin' clever with me, or you'll be feelin' the back of me hand.' Danny towered menacingly over her. 'You're getting too big for yer boots, like Miss High and Mighty next door!'

Vera frowned as she pressed her daughter's head into her shoulder for protection. 'What's Mary done to you? You hardly ever see the girl.'

'I saw her tonight and she treated me as though I was a piece of muck.'

Vera could smell the beer and the nicotine as his face loomed closer. She took in the bloated face, the bleary eyes, and the stomach swollen with drinking too much beer for too long. He never had any money for sweets for the kids, or to mug them to the Saturday matinee, but he always had enough to prop the bar up in the pub every night. Suddenly she was filled with loathing for the man she'd married. The man who'd punched her around for the last three years, treating her like a lackey because she dared to have a child who was mentally retarded.

'Shall I tell you why Mary treated you like a piece of muck?' Vera's words were slow and deliberate. 'She saw me face the last time you gave me a belt, and she probably thinks that's what you are ... a piece of muck!'

Danny's head came closer. 'So you went cryin' to the neighbours, did yer?'

'I didn't have to; Mary came here!' Vera was surprised how calm she felt. There was no fear in her now. 'Why? You're not afraid of your boozing pals finding out you hit your wife, are you? The great Danny Jackson's not ashamed of people knowing he's a coward, surely?'

Danny's nostrils flared as his two hands reached for her.

'Sshh!' Harry put a finger to his mouth as Mary came through the door. He was standing at the bottom of the ladder with the paste brush in his hand and his head cocked to one side. 'Listen!'

Through the wall Mary could hear Danny's loud voice, and her hand went to her mouth. 'Oh, God, don't let him hit her again!'

'Don't let him what?' Harry came alive. 'You mean he knocks Vera around?'

Mary nodded. 'Last time he took off she ended up with a terrible face.' She started to tremble. 'This might be my fault, because when I went out tonight Danny came out of their door at the same time. He started to speak to me, but I couldn't bear to be near him after what he'd done to Vera, so I ran away from him.'

Harry was bending to put the brush on a piece of newspaper he'd spread on the floor when they heard Danny's cry of rage. 'To hell with that!' Harry was at the door when Mary touched his arm. 'Don't go in, Harry! You'll end up fighting with him.'

He shrugged her hand away. 'It'll do him good to have a man to fight for a change! He won't find it as easy as picking on a woman!'

Chewing nervously on her lip, Mary dashed out after him. She was on his heels when he reached the Jacksons' and was surprised to see the door open and young Colin and Peter crying on the step. 'Me dad's hitting me mam,' young Colin cried. 'Make him stop, mister!'

'Take the boys to your house, Mary.' Harry's voice was tight with rage. 'Keep them there till I come back.'

'Be careful! Vera said he's like a madman when he's drunk.'

'Don't worry about me! Take the boys.'

Mary drew the boys away as Harry stepped into the hall. He threw the living-room door open, and in a split second saw Danny's clenched fist crash down on the back of Vera's head which was bent over to protect Carol. Burning with rage, Harry grabbed him by the back of the neck and flung him backwards against the table which moved under his weight. A look of surprised anger crossed Danny's face. 'What the hell d'yer think you're doin'? Get out of my house!' He straightened up and gave Harry a push in the chest. 'D'yer hear me . . . I said get out!'

'I'll get out, and I'll take you with me!' Harry grabbed him by the neck of his shirt. 'Me and you are going to have a little talk outside!'

'I'll break yer bloody neck if yer don't get out of my house!' Danny blustered as he tried unsuccessfully to loosen the grip on his shirt. 'I'll have the police on to you . . . you're trespassin'.'

'You can get the police after we've had our little talk.' Harry couldn't remember ever being so angry as he was now. 'In fact I'll get them for you; I'm sure they'd like to know you beat your wife.'

'You've no right interferin' between man and wife.' Beer had so dulled Danny's senses he didn't heed the warning in Harry's eyes. 'Now get!'

Grasping the shirt neck tighter, Harry pulled him forward until their faces were almost touching. 'Are you coming outside, or do I have to drag you out?'

'I'm not going . . .' That was as far as Danny got before he was pulled through the door and into the street. Harry slammed him up against the wall then deliberately let his own arms fall to his sides. He didn't move or speak, and his calm lulled Danny into a sense of false security. Roaring like a bull, he pulled his arm back, and throwing all his strength into the punch, aimed at Harry's head. When Harry neatly sidestepped, the blow landed in mid-air, throwing Danny off balance. Harry waited for him to regain his balance, then said, quietly, 'Well, you started it!' He aimed a right-handed punch to Danny's face and heard the blow land at the same time as Danny cried out in pain. 'Explain that to your mates in work!' Harry turned on his heels and walked back into the house, where Vera was sitting in the chair crying as she rocked gently with Carol held tight in her arms. 'Come on, Vera! The boys are in Mary's.'

'Where is he?'

'Outside! I don't think he'll be hitting anyone again.'

'He's going to work tonight.' Habit made Vera hesitate. 'I should be doing his carry out.'

'Let him do his own!' Harry pressed her towards the door. 'You can bring the kids back when he's gone.'

Vera shot a glance at Danny, who was still standing against the wall nursing his face. She knew she should feel pity for him, but couldn't. He'd shamed her too often. As soon as she'd reached the safety of Mary's house, Harry went back to Danny.

'They'll stay in Mary's till you've left for work. And don't try and take it out on Vera tomorrow, because what you've had tonight is only a taste of what you'll get if you ever lay hands on her, or the kids, again.'

All the neighbours were standing at their doors. They'd come out to see what the noise was about, but not one had interfered as Danny Jackson got what someone should have given him years ago. But Danny knew he couldn't let Harry get away with it or he'd never be able to lift his head up again. So Danny did what Danny always did . . . he tried to bluff his way out.

'I'm not frightened of you, mate! If I didn't have to go to work I'd give yer the hidin' of yer life!'

'I'll be here any time you like!' Harry's voice was low. 'Just remember you've been warned!'

Vera's face looked weary as she lifted the sleeping Carol from Mary's couch. 'Thanks, Harry! I'm just sorry you had to get involved in my troubles.' She looked across at her sons. 'It's time you two were back in bed. Say thank you to Auntie Mary and Uncle Harry.'

Harry ruffled the boys' hair as they passed. 'Sleep well.'

'Thanks, mister!' From that night on Harry Sedgemoor took over from Tom Mix as their hero.

When Vera was thanking him again at the door, Harry grinned as he made a fist of his right hand.

'I quite enjoyed it! But I'll tell you what . . . if his face is as sore as these, he'll have a right shiner!'

Vera managed a weak smile. 'I can see him now, explaining to his friends how he walked into a door!'

'Well, that bit of excitement put a halt to me gallop!' Harry faced Mary across the room. 'At least I got the border up, but I was hoping to get the ceiling done as well! Still, it's too late now, so we'll leave it for another day, eh?'

'Yes, please! I've had enough for one day.' Mary was collecting the Jacksons' used tea cups and she felt worn out. She'd gone to work that day to get some overtime in and was ready now for bed. 'I'll just rinse these through, then it's up the wooden hills for me.'

There went Harry's hopes of a quiet chat with her. 'I'll

clear up then, and leave you in peace.' He carried the ladder down the yard, cursing Danny Jackson for spoiling his chances.

Eileen had never seen Mary so animated for a long time. They were on the bus on the Sunday morning and Mary was talking fifteen to the dozen as she described the events of the night before.

'I met Mr Williams from across the road this morning, and he said it was about time someone taught Danny a lesson.'

'Ooh, I wish I'd been there! Why is it that I miss all the fun?'

'The whole street was out! I was terrified, but I popped me head out to see what was happening, and was just in time to see Harry give Danny a fourpenny one!'

'Wasn't it a blessing that Harry was in your 'ouse? Yer see, kid, I told yer Harry would come in useful, didn't I?'

'I was frightened in case he got hurt.'

The bus came to a stop and Eileen stood up. 'I wouldn't worry about Harry Sedgemoor! He's no mammy's boy, that's for sure!'

They'd been in work an hour when Eileen saw Harry approaching Mary and she cupped her hands to her mouth. 'Yer'll be takin' Joe Louis on next, will yer?'

Harry grinned. 'Don't you start or I'll have you outside!'

'Yer wouldn't have to drag me out, big boy! I'd come willingly!' Eileen laughed at her own joke. 'But I've got a bone to pick with yer, so when yer've finished with Mary, get over here.'

'I'll be round in a minute.' Harry's face straightened. 'Did you hear anything, Mary?'

'Not a sound! I kept me ears open, but didn't hear a thing. Mind you, I don't know what time Danny gets in, so I might have left for work before he got home.'

'If you do hear anything, or if he comes near you, you let me know.'

'Don't worry . . . if he came near me I'd scream the place down!'

'Don't be frightened of him. He only picks on those in his own house, where no one can see him.' A sheepish grin covered Harry's face. 'If my fingers are anything to go by, he should be sporting a black eye by now.'

'Have you hurt your hand?'

'No, not really! But me fingers feel as though they've been in contact with a brick wall! Anyway, I'll see you later.'

Eileen was waiting for him. 'I believe yer gave him a belter.'

Harry waved his hand dismissively. 'What do you want me for?'

The trolley for faulty shells was usually emptied half way through each shift by Willy Turnley. But they'd only been in work an hour and Eileen's trolley was nearly full. She nodded towards it.

'What's the matter with the dozy buggers in there? Are they all asleep or something? If we were as dozy as them, our soldiers would be tryin' to fight a war with dud shells! Tell 'em to get off their arses if they don't want Hitler to win this bloody war!'

Harry shook his head at the loaded trolley. 'I'll go and see them now.'

They were at their dinner break when Mary started to feel sick. Telling Eileen she was going to the toilet, she locked herself in one of the cubicles and, just in time, bent her head over the lavatory. Afterwards, feeling as weak as a kitten, she leaned against the cool, tiled wall, wiping her mouth on a piece of toilet paper. She took half a dozen deep breaths before opening the cubicle door and felt a sense of relief when she found the place empty. Quickly rinsing her mouth out with cold water, she made her way back to the canteen.

'Bloody hell, kid! I was beginning to think yer'd flushed yerself down the lavvy!' Eileen screwed her eyes up as she took a good look at Mary's face. 'What's the matter? Yer look as though yer've seen a ghost.'

'Having a baby doesn't seem to agree with me. I've been sick.'

'I think yer should go home, kid.' Mary's white face frightened Eileen. 'Yer not fit to stand beside the machine in case yer 'ave an accident.'

'I'll be all right! I should have gone to the doctor's yesterday but I came in to work instead, thinking I could go and see him tomorrow with us starting nights. I'll ask him if he can give me anything to stop the sickness, because I'm sick every morning.'

Eileen looked doubtful. 'If yer feel the least bit faint, for God's sake give us the wire, won't yer?'

Every few seconds Eileen looked across the machine,

worried for her friend. She was doing this when she saw Harry walk up to Mary. 'Oh, bloody 'ell,' she muttered. 'He's all she needs right now!'

If Mary's hair had been loose, Harry probably wouldn't have noticed her pallor. But with the turban dragging her hair back from her face, he'd have had to be blind not to notice.

'Feeling OK, Mary?'

She nodded without lifting her head. 'Fine, thanks.'

Harry rounded the machine quickly, and when Eileen saw him walking towards her she asked herself, 'What do I do now? I'd better tell him the truth and put him out of his misery.' But as he came closer and she saw the anxiety on his face, she knew she wouldn't be putting him out of his misery . . . she'd be dropping him right in it!

Harry didn't waste words. 'Eileen, is Mary pregnant?'

'Ah, ay, Harry! What d'yer think I am? It's none of my business, so why ask me?'

'I can hardly ask her, can I?' He turned his back to the machine, and Mary.

'You know how I feel about her, don't you? How I've always felt!'

'I'd have to be blind not to!' Eileen kept a smile on her face in case Mary was watching. 'I think yer a smashing feller, but Mary's me mate.' Sighing, she stuck a finger under her turban to scratch her head. 'OK, Harry! Mary is pregnant! But if yer tell her I've told yer, I'll never speak to yer again.' When his mouth opened to speak, Eileen held her hand up. 'No, Harry, let me finish! I've let the cat out of the bag now, so I may as well go the whole hog. I know how yer feel about Mary, but I think the world of her too, and heaven help anyone who hurts her.' She saw Mary watching them with curiosity, and waved across to her. 'We're talkin' about when the war's over, and we start our own decorating business.'

Satisfied, Mary smiled back before lowering her head again. Harry waited a few seconds. 'Well, go on!'

'It happened when Bob was on embarkation leave, and she told me they got carried away. I believe her too, 'cos she's so bloody innocent it just isn't true! She's not a hard girl, and when the gossips find out, they'll crucify her. She's not strong enough to stand up to that, so if ever anyone needed a friend, it's Mary Bradshaw. And right now I feel like a traitor!'

Chapter Fourteen

Lizzie Sedgemoor watched her son out of the corner of her eye. He'd been in a bad mood when he came in from work, and when she'd asked him what was wrong he'd nearly bitten her head off. When he worked days at the weekends he usually went for a pint, or to a dance, but here he was sitting quietly listening to the news on the wireless. The commentator's voice was telling them how Hitler was pushing the Allies back on all fronts and her husband grunted in anger. 'When our lads get started he won't know what's hit him, you mark my words! Him and his Heil Hitler salute . . . I'd bloody Heil Hitler him!'

Lizzie tried again with Harry. 'You're very quiet, son.'

'I'm trying to listen to the wireless, if you don't mind!' Harry spoke sharply, and George lifted his head in surprise. He opened his mouth to rebuke his son, but Lizzie's eyes warned him off. It was when Harry had gone up to bed early, George asked. 'What's up with him?'

'I think he's sweet on Mary Bradshaw.' Lizzie picked her knitting up. 'From the looks of him, I'd say he's not having much luck.'

'He'll get over it! He'll be out dancing again in a few days, just you see.'

'I don't know so much.' Lizzie's nimble fingers flew along the row of stitches. 'I've never seen our Harry like this before.'

Upstairs, Harry lay on his bed staring at the ceiling. He'd had so many dreams over the last few weeks, and now those dreams were shattered. He imagined Mary in his mind, and his head and heart went through conflicting emotions. He still loved her . . . God, how he loved her! Since Eileen had told him she was expecting a baby he'd tried to push her out of his mind, but couldn't. He'd tried to feel disgust, but couldn't. When he thought about the baby the hatred in his heart was for Bob, not Mary.

Slipping his legs over the side of the bed, Harry dropped his head in his hands. He loved her so much, if she'd have him, he'd go down on bended knee and ask her to marry him. OK, she didn't love him, but in time he was sure she could come to care for him. And if she'd marry him he could protect her from the shame and the spite of the wagging tongues.

Through these thoughts, ran others. What about his mam and dad? They'd go mad if they knew she was expecting Bob West's baby and their son wanted to marry her! And Mary was a Catholic, too! That was another argument they'd have against him marrying her.

Harry flung himself down on the bed again. What the hell am I thinking like this for? I'm talking about her being a Catholic and me marrying her, and she only knows I exist because I happen to be a neighbour! Still, I can hope, can't I? Nobody can stop me from doing that. And they can't stop me from loving her, either! If I ever get the chance to marry Mary Bradshaw nobody will stop me . . . baby or no baby . . . Catholic or no Catholic!

Eileen missed the usual bus on the Monday night and there was only Mary left in the cloakroom when she pushed the door open. 'That bloody clock of ours is away to hell!' Struggling into her overall, beads of sweat running down her face, she glanced at Mary. 'You don't look too good, kid! How did yer get on at the doctor's?'

Mary took her arm and hurried her from the cloakroom. 'I've got lots to tell you, but we'd better get to our machines. Can we eat our dinner quick, and go outside for ten minutes in the break?'

'Is it bad news, kid?'

'Not bad news, no! But in my condition there's not likely to be any good news, is there?'

While Eileen kept glancing across, wondering what Mary had to tell her, Mary's thoughts were on Bob. He was always on her mind, but she never spoke of him to anyone. Only when she was alone in the house or standing by the machine as she was now, did she allow her head to fill with memories. Bob's arms around her as they sat on the back row at the pictures, or laughing into each other's eyes as they twirled around the dance floor in a quickstep. Their world was full of happiness then, and they thought it would last forever. But he'd gone now, and the happiness had gone too. All that was left was heartache.

'When I got to the surgery yesterday, Doctor Greenfield had been to the hospital and told me mam everything.' They were sitting on a grass verge outside the factory and Mary pulled at a blade of grass.

'Go way!' Eileen's eyes widened in surprise. 'What happened then?'

'I was terrified going to the hospital. Me heart was beating fifteen to the dozen. And when I got to the ward and saw screens round me mam's bed, I nearly died of fright. I thought she'd had another stroke with the shock.' Mary closed her eyes as she re-lived the scene. 'I was that frightened, thinking it was all my fault, I nearly ran out of the ward! I would have done if the Sister hadn't pushed me through the screens.'

The drama was too much for Eileen. 'Go on, kid! Had she had a stroke?'

Mary shook her head. 'The doctor had told Sister we'd need some privacy and she'd put the screens around. He told me to take plenty of hankies, and he was right. The pair of us cried our eyes out.'

'What did she say about the baby?'

'We never mentioned the baby! I couldn't stop crying and saying I was sorry I'd let her down, and me mam was crying and telling me not to worry.'

'My God! Yer can be a real pain in the arse, sometimes, kid!' Never one to mince words, Eileen went on. 'Yer mam's ill in 'ospital, and you go in and make her more ill!' She tutted in exasperation. 'Buck yer ideas up, kid!'

'You expect me to laugh when I'm telling me mam I'm expecting an illegitimate baby?'

'I'd expect yer to put a brave face on, for her sake. She's probably worried sick about yer.' Eileen sucked in her breath. 'Does she know I know?'

'I told you, we never mentioned the baby!'

'I'll go in with yer tomorrow. She might feel better if she knows I know about the baby.'

Mary's eyes lit up for a second, then dulled again. 'I can't take any more of your time up. Your mam must be cursing me.'

A laugh rumbled in Eileen's tummy as she rolled on to her knees. 'My mam's like your mam, she never curses! It's a pity I don't take after her, isn't it?' Her clenched hands dug in the grass as she tried to lift herself. 'Give us a hand up, kid! Otherwise I'll be here all night.'

Eileen dragged a chair noisily across the floor and positioned it near the bed. 'How's it going, Mrs B? Yer look the picture of health to me.'

'I'm not too bad.' Martha's face was pale but her eyes had lit up at the sight of Eileen. All night she'd been wondering how she could get a message to the big woman to ask her to keep an eye on Mary for her, and now here she was.

'And how d'yer like the idea of being a granny?' Go to it like a bull in a china shop, Eileen had told herself. If it's left to Mary, we'll sit through the whole visit without the baby being mentioned.

A shadow crossed Martha's face. She hadn't thought of the baby as being a living thing; only something that was going to ruin her daughter's life. Now Eileen was bringing

211

the baby to life and Martha felt a strange stirring in her heart. When she didn't answer, Eileen looked across to Mary. 'What d'yer want, kid? A boy or a girl?'

Colour flooded Mary's face. 'I don't mind! What about you, Mam?'

There was no hesitation. 'A little girl named Emma.'

'That was your mother's name, wasn't it?' Mary's relief was mixed with surprise. 'D'you like that name?'

'I wanted to call you Emma, but your dad wanted Mary.'

'Your mam's got it all worked out.' Eileen was laughing as the bell went, and she gripped Martha's hand. 'Don't worry about tatty head here, Mrs B! I'll keep an eye on her.'

'Thank you! You're an angel!'

Eileen grinned. 'Some angel!'

Mary hovered over the bed. 'Don't let on if any of the neighbours come in, will you, Mam? Only Eileen knows.'

Martha nodded. 'Don't worry, lass!'

Mary linked her arm through Eileen's as they left the hospital. 'You've done more in half-an-hour than I'd have done in a month of Sundays.'

'Yer'll have to learn to have a big mouth like me, kid!' Mary could feel Eileen's body shake before the laugh came. 'On second thoughts, I wouldn't wish my mouth on me worst enemy! Janet Griffiths said I had a mouth as big as the Mersey Tunnel, an' I couldn't argue with her.'

As she passed the Smiths' house, Mary remembered how good Fred had been to her mother, and on impulse decided to give a knock. She hadn't seen any of the family since the day she'd shut the door in Elsie Smith's face, and she'd been feeling guilty about it ever since. She didn't like the woman, but that wasn't a good enough reason for being so rude to her. The door was opened by Fred, and he quickly invited Mary inside. 'We don't see anything of you these days, lass!'

'I won't come in, if you don't mind, Mr Smith! I'm on nights, and I've got to be leaving for work in an hour. I only called to tell you that me mam knows about Bob now; the doctor told her. So if you or Mrs Smith want to go in and see her, she'd be made up.'

The living room door opened and Elsie's head appeared. Curiosity was written all over her face, but Mary left it to Fred to satisfy her. She'd called to make peace, that was all. 'I'll be off then, and get ready for work. Ta-ra.'

'I suppose yer know I'm seeing more of you than I am of me own kids, don't yer?' Eileen grinned as she took her seat next to Mary on the bus. 'It's only a bloody hour since I left you.'

'I know! I'm disrupting your whole life.' Mary's wide blue eyes gazed with affection at her friend. 'I honestly don't know what I'd have done without you the last few weeks.'

'Oh, you'd 'ave got by, kid! And anyway, now yer mam knows, the worst is over for yer.'

'It's certainly a big load off me mind; but I think the worst has still to come, hasn't it? What's wrong with me isn't going to go away ... it's going to get bigger every day.'

'Yer'll get over that too! I'll be here, and yer'll have yer mam and yer friends to help.'

Mary's laugh was hollow. 'What friends? I haven't got any!'

'Kid, yer don't know who yer friends are till yer need them. You might get a big surprise.'

'To use your words, Eileen, it would be a big bloody surprise!'

'Eh, don't you start swearin', or I'll get the blame for it.' Eileen's nose twitched. 'Gets it out of yer system though to have a good old swear, doesn't it? It's either that or kickin' the cat.'

'What do you want, lover boy?' Eileen glanced sideways to where Harry was standing. 'Yer look as though yer've found sixpence and lost a pound.'

'I was wondering what you think my chances are with Mary?'

'Oh, what a pity I haven't brought me crystal ball with me! If I'd known yer wanted yer fortune told, I'd have brought it.'

'I'm serious, Eileen!'

'In that case, I suggest yer go and ask Mary! I'm not her bloody keeper, yer know.'

'I want to marry her!'

Eileen saw he was deadly serious. She blew out a deep breath and thought what a marvellous solution it would be for all Mary's troubles. But it wasn't that simple. 'Do yer mam and dad know how yer feel about Mary?'

'It's my life, Eileen! I want Mary, and I don't care what

anyone else wants or thinks. All I need is a little help from a friend to get near to her. To see her somewhere outside of work, so we could have a chance of getting to know each other. Will you help me . . . please?'

'Harry, we can't plan Mary's life for her!'

'I know that! But just give me a chance to make friends with her! That's all I ask!' His eyes were so pleading, Eileen felt pity for him. She didn't think he stood a snowball's chance in hell with Mary . . . no one did . . . but it wouldn't hurt to try. If it didn't do any good it couldn't do any harm. 'I'll see what I can do.'

'Make it soon, will you?' Harry was turning to walk away. 'You see there isn't much time.'

Eileen racked her brain for a way to get the two of them together outside of work, but by break time had come up with nothing. It was only when they were in the canteen that the germ of an idea was born. Her fat arms leaning on the table and her docker's sandwich clutched in her hands, she viewed Mary out of the side of her eye. 'Have yer seen anything of Vera Jackson since the big fight?'

'I haven't had time to call. I seem to spend all me time either in work, in the hospital, or in bed!' Mary speared a chip with her fork. 'There's been no sound from their house, so I imagine everything's all right.'

'I'll come to the 'ossie with yer again tonight.' Eileen changed the subject. 'Make sure yer mam's OK, then I won't go again till next week when we're on mornings.'

'You don't need to! You've got enough to do!'

'I'll get the kids ready for bed before I go out, so me mam won't mind.'

Mary didn't argue. She always felt safe when Eileen was with her, and so alone when she wasn't. Every night in bed she thanked God that she'd got through another day, and she knew it was only Eileen that made it possible.

After the dinner break Eileen tried unsuccessfully to catch Harry's eye. Muttering to herself that he was always there when you didn't want him, she bawled across the machine. 'I'm dying to go to the lavvy ... I won't be a minute.'

She found Harry outside the manager's office and didn't waste time. 'For what it's worth, I'm goin' to the 'ossie with Mary tonight. If yer 'appened to knock about half six to ask if she's seen anything of the Jacksons, I could suggest yer come with us.'

The cleft in Harry's chin deepened when he smiled. 'You're on!'

As she hurried away, Eileen called over her shoulder. 'Don't ever say I never did nothin' for yer!'

Mary was rinsing her face when the knock came and she dashed through to the door thinking it would be Eileen. But it was Vera standing on the step with Carol in her arms. 'Can I come in a minute, Mary?'

'Sure!' Mary planted a kiss on Carol's face. 'Hello, sweetheart.'

'I won't keep you.' Vera pulled Carol's hands back as they made a grab for Mary's blonde curls. 'I know you'll be getting ready for the hospital.'

'I'm all right for a few minutes.' Mary took her make-up bag out of the sideboard drawer. 'Eileen's not coming till half past.' Her eyes looked up from the small compact mirror. 'How did you get on?'

Before Vera could answer, the knocker sounded again. 'This'll be her.' Mary had her hand on the door knob when she remembered Eileen never knocked on the door, she always rapped on the window. There was a puzzled expression on her face when she swung the door open, and it quickly turned to one of impatience at the sight of Harry Sedgemoor.

'I wondered if you'd heard anything of next door.' Harry slipped past without waiting to be asked in. 'Have you seen Vera?'

'That's the second time I've opened the door expecting to see Eileen.' Mary made no effort to hide her annoyance. 'Vera's here now.'

'Oh, I'm glad it's you.' Vera's eyes lit at the sight of Harry. 'I've been wanting to thank you and Mary for the other night.'

'It was just lucky I was here.' Harry looked bashful. 'Actually, that's why I've called . . . to ask if Mary had seen you.'

'She's only been here two minutes,' Mary's lips were pursed as she applied lipstick. 'I haven't had time to ask her anything yet.'

'Danny never said a word when he got in from work. He had his breakfast, smoked a few Woodies, then went to bed.' Vera bit on her top lip to keep a smile at bay. 'He's got a beautiful black eye.'

'You mean he hasn't mentioned it at all?' Mary sounded disbelieving.

'Not a dickie bird! He hasn't raised his voice since, even when Carol's making a din with the pan lids I give her to play with.' Vera jumped when the loud rap came on the window. 'This'll be for me.'

'No.' Mary smiled. 'This is definitely Eileen.'

'What a bloody rush!' Eileen's smile covered everyone as she bent to kiss Carol. 'Hello, chuck! Aren't you a little beauty!'

When Mary slipped upstairs for her coat, Eileen stared hard at Harry. He could see the question in her eyes and shrugged his shoulders. 'I only just got here before you. Vera was here when I arrived.'

'How's it goin' then, Vera?' When Vera related the story, Eileen made all the right noises, as though it was the first time she'd heard it. 'So he hasn't mentioned it at all, since?'

'Not a word! I don't know whether it'll last, but the funny thing is, I don't feel frightened of him any more.'

'I should bloody well think not!' Eileen's snort was like that of a raging bull. 'You stick up for yourself! Don't yer take nothing from him!'

Mary came into the room at that moment struggling into her coat. 'I've missed it all now! I'll slip in tomorrow, Vera, and you can tell me everything.'

There was a look of pure innocence on Eileen's face as she asked Harry, 'Are yer comin' to the 'ossie with us?'

Mary got in quickly, her eyes sending urgent messages to Eileen. 'Harry doesn't want to be bothered! He's probably got better things to do!'

218

'I haven't, as a matter of fact! I was going for a pint, but I'd rather go and see your mam.'

'How about you, Vera?' Eileen asked. 'Would you like to come, too?'

'I'd love to, but there's no one to mind the baby.' Vera kissed the top of Carol's head. 'The boys are too young to leave her with.'

'Your feller's home, isn't he? Let 'im mind her for a few hours.'

'I wouldn't ask! I couldn't trust him with her!'

'My mam would mind Carol,' suggested Harry. 'She'd be made up having a baby to fuss over.'

'I couldn't.' Vera's bravado was slipping under the challenge. 'Danny's going to work and I've got his carry out to do.'

'Bloody hell, woman, what's the matter with yer? Just you get in there an' tell him yer comin' to the 'ospital with us, and tell him to do his own carry out.' Eileen pulled Carol from Vera's arms. 'Get going, while Harry goes and see his mam.'

'He won't let her come with us!' Mary faced Eileen when they were alone. 'Not after the other night.'

'I think yer wrong! He won't have the guts to refuse when . . .' Eileen shut up when Harry's smiling face rounded the door. 'Is it OK with yer mam?'

'She's tickled pink! She's standing by the door, waiting!'

Mary's lips were clenched as she shook her head. 'Your mam won't be seeing the baby! Danny won't let her come with us after what happened.'

Carol's infectious laugh filled the air as Eileen tickled her tummy, and there was a catch in the big woman's voice as she asked, 'How could anyone hurt her! If she was mine, I'd love the bones of her.'

Four sets of eyes turned when Vera walked in wearing her best coat and a smile that lit up her face. 'That belt you gave him must have affected his brain.' She grinned at Harry. 'He was as meek as a kitten! I told him to do his own carry out, and he just asked what there was to put on the bread!'

Lizzie Sedgemoor held her arms out and Carol reached for her. She didn't understand what was going on, but she did recognise a friendly face. 'Don't hurry back,' Lizzie told Vera. 'Me and George will take care of her.'

'Gerra load of yer mam's face,' Eileen whispered. 'She thinks she's seein' things.'

Martha was thrilled. It was only supposed to be two visitors to a bed, but she didn't care. She was so happy to see her daughter surrounded by friends, and when a little niggle at the back of her head reminded her that two of the friends didn't know about the baby yet, Martha pushed it aside. Vera and Harry weren't the type to turn against Mary when they found out.

'Who's got Carol?' This was Martha's first thought. God forbid she'd been left with Danny.

'It's all right, me mam's minding her,' Harry answered. 'She'll be getting spoilt right now ... me mam and dad always wanted a daughter.'

Martha couldn't suppress a smile when she turned to

Eileen. You couldn't see the hospital chair under her enormous bulk, and Eileen appeared to be sitting on air. She returned Martha's smile as she rummaged in her pocket and brought out a small slab of Cadbury's chocolate. Sliding it across the bed, she spoke out of the side of her mouth in an imitation of an American gangster. 'Hide it, kid!' When Martha went to protest, thinking she was depriving the Gillmoss children of their sweet rations, Eileen stopped her. 'Don't worry! I know the feller in the sweet shop.'

'Is there anyone you don't know?' Harry asked.

'If there is, sonny, then he ain't worth knowin'!' Eileen gave him a cheeky wink as Mary said, 'She wonders where young Billy gets his mischief from! He takes after his mam!'

'I'll tell yez what.' Eileen nodded her head knowingly. 'When our Billy's older, he'll knock spots off them spivs down in Cazneau Street market! I can see him now, standing on a street corner with a ciggie hanging out of the side of his mouth, wearing a long camel coat, a trilby 'at pulled down over his eyes, and floggin' black market watches.'

'He'll end up rich, then, won't he?' Harry asked, his eyes bright with laughter.

'He'll need to, to keep himself in kecks!' Every head in the ward turned when Eileen's laugh erupted. 'I know I can't!'

'I've told you to get him a pair of corrugated iron ones,' Harry said. 'Even your Billy's not tough enough to wear them out.'

'D'yer wanna bet!? He's ripped the arse out of the

221

pair I bought him last week, sliding down the railway embankment.'

Four sets of eyebrows raised when Vera started to laugh. It was a high-pitched laugh, broken off at intervals while she noisily drew breath. Tears of laughter ran down her cheeks, and as she wiped them away she looked at the big woman she'd known by sight for years, and had always thought of her as being common and loud mouthed. Now she was seeing her as a warm, friendly, and very funny woman. 'You're a proper case, you are!'

'You'll get used to her in time, Vera.' There was genuine affection in Harry's eyes as they rested on Eileen. 'But too much of her can damage your health. She needs to be taken in small doses.'

Eileen squared her shoulders, thrusting out her enormous bust. 'There's nowt small about me, sonny! Come up and see me sometime, an' I'll show yer!'

'Ooh, I'll take your word for it, Eileen! You're too much of a woman for me!'

'Well, go on,' Martha asked eagerly. 'What about Billy's trousers?'

Eileen grinned at the memory. 'I told him I didn't have any coupons left for a new pair, and he'd have to go to school in one of our Joan's gymslips. He thought I meant it, an' yer should have seen his face! He kept eyeing our Joan's gymslip with a gleam in his eye, an' I don't know how I kept me face straight!' Eileen's gaze swept round the rapt faces of her audience. 'I asked him if he was going to have pains in his tummy so he wouldn't have to go to school, an' d'yer know what the cheeky monkey said? He grinned, as bold as brass, and said, "No, I'm gonna have a sore throat!"'

The half hour flew by and disappointment was written on Vera's face. For the first time in three years she'd felt her old self again. Laughing and talking to nice people ... she couldn't remember the last time it happened.

Mary, Vera and Harry were still talking about Eileen as they walked up their street. 'She's so funny!' Vera chuckled. 'I haven't laughed so much in years.'

'She's a smashing person,' Mary said. 'She'd give you her last ha'penny.'

Vera's high laugh rang out in the silent street. 'That's if she hadn't spent it on a new pair of kecks for their Billy!' She'd stopped automatically outside her own front door, then remembered she had to pick Carol up. 'I'll get the baby, then see how the land lies at home.'

Six steps on and they were outside Mary's. Harry would have lingered but Vera was anxious to get home now ... butterflies were starting in her tummy in case Danny's mood was merely a lull before the storm. 'I'll come in again with you to see your mam, Mary.'

'OK! Ta-ra Vera, ta-ra Harry.'

'See you in work later, Mary! Goodnight!' Harry would have skipped the few yards to his front door. He was so happy he felt like a seventeen-year-old after his first kiss. But he straightened his face before following Vera into the living room. If he went in grinning like a Cheshire cat his mam would think he'd gone barmy.

Carol was sitting on George's knee, catching a coloured ball that Lizzie threw to her. She looked happy and contented and Vera let out a sigh of relief. She wouldn't stay for a cup of tea . . . nervous about the reception waiting for her at home.

Lizzie walked to the front door with Vera, and when she came back she cocked an eyebrow at Harry. 'Not going for a pint tonight?'

'No! I'll have to be getting ready for work soon.'

George lowered his newspaper. 'Isn't it about time you found yourself a steady girlfriend and settled down?'

Harry grinned. 'I'm waiting for the right one to come along.'

'She's a long time coming,' Lizzie said dryly. 'I'm beginning to think I'll have to knit you one.'

'It sounds as though you and me dad want to get rid of me!'

Lizzie reached for her knitting needles. 'We just want to see you settled down, that's all.'

Harry glanced around the room. 'Where's the morning paper? I haven't had a chance to look at it.'

George folded the *Echo*. 'Your mam's given it to next door. You can have this, son, and I'll read it when you've gone to work.'

Harry put the folded paper under his arm. 'I'll lie on the bed and read it.'

Harry threw the unopened paper on a chair and lay on the bed. The paper had been an excuse to get to the privacy of his own room. He crossed his arms behind his head and a smile started as he re-lived every second of the last two hours. Every word Mary had spoken, every gesture, every expression on her beautiful face; all were imprinted on his mind. Eileen had done her bit by getting them together tonight, but she couldn't do that very often. He'd have to think of something himself. And he didn't have a lot of time. Once Mary had the baby, and the gossip had died down, she wouldn't need him. And he was under no illusions. If he was to get anywhere with Mary, it would only be because she saw him as a way out. But he didn't care! He wanted her so badly he didn't care what her reasons were. But how was he going to get close to her if he never saw her outside work?

usual. Oliver had done her ... by ... that, together,
tonight, just the ... and her very ... time. He'd done it
finally, or made him himself. And he didn't want a lot of
... Once Mary had the baby, and the postnatal third
phase, she wouldn't need him. At last she would be ...
mother ... If it was to ... properties with Mary, self would
only be because she saw him as a part of that. he didn't
... that. He wanted her so badly he didn't care what ...
reason. Even her how was he going to persuade to her the
above, or ... ... a get out. The ... to play in for ...
... in which reached as others fell inside ... reaching, ...
and ... poetry. Her ... he ... and ... a ... way.

Chapter Fifteen

'Hang on a minute till I get me breath.' The springs in the worn-out couch creaked as Eileen fell back, her breathing loud and heavy. Her legs were wide apart and her knickers could be seen just above the dimpled knees. 'This hot weather's no good for me.' She pulled the neck of her dress forward and blew down the valley between her breasts. 'Ooh, that feels good! Now, how did yer get on at Oxford Street?'

With a smile of smug satisfaction, Mary dipped her hand into her bag and brought out a card. 'I told you I would, didn't I?'

'Well, you jammie bugger!' Eileen gazed at the large heading on the card. Oxford Street Maternity Hospital. 'Your face would get yer the parish!'

'I don't need to go back till the week after Christmas, but I've got to see Doctor Greenfield every fortnight for a check-up.' Mary returned the precious card to her bag. 'They warned me they might not have a bed for me when the time comes, but I'll worry about that when it happens.' She stretched the fingers of her left hand and laughed nervously. 'I kept me hand out of sight because all the other women had wedding rings on.'

'Get yerself a ring from Woolies, yer daft nit! They only cost a tanner and no one would know the difference.'

'It's not so bad walking round without a ring now, but when I'm as big as some of the women at the clinic today, I'll feel ashamed.'

'I won't mind walking down the road with yer when yer eight months, kid! Yer'll be waddlin' like me! The difference is, you'll be gettin' rid of your fat while I'm lumbered with mine.'

'I couldn't imagine you any different.' Mary eyed the mousey, limp hair, the fat, rosy cheeks that were creased into laughter lines, the old grey swagger coat that was worn summer and winter. 'You wouldn't be the same old Eileen!'

'No! Fat and jolly, that's me!' Eileen sighed. 'I'm glad you've got some good news, kid, because our Rene came this morning with bad news. Alan's in hospital down South, an' he's had his right arm amputated.'

'Oh, my God!' Mary gasped. 'Isn't that terrible!'

'Our Rene's out of her mind! She wanted to go down to him, but Mr Crowley told her not to. How the 'ell he finds things out I'll never know, but he said Alan will be getting transferred to a hospital up here soon.' Eileen pinched the bridge of her nose. 'Me bloody head's killing me! There seems to be nowt but trouble these days.'

'D'you want a drink?'

'I could murder a cup of tea, kid! I've got a sore throat with tryin' not to cry. Can yer imagine the size of me, and every time I looked at our Rene I felt like bawlin' me head off.'

'It's a person's heart that cries, Eileen, and the bigger the heart the bigger the tears.'

'Oh, go and make the bloody tea before I start blabberin'! All I need is a bit of sympathy an' I'll be off!'

Eileen was more serious than Mary had ever seen her. 'It doesn't bear thinking about! Alan used his right hand all the time in work, so what's he goin' to do now?'

'Better to have Alan back without an arm than never have him back at all.' A tear rolled down Mary's cheeks. 'I wouldn't care what was wrong with Bob if I could just have him back. Tell Rene she's one of the lucky ones.'

Eileen plodded up the road, deep in thought. Perhaps she shouldn't have told Mary about Alan ... she had enough trouble. Then again, hearing about someone else's problems might take her mind off her own.

'Hello, Eileen.'

Eileen jumped. 'Bloody hell, Harry! Yer nearly gave me a heart attack!'

Harry moved nervously from one foot to the other. 'I know I'm acting ridiculous for someone of my age, so don't start being funny.'

'Who's bein' funny?' Eileen squinted up at him. 'What yer doin' hanging round here?'

'I saw you passing the window on your way to Mary's and I knew you wouldn't be long.'

'Well, I know yer not hanging round to ask the state of me health, so what are yer after?'

'I want to talk to you about Mary.'

'Oh, my God! We're not on about that again, are we? Yer a big boy now, an' yer don't need me to hold yer hand.' Eileen tutted. 'If yer want to ask anything, then ask Mary!'

'D'you think I'd be standing here now if I had the nerve to ask her meself?'

'For cryin' out loud, Harry, if yer want to do anything, then for God's sake do it, an' we can all get some peace!'

Harry dug his hands in his pockets and shrugged his shoulders. 'Easier said than done.'

He made to move away and Eileen grabbed his arm. 'Do yer mam and dad know how yer feel about Mary?'

'I'll tell them when there's something to tell. But they won't put me off! It's my life and God knows I'm old enough to know what I want.'

'Strong words, Harry! But it's action you want, not words.'

Harry opened his mouth, then thought better of it. He walked to the pub on the corner and leaned against the bar. Eileen was right! It *was* action that was needed now.

When Mary opened the door at six o'clock and saw Harry standing on the step looking pale, she thought something was wrong. 'What's up?'

Almost losing his nerve, Harry started to say he'd come about painting the ceiling. Then he steeled himself. If he didn't do it now he never would. 'Can I have a word with you?'

Mary felt his tension as he passed. There was definitely something wrong but it couldn't be her mam because she'd seen her a couple of hours ago. Harry made straight for Martha's chair, so Mary sat on the couch. She'd been changing the bedclothes and a couple of feathers hung from her hair. Her eyes were questioning but she didn't speak and the silence was deafening. In the end she lost her patience. 'What is it, Harry?'

'I don't know where to start.' Harry ran a hand through his hair. 'It probably isn't the right time or place, or even the right way to say it, but it's the only way I know. Will you marry me, Mary?'

Mary had been sitting on the edge of the couch leaning forward. Now she sprang back, putting as much distance between them as possible. Her back was pressed against the couch and her mouth gaped open in surprise. When he saw her reaction, Harry's heart sank. But he'd come so far, he had to carry on.

'Will you marry me, Mary?'

'Marry you?' Mary's voice was shrill. 'Are you crazy?'

'I've always been crazy about you! I never stood a chance before, but now I'm asking for that chance.'

'There must be something wrong with you.' Mary was staring at him in disbelief. 'I don't want to marry you!'

'Hear me out . . . please?'

Mary was shaking her head from side to side, her hands covering her ears to blot out the sound of Harry's voice. Frightened by the wild look in her eyes, he stood up. It was the movement that made Mary look up at him, and although she couldn't hear his voice, she could read his lips. He was asking her to listen to him, but she waved her hand, telling him to go.

'Just hear me out, then I'll go.' Harry sat down again. 'I know you don't love me, but I love you. I always have done. And I think you could come to care for me in time. If you married me I could look after you and your mam.'

Mary's head was screaming, tell him . . . tell him! He'll go away then! He wouldn't want to be in the same room as you, never mind asking you to marry him. Her heart was thumping as the words raced round in her head, but shame stopped her from blurting them out.

'I'm only asking you to think about it.'

It was the pleading in Harry's voice that told her she had to put an end to this madness. 'I can't marry you! I don't love you, and even if I did I couldn't marry you!'

'Because of the baby, Mary?'

Mary gasped as though she'd been slapped in the face. 'Did Eileen tell you?'

When he shook his head, she cried, 'If you know, what in God's name are you asking me to marry you for? You should be running miles away from me!'

'I'm here because I want to marry you and because I want to help you.'

'And put up with all the gossip from neighbours, and your mates in work?'

'I don't owe any of them anything.' Harry's voice was stronger now. 'Nobody worries me, only you. I want to help you and look after you.'

'I don't need your pity!' Mary hurled the words across the room. 'And I don't want to marry you!'

Harry hung his head. 'I don't pity you, Mary. I love you!'

'But I don't love you! You don't seem to understand I'm carrying Bob's baby!'

'That's why I'm asking you now. Otherwise I would have waited and tried to court you.' He looked deep into her eyes. 'We could get married soon, and I'd be able to give you a hand with everything. I get a good wage and I've got a few bob in the bank, so you'd want for nothing.'

'D'you think I'd marry you for money! No, thanks, Harry; I've still got some pride left. I've made me bed, and I'll just have to lie on it.' Mary closed her eyes to shut out the sadness on his face. Why am I shouting at him? she asked herself. Instead of being disgusted, he's come to ask me to marry him, and all I'm doing is shouting at him. 'I'm sorry! You'll make someone a fine husband, but you deserve better than me.'

'As far as I'm concerned, there is no one better than you! That's how I've always felt, and I'll never change. So will you at least think about it?'

'No, Harry!' Mary shook her head vigorously. 'I made up me mind when Bob got killed that I'll never get married, because I could never love anyone like I loved him.'

'There are different kinds of love, Mary. I wouldn't expect you to feel the same about me as you did about Bob. But I do think you could come to care for me.' When she seemed about to protest, Harry lifted his hand. 'You say you'll never love anyone again, so why not marry someone who understands this and is willing to accept it? At least the baby would have a father.'

'But it's not your baby! It's mine and Bob's!'

Harry pressed his knuckles to his eyes as he stood up.

'I'm just asking you to think it over, and have a word with your mam.'

'I'm not telling me mam!' Mary faced him. 'She'd have a fit!'

'She wouldn't, you know, because I've already told her.' Although his voice was low, to Mary it was like the exploding of a bomb. 'You've what!' she shouted. 'When did you see me mam?'

'I've just been to the hospital, and they let me see her for a few minutes.' Harry ran his tongue over lips dry with nerves. 'I've got a lot of respect for your mam, and I thought it only right to tell her.'

Mary's nostrils flared. 'You had no right to see me mam before asking me! If you've upset her I'll never forgive you!'

Walking towards the door without a backward glance, Harry said, 'Don't worry, your mam wasn't upset.'

Elsie Smith heard the slam of the Bradshaws' door and waited for Harry's figure to pass the window. Her eyes were like slits; her thin lips pressed into a tight, straight line. 'There's something fishy going on next door. Harry Sedgemoor's never away from Mary's these days, and it's not proper with her being in the house on her own.'

Fred sighed, but didn't look up from the paper he was reading. He didn't need to see his wife to know exactly what she'd look like. Her arms would be folded across her thin chest, and there'd be a mean look on her face. 'Don't you ever tire of pulling people to pieces? You never have a good word to say about anybody; but I never thought even you would say anything bad about young Mary.'

'No; she looks like an angel, doesn't she? But you mark my words, there's something goin' on between her and Harry Sedgemoor.'

Fred sighed as he raised his head to see the vindictiveness in her eyes. She was his wife, and she'd borne him the two sons he idolised, but there were times when he almost hated her. People remarked about how thin she was, but Fred would have used another word to describe his wife. The word was narrow! Everything about her was narrow ... particularly her mind. It was because of her bad mindedness they had no friends. People didn't want to be listening to gossip all the time. Especially when they knew that as soon as their back was turned they would be the target of her wicked tongue.

'I'm sorry I'm late, Mam! Did you think I wasn't coming?'

'Don't worry, lass! I know you've got your hands full.'

'How's the treatment going?' Mary was out of breath with running from the bus stop. 'Are you still winning?'

Martha searched her daughter's face. She didn't answer the question because she had one of her own that wouldn't wait. 'Did Harry come?'

'Yes! He had no right to come and see you, and I told him so!'

'He had every right to come and see me, and I respect him for it! He's a good man, Mary, as straight and honest as they come. You could do a lot worse than marry Harry Sedgemoor.'

'Mam, I don't believe this is happening! Bob's only been

dead a couple of weeks! Am I just supposed to forget all about him? He's never out of me mind, I'm crying over him all the time, and you expect me to marry someone else!'

'Lass, I know, and I understand. Bob's in my mind all the time as well, because he was like a son to me.' Martha sighed. 'But it's the baby I'm thinking of. She'll be illegitimate, and you know how cruel people can be. If you married Harry, she'd have a father, and a name.'

'But I can't get married just to give the baby a name!'

'I'm not going to try and talk you into anything you don't want, but I am going to ask you to think hard on what life's going to be like for you and the baby. I'm not going to be any help to you, and I'm worried how you'll manage. Harry knows you don't love him ... he told me so. But he must love you very much, otherwise he wouldn't want to take on another man's baby. And many marriages have survived on respect.' Another sigh escaped before Martha went on. 'If you are to get married, I would rather it was Harry Sedgemoor than anyone else because I know he'd be good to you.'

'It wouldn't work out, Mam! Apart from the way I feel, what about his mam and dad? They'd go mad when they found out I was pregnant!'

'I asked him about that, because of course they'd be upset; they wouldn't be normal if they weren't. But Harry said he thinks they'd come round, in time.'

'It's no good talking about it, Mam! I just couldn't do it!'

'All right, lass! It's your life, and anything you do is fine by me. I was only thinking about what was best for you and the baby.'

For once Mary was glad when the bell went. 'I'll see you tomorrow, Mam.' She didn't see the disappointment in Martha's eyes as she bent to kiss her. She wasn't to know that since Harry's visit, Martha had been building her hopes on her daughter appreciating what he was offering. Now those hopes had been dashed. What worried her was that Mary was so naive she had no idea what life would be like as an unmarried mother. No idea of the shame when she had to face neighbours, or when strangers asked her about her husband. Still, it was Mary's life, and she couldn't live it for her!

'I've had the feet walked off me.' The legs on the kitchen chair wobbled as Eileen twisted round to stick her two feet out. 'Just look at the state of them! They look like ham shanks . . . if yer can remember what ham shanks looked like!'

'Where did you end up going?' Mary was agitated inside. She'd have to tell Eileen about Harry before they left for work in case he told her himself. But where to start?

'The kids wanted to go to New Brighton.' Eileen swivelled round again. 'Our Edna had never been on a boat, and when Billy mentioned it, well, that was that! She'll get her own way, if it kills her!' Eileen was shaking her head but pride was written all over her face. 'She's two years younger than Joan, but she can knock spots off her for brains. She's nearly as tall as her, too! She had one of our Joan's hand-me-down dresses on today, and it was up to her arse.'

Mary sat on her hands to keep them still. 'Did you have a nice time?'

'The kids enjoyed it, because they didn't know any different. But it saddened me. Everywhere yer look there's sand bags piled high, and along the beach there's signs warnin' yer about bombs and mines. Not a bit like the old days when the shore was full of people on deck chairs and lickin' ice creams. Still, the kids enjoyed it, and that's what counts. They've been on holiday for weeks and the furthest they'd been till today was the back jiggers.'

'You'll be tired in work tonight,' Mary said. 'You'd have been better having an hour's sleep than coming here early.'

'I'll need a couple of matchsticks to keep me eyes open.' Eileen grinned. 'Anyway, what have you been doing with yerself? How was yer mam?'

Mary lowered her head. 'If I tell you something, will you promise not to laugh?'

'How the hell can I promise that!? If it's funny, then I'll laugh!'

'Harry called here today.'

'Oh, aye! What did lover boy want?'

'You won't believe it.' Mary could feel her face burning. 'He asked me to marry him.'

Instead of the laugh she expected, Eileen said softly, 'So he finally got round to it, did he?'

Mary's brow creased. 'You mean you knew he was going to?'

'I knew he wanted to, but I didn't think he'd have the guts.'

'Well he needn't have bothered!' Mary ground the words

out. 'I think he had a flaming cheek, and I told him so.'

Eileen studied Mary's face for a while before saying. 'You're pregnant with another man's baby, and yer think Harry's got a flamin' cheek because he asked yer to marry him? It's not Harry who's got a flamin' cheek, kid, it's you!'

'You're as bad as me mam!' Mary was close to tears. 'You both knew Bob, and you both know how I felt about him! But to hear you both talk, he never existed! You've wiped him out of your minds! He's dead now, so why don't I marry Harry Sedgemoor!'

'Haven't yer stopped to ask yerself why me and yer mam are actin' the way we are?' Eileen's voice was low. 'We haven't forgotten Bob! How could we? And if you weren't expecting his baby, none of this would be happening. But you are expecting, kid, and that makes all the difference.'

'But I can't marry Harry just because I'm pregnant!' Mary cried. 'I thought you were supposed to get married for love!'

'Most people do get married for love, kid. But in your case it's a bit different, isn't it? I think Harry Sedgemoor's got guts to want to marry a girl who's expectin' another man's baby. And what do you do? You spit in his face! I'd have thought he deserved better than that . . . but it's your life, not mine.'

'Yes, it is my life, and the . . .' Mary's words petered out as Eileen held her hand up.

'I'm not going to fall out with you over this, kid, but I wouldn't be a friend if I didn't try to warn yer about what lies ahead.' Eileen searched for the right words. 'You said yer were ashamed when yer went to the clinic because yer

239

didn't have a wedding ring on. Think a bit further ahead, when yer can't hide it any more and yer've got to face the neighbours with their sly grins and their gossip. And you're not the only one who's got to face that ... there's your mam, too! I bet she's lying in the 'ospital bed, right now, worrying about how you're goin' to manage to bring a baby up on yer own, 'cos she won't be able to help.' Eileen rubbed a hand across her eyes as though to clear her mind. 'And what about the baby? What are yer going to tell her when she asks why she hasn't got a daddy, like all her friends? And when she comes in cryin' 'cos the other kids have been making fun of her, what are yer going to tell her?' Eileen sighed. 'I'm sorry, kid, but these things happen and I think yer should be warned. I just hope yer don't live to rue the day yer turned Harry Sedgemoor away.' She patted Mary's hand before standing up. 'I've got it all off me chest now, kid, an' I won't mention it again. So let's get off to work.'

Mary's nerves were frayed as she waited for Harry's routine stop by her machine. She was filled with guilt and shame, and in her highly emotional state she blamed Harry for it all. She was so deep in rebellious thought she didn't see him approaching, and she jumped when he spoke. 'Everything all right, Mary?' His question and his voice were the same as they were every day, and no one watching would have believed that only yesterday he'd asked her to marry him and she'd thrown the proposal back in his face.

'Fine, Harry!'

He didn't look any different, but when their eyes met

briefly she saw an expression in his that she couldn't put a name to. 'That's good.' With those two words Harry turned on his heels and rounded the machine to where Eileen stood. 'I suppose you know?'

Eileen shrugged her shoulders. 'Not all the details, but, yeah, she did tell me.'

'Did she tell you she did everything but throw me out?'

Eileen couldn't understand why Harry wanted to marry someone who was carrying another man's baby, but she did know he deserved better than the treatment Mary had dished out to him. 'What can I say, Harry?' A mischievous smile played around the corners of her mouth. 'Except that if yer'd like to ask me, I'll grab yer with both hands.'

Chapter Sixteen

Mary sat up with a start, her heart thumping. Beads of sweat ran down her neck as she woke from the same nightmare that had haunted her sleep for the last three days. Nightmares in which a little girl with the same colour hair as her own, sobbed, 'Why haven't I got a daddy?' And the same little girl, with tears streaming down her face, being chased home from school by children who were taunting her.

Running a hand across her tummy, Mary fell back on the pillow. Tears escaped to run down her cheeks and she wiped them away with the corner of the sheet. Was it fair to let her mam and the baby suffer all their lives when, by marrying Harry Sedgemoor, she could spare them? Was she being selfish putting her own feelings first? What would Bob want her to do? Would he want their baby to have an unhappy life because of something they did? Mary swung her legs over the side of the bed. If she didn't get a decent sleep soon, she'd be dropping. Her body felt leaden as she stumbled down the stairs, and when she was swilling her face in the kitchen sink and glanced in the small cracked mirror, she was horrified at the drawn face staring back at her. She was meeting Eileen at the shops at three o'clock and she was sorry now she'd agreed to go. If Eileen saw her looking like this she'd start asking questions.

'Five pound of spuds, two pound of carrots and a turnip.' Eileen grinned at the assistant behind the counter. 'Oh, an' a bunch of bananas.'

'We'll put the flags out when that day comes.' The woman smiled back as she reached for Eileen's basket. The war had put a stop to giving customers their groceries in paper bags. They either brought their own bags or carried their shopping home wrapped in newspaper brought in by customers. 'One and three ha'pence, please.'

Eileen handed the right money over and followed Mary out of the shop. 'Have yer got everything yer want, kid?'

'I could do with butter and sugar, but I've used all me coupons so I'll have to wait till the weekend.'

'How the hell they expect us to manage on two ounces of butter a week I'll never know! My lot are in and out by the minutes askin' for butties, an' I only get half a pound a week between the four of us! It's a good job I'm well in with Milly Knight, or we'd starve.' Eileen stopped and put the heavy basket down. 'Let's have a breather. Me arms'll be down to me knees by the time we get home with the weight of this.' She looked closely at Mary. 'Yer look pale, kid! Are yer gettin' enough to eat?' She lifted the heavy basket again. 'Don't forget yer eating for two.'

'I get enough to eat.' Mary fell into step beside her friend. 'Clark Gable saves me a piece of fish every week that does me for two days, and I get me meat ration . . . such as it is. And I get a hot dinner in work nearly every day, don't forget.'

'There's no goodness in canteen food, kid! It's nourishment yer want, not punishment.' Eileen puffed as she waddled along. 'Yer look peaky to me.'

'I don't feel so good.' Mary admitted. 'I'm all mixed up inside.'

'Want to talk about it, kid?' The basket was lowered to the ground again. 'Sometimes yer feel better if yer can get things off yer chest.'

Mary nodded. 'If I don't sort meself out soon, I'll go crazy.'

'I'll call for yer tonight, and we can go to work together. If I come half-an-hour early, we can have a natter.' Eileen assumed a solemn expression. 'You know the consultation will cost you two guineas, don't you, Modam? Har you sure you can hafford it?'

Mary responded by widening her eyes. 'But that's nearly a week's wages!'

'Worth hevery penny, I can hassure you! My services har very much sought hafter.'

'D'you take weekly payments, or can I pay by Sturla's cheque?'

'A Sturla's cheque will do nicely, thank you, Modam!' The posh accent went as Eileen spluttered. 'I can get our Billy a new pair of kecks on it!'

'I'll leave it to brew for a while.' Mary slipped the knitted cosy over the pot and sat down. Leaning her elbows on the table she looked directly into Eileen's eyes. 'I keep thinking about what you said, and I'm frightened the baby will suffer because of me. She didn't ask to be born, but she's the one that'll be hurt the most.' Eileen was watching intently, but when she didn't speak, Mary went on. 'What do I tell her when she grows up?' She was picking nervously at the skin round her nails and Eileen slapped her hand away.

'Yer'll end up with a whitlow doin' that! Get it all off yer chest while yer've got the chance.'

'I've been wondering whether to marry Harry, so the baby will have a name.' Mary got the words out quick before she lost her nerve. 'I would do, but I don't think I could live with him, you know, like a real wife.'

Eileen's eyebrows nearly touched her hairline as they shot up in surprise. 'Yer mean yer'd marry him if he stayed with his mam, and you live here?'

'No, I don't mean that!' Mary was impatient that Eileen didn't understand. 'I just don't think I could sleep with him.'

'Well, I've heard everything now! What the hell d'yer think Harry is . . . a bloody monk! He might be crazy about yer, but that doesn't mean he's daft in the head! You're not askin' for much, are yer, kid?'

Mary kept her eyes down and went back to scratching her nails. 'It's not just Harry! I couldn't bear any man to touch me.'

Eileen clamped her lips together before she said something she'd regret. Marrying Harry would solve all Mary's problems, but what about Harry himself? Would he still

want to marry her if he'd heard what she'd just said?
Sleeping with him would be one of the reasons most girls
would marry him . . . but then, Mary wasn't like most girls.
'The only advice I can give is to talk to Harry. Tell him what
yer've told me and leave it up to him.'

Mary gave a mirthless laugh. 'I'll stop him in the street
and tell him I'll marry him if he promises not to come near
me! He'd think I was mental!'

'Forget it then!' Eileen shrugged. 'Yer've shown him the
door once, so he won't be back for a second helping unless
yer give him some encouragement.'

'Shall I knock on his door and ask for a date?'

'Sarcasm won't get yer anywhere, kid! It's you that's in
trouble, not me or Harry!' Eileen tutted. She'd come to
help, and here she was losing her temper. 'Look, treat
Harry like a human being and he'll do the rest.'

'You think I'm selfish, and I know I am! But it's not
meself I'm thinking about.' Mary was so close to tears,
Eileen didn't have the heart to say what she really thought.
So she held out her hand and asked, 'Do I get that cup of
tea, or not?'

'Oh, lord, I'd forgotten! It'll be stiff by now!'

'If it's wet and warm, it'll do me.' Eileen reached for the
cup. 'Treat Harry decent, kid, and leave it to him.' She
took a mouthful of tea. 'Tell yer what! Yer could send
Harry round to our house every night, and I'll send him
back with a permanent smile on his face.'

'But what makes you think she won't tell me to take a
running jump if I ask her for a date?' Harry's face was

creased in a frown. 'If this is your idea of a joke, I don't think it's funny.'

'Yer don't see me laughin', do yer? Anyway, please yer bloody self!' Eileen moved down the machine leaving him looking bewildered. He stared at her back for a few seconds then moved towards her. 'Just three words, Eileen! Were you serious?'

'I'm too old to play games, Harry!'

There was determination in his step as he rounded the machine, but when Mary looked sideways at him he nearly chickened out. 'How's things, Mary?'

Mary didn't turn her head away like she usually did. 'Dull and boring.'

Harry's mouth felt like emery paper. 'How d'you fancy going to the flicks one night, to break the monotony?'

Can I go through with this? Mary asked herself. If I can't, it's not fair on him. Her mind was divided into two camps, her Mother and the baby in one, far outweighing her own feelings in the other. 'It would make a change.'

'How about tomorrow night? We could go for a drink before the pictures, and come straight on to work?'

'What about me mam? It means she wouldn't have a visitor unless Eileen would go in and see her. Wouldn't it be better to wait till next week, when we're on mornings?'

'No!' The word shot from Harry's mouth. 'Let's make it tomorrow.'

Mary sounded calm but there were hundreds of butterflies flying from her tummy up to her throat. 'I'll ask Eileen at break time.'

'I'll go and ask her now.' Before Mary could stop him he

was whizzing round the machine to where Eileen had been sneaking glances at them, trying to figure out from their expressions what was going on.

'I owe you a lot of favours, Eileen,' Harry started. 'But would you do me one more big one? Would you go in and see Mrs B tomorrow night, while I take Mary to the pictures?'

Eileen looked at his face, shining with happiness, and her own heart felt lighter. 'What's in it for me, big boy?'

'A big kiss, when she's not looking.'

'I'll keep yer to that!' Eileen waved across to Mary. 'OK, kid!'

Mary waited patiently for the other women to leave the canteen. 'Me mam'll start building her hopes up, you know! Don't let her think there's anything in it, or she'll have me married off!'

'Leave it to me, kid. I'll be the soul of discretion.' Eileen looked at Mary and rolled her eyes. 'Yer will try and smile temorrer night, won't yer? The miserable gob on yer now is enough to curdle the milk!'

Mary slammed the door behind her and fell into step beside Harry. The hairs on the back of her neck were tingling with embarrassment as she imagined eyes peering through the windows they passed. This should give the neighbours something to talk about. She could almost hear Elsie Smith's voice, 'It didn't take her long! And young Bob only dead a matter of weeks!'

Neither of them spoke until they reached the main road,

then Harry asked, 'Shall we go to the Prince Albert for a drink?'

Mary was wishing she was miles away. 'If you want.'

Harry felt her flinch as he put a hand under her elbow, but he left it there till they reached the pub and sat at a corner table. 'I'll take you somewhere nice next week, when we don't have to worry about getting back early for work.' He studied her face as she sipped her drink, and thought how pretty she looked in the blue and white floral dress with a white cardi slung across her shoulders. Her lovely blonde hair had been brushed till it shone and bounced with every move of her head. It was on the tip of his tongue to say how nice she looked, when he remembered Eileen's warning to 'play it cool'.

The silence between them was becoming embarrassing as each tried to think of something to say. In the end both started to talk at the same time, and Harry laughed. 'You first.'

Mary stared into her glass. 'Do your mam and dad know you're out with me?'

'Of course they do! Why?'

'I just wondered.'

'Mary, I don't have to ask me mam every time I go out! I don't even have to ask her who I can marry!'

Looking through her long black lashes, she asked, quietly, 'You would really marry me, knowing I'm expecting Bob's baby?'

'If you'll have me, yes!'

Mary put her empty glass down. 'Shall we go?'

As he stood up, Harry groaned. At this rate we'll never

get a chance to talk properly. It'll be next week before I can take her out again, and the way things are going the baby will be due before we get anywhere. The thought acted as a spur. 'Mary, we've got to talk. Can I come up to yours in the morning?'

Mary nodded. She was willing herself to feel something for this man who was offering her a way out of her troubles, but there was no spark and she doubted if there ever would be.

They didn't sit on the back row as she usually did with Bob, but halfway down the front stalls. Harry felt his arm brushing hers on the arm rest and had to steel himself not to take her hand in his. The picture had started but he never knew what it was about because his mind was on the girl sitting next to him, and his eyes kept sliding sideways to watch the changing expressions on her face.

When the lights went up, Mary turned to him. 'Did you enjoy it?'

'Yeah, it was great,' Harry lied as he looked at his watch. 'It's only ten to eight. D'you want to see what we've missed, or can we go back to yours?'

Mary didn't hesitate. 'If you want to.'

Their conversation was desultory as they walked home, and as soon as they were in the house Mary made for the kitchen. She needed time to sort her thoughts out. In the other room Harry paced the floor. There was no sound from the kitchen and he knew the tea making was just an excuse to buy Mary time. He was impatient, but he knew she couldn't stay out there indefinitely so he waited. His hopes were riding high, but when she came through the door, her face full of doubt, his hopes began to flounder.

The tension was almost tangible. They were more like strangers than two people with marriage on their mind. Suddenly Harry could stand it no longer. 'We haven't got much time, Mary. Have you thought about what you want to do?'

'If I told you what I'd like, you'd think I needed certifying!'

'Try me!' Harry looked at the pale face and saw the trapped look in her eyes. He wanted to take her in his arms and tell her she didn't have to be frightened of him . . . he'd never hurt her. 'Tell me what's on your mind, and I'll tell you whether you're crazy or not.'

'I've got to be honest, otherwise it wouldn't be fair on you.' Mary looked down at her clasped hands. 'I do like you, Harry . . . but I don't love you. It's too soon after Bob, and my thoughts are still filled with memories of him. I can't forget him, and I don't think I ever will.'

'I don't expect you to forget Bob, but you've got your whole life in front of you!'

'Bob's always with me! He's never out of me thoughts! It's his baby I'm carrying, and it's his baby I'm trying to protect. You say you want to marry me, but I think it's only fair you should know I'd only marry you to give his baby a name.' Mary's beautiful face was full of sadness. 'I'd be using you, Harry, and you don't want that, do you?'

'You can't love a dead man for ever.' Harry's eyes didn't waver. 'As time passes you'll learn to love again. I'm willing to take that chance if you are.'

Mary turned her face away. He really was too good a

man to be used like this. She searched her mind for the right words to warn him of the obstacles he'd have to face. 'What about your parents? They'll go mad when they know about the baby . . . and then there's the difference in our religion! With you being a Protestant, they wouldn't marry us in church and I couldn't get married in a registry office.' A long drawn out sigh escaped. 'On top of all that you'd be the laughing stock of all the neighbours and your mates in work.'

Harry waved his hands. 'I've got a strong back! Anyway, to hell with them! It's what you and I want, not the neighbours or me mates!'

'There's me mam, too!' Mary was determined he would know exactly what he was taking on. 'If she doesn't get better I'll have to take care of her, as well as the baby. You'd be taking the whole lot of us on, so you'd best give it a lot of thought.'

'I don't need to! I know what I want, and that's you!' Harry pleaded with his eyes. 'Will you marry me, Mary?'

Mary's head shook from side to side. 'I couldn't face your mam and dad! How d'you think they'd feel, living a few doors from a grandchild that wasn't really theirs?'

'I'll find us a house away from here, where people won't know I'm not the baby's father.' Nothing would stand in Harry's way now. 'A six-roomed house where your mam could have her own room downstairs.'

Mary bit back the retort that it wasn't his baby, and she could never pretend it was. What a mess she'd made of her life! 'What happens if it doesn't work out? I do like you, but I don't love you.'

'It will work out! I'll make it! Just give me the chance, Mary.'

It was a mental picture of her mother's face that made Mary consider her answer. 'Think about it first, and have a good talk with your parents.'

'I could spend till Doomsday thinking about it, and I still wouldn't change me mind. Tell me you'll marry me and I'll sort everything out.' He moved to sit next to her on the couch. 'Tell me now, Mary!'

'Don't say any more till you've told your mam and dad,' Mary insisted. 'If they don't talk you out of it, and you're still prepared to take me, and me mam, and the baby on, then, yes, I'll marry you.' She glanced at the clock on the wall over the firegrate and stood up quickly. 'We'd better start making tracks or we'll be late.'

'Shall we tell Eileen?' Harry felt like running into the street and shouting it to the world.

'Not till you've talked to your parents. After that, if you still want to go ahead with it, we'll tell me mam and Eileen.'

There was a nagging doubt in the back of Harry's mind that said for someone who'd just accepted a proposal of marriage, Mary didn't look very happy. But he brushed it aside. She'd gone through a lot in the last few months, but once she'd got used to the idea, and they'd told everyone, she'd be OK.

Chapter Seventeen

'Have you lost the run of your senses?' Lizzie Sedgemoor faced her son across the table. 'All the girls around, and you want to marry one who's expecting another man's baby! You must be out of your mind!'

George Sedgemoor saw the anguish on his son's face. He hadn't spoken since Harry dropped the bombshell, but now he asked, 'Are you sure you know what you're doing, son?'

'Yes, Dad! I love Mary, and always have done. If I can't have her, I'll never marry anyone else.'

Lizzie was standing now, her knuckles white as she leaned her weight on the table. 'And what about us? Don't you care about us, and the laughing stock we'd be?'

'I've got me own life to think of.' Harry's voice was weary. 'I'm sorry if you and me dad are upset, but it won't change me mind! If Mary Bradshaw will have me, then I'm going to marry her.'

'Well, don't bring her here because she won't be welcome!' Lizzie spat the words out. 'And don't expect us to come to your wedding, either!'

'Now, Lizzie!' George appealed to his wife. 'Don't say

anything you'll be sorry for later. We've always liked young Mary, haven't we?'

'Oh, I liked her all right! Thought butter wouldn't melt in her mouth! But she's not as innocent as she makes out, is she? She's got herself pregnant, and now he . . .' Lizzie's voice was choked as she nodded her head towards Harry, 'is daft enough to want to marry her!'

Harry jumped to his feet and mother and son faced each other. 'She's not a bad girl! She made a mistake, once, and now she's a slut as far as you're concerned.'

'Huh! Told you that, did she? And you fell for it! Well, all I can say is that you're a bigger fool than I thought you were!'

Harry dropped his head in despair. He loved his parents deeply and didn't want to hurt them. But why couldn't they see that his happiness lay with Mary? They were always teasing him about being single at twenty-seven, and now he had the chance of marrying the only girl he'd ever loved, why couldn't they be happy for him? 'Please, Mam! I don't want to fight with you, but I'm going to marry Mary no matter what you say. Can't you see it's what I want, and be happy for me?'

George spoke before Lizzie could answer. 'We knew you were sweet on Mary, son! And we'd have been over the moon with you marrying her if it wasn't for the baby. It's come as a shock to me and your mam, you must see that! Give us a chance to get used to the idea. We only want what's best for you, you know that.'

Lizzie glared at her husband. 'And you think marrying Mary Bradshaw, and her being pregnant, is the best thing for him? She's a scheming little bitch, that's what she is! She's using him, and you're both too thick to see it!'

'It's me that wants to marry her, Mam; not her wanting to marry me!' Harry was trying not to lose his temper because he knew he was hurting them deeply. But he couldn't stand by while his mam called Mary a scheming little bitch. 'She knew you'd take it like this, and she told me she wouldn't blame you one bit. She wouldn't even tell her mam until you'd had a chance to talk me out of it. That's the scheming little bitch you're talking about!' His voice was tired and he had a headache. He'd stayed up after he came in off night shift to tell his parents, and now he felt physically and mentally worn out. 'I love her, Mam, and I had hoped that you and Dad would be happy for me. But if you won't accept her, I'll still marry her and consider meself a very lucky man.' Without waiting for a reply, Harry turned on his heels and left the room, leaving his parents staring at the closed door.

'Well, I never thought the day would come when I'd hear that coming from me own son.' Lizzie covered her face with her hands and dropped back on the chair. When the tears started to flow, George stood up and put a hand on her shoulder. 'Now, Lizzie, there's no need to carry on so. It's not the end of the world, you know.' When his wife didn't answer, he went on, 'He's our only son and if we're not careful we could lose him.'

Lizzie lifted her tear-stained face. 'He's not worried about losing us, is he? He doesn't care what we think!'

'Would you have taken any notice if your mam and dad had said you couldn't marry me? And we both know, deep down, that Mary's not a bad girl. She only ever had one boyfriend, and Bob West was as fine a boy as you'd get.'

Lizzie sniffled, then blew her nose into a hankie. 'But she doesn't love our Harry! Bob's only been dead a matter of weeks, and you don't fall in and out of love that quick! She's using our Harry for a convenience, and what sort of a marriage is that for him? It's not only the baby, either . . . he's talking about changing his religion.'

'That's for him to decide, not us!' George patted her shoulder. 'I'd better be off or I'll be late clocking on.' He went into the hall for his coat, and when he came back he closed the door behind him so his words wouldn't carry up the stairs. 'You said some nasty things, Lizzie! We all say things we're sorry about afterwards, but the trouble is, once you've said them, you can't take them back. So think on, Lizzie!'

Mary's nerves were stretched to breaking point when Harry knocked. In work he'd suggested not telling his parents about the baby until after they were married, but Mary had insisted. She'd never be able to look them in the face again if they started married life on a lie.

She closed the door and followed Harry into the room where he stood with his back to the fireplace. He took a few steps towards her, then changed his mind. He looked tired, Mary thought, and when he smiled there was no warmth in the smile. They faced each other for several seconds then Mary asked in a faltering voice, 'Are we still going to the hospital?'

'Of course we are! Why?'

'Did you tell your parents?' When he nodded, she asked, 'What did they say?'

'Me dad didn't have very much to say, but me mam was upset.' Harry knew he'd have to tell her most of the truth in case his mam came to see her. 'She's been very quiet since I got up,' he spread his hands out. 'In fact she hasn't spoken a word in two hours.'

'You can't blame her! Any mother would feel the same.' Mary pushed her hair back in a gesture of helplessness. 'I think you'd be better walking out of that door and forgetting the whole thing. Too many people are going to be hurt.'

Harry crossed the space between them and took hold of her hands. 'We're going to the hospital to tell your mam we're getting married! If I walk out of that door, I'm the one who's going to get hurt! We're getting married because I want to, Mary. And, although for different reasons, so do you. Don't worry about me mam, because I think she'll come round.'

Mary withdrew her hands and turned her back on him. Picking up a cushion, she hugged it to her. 'I'm making everyone unhappy. If I only had meself to worry about, it wouldn't be so bad. But I'm not the only one, am I?'

Harry took her by the shoulders and turned her round. 'I've faced my mam, now let's go and face yours.'

The look on their faces told Martha that this was no ordinary visit. Harry could barely suppress his excitement as he took hold of her hand. 'Didn't think you'd be seeing me again so soon, did you, Mrs B?'

'No! This is a surprise.' Martha looked towards Mary for an explanation, but Harry got in first. 'We've got some good news for you! At least I hope you'll think it's good news! Me and Mary are getting married.'

Martha closed her eyes briefly, and when they opened they were glistening with tears. 'Oh, lad, I'm so happy!' She stretched her hand out to Mary who was standing by, white faced. 'I'm glad for you, lass.'

If Mary wasn't brimming over with happiness, there was no concealing Harry's. He had a grin on his face like a Cheshire cat, and when Martha asked if he'd told his parents, the smile didn't slip. 'Yeah! I told them this morning.'

'Are they pleased?' Martha couldn't help but see the look exchanged across the bed. 'They'd get a shock, wouldn't they?'

'You can say that again! Me mam hasn't got over the shock yet! She thought she was never going to get rid of me.'

'When are you getting married?'

'Not so fast, Mam!' Mary did her best to smile. Her mam and Harry looked so happy she didn't want to spoil it for them. 'Harry's going to try and get a six-roomed house, so you can have a room of your own. We won't be getting married until we've got a house.'

Martha knew her daughter inside out. She knew Mary would want to move before the neighbours found out she was pregnant. She didn't blame her for this, but she wondered if Mary knew how much she had to thank Harry for?

'I got some good news myself, today! The doctors say I should be ready to go home soon.'

For the first time, Mary didn't have to force her smile. 'Oh, Mam, that's marvellous! They must be really pleased with you.'

'It's more a case of them not being able to do any more for me. I can move me hand a bit, but there's no strength in it and it'll never be any good to me. And me leg is just useless.' Martha's face brightened. 'Still, I've got a lot to be thankful for! I can get about fine on me crutches, and the doctor says I'll get around better when I'm at home.' She smiled at Harry. 'When d'you think you'll be getting married?'

'Give us a chance, Missus! She's only just said yes, and we haven't got down to making plans yet.'

'It'll be lovely if I can see me daughter getting married.'

The thought flashed through Mary's mind that the way things were with Harry's parents, there might only be her mam and Eileen at the wedding.

'You don't think I'd get married without me mam there, do you?'

'And Eileen?'

'Oh, it wouldn't be a show without Punch, now would it? Of course Eileen will be there ... she's me best mate!'

Martha was smiling when they left. She felt as though a heavy burden had been lifted from her mind, and there was only one small cloud on her horizon. The haunted look on Mary's face. Please God it would disappear when she started making plans for the wedding.

* * *

'We've got bags of time before we need to get ready for work.' Harry's hand was cupped possessively under Mary's elbow. 'Shall we go back to yours for an hour?'

Some of the neighbours were standing at their doors talking, and by the time she'd unlocked the front door, Mary's face was bright crimson. 'You can imagine what they're saying, can't you? It didn't take me long to find someone else.'

Harry didn't care what anyone said, or did. He was going to marry the girl he thought was out of his reach, and his mind was too full of his newfound happiness to worry about other people. They'd just sat down when he asked, 'When's the baby due?'

The question was unexpected and Mary's head went down. 'In about six and a half months. Doctor Greenfield said you can never tell with a first baby, they sometimes come two weeks early or two weeks late.'

'Shall I start looking for a house, then?'

'We're going to have to see a priest before we do anything.' This was the one thing Mary dreaded. It would have been bad enough telling Father Murphy about the baby, but to tell him she was marrying Harry, who was a Protestant, was a million times worse. But rather tell him than Father Younger! He'd lecture her something terrible. 'Are you sure you want to become a Catholic?'

'Mary, I'd be quite happy getting married in a registry office . . . but if you've set your heart on a church wedding, then I'll change me religion.'

'I wouldn't be married in the eyes of the Church if I got

married in a registry office. And we'd have trouble getting the baby christened.'

'Then we go and see the priest! I've never been one for going to church, but I want to do everything that will make you happy.' Harry was twirling his thumbs round, his face thoughtful. 'I would like you to pack in work.'

Mary was shaking her head before he'd finished speaking. 'No! I need the money to buy things for the baby.'

'I can see to everything you need for the baby! I get good money, and once we're married you can buy what you want.' Harry felt like pinching himself to make sure he wasn't dreaming. 'Pack your job in, Mary, please? I don't think you should be standing on your feet for so long in your condition.'

Mary felt as though she was being pulled along against the tide. Things were happening so fast she couldn't take it in. But the thought of packing in work did appeal to her. It wouldn't be long before some sharp-eyed woman recognised the signs, and it was a fear she went to work with every day. Her face was filling out, her hips wider, and her breasts fuller. Tell-tale signs to any woman, and she was only surprised that no one had noticed before now.

Harry crossed the room to sit next to her. 'We're talking about getting married and I've never even kissed you.' When panic showed in the wide eyes, he coaxed. 'Just one kiss to seal our engagement.' He put his hand under her chin and turned her face towards him.

Mary sat rigid as his mouth came down on hers. She tried to respond but couldn't. She'd always closed her eyes when Bob kissed her, but now they were wide open, and as Harry lifted his mouth from hers she saw the sadness and disappointment reflected in his. 'I'm sorry, Harry,' she said softly. 'Just give me time. Everything's happened so quickly.'

'I won't rush you, love! We'll have plenty of time to get to know one another when we're married.'

Mary prayed under her breath, I hope so!

'I'll slip home and get me overalls and we can travel to work together.'

'No!' Mary spoke sharply. 'Let's leave things as they are, otherwise people will start putting two and two together.'

'I've told you, I don't care what people think!'

'Look, I'll pack in work soon if that's what you want, but I'd rather the girls thought it was because me mam's coming home. I don't care what they think after I've left.'

Harry shrugged. 'Have it your own way. I'll see you in work, then!'

'Me and Harry are getting married.' Mary blurted it out as they neared the Black Bull and Eileen stopped in her tracks. 'Well, they say the quiet ones are the worst, and in your case they're bloody right! Still, I'm glad for yer, kid, an' I think yer doing the right thing.'

'You're probably the only one that does, except for me mam! I'm not the most popular girl in the world in the Sedgemoor house.'

'What did yer expect? Yer can't blame them, now can yer?' Eileen put her arm across Mary's shoulders. 'It'll only be a nine days' wonder, so don't worry. Everyone will have a real good jangle about yer, then it'll be forgotten in a few days. The women will be jealous 'cos yer've got yerself a crackin' good feller.'

'He's too good to be made use of, like I'm doing.'

'Harry's got his head screwed on the right way, kid, an' if he didn't want to marry yer, then he wouldn't marry yer!'

Mary was squashed up against the side of the bus when Eileen whispered, 'Is it a secret, or can anyone know?'

'Definitely a secret,' Mary whispered back. 'Me mam's coming out of hospital soon, so when I give me notice in, I can say it's because I've got to stay home and look after her.'

Eileen wagged her head. 'I'll say this for you an' Harry; when yez make up yer mind to do something, yez don't hang around, do yez?'

They were walking through the factory gate when Mary asked, 'Will you be my maid of honour?'

Every feature on Eileen's face showed her amazement. 'You must want yer bumps feeling! I'd look like a baby elephant standin' next to you! I'd spoil yer weddin'!'

'I want you, Eileen; you're me best mate!'

'Well, in that case, I'll be happy to oblige, an' thank you for asking me.'

Mary could feel the laugh building up in her friend's body and was ready for the roar when it came. 'I might even buy meself a new coat and surprise the lot of yer.'

They had reached the cloakroom, where all the gossiping went on, and Mary lowered the tone of her voice. 'After the last few days, nothing would surprise me.'

Harry's grin stretched from ear to ear. 'It was all your fault, so if I've got any complaints I'll bring them to you, shall I?'

Eileen's grin matched his. 'Yer don't believe in messin' about do yer?'

'I can't believe it meself! It's like one of those sloppy films you see, where the goodie always gets the girl.'

'Things'll work out if yer give them time.' Eileen dropped the cloak of toughness she wore as a shield. 'I'm very fond of her, Harry, so you take care of her or yer'll have me to answer to.' Embarrassed by her own show of emotion, she reverted to type. 'If yer go round with that grin on yer face, yer'll be gettin' locked up.'

'I just wish Mary looked a bit happier,' Harry confided. 'She doesn't look like someone about to be married, does she?'

'Bloody hell, Harry!' Eileen placed her hands on her ample hips and glared at him. 'What d'yer expect? Bloody miracles?'

'You're right.' Harry's grin reappeared. 'It's just that I'm so happy I want everyone else to be happy as well.' As Eileen moved down the machine he caught her arm. 'What's the priest's name at the Blessed Sacrament?' Eileen's small eyes practically disappeared in the folds of flesh as her brows drew together. 'What d'yer want to know that for?'

'Mary wants to get married there.'

'There's three priests, but one of them hasn't been there very long, so I don't know him. Father Younger's the oldest ... he's been there as long as I can remember. I used to be terrified of him when I was a kid, 'cos it was woe betide yer if yer didn't know yer catechism off by heart. An' if yer missed Mass on a Sunday and didn't have a letter from our Lord to excuse yer, he'd frighten the living daylights out of yer.'

'What about Father Murphy that Mary talks about?"

'Oh, he's a lovely feller! As Irish as the blarney stone itself! If you're goin' to see one of them, make it Father Murphy . . . he's more understanding.'

Mary was due for her monthly check-up at the doctor's on the Saturday, but she went in to work for the day, telling herself she could go on Monday when they started early shift. It was an excuse, and she knew it. But how was she going to tell the doctor about Harry?

She was thinking this when a knock came on the door just after she got in from visiting her mother, and thinking it was Eileen, she opened the door with a smile on her face. But the smile froze when she recognised Father Murphy. 'Come in, Father.' Her heart thumping, she followed the black-coated figure into the living room. 'I've just got back from the hospital.'

'That's why I left it till this time.' The priest took his hat off and smoothed down his shock of fair hair. 'Can I sit down?'

Mary hastily moved her coat. 'Of course, Father! I was just surprised to see you.'

Settling himself in Martha's chair, the priest looked up at Mary, whose fear was written on her face. 'I believe you have something to tell me, Mary? Is that right now?' His soft Irish voice rolled the words gently. 'I know you've a lot on your mind with going to work and visiting your mother,

267

but I don't think that's a good excuse for not coming to church. D'you not think I'm right, now, Mary?'

Mary stood petrified, like a statue. This had to be the worst moment out of all the thousands of moments in the last few months. It had been bad enough confessing her sin to a priest in the darkness of the confessional box, but to face someone across her own living room, someone she knew and admired, was not to be contemplated.

'Shall I tell you why I've called, Mary? I had a visit this evening from a Mr Sedgemoor.'

'Harry!' Mary swallowed hard. 'We were supposed to be coming to see you together! He didn't tell me he was going tonight.'

'He'll be down shortly, so we can discuss things together.' Father Murphy sat back and stretched his legs out. 'I came early because I wanted to have a talk to you on your own. Why haven't you been to confession, Mary?'

'But I have, Father!' Mary couldn't meet his eyes. 'I went to the Holy Name because I was too ashamed to come to you or Father Younger.'

'Oh, Mary, you poor child! You aren't the first person to have committed a sin, and you certainly won't be the last. We human beings are fallible, and we're all sinners. But the good Lord forgives those who repent. Surely you haven't forgotten all the things you were taught, Mary?'

His softly spoken words were seeping through to Mary's troubled mind, easing the shame and guilt she'd carried with her for so long. Slowly the tension in her body started to unwind, and she was able to face him as he leaned forward to rest his elbows on his knees. 'Mr Sedgemoor tells me you want to get married and he wants to become a Catholic. What I want to know is, does he really want to become a convert or is he only doing it to please you, so you can be married in the church? If that is his only reason, and he doesn't intend to become a practising Catholic, then I can't agree to giving him instruction.'

'I can't speak for Harry, Father! You'd best ask him yourself. He's a good man and he won't lie to you.'

'No, I don't think he would.' The sound of the letter box rattling brought a smile to his face. 'It's himself here now! Let's find out what he's got to say.'

Chapter Eighteen

'Yer've had a busy week, what with one thing and another, 'aven't yer, kid?' Eileen was hanging on to Mary's arm, puffing as she tried to keep up with the younger girl's pace. 'I bet yer glad it's over.'

'You're not joking! But it's been a load off my mind, and I've got Harry to thank for it! I was terrified of seeing Father Murphy and Doctor Greenfield but he saw them both with me, and it's a relief.'

'I know about Father Murphy 'cos Harry told me. He went for instruction yesterday, didn't he?'

Mary nodded. 'Father Murphy knows we want to get married soon, and he's promised to give Harry instruction two or three times a week so we can be married at the altar. He read the banns out for the first time yesterday.'

'I know . . . me mam heard them! The whole neighbourhood will know by now.' Eileen shook with laughter. 'Except the Proddy dogs.'

'Yeah! Thank goodness Elsie Smith isn't a Catholic.'

'Oh, she'll find out, don't worry! The Germans don't know what they're missing with Elsie Smith . . . she'd make a bloody good spy!'

'Doctor Greenfield was giving me a lecture about getting married for all the wrong reasons, but when I told him me mam was over the moon he was all right about it. And I think Harry made a good impression on him.' Mary stifled a yawn. 'I'm dead tired! When I've had something to eat I'm going to try and put me feet up for an hour before I go to the hospital.'

'Where did Harry disappear to this afternoon? I didn't see 'im after the break.'

'He probably went to a bosses' meeting.' Mary loosened her arm from Eileen's as they reached the corner. 'I'll see you tomorrow.'

'OK, kid! Try and get those feet up an' have a rest.'

Mary made herself a sandwich before making the bed and dusting the living room. Then she decided to soak her swollen feet in a bowl of warm water before having a lie down, and she was walking towards the kitchen when a knock sounded. No peace for the wicked, she sighed as she opened the door to Vera Jackson.

'Guess what's happened?'

Too tired for guessing games, Mary said, 'Go on, I give in.'

'Danny's got his calling up papers.' The news was delivered in a dramatic voice as Vera pulled at the buttons on her cardigan. 'They came in the post this morning and I opened the letter. He's got to report to the recruitment office next week.'

'Does he know?'

'Not yet!' Vera grimaced. 'He'd gone to work when the post came.'

'I thought they were only calling young men up!'

'He's only thirty-eight! I know he looks older, but that's with all the beer he drinks.' Vera sighed. 'I don't know whether to laugh or cry. For all his faults, I wouldn't wish him any harm.'

'It's to be hoped he doesn't take it out on you.'

'He won't! I didn't tell you, but after Harry gave him that belt, I had a good talk to him. I told him straight that I was fed-up being his punch bag. I said if he ever raised his hand, or his voice again, to me or the kids, I'd leave him. I meant it too, Mary, because I'd had it up to here.' Vera put her hand on the top of her head. 'Since then he hasn't been too bad. He's not exactly a barrel of laughs, but he's better than he was. And perhaps the Army will knock him into shape ... if he passes the medical.'

Mary felt guilty for not asking Vera to sit down, but she had to put her feet up for an hour before she went to the hospital. 'Let me know what he says, won't you?'

'I'll slip in tomorrow.' Vera was waving goodbye when Mary heard a door slam, and she turned her head to see Harry coming towards her. Vera saw him too, and called, 'Mary's got some news for you.'

Harry waved in acknowledgement, saying under his breath, 'Let's get inside, quick! I've got something to tell you.'

As soon as they were in the living room he gripped Mary's arm. 'We've got a house!' In his excitement the words poured from his mouth. 'It's in Orrell Park, just off Moss Lane, and it's a cracking house! I went to see it yesterday but didn't say anything in case nothing came of it. But I've been to see the landlord and he gave me the key. It's ours if we want it, but I've got to let him know by tomorrow.'

Mary stared at him. Getting married was now becoming a reality, and her feelings couldn't cope with the speed things were moving.

'Mary!' He was shaking her arm. 'Aren't you pleased? It's a lovely six-roomed house, and it doesn't need a thing doing to it.' From his pocket he produced a key which he dangled before her eyes. 'We can go and see it now, and if you like it I can tell the landlord definitely we'll have it. You'll love it, Mary! Honest to God, you'll just love it!'

'I haven't got time to go and see it now!' Even as she spoke Mary knew she was being contrary, but she felt so tired. 'I've got to go and see me mam.'

'We've got a chance of a lovely house and you haven't got the time to go and see it!' Harry look stunned. 'I've got to give the keys back tomorrow and tell the man whether we want it or not.' He clicked his tongue. 'Make up your mind, Mary! D'you want to move or not? We'll never get another chance like this, I'm telling you! It's a lovely house, in a nice area, and it's as clean as a whistle. There's a sitting room for your mam, and a row of shops at the top of the road. What more d'you want? So, are you coming to see it, or not?'

Harry had never used this tone to her before, and without thinking she reacted. 'Yeah, OK! We can go on the way to the hospital and then we can tell me mam about it.'

Letting his breath out slowly, Harry felt the knots in his tummy loosening. He'd been so excited about the house that Mary's lack of enthusiasm had disappointed him. 'What time shall I call for you?'

Mary looked down at her swollen feet. 'I wanted to put me feet up for an hour, 'cos they're aching. With standing all day, me ankles are swollen. Will half five be time enough?'

Harry looked at the puffiness hanging over her shoes and was angry with himself for being so sharp with her. 'I'll be glad when you've packed in work. It's far too much for you!' He pecked her cheek. 'Get on the couch for an hour and I'll call at half five.'

When they got off the bus in Moss Lane, Mary gazed at the tree-lined road. Oh, it was nice around here! She could visualise herself pushing a pram under the branches of the trees and admiring the neatly kept gardens in front of the houses. It was what Eileen would call 'proper posh'.

They turned into a side road, and a few doors down, Harry stopped. 'Well, this is it!'

While he was opening the door Mary looked at the well kept houses on either side. She could feel her interest growing, and when Harry stepped aside to let her go in first she felt a stirring in her tummy as though the house was welcoming her. The hall she found herself in was long and narrow, with the stairs facing and two doors on the right.

Harry opened the first door with a flourish. 'Your sitting room, Madam!' It was a square room and the first thing to catch Mary's eye was the tiled fireplace on the wall opposite. No more blackleading or polishing the brasses, she thought. Then she saw the tall bay windows, which had

275

pretty floral curtains hanging from them. 'Ooh, aren't the windows lovely!' She turned to Harry who was watching her face intently. 'Who do the curtains belong to?'

'They go with the house! The previous tenants moved out quickly when the blitz was on, and they didn't take them down.'

'It's a lovely room.' Mary was almost talking to herself. 'Me mam would love it because it's so bright, and she'd be able to watch the people passing.'

'Come and see the rest of it.' Harry took her hand and led her into the next room. To Mary, who was used to the small space in their two-up-two-down, the room seemed enormous. It had a tiled fireplace the same as the one in the front room, and there were cupboards built into the recesses on either side of the chimney breast. She hardly had time to take it all in when Harry opened a door at the far side of the room, and she gasped with pleasure. The kitchen was twice the size of the one at home, and there were shelves fitted along the walls, and a tall blue and white kitchen cabinet beside a large white sink. 'Ooh, it's beautiful!'

'Wait till you see upstairs.' Harry's spirits were rising as he pulled Mary up the stairs. 'There's a bathroom, so you won't have to be running down the yard for much longer.'

There were two large bedrooms and a small box room. The rooms were all light and airy, and there were gay coloured curtains on all the windows. Harry left the bathroom till the last, and was rewarded by the pleasure on Mary's face as she imagined herself soaking in the large white bath. No more tin bath in front of the fire while her mam sat in the kitchen, worrying in case anyone called.

'We can make the box room into a nice bedroom for the baby,' Harry said. 'And if your mam ever gets well enough to climb the stairs she can have the back bedroom.'

Even the implication that she and Harry would be sharing the front bedroom didn't dampen Mary's spirits. She'd fallen in love with the house.

'You like it, then?' His voice was anxious. 'Everywhere's nice and clean so we could move in and decorate at our leisure.'

'Are all the curtains being left? Ours wouldn't go anywhere near these windows.'

'They're all being left! And have you noticed all the rooms have got oilcloth on the floors?' In his excitement Harry had put his arm round Mary's waist, and now he drew her closer. 'We wouldn't have to do much, really. If we can use some of your mam's stuff till we get settled in, then there's no reason why we can't get married as soon as you like.'

'The rents round here are pretty high, aren't they? Can you afford it?'

'If I couldn't, I wouldn't be going for it! If you like the house I'll put a month's rent down tomorrow, and it's ours.'

'It is a lovely house.' Mary's voice was wistful. 'It's got a nice feel to it, as though the people who lived here before were happy.'

Harry looked at his watch. 'You haven't got time to see down the yard or you'll be late for the hospital. But there's another lavatory down there, and a wash house with a boiler and running water.'

'Me mam will love it!' It was so long since anything nice had happened, Mary felt like bursting into tears. 'I can't wait for her to see it.'

Harry forced himself to take his arm from her waist. If they didn't go soon he wouldn't be able to resist the temptation to kiss her. And he knew she wasn't ready for that yet. 'We won't tell your mam about it tonight. Wait till we've got the key and the rent book. I'll come in with you tomorrow because I want to see her face when you tell her.'

'Don't forget I knew yez when yer had nowt! So don't be puttin' airs and graces on with me!' Eileen had been with them to see the new house and had insisted on going to the hospital with them, saying she wanted to see Martha's face, too. They were walking up the long path and Eileen was puffing and blowing. 'This bloody path seems to get longer every time I come.'

'If you didn't talk so much, you wouldn't get out of breath.' Mary took hold of her friend's arm and looked across at Harry who was walking on the other side of Eileen. 'Get hold of her arm and we'll give her a push up.'

As Harry took her arm, Eileen doubled up with laughter. And the more she laughed the more she gasped for breath. 'I've got a stitch in me side now! For God's sake don't make me laugh any more, or I'll wet meself.'

'We haven't said a word!' Both Mary and Harry were laughing without knowing why. But Eileen's laugh was so infectious, even people passing them on the path were turning to smile.

After a few minutes Eileen stood up straight. Taking a

deep breath, she said, 'Not a word out of either of yer, or yer'll start me off again.'

'What are you blaming us for?' Mary asked. 'We haven't opened our mouths.'

'It wasn't what yez said that started me off. It was what me imagination added to it!' Eileen looked from one to the other. 'D'you remember when we were kids, and we used to give each other a piggy back?' She looked at the puzzled expressions on their faces and shook her head. 'Yer a miserable pair of buggers, you are! Anyway, I imagined Harry giving me a piggy back, an' he ended up in 'ossie, and I had to come and visit him every night.'

Mary was the first to recover from a laughing fit. 'Come on, you two! They've got notices up all over the place asking people to be quiet in the hospital grounds, and here's us laughing our heads off!'

'Then make her shut up!' Harry was holding his side. His imagination was as vivid as Eileen's and he could picture himself struggling up the path with the big woman on his back.

'I'll be as good as gold.' Eileen put her hand on where she thought her heart was. 'As our Billy would say, I cross me heart and hope to die.'

Martha got a shock when she saw the trio walking towards the bed with red-rimmed eyes. They didn't greet her, either, but stood silently at the bottom of the bed. Then, unable to contain themselves any longer, they all burst out laughing. 'What's up with you three?'

'Two of us are all right,' Harry told her. 'But the third should be in a looney bin.'

'You frightened the living daylights out of me! I thought something was wrong.'

'Nothing's wrong, Mrs B! In fact everything's hunky-dory!' Harry looked at Mary. 'Go on, tell her the news.'

Martha had to keep asking Mary to stop because she couldn't take it all in. Her head was spinning as her daughter described all the rooms in the house, the big windows, the lovely curtains and the wash house. 'It sounds lovely, lass!'

Eileen had been dying to get her two pennyworth in. 'Yer've got a bathroom upstairs with a lavvy in! No more sittin' down the yard in the freezin' cold gettin' yer backside frozen while yer've got yer foot against the door in case someone bursts in while yer 'aving a sweet one! An' no bits of newspaper hanging on a nail in the wall, either! Yer'll have to have proper toilet paper, an' yer backside'll think it's its birthday!' An arm under the mountainous bosom, she pushed it upwards. 'It'll be me best hat an' coat when I visit yez there!' Her cheeks moved upwards as her forehead came down in a frown. 'Talkin' of coats . . . which we wasn't . . . when do I 'ave to buy me Paris model for the big day?'

'We haven't made any definite plans yet.' Mary's answer was quick, but Harry's was quicker. 'There's nothing to stop us! You can give your notice in tomorrow, leave work next Friday, and move on the Saturday. We could be married the following Saturday because the banns will have been read out three times by then.'

'But there's so much to do!' Mary argued. 'I'll never get all the packing done in time.'

Martha shared the frustration she saw on Harry's face. 'You'd be best sitting down, just the two of you, and sorting things out.' Her eyes held those of her future son-in-law. 'But you'll have to put your foot down with her, Harry! I've always seen to everything, and Mary's never had any responsibility.'

'I'm not a child!' Mary was indignant. 'I can look after meself.'

Eileen heard Harry mutter under his breath, 'You could have fooled me,' and decided it was time to change the subject, quick. 'With all the excitement, Mrs B, we haven'i even asked 'ow yer are?'

Martha smiled gratefully. 'I'm fine, thanks, Eileen! Looking forward to coming home.'

Eileen tried to bring back the pleasure they'd all felt when they'd entered the ward, but even her tales of young Billy did little to lighten the tension. And when she bent to say goodbye to Martha, she winked and whispered, 'Yer'd think these two were plannin' a wake, instead of a wedding!'

As soon as they got home Mary made a beeline for the kitchen. 'I'll stick the . . .' her words were cut off as Harry grabbed her arm and swung her round. 'Oh, no you don't! You think a cup of tea is the answer to everything! You'll sit down and listen to what I've got to say, and like it! I'm fed-up being treated like a little boy, and I don't intend to take any more of it.' He pushed her down on the couch and stood over her. 'I've been as patient as I can be, and I've made allowances for what you've been through. But we're not playing Mothers and Fathers, Mary! You've got to make up your mind, once and for all, what you want to do.' This was the Harry who was used to giving orders and having them obeyed, and Mary was stunned into silence. 'I can give the key back tomorrow, even though I'll lose the month's deposit, and forget the whole thing, if that's what you want.' His face told Mary he meant every word of it. 'It's not what I want, but I'd rather do that than go on as we are now. I just can't win with you, no matter what I do! You shut me out as though I don't exist, and I will not be ignored, Mary! Either you meet me half way or we call it a day. It's up to you, but I want your answer now! If I take that key back, I'll never look for another house.'

'I've said I'll marry you.' Mary looked up at him. 'It's just that I don't think we can do things as soon as you think.'

'You've said you'll marry me!' There was no mirth in Harry's laugh. 'You sound as though you're buying a three piece on the never-never! We're talking of marriage, Mary, and that means spending our life together! So, we sit down now and make all the arrangements for the wedding, or we call the whole thing off.'

Mary's mind was racing as she considered life with Harry, and what her life would be like without him. 'We'll get married when you want to.'

'Not just like that we won't! You make it sound as though I'm asking you to sign your death warrant, instead of asking you to marry me!'

'What d'you want from me? D'you want me to crawl!?'

'That's what you're expecting me to do! You want me to give, but you don't want to give anything in return! How can a marriage work if we're not even friends? If we don't even have a friendship going between us, what chance do we have of being happy together?'

'I've asked you to give me time.' Mary's wide eyes almost melted Harry's resolve. 'I'm not as outgoing as you, and I don't make friends easy.'

'But you don't even try to be friends with me! I watched you tonight with your mam and Eileen. You're a completely different person when you're with them.' He ran his fingers through his hair. 'I love you, Mary, but I couldn't live with you if you're going to treat me like a stranger. I'm only human and I need more than that.'

'You deserve more than that, too!' Mary whispered. 'Just be patient with me, Harry, and I promise I'll change.'

'Prove it! Give your notice in tomorrow, let me make arrangements with the removal man to move house a week on Saturday, and see Father Murphy about getting married the Saturday after.'

It was midnight when Harry left for home ... every last detail planned. As he was going out of the door, he said, 'I'll take an hour off in the morning and go and tell your mam.'

'But why? We can tell her tomorrow night!'

'Your mam was worried when we left her tonight, Mary! Let's not keep her worrying any longer than she has to, eh?'

It was a lovely sunny day and Mary and Eileen were sitting outside after they'd had their dinner. 'He's a long time! He said he'd only be gone an hour, but he's been missing nearly all morning.'

Eileen's eyes swivelled sideways. 'I'll tell yer what, kid,

he doesn't let the grass grow under his feet, does he? In the 'ospital last night I wouldn't have given him a snowball's chance in hell of getting yer to the altar in two weeks. If looks could kill, he'd have been a dead duck with the look you gave 'im.'

'I wondered where you'd got to.' Harry appeared at their side. 'I've been looking all over for you.'

'We've been wondering the same about you!' Mary answered. 'Where've you been all this time?'

'Everywhere!' Harry's white teeth flashed in the sunlight. 'I decided if it was left to you we'd never get anything done, so I've done the lot!'

Mary's mouth gaped. 'What d'you mean, you've done the lot?'

'I've arranged for the furniture van to move you next Saturday, and your mam's coming home on the Sunday. I went to see Doctor Greenfield, and he's going to call and see her in the new house, to make sure she's all right.' He took a deep breath. 'Your mam's over the moon!'

'I never thought I'd see a real live flash Harry!' Eileen was tickled by the stunned look on Mary's face. 'You can certainly move yer backside when yer want, can't yer?'

'That's not all!' Harry looked hard into Mary's eyes, daring her to object. 'I've been to see Father Murphy. He can't marry us the following Saturday because he's already got a few weddings on, but he can do it on the Friday. I said that would do, so we get married a week on Friday, at the Blessed Sacrament, at eleven o'clock.'

'I'll never get everything done in time.' Mary's voice rose. 'How can I get all the packing done to move on

Saturday when I don't finish work till Friday?'

'It can be done! I'll do all the heavy work, and your mate here,' Harry winked at Eileen, 'she'll give you a hand, won't you, Eileen?'

'I sure will, kiddo!' Eileen wouldn't have missed this for the world. 'We'll get yer moved, don't worry.'

'But the house won't be ready for me mam the day after we move in! It can't be done!'

'It'll be done!' Harry wasn't listening to excuses. 'We'll have that house like a palace for your mam! There's curtains up, lino on the floor, and the place is spotless. All we have to do is move the furniture in.'

As they walked back into the factory Mary was still shaking her head, while Eileen was still grinning.

Chapter Nineteen

'Where yer off tonight, Willy? Flyin' yer kite, as usual?' Eileen watched Willy Turnbull pulling the loaded trolley away to make room for the empty one. 'Got a date, have yer?'

'Aah, that would be tellin', wouldn't it?' Willy smirked. He loved to be thought of as a lady killer and had no intention of telling Eileen he didn't have a date but was hoping to pick up a girl at the Grafton dance hall. 'I don't kiss and tell.'

'I'm not interested in yer kisses, Willy! It's what the rest of yer body gets up to that I want to know about.'

Willy's mouth was open to reply when a large explosion shook the ground beneath their feet, followed by several smaller bangs. Then came the sound of shattering glass and shouting and screaming. Eileen looked across the conveyor to see Mary standing white faced and open mouthed.

'Turn the bloody machine off!' Eileen pushed a dazed-looking Willy. 'Go 'ed, switch the bloody thing off!' Willy's eyes looked glazed as he remained rooted to the spot. Eileen put a hand in the middle of his back and pushed hard. 'Get a move on, will yer!' She waited till he made a move towards the end of the machine where the lever was for switching off the conveyor, then dashed round to Mary. 'It's all right, kid! Probably nothing to worry about.'

'It was a bomb!'

'Nah! The alarm would have gone if there was an air raid.' All the machines had stopped now, and women were gathered in groups at the end of their machines. Men were running from different parts of the shop floor in the direction of the glass-fronted offices which lined the side wall. Eileen took Mary's arm and steered her forward. 'Let's find out what's up.' They could see Harry outside the office, a head taller than most of the other men, and his face was serious as he waved his arms about, talking quickly. Then, a troubled look on their faces, the men ran after him out of the shell inspection department. 'There's definitely something up,' Eileen muttered. 'But it can't have been a bomb or they'd have us all out.' Her nose twitched. 'Can yer smell anythin' burning?'

'It smells like gunpowder.' Mary was shaking. 'I wish someone would tell us what's going on.'

Just then Willy came hurrying down the passage between the machines. The long hair, usually carefully combed up from the side to hide his bald crown, was hanging down his shoulders, but for once his vanity was forgotten. The women converged on him, all talking at once and demanding to know what had happened. He brushed their questions aside. 'Harry said I've to switch the machines on, and yer've to get back to work.'

'Sod that!' Eileen snorted. 'The bloody place is nearly

blown up and he tells us to get back to work! If I'm to be blown to smithereens I'd like to know in advance.'

'There was an explosion in the powder shop.' Willy licked his dry lips. 'But there's no danger.'

Maisie Phillips' face was white beneath her thick make-up. 'No danger! You don't get an explosion like that without someone being hurt!'

'All I know is, I've been told to start the machines up, and that's what I'm doin'.' Willy threw the lever on Maisie's machine, forcing her to take her place at the side of the conveyor before the shells began to roll. Eileen and Mary walked behind him as he made for their machine. 'You'd think someone would tell us what was goin' on!' Eileen stormed. 'I think they've got a bloody cheek!'

'They don't know themselves how bad it is.' Willy looked round furtively. 'I think some of the girls have been injured 'cos they've sent for ambulances.'

Rumours were rife for the next hour. Every time a woman went to the toilet she came back with a knowing look on her face and a higher number of deaths. It was much later that Harry appeared, looking ghastly. No one had been killed, he was quick to assure everyone, but some had been injured. He managed a smile when Mary asked him what happened, and he convinced her the rumours she'd heard were wrong. Then he went round to Eileen, where the mask slipped. 'It's hell in there!' He wiped the sweat from his brow as his eyes blinked rapidly. 'If you saw the injuries you'd think this was the battlefield!' He glanced across the machine. 'Don't tell Mary, but one of the women has had half her face blown away!'

'Oh, my God! Who was it?'

'Iris Brown.'

Eileen screwed her eyes up. 'She's got three young kids, and her feller's in the Navy.'

'We don't know what happened yet, but all the women on that machine were injured and have been taken to hospital. The rest of them are being treated for shock.' Harry breathed in deeply, then let it out slowly. 'I can't get Iris Brown's face out of me mind. I don't see how she can live with those injuries! Honest, Eileen, half her face was blown away!'

Eileen inspected a suspect shell then returned it to the conveyor. 'They can't take cigarettes or matches in there, can they?'

'No! The precautions are very strict, but I suppose any friction could have caused it. The only ones that might know are the women who were working on the machine where it happened, and they won't be talking for a long time. The inspectors are sifting through the rubble now to see if they can find out the cause, but it's just like a bomb crater in there.'

'Let's know if yer hear anything about Iris, won't yer?'

'Mr Morgan's gone in the ambulance with her, but I don't think we'll get any news today. If we do, it'll be bad news.'

Eileen watched him walk away. 'What a bloody life!'

Mary was rummaging in her bag for the door key when Vera Jackson came hurrying up. 'I've been watching for you. You're late today.'

'There was an accident at work.' Mary was too upset to talk about the awful morning. 'How did it go with Danny?'

'He went as white as a sheet when he read the letter. I thought he was going to pass out.' Vera shook her head, 'No ... I'm being unfair! He seemed a bit shaken, but not as bad as I'm making out. He's been very quiet since, and he keeps looking at the kids with a funny look on his face. I've even caught him looking at Carol, and he never does that ... he usually ignores her. Anyway, he's got to report to Central Hall in Renshaw Street for his medical. If he passes, he reckons he'll probably be called up in a few weeks.'

Mary was studying Vera's face. She was a good neighbour and they'd always been friends. It would be a lousy trick not to tell her they were moving.

'Can I come in yours for a few minutes? I've got something to tell you.' They stood in Vera's tiny hall and Mary kept nothing back. 'We're moving on Saturday, Vera, and I'm telling everyone it's because me mam's coming home and we need a six-roomed house. But the real reason we're moving is because I'm pregnant and I'm marrying Harry Sedgemoor.' Without giving the shocked Vera time to comment, Mary went on. 'It's Bob's baby, but Harry knows and still wants to marry me. We're moving to get away from gossiping tongues, but I wanted you to know the truth.'

'You poor kid! I won't breathe a word, you know that! But I've got to say I think you're getting a smashing feller in Harry Sedgemoor. Perhaps you're going to have some good luck for a change.'

'I could do with it!' Mary threw her head back. 'Me mam's coming out of hospital the day after we move, so that's good news, isn't it?' Evading Carol's outstretched arms, Mary kissed her. 'I'm sorry, sunshine! But I've got so much to do I don't know where to start! I don't see how we can get everything done in time, but Harry and Eileen said they'll do all the hard work.'

Vera laughed as she imitated Eileen's voice. 'If I say yer can do it, kid, then yer can bet yer bottom dollar yer'll do it!'

By Friday Mary was worn out and had to summon all her energy for that last shift. It had been hard going getting all the packing done, but Eileen and Harry had been round each day for a few hours, and between them they'd done most of the donkey work.

Mary had no regrets at leaving work, because apart from Eileen she hadn't made any real friends. The women had been surprised when she gave her notice in, but because her mam was coming out of hospital nobody questioned it. As she stood by the conveyor on her last shift, she imagined some of the remarks that would be passed in the cloakroom when they found out she was pregnant. 'Fancy her! Going round with her nose in the air, an' all the time she had a bun in the oven!'

Harry got away early that night and travelled home with the two women. Eileen left them at the corner, shouting, 'I'll see yez tomorrer, kids! Don't worry if yer sleep in, tatty head! Me and Harry will wake yer up. Ta-ra!'

Once Mary's door swung open Harry didn't linger.

'Don't you do anything tonight. We'll see to everything in the morning. Get a good night's sleep and you won't be so tired tomorrow.'

He'd walked a few steps when Mary called him back. 'Are your mam and dad coming to the wedding?'

'I haven't told them yet!' Harry admitted. 'They know you're leaving in the morning, but I haven't told them about the wedding. I'm going to tell them now, if they're still up.'

'I've been worrying meself to death about them. They're your parents, and I don't want you to fall out with them because of me.'

Harry walked back and squeezed her arm gently. 'Don't you worry, everything will work out fine, I promise! You get a good night's sleep and forget everything else.'

'You're my parents, and you should be at me wedding. But I can't make you come if you don't want to.' Harry spread his hands out in despair. 'All I can say is, you'll make my wedding day complete if you're both there to see me marry the girl I love.'

George Sedgemoor was scraping the bowl of his pipe with a small pen-knife. He stretched across to knock the pipe against the bars of the grate and watched as the charred remains of his last smoke fell into the fire. 'I'll be there, son.' He spoke quietly. 'Your mam will have to do as she wants, but I'm not missing me own son's wedding.'

There was a heavy silence before Lizzie asked, 'Are you having a reception afterwards?'

Harry shook his head. 'There'll only be a few people

there and we couldn't go anywhere because Mrs B will be in a wheelchair. We'll just have a bite to eat and a few drinks at home.'

Lizzie's head was bowed, and as she studied the red bob on her bedroom slippers her mind flashed back over the last thirty years. Martha Bradshaw had always been a good neighbour and friend. In the early thirties, when a lot of men were out of work, it was always Martha that people went to for help and they were never refused. Lizzie had often gone to her when George was out of work and they didn't know where the next meal was coming from. It was only since the war started, and she'd had a regular wage coming in off George and Harry, that Lizzie had been able to go to the shops and buy what she wanted without having to count every penny. But Martha must have had a struggle bringing Mary up with no man's wages coming in. Yet never once had she complained or asked for help.

Lizzie sighed. Since Harry's shock announcement last week she'd never even asked how Martha was. Now, pocketing her pride and her stubbornness, she asked, 'Martha no better, then?'

'She'll never walk without crutches, but she never moans.' Harry stifled a yawn with the back of his hand. 'I'm going to bed! I feel worn out, and I've got to be up again at seven. The furniture van's coming to Mary's at eleven, and there's still loads to do. If you're awake, Mam, will you give me a shout?' He had turned to the door and didn't see the look exchanged between his parents. But he stopped in his tracks when Lizzie said, 'I'll give you a hand in the morning, if you like! An extra pair of hands won't go amiss.' After a slight pause, she added, 'Me and your dad will both be at your wedding.'

Harry squeezed his eyes tight. 'That's the best wedding present you could give me. Both me and Mary want you there. She's been worrying herself sick about the pair of you. Thanks, Mam and Dad! I'll sleep tonight, now.'

But Harry couldn't sleep. The explosion at the factory two days before had affected him badly. He couldn't get Iris Brown's face out of his mind. The supervisors had been told to play it down so as not to frighten the other workers, but he knew they were all as shaken by it as he was. Three women had been so badly injured in the explosion they'd never work again, and ten others had been kept in hospital suffering from minor injuries and shock. The gunpowder had blown up in Iris Brown's face and she'd borne the brunt of it. She wasn't expected to live. The explosion had been caused by friction and couldn't have been prevented, Harry had been told. It was one of the risks of working with gunpowder.

Harry pulled the bedclothes round his shoulder. If he didn't get some sleep he'd be in no condition to lug furniture round in the morning. His last conscious thought was that women certainly weren't the weaker sex. Some of them had more guts than many men he could name. They must have been terrified after the explosion, but not one woman working on filling the shells with gunpowder had asked to be taken off the job.

Two doors away, Fred Smith couldn't shut out the sound of his wife's whining voice. 'I told you there was something fishy going on, didn't I, but you wouldn't have it! Well, perhaps you'll believe me now after what we've just heard. Fancy, after being neighbours all these years, they only tell us the night before they move house! And if Mary's packing in work to look after her mam, as she says, where's the money coming from to pay the rent on a house in Orrell Park? We couldn't afford it, never mind them!'

'Is it any of your business?' Fred seldom raised his voice, but he did now. 'I've never lifted a hand to you in all the years we've been married, but I'm sorely tempted to now! So remember that before you open that mouth of yours again to pull decent people to pieces.'

Eileen had to bang hard before Mary's tousled head appeared round the door. 'There's no need to panic, 'cos it's only seven o'clock.' She pushed Mary towards the stairs. 'But yer don't want yer future husband to see yer lookin' like a wet week, do yer?'

Mary was halfway down the stairs when the knocker sounded. 'I'll get it!' She swung the door wide, expecting to see Harry standing on the step alone. When she saw Lizzie with him, a flicker of fear crossed her face and she was frozen to the spot. They'd come to tell her it was all off.

'Are you going to keep us on the step all morning?' Harry was trying hard to keep his nerves under control. 'Me mam's come to give us a hand.' Mary stood aside and as Lizzie stepped into the hall she looked into the scared, white face. 'Hello, Mary.'

Harry didn't know how it happened, but the next thing he knew his mam had her arm around Mary and they were both crying. Eileen ran to the door to see what was going on and when she took in the scene she looked at Harry in amazement. He couldn't remember crying since he was a kid, but he was near it now as the two women he loved most in the world embraced each other.

'Eh, come 'ed you two!' Eileen smacked Mary's bottom. 'The van'll be here before we've even started!'

The two women broke apart, sniffing and rubbing their eyes with the backs of their hands. 'Can I come in now, please?' Harry asked. 'The neighbours will be wondering what's going on.'

'D'you know Eileen, Mrs Sedgemoor?'

'Course I do! I've known Eileen and her mam for years! How is your mam, Eileen? And the kids?'

'Don't ask her about the kids or we'll never get any work done.' Harry lifted his arm to fend off Eileen's blow.

'Har you hinsinuating that my darling little children har not hangels? I'll have you know I wash their halos hevery night.'

The ice was broken and work started in earnest. At half nine Mary called a tea break. 'We've only got odd cups, Mrs Sedgemoor, d'you mind?'

'Yer won't be usin' odd cups in Orrell Park!' Eileen nudged Lizzie. 'Proper tu'penny ha'penny toffs down there! All fur coats and no knickers!'

Lizzie had been dying to know where her son was going to live but had been too stubborn to ask. 'D'you like the house, Mary?'

Mary felt as though she was in the middle of a dream. Harry's mother was sitting in their house drinking tea! 'It's beautiful! Why don't you come and see it this afternoon.'

Lizzie beamed. 'I'd love to! I'll slip home and get something ready for George's dinner, and I'll make us some butties while I'm at it so you won't have to worry.'

'Thank God someone remembers we've got to eat!' Eileen clapped her hands. 'Me belly thinks me throat's cut!'

Harry, like Mary, felt light with relief as he laughed at Eileen. 'Don't you ever think of anything but your tummy?'

Seeing the cheeky grin start on Eileen's face, Mary knew she was going to say something embarrassing and made a beeline for the kitchen. She was just out of the door when she heard, 'Yer know I've got something else on me mind all the time! But I'm not getting any, am I, so I'll have to stick to food till my feller gets 'ome.'

Harry jumped from the taxi and hurried to the space beside the driver where the wheelchair was propped. He dragged it down and was fumbling with the arms when Eileen pushed him aside. 'Move over, kiddo, and let the expert show yer 'ow.' With a twist of the wrists she had the chair open. 'It's the way yer 'old yer mouth, kid!' She grinned before popping her head in the taxi to see Martha sitting next to Mary, her eyes shining with excitement. 'Acting the part already, are yer? Rollin' up to yer new house in a flippin' taxi!'

All Harry could see was Eileen's enormous backside, and he had to knock on the window to ask Mary to tell her to move. 'Give us a hand with Mrs B will you?' He slipped Mary a ten shilling note to pay the driver, then with

Eileen's help got Martha from the taxi and into the wheelchair.

Martha only had time to glance quickly at the outside of the house before Harry tipped the chair and wheeled her over the two front steps. She gasped in amazement at the length of the hall, and her 'Oh, isn't it huge?' brought a smile to Mary's face.

'This is your room, Mam.' Mary watched her mother's face. 'D'you like it?'

'Oh, it's beautiful! So big and bright.'

It was the kitchen Martha fell in love with. 'Just to think, if I was all right I could do all me baking and washing in here.'

'Washing, did you say, Missus!?' Eileen asked in mock horror. 'Yer don't do yer washin' in here! It's easy to see you're not used to anything! Yer've got a proper wash house now, not like us common people!'

The wheelchair was too wide to go through the back kitchen door, and Harry winked at Eileen. 'One either side?'

There was so much laughing over their clumsy attempts to get Martha through the door, Eileen had tears in her eyes. 'If we kill yer between us, at least yer'll die laughin'!'

When they were all squashed into the wash house, Eileen nudged Martha. 'You'd better hurry up and get well, so yer can start takin' washin' in! But don't have yer customers comin' to the front door, 'cos it'll lower the tone of the neighbourhood. Make 'em use the back entry. And don't forget it's entry round here, and not jigger!'

Martha was tired with all the excitement so they settled

her in her own chair, in her own room. She looked at the beloved photographs lined up on the sideboard and breathed a sign of contentment. 'It's funny, but I feel this house is going to be lucky for us. It's so warm and friendly, I don't feel a bit strange in it.'

'D'you know, that's just how I felt when I first walked in!' Mary's voice held surprise. 'I know it sounds daft, but it seemed to welcome me.'

'It was only by a stroke of luck I got it, too!' Harry was looking smug. 'Ten minutes after Mr Armstrong gave me the key another couple came along and said they'd take it without even seeing inside.'

'Go 'ed!' Eileen wagged a finger. 'Tell the truth . . . yer gave him a back hander.'

'Eileen thinks everything falls off the back of a lorry.' Harry grinned at Martha. 'Either that, or it comes from under the counter.'

'Well, I never 'eard of a house falling off the back of a lorry! And even if they did, I couldn't afford one like this! I bet the rent's high!'

'Twelve and six a week,' Harry told her. 'And I think it's worth it.'

'All right for them what can afford it, eh, Mrs B?'

Martha was smiling as she nodded at Eileen, then she turned to Mary.

'Have you got your wedding dress yet, lass?'

'Ah, ay, Mam! Give us a chance! I haven't had time to breathe, never mind worry about me dress!'

'How are yer off for coupons?' Eileen asked. 'I can let yer 'ave some.'

'I should be all right, because I haven't bought anything for ages.'

'Don't forget yer'll need a lot!' Eileen didn't worry that Harry was listening. 'Yer need some glamorous undies and nighties, as well as a dress. And yer mam needs an outfit.'

Mary blushed. 'What I can't afford, I'll do without!'

Harry stepped in before Eileen went too far. 'I've got some coupons you can have. And I'm coming tomorrow so you could slip into town while I'm here with your mam.'

'But you start nights tomorrow night,' Mary protested. 'You'll need to get some sleep.'

'I can't sleep day and night! Anyway, I was coming tomorrow for a couple of hours to unpack some of the crates. There's plenty to do to keep me occupied while you go shopping.'

'I'll come with yer!' Eileen said, eagerly. 'I can look for a dress for meself.'

'Go on, lass, while you've got the chance,' Martha coaxed. 'You've only got a few days to get everything you need.'

'If you're sure you'll be all right.'

'That's settled then.' Eileen rubbed her hands together. 'Isn't it exciting, going for yer wedding dress! Mind you, when Harry sees me all dressed up you won't be in the meg specks!'

'You behave yourself when you're out with me,' Mary laughed. 'Don't go making a fool of me!'

Chapter Twenty

They stepped off the bus in Clayton Square and Mary's eyes swept the shops on either side of the busy shopping centre. 'Where to first?'

'Let's go to Etam's for yer undies while we're on this side of the road, then we can look for yer dress.' Eileen tucked her arm through Mary's. 'Are yer OK for money, kid?'

'Harry made me take ten pound off him as we were coming out. I didn't want to take it, but he made me.'

'Good for 'im! Now yer can buy something special to get married in.'

'I don't want anything special! Just something nice and plain that I can get some wear out of afterwards.'

Half an hour later, when they walked out of Etam's, Mary was in a daze. None of the things in the bags she was carrying would have been bought if Eileen hadn't been with her. The big woman had had the shop assistants in stitches when she saw the size of the undies Mary chose. The pretty bra, in a size thirty-four bust, had her spluttering. 'Blimey! the only way I would wear them would be for ear muffs!'

Mary had picked out a floral cotton nightie which was

pretty and practical, but to Eileen it was definitely not a honeymoon nightie. Much to Mary's embarrassment, and fits of giggles from the assistants, it had been tugged from her hand and thrown back on the counter in disgust. 'Yer'd look like Old Mother Riley in that!' A beautiful low cut, satin nightdress in pale blue had caught her eye, and without a 'by your leave' to Mary, Eileen had handed it over the counter. 'She'll take that!'

Clutching the bags, Mary asked, 'Where to now?'

'Let's go mad and try Henderson's and the Bon Marche. I've never bought meself a decent coat in me life, but I'm goin' to break eggs with a big stick for me mate's wedding.'

Eileen whistled when Mary came out of the changing cubicle. 'Kid, yer look like a million dollars in that!'

The dress was a pale blue crepe that matched perfectly the colour of Mary's eyes. It had three quarter length sleeves, a high mandarin collar and a dropped waistline with a bow either side. The assistant looked on in admiration as Mary surveyed herself in the long mirror, and as their eyes met, she smiled. 'It looks lovely on you, Madam.'

'It's a beautiful dress, but I wouldn't get much wear out of it.'

They both turned at Eileen's snort. 'To hell with gettin' much wear out of it! It's yer weddin' dress!' She could see Mary wrestling with her conscience. 'If yer don't buy that one, kid, then yer can go home on yer own! Yer only get married once, for Christ's sake!'

Mary took one more look at herself in the dress she'd

fallen for as soon as she'd set eyes on it, then smiled at the assistant. 'I'll take it.' The dress Eileen chose was in a light beige, with covered buttons down to the waist, a round collar and tie belt. 'It'll be bloody filthy in five minutes, but what the hell!'

They took special care in choosing Martha's dress. In the end they agreed on one with a light grey background, covered in small white flowers. It was buttoned right down the front which meant it would be easy for her to take off and on.

Weighed down with parcels, they made for Reece's and a pot of tea with toasted teacakes. 'Yer looked lovely in that dress, kid!' Eileen spoke through a mouthful of teacake. 'Wait till Harry sees yer on Friday.'

'It was a lot of money to spend on a dress I won't get much wear out of.' Mary stared down at her plate. She never mentioned Bob's name to anyone these days, but he was never out of her thoughts. If only it was him she was wearing the dress for ... but what good did it do to dream? 'I shouldn't have let you talk me into spending so much money, 'cos we need things for the house.'

'Stop yer moaning! I'll take yer down to Paddy's market one Saturday an' yer can get everything yer need from there, without coupons!' Eileen became exasperated. 'Don't yer want yer mam to be proud of yer? She's only got you, so don't begrudge her wantin' to see her daughter looking nice on her wedding day.' Wiping the grease from her chin with a hankie that had seen better days, she went on, 'There's a hat shop round the corner, an' we're going to buy you the most glamorous hat in the shop. And don't bother arguing, kid, 'cos yer goin', even if I have to drag you there! OK?!'

Harry looked pleased when he opened the door and saw them weighed down with parcels. 'Did you get what you wanted?'

'It's a good job yer paid a month's rent in advance.' Eileen nodded at Mary's back. 'That one there has just spent a month's wages on a bloody hat!'

'I'd better tell me mam to get all togged up then, hadn't I?' Harry stuck his tongue out at Eileen before looking at Mary. 'I forgot to tell you, me mam asked if you needed a hand on Friday morning to get the table ready?'

'No, I'll be all right. Eileen's coming early to give a hand, and there'll only be six of us, anyway!'

'Twelve!' Harry contradicted. 'I've asked Johnny Griffiths to be me best man, so him and his wife are coming. I've also asked the Smiths and the Jacksons.' When Mary closed her eyes, he went on, in a firm voice that advised no opposition, 'They've been our neighbours for years, Mary, and you couldn't not ask them! We all know Elsie Smith is a nosey so-an-so, but you can't take it out on Fred. He's a good bloke, and he was over the moon when I invited them. And I want to make it up with Danny, seeing as he's going in the Army, so I've asked him and Vera. I told them to bring Carol, as well.'

'Oh, I'm so glad!' Martha breathed a sigh of relief. 'I've been worrying about the neighbours.'

'I've ordered the cars, the flowers, and something to

drink. And thanks to Eileen, here, we've got tins of salmon for the Catholics and boiled ham for the Protestants.'

Eileen's shoulders moved, taking her whole body with them. 'All we've got to do, is get Tilly Mint here, down to the church on time.'

When Mary was alone with her mother, she took the dresses out to show her. 'They're lovely, lass! Try yours on for us.'

'I'll try it on later,' Mary promised, before kneeling down at the side of Martha's chair. 'I've been thinking about Bob's mam and dad. D'you think I should tell them about the baby?'

'I've been asking meself the same question for weeks, and still don't know the answer. They're bound to find out sooner or later, and they'll be upset if you haven't told them.' Martha sighed. 'I feel so sorry for them! Bob was their only child, and they've gone through so much.' She stroked Mary's hair. 'But what about Harry? You can't expect him to welcome the Wests coming to see their grandchild when he's your husband! You'll be married to him, lass, and he's the one should come first.'

'The baby comes first, Mam!'

'Even so, don't you think it would be best if the baby grew up thinking Harry was its father?'

'I'm so mixed up I don't know what to think. I don't even know if I'm doing the right thing by getting married!' Mary saw concern in the faded blue eyes. 'Don't worry, Mam. I'm just tired with traipsing round Liverpool all day. Everything will work out.'

'If you want my advice about the Wests, I'd say do nothing until after you're married. Then have a good talk to Harry about it. He'll be your husband then, and you shouldn't have any secrets from him.'

Eileen pulled a face when she got home and found the house empty. She'd been looking forward to showing her dress off. Still, she could try it on for her mother later, when the kids were safely in bed. Remembering the grubby hands that would go with curious minds, Eileen put the bag with her new dress in under the ironing on the sideboard. It was as she was turning to go out to the kitchen that she saw the letter. It was propped up in a prominent spot on the mantelpiece, and she knew right away who it was from. All the pleasure she'd felt during the day drained away from her as she spoke to the empty room. 'I wish you were 'ere, Bill, to see me in me new dress.'

She was still standing with her coat on, clutching the letter, when Maggie walked in. 'What does Bill have to say?'

'Not much! But at last he's had a couple of my letters, so that's something to be thankful for, I suppose.' Eileen stuffed the letter back in the envelope. 'I've had a smashing day out with Mary, and came home feeling full of the joys of spring with me new dress. Now I feel like blabberin' like a baby 'cos Bill's not here to see it.'

'Let's see it!'

'Leave it till later, in case the kids come in. If they get their filthy hands on it they'll ruin it.'

'Did Mary get her dress?'

'Yeah, she got a beauty!' Eileen grinned. 'Mind you, the dress had a head start when she got into it! She'd look good in a coal sack!'

'Our Rene's been! Alan's being transferred to Liverpool today, and she can visit him tomorrow. She said you'd promised to go with her, but I told her you were on nights, so she's going to leave it until about two o'clock.'

'Which hospital's he coming to?'

'Mossley Hill.' Maggie chewed on her bottom lip. 'She said it's where a lot of the wounded are being sent.'

'Where the 'ell is Mossley Hill 'ospital?' Eileen frowned. 'I've never heard of it.'

'I hadn't either! But Rene's got directions on how to get there.'

'What am I going to wear? I haven't got a decent coat to me name.'

'The weather's nice, so you don't need a coat.' Maggie's eyes travelled the room for sight of a shopping bag. 'What's wrong with your new dress?'

'It's Hobson's choice, 'cos I've got nowt else! But can yer imagine me goin' out in me figure? It's years since I went out without a coat.'

Maggie tutted impatiently. 'Everybody else does, so I don't see why you can't!'

'Everybody hasn't got a figure like mine, Mam!'

'Oh, go on with you! You're just a bit on the, er, bonnie side.'

Eileen's laugh rang out. 'The word yer lookin' for, Mam, is fat!'

'I know the word I'm looking for!' Maggie retorted hotly.

'And it's bonnie! I bet you'll look every bit as nice as our Rene tomorrow!'

'Seein' as I'm twice as fat, I should look twice as nice, shouldn't I?'

Eileen nudged her mother in the ribs. 'Thanks for tryin', Mam, but I'll never be a Veronica Lake, so why worry?'

Eileen was wearing a pair of high-heeled shoes she hadn't worn for years and they were crippling her. Her feet were always swollen with the extra weight she was carrying, and as she tottered on the slim, high heels, she groaned in agony. 'How much further is it, our kid? Me bloody feet are killing me!'

'It's just a bit further along, then we turn into North Mossley Hill Road and it's the first turning on the right.' Rene glanced down at her sister's feet. 'You should have put a pair of flat heels on.'

'D'yer think I wouldn't have done, if I'd had a pair?' Eileen asked through clenched teeth as she thought how ridiculous it was to go through agony just to look nice. Then her sense of humour surfaced as she cast her eyes down to her enormous bust. 'I haven't seen me bloody feet in years, but I don't half know I've got them now! They're practically talkin' to me!' They were walking through a lovely area with large detached houses in their own grounds. High walls surrounded the large gardens giving the owners privacy from their neighbours. 'Must have a few bob to live round here.' Eileen stopped to peer through the railings of a pair of huge, wrought iron gates. 'Yer could get the whole of our street in that one garden.' Rene was too keyed up with nerves to answer. And when they stopped outside the gates of a building that had at one time been a church, but now had a hospital sign outside, she was shaking. 'I'm terrified, Eileen!'

Sore feet forgotten, Eileen put a hand on each of Rene's shoulders and turned her round to face her. 'Let's just calm ourselves down before we go in, shall we? Alan's got enough on his plate without you cryin' yer eyes out in front of him, so for Christ's sake pull yerself together! You know what's wrong with him, so prepare yerself!'

Dropping on to a chair, Eileen screwed her eyes up and blew out a sigh of relief. 'Me feet'll never be the same again!' She circled one of her fat legs with her two hands, and struggling, pulled the leg across her lap. 'Ooooh!' She pulled off the too tight shoe and groaned in pain. 'I've been in bloody agony since I left the house!' Through her stockings angry red marks could be seen where the shoe had bitten into the flesh, and she winced as she rubbed her foot. 'What we go through for bloody pride!'

Maggie watched the other shoe being taken off and flung across the floor in disgust. 'Get yourself a decent pair of comfortable shoes for heaven's sake! We're not so poverty stricken you can't afford a pair.' She waited till Eileen stopped groaning, then asked, 'How was Alan?'

'I didn't half get me eye wiped, Mam! There was me, the big tough guy, telling our kid not to be such a baby. Prepare yerself, I told her!' Eileen huffed. 'The trouble was, no one had prepared me!'

'Is he very bad?'

'What can yer expect? He says he's worried about not being able to work again, but I think it's more than that. I'm not very good with words, Mam, but he seemed to 'ave a haunted look in his eyes, as though he's got something on his mind.'

'We don't know what he's got on his mind.' Maggie was crying softly. 'Don't know what he's gone through or the terrible sights he's seen.'

'He's lucky compared to some, believe me! If yer'd seen some of the other fellers in the ward yer'd realise just how lucky he is! The poor feller in the next bed is twenty-four years of age, he's got a twelve-month-old baby, and he's lost both his arms.'

As Maggie's cries became louder, Eileen cursed herself for being stupid, and kept quiet about the other men she'd seen. The ones suffering from shell shock, who wandered round in a little world of their own. And the man in the bed opposite Alan, whose face was covered in bandages. When she'd asked what was wrong with him, she'd been told half his face had been blown away. The memory of those men would be with Eileen for a long time, but there was nothing to be gained by upsetting her mother.

They heard footsteps running along the hall before young Edna burst through the door. 'I can do it, Mam! Come an' see me, Mam!'

'What can yer do, pet?'

Edna pulled on her mother's arm. 'Come outside, an' I'll show yer!' Eileen's lips curled upwards. 'Life goes on, Mam!' She allowed herself to be pulled, in her stocking feet, into the street. 'Stand there, Mam, and watch me.'

Bouncing a red rubber ball, Edna began to sing. 'One, two, three, Oleara.' At the count of three, she cocked a thin leg over the ball, 'four, five, six, Oleara', again she cocked her leg over the ball, 'seven, eight, nine, Oleara.' This time her little leg just made it back to the ground in time to bounce the ball higher as she sang, 'ten Oleara, catch the ball!' and twirl round before catching the falling ball in her hands. 'There yer are, Mam! Aren't I clever?'

Looking at her daughter's happy, innocent face, Eileen silently thanked God for her, and Joan and Billy. Without them life wouldn't be worth living right now. Ruffling Edna's hair, she said, 'You are clever, and that's a fact! Yer deserve a penny for some sweeties after that!' Holding the thin hand in hers, she walked back along the hall thinking that there was still a lot to be thankful for. Nice things still happen . . . like our Edna being able to cock her leg over the ball without falling flat on her backside. And me best mate gettin' married on Friday!

Chapter Twenty-One

The flickering candles at the foot of the statue of the Virgin Mary on the small side altar caught Harry's eyes as he turned to whisper to his best man, 'They're late.'

'It's not quite eleven, yet.' Johnny Griffiths smiled at Harry's unease. 'It's the bride's prerogative to be late, anyway.'

'My watch must be fast.' Harry ran a finger round the inside of his shirt neck. It was new, and the collar was stiff and uncomfortable. He could hear the low voices of his mother and father behind him as they chatted to Elsie Smith, and on the opposite side of the aisle Martha and Eileen were turned round whispering to Vera and Danny Jackson. There weren't many people in the large, beautiful church, only the ten invited guests, a few of their neighbours, and a handful of daily worshippers. Fred Smith wasn't there, because at the last minute he'd been asked to give Mary away. She had no relative to walk her down the aisle, so with Fred being a Catholic he'd been invited to take the place of her father.

Up till four weeks ago Harry had never been inside a Catholic church. But since then he'd been to see Father

Murphy eight times for instruction, and the priest had brought him through from the vestry, into the church, as part of his introduction into the Catholic faith. Harry hadn't been nervous then, but he was now! He wouldn't be content until the wedding was over and Mary had his ring on her finger. The ring! Forgetting to lower his voice, Harry grabbed Johnny's arm. 'You have got the ring, haven't you?' Johnny let his face look blank for several seconds, then grinned as he patted his breast pocket. 'All present and accounted for.'

There was muted laughter and Harry turned his head to see Martha and Eileen trying to keep their faces straight. 'He 'ad yer worried then, didn't he?' Eileen, to use her own words, was feeling like the fairy on top of a Christmas tree. Dressed up to the nines in her new dress, a wide-brimmed hat that had been borrowed from their Rene, a new pair of shoes and matching gloves, she'd told her mother, 'I wouldn't call the Queen me aunt in this gear!'

Harry tried to raise a smile. 'I've got a spare . . .' he heard the whispering stop as all heads turned towards the back of the church. A hand in his back pushed him out of the pew and Johnny hissed, 'They're here! Move out!'

Harry, his hands clasped tightly together, squared his shoulders as he stood in front of the altar. He bent his head and turned it slightly to see Mary walking down the aisle on Fred Smith's arm. She looked neither left nor right, her face pale. But Fred was beaming with pride and enjoying the importance of the role.

Father Murphy, who had appeared from nowhere, was smiling encouragement as Mary reached Harry's side, and indicated where they should stand. Mary's mind and body were numb. The short service was a blur ... her voice a faltering whisper as the priest asked her to repeat the vows after him. And when Harry was slipping the ring on her finger, the hand wearing the new gold band looked like a stranger's hand. 'I now pronounce you man and wife.' Harry cupped his hand under Mary's chin and bent to kiss her; then they were being led through to the room where the registrar was waiting for their signature on the marriage licence.

Harry's heart was bursting with pride as he walked back up the aisle with his new bride on his arm. He bent his head sideways to whisper. 'You look lovely, Mary.' The dress suited her to perfection, as did the small hat perched on top of the long blonde hair. The eye veil, as delicate as a spider's web, did little to hide the wide blue eyes beneath it. They walked from the darkness of the church into bright sunlight, and a shower of confetti from Eileen, Vera and Elsie Smith. Eileen hugged Mary in a bearlike grip, grinning over her shoulder at Harry. 'Well, yer've been and gone and done it now! No more gallivanting for you, me lad!'

Mary disengaged herself from Eileen's arms. 'Is me mam all right?'

'The men are seein' to her, so don't be worrying. Yer car's holding the traffic up, so get going! The bride and groom should be there to welcome their guests, so don't show yer ignorance an' get home an' have the sherry poured out for us.'

Mary slipped into the back seat of the car. She tried to

return the driver's smile but her lips were so dry she thought they would crack when she stretched them. 'Well, that's over!' Harry took her hand. 'I can't say I'm sorry, either! I was as nervous as a kitten.'

Within minutes they were stepping out of the car and Harry turned to slip some money into the driver's hand. Then he opened the door and stepped aside to let Mary pass. He caught her up in the middle of the hall, his arm round her waist. 'How about a kiss for your new husband, Mrs Sedgemoor?'

Her heart doing somersaults, Mary lifted her face. The kiss was gentle at first, then more demanding, and Mary pulled away. 'They'll be here any minute, and I want to see to the table.'

'Would it be so terrible if they saw a man kissing his wife on their wedding day?'

'I've got the table to see to.' Even to her own ears Mary's excuse sounded childish. 'I want everything to look nice for when they get here.' She moved plates that didn't need moving, and straightened chairs that were already straight. Anything to avoid Harry's watching eyes. And when the bell rang she sighed with relief as she dashed to let their guests in.

Even with the two extending leaves in Martha's table it wasn't big enough for them all to sit round, so after helping themselves to food from the table, they sat with their plates balanced on their knees and wine glasses in their hands. It was a noisy, happy atmosphere, and slowly the strain on Mary's face relaxed. She didn't have much to say, but then neither did anyone else with Eileen there. Her tales of young Billy kept them all amused. 'Yer know this secret weapon that Hitler's supposed to have? Well, Winston Churchill doesn't know it yet, but we've got a better one! If they dropped our Billy behind enemy lines the war would be over in a week, 'cos he'd talk the bloody Germans to death!'

When Vera's high-pitched laugh sounded, Mary happened to be facing Danny, and her brow creased when she saw the look on his face as he watched his wife. It was a look of affection. Something Mary hadn't seen for years. Vera had told her he'd changed since he got his calling up papers, but Mary hadn't believed it possible he'd changed this much. He was so good with Carol, sitting her on his knee and even kissing and hugging her. And it wasn't put on for the benefit of the company either, because you could tell by Carol's face that she was no longer afraid of him. Perhaps the thought of going away had made him realise what he was leaving behind. Whatever had changed him, Mary was glad for Vera's sake. She returned to the conversation going on round her, to hear Harry asking, 'I was never as naughty as young Billy, was I, Mam?'

'That's what you think!' Lizzie clucked. 'Remember when you had that catapult? There wasn't a bird, cat or dog safe when you had that thing in your hand! We never had any pigeons on our roof, 'cos you used to knock them off!'

'I was a good shot, though, wasn't I, Mam?' Harry teased.

'Too bloody good!' George remembered. 'When Mr Watson kept pigeons he was never away from our door, complaining about you hitting his blasted birds! He wouldn't leave till I'd given you a good hiding, either!'

Harry's laugh was loud. 'I've often wondered why I didn't like that man.'

Eileen wasn't going to let her Billy be outshone by anything Harry had done. So she got into her stride, doing what she was best at and that was making people laugh. 'I'll give yez an example of 'ow crafty the little bugger is, shall I? The other day I was rushin' round like a blue-arsed fly tryin' to get me work done, and I heard him arguing with me mam. She couldn't get a word in edgeways ... everything she said he had an answer for. I put up with it for a while, then I lost me rag an' grabbed him by the scruff of the neck. "Will you put a stopper in that gob of yours," I said, "before I put me fist in it!" D'yer know what the cheeky little monkey did? He looked up at me, as cool as yer like, an' stuck his hand out. "Giz a penny then," he said, with such a smirk on his face I felt like thumping him one. "Yer cheeky little sod," I said, "why should I give yer a penny when yer've been naughty?"' Eileen's whole body was shaking so much with laughter the floor boards creaked. 'I know I shouldn't be laughing, but when I think of the look on 'is face, I can't help meself. He said, "Well, yer told me to put a stopper in me gob, so if yer give us a penny I can buy meself some gobstoppers!"' Martha was laughing with the rest of them, but Lizzie noticed her tired eyes and the sag of her shoulders. Scraping her chair back, Lizzie stood up. 'I think it's time we went. It's been a lovely day, but Martha's had enough.'

'Yes, we'd better be making tracks too! We've left the

boys with the McDermots.' When Fred stood up, Elsie got up too. For once she looked happy, but whether it was because she'd enjoyed herself or whether she was thinking of all the gossip she had to tell the neighbours, no one would ever know. Her eyes had been everywhere, and her three trips to the bathroom had been to make sure she saw everything there was to see.

Lizzie was nudging her husband's arm. 'Go on, tell them!'

George grinned sheepishly. 'We didn't know what to buy you for a wedding present, so we all clubbed together and bought you one decent present between the lot of us.' His wave took in the Smiths, the Jacksons and Eileen. 'It's a surprise though, so we're not telling you what it is. Just don't go out on Monday morning, 'cos it's being delivered.'

'Oooh, I can't wait till Monday.' Mary clasped her hands. 'Go on, tell us what it is, please!'

'Just 'old yer horses, young Mrs Sedgemoor,' Eileen mocked. 'Yer'll see it soon enough! In the meantime, put in a good word for me with yer old man, will yer? Get him to move that bloody Jean Simpson on to another machine, for God's sake!'

Mary blushed. 'You'd better sort that out with Harry.'

'Ah, come on, kid! I thought yer were me mate! If yer can't get him to do yer a favour on yer weddin' night, then yer mustn't be doing it right, so come to yer Auntie Eileen for some advice.'

Harry bit his lip to stop himself from laughing. He could see by Mary's face that she wasn't amused, so he came to her rescue. 'You'll be having us divorced before we've been married twenty-four hours! And you wonder where young Billy gets his cheek from !'

'Come on, let's get going.' Lizzie led the way into the hall. She was about to step into the road, then turned back to Mary. 'You will make sure he gets plenty to eat, won't you?'

This started everyone off laughing again, and it was a happy group that waved goodbye.

Harry helped Mary clear the table, then they put all the furniture back before starting on the dishes, working in an awkward silence. As soon as they were finished Mary automatically walked into the front room where Martha was sitting with a contented smile on her face.

'All back to normal again, Mam.'

'It's been a grand day, lass! It was nice seeing the neighbours again, and I think they all enjoyed themselves.' Martha looked towards the door. 'Where is Harry?'

Mary looked surprised by the question. 'In the other room, I suppose.'

'Don't you think you should go and see? He might want to be alone with you for a while! I'll be all right here with me wireless.'

'He can come in here if he wants to.' Mary's voice was petulant.

'No, lass! You got married today, and your place is in your own room with your husband.' Martha knew she was treading on thin ice and chose her words carefully. 'It's been a hectic day, lass, and I'd like to be on me own for a while.'

Mary's head hung as she walked towards the door. 'Give me a shout if you want anything.' In the back room she found Harry setting the alarm clock that had been a present from Eileen's mother. 'Shall I make a cup of tea?'

Harry looked up. 'A cup of tea's your answer to everything, isn't it, Mary?' He smiled to take the sting out of his words. 'Why don't you just sit down and talk?'

Like a little girl doing as she was told, Mary sat in a chair facing the couch. 'D'you think they all enjoyed themselves?'

'Never mind them! Did you enjoy yourself?'

The direct question had Mary floundering for words. 'I thought everything went off great!'

In a gesture of despair, Harry shook his head. 'The difference in you when you're with other people and when you're with me, is unbelievable! You're not frightened of me, are you, Mary?'

'Of course not! Don't be silly!'

Harry patted the empty space at the side of him. 'Then come and sit next to me.'

'I'll go and change me dress first. I don't want to get any marks on it.' Mary ran from the room leaving Harry hurt and bewildered. He'd married a woman who wouldn't even talk to him! Making a quick decision he put the clock down and went to Martha's door. He knocked softly, and walked in when she answered. 'I don't know how to handle it, Mrs B! She treats me as though I've got the plague!'

Martha nodded her head sadly. 'I know, and I understand how you must feel. But she's been through hell for the last few months and needs time to get it out of her mind.'

'How much time, Mrs B? A month, a year, ten years? And what am I supposed to do if she never changes?'

'She will, Harry! I know she will! She's all frightened and mixed up inside, and my heart breaks every time I look at her. She used to be so happy, and always laughing; then everything suddenly went wrong, and she doesn't know how to come to terms with it.' Martha ran a hand across her forehead. 'You do love her, don't you Harry?'

'D'you think I'd be here if I didn't?'

'Then be patient, and give her time.'

Mary took the dress off and hung it in the wardrobe, followed by the pill-box hat which was placed carefully in a bag and put on a side shelf. Her movements were deliberately slow as she stretched out the minutes until she'd have to go back downstairs. She was dreading sitting alone with Harry and trying to think of something to talk about. As she slipped into a new navy blue skirt she talked to the empty room. 'This is his home now, and he'll be living and sleeping here.' Her eyes were drawn to the double bed. In a few hours they would be lying together in that bed. She had to pull the waistband across her thickening waist to fasten the side button, and the action reminded her why Harry would be sleeping in her bed tonight. He was so good, why couldn't she at least be civil with him? I'm going to have to try, she thought as she made her way down the stairs, because I'm not being fair to him.

The living room was empty and the kitchen in darkness. Mary's face wore a puzzled look as she stood in the middle of the room. Where had he gone? Then she heard voices coming from her mother's room, and when she walked in it was to see Harry sitting on the bed, chatting away to Martha. 'Hello, lass! Me and Harry were just talking about having a game of cards to pass an hour away. D'you feel like playing?'

Mary felt a stab of jealousy, then told herself she was being childish. What was wrong with Harry talking to her mother? After all, where would they be without him? 'Are we playing for money or matchsticks?'

Harry had never played cards before, so they had to teach him as they went along. It was a slow game because Martha could only use one hand and had to spread the cards out on her lap, under the cover of the small, green, baize-topped card table. Harry lost every hand and had to keep borrowing matchsticks off Mary to stay in the game. 'I think you're a couple of card sharks.' Harry pulled a face, and Mary's laugh rang out. 'If we were playing for real money you'd owe me about two pound.' She was completely at ease with him now, but when her eyes met his there was only friendliness there. The special look that passes between lovers, especially newlyweds, was missing.

Martha put her cards on the table at the end of a game that Mary had won. 'I don't know about you two, but I'm dead beat. I'm going to bed.'

Harry stretched his arms over his head. 'I'm whacked, too! Thank God I've got a week's holiday in front of me. No getting up at five in the morning.'

'I'll give you a hand, Mam.' Mary's smile had disappeared.

'There's no need, lass! I can manage fine on me crutches. I had to do it in the hospital, so I can do it here.'

Harry said goodnight, but Mary lingered, listening to his footsteps climbing the stairs. 'Go on, lass!' Martha pushed her gently. 'It's been a long day, and you must be worn out.'

Harry was getting undressed when Mary entered the bedroom, and keeping her eyes averted she grabbed her nightdress from the chair and fled along to the bathroom. She wasted time cleaning her teeth and washing her face; then when she couldn't reasonably put it off any longer, she crept back along the landing. Harry was lying on his back staring at the ceiling, when he heard the sound of the door closing. His head turned, and Mary felt his eyes burning through the flimsy material of the nightdress that did nothing to hide the fullness of her breasts. Her hand went to the switch on the wall. 'I'm putting the light out.'

The room was plunged into darkness and Mary moved slowly across the room until her knees came into contact with the bed. Slipping between the sheets she lay on her back and pulled the clothes up to her chin. She could feel Harry's leg touching hers, but he didn't move, and for five minutes the only sound in the room was the ticking of the clock and the beat of Mary's heart. Then Harry turned on his side and slipped an arm under her shoulder, pulling her towards him. He heard her crying softly and put his other arm around her and held her close. 'Don't cry, sweetheart! I wouldn't hurt you for anything in the world.'

Chapter Twenty-Two

'Wake up, sleepy head! I've brought you a cuppa.'

Mary opened her eyes to see Harry standing at the side of the bed wearing a dressing gown over his pyjamas. The intimacy of the scene caused her to sit up like a bolt, her face flaming and a hand clutching the sheet up to her neck. She reached for the cup, and as she did so the narrow strap of her nightdress slipped from her shoulder. Pulling her hand back quickly to cover herself she nearly sent the cup flying out of Harry's hand and he stepped back. 'Steady on!'

'I'm sorry.' Mary took the tea and kept her eyes down as she sipped slowly, wishing he would go away and leave her alone. But to her dismay he sat down on the side of the bed.

'About last night, Mary, I'm sorry but I got carried away.' There was no mirth in his laugh. 'Fancy a man getting carried away on his wedding night!'

'It doesn't matter.' Mary refused to meet his eyes. 'We're married and you're entitled to your rights.'

'Oh, I know what I'm entitled to! But I don't want to make love to you just because I'm entitled to!' Harry stood

327

up and dug his hand in the pocket of his dressing gown. 'I'm not going to make any promises because I'm only human. But I'll bother you as little as possible until you come to me of your own free will.' With this he turned on his heels and left the room.

Mary stared at the closed door. 'You'll be waiting a long time if you're waiting for me.' Her mind went back to the time when she'd switched the light out last night. She remembered how tense her body had been when Harry took her in his arms. But he'd been so gentle, and when she'd cried it was because all through the heartache of the last three months she'd had no shoulder to cry on. And last night Harry had provided that shoulder. When the needs of his body took over she hadn't pushed him away because they were married now, and it was expected of her. She didn't want him to make love to her, but if that was the price she had to pay for the sake of her baby, then she would pay it.

Martha understood when Mary couldn't meet her eyes. Hadn't she felt the same when she'd had to face her mother for the first time after her wedding night? So Martha chatted away as though it was an ordinary day and she and Harry got on like a house on fire. It was to Harry she posed the question, 'What about today's dinner? Mary's never cooked a roast dinner in her life.' Harry had the Sunday paper propped up in front of him as he ate his breakfast, and he peered over the top. 'I'll see to the dinner.'

'You will not!' Mary glared. 'I'm quite capable of doing it meself.'

There was doubt on Martha's face but the shrug of Harry's shoulders told her it was best not to interfere. So she went back to her room and her beloved wireless, while Harry set about cleaning out the wash-house and Mary began cooking her first roast dinner.

The roast potatoes looked lovely and golden, the mashed carrot and turnip looked good, and at the side of the plate lay a strip of the lamb Eileen had brought for them yesterday. Martha and Harry exchanged raised eyebrows, while Mary surveyed the plates with pride. She was watching as Martha tried unsuccessfully to cut one of the potatoes. 'Did you remember to par boil these first?' Martha hated having to ask the question and spoil her daughter's happiness, but there was no way anyone could eat the potatoes which were raw inside.

'I didn't think you boiled roast potatoes.' Mary looked downcast. 'I put them in the oven, in hot fat, and turned the oven up high. They were brown in ten minutes.' She glared when her mother and Harry burst out laughing, then it crossed her mind that she hadn't heard her mother laughing so whole heartedly for a long time, and a smile lit up her face. 'OK, Harry! You're so clever, you can do the cooking from now on.'

'I've got a better idea,' Harry spluttered. 'I'll put your mam's chair in the kitchen and she can supervise.'

Martha wiped a tear away. 'Don't worry, lass! I couldn't boil water when I first got married. Everyone has to learn.'

In the afternoon Mary wanted to spend some time sorting the drawers out in the bedroom so she could empty one to make room for Harry's clothes. When they'd moved in, everything had been done in such a rush that things had been stuck anywhere for quickness. She was kneeling on the bedroom floor folding underwear and jumpers when she heard the bell ring, and a few seconds later Harry called her down. Humming softly, she ran down the stairs, and hearing voices from her mother's room her hand reached for the knob. Then she recognised the voice of Father Younger and she froze on the spot, her mind being transported back to when she was a child in the classroom. Even those who hadn't done anything wrong shivered behind their desks when the awesome figure of Father Younger strode down the classroom, his stern eyes running down each line of girls as he walked. And as he stood in front of the class, a giant of a man to the young children who gazed at him with eyes round with apprehension, his voice sounded like thunder in the silent classroom as he asked those who hadn't been to Mass on Sunday to put their hands up. Mary had never been the victim of his acid tongue, but had always felt sorry for those who were. Their punishment was being shamed in front of their classmates, three strokes of the cane, and a letter to take home to their parents. No excuse they gave was good enough for missing Mass.

All these memories flashed through Mary's head before she took several deep breaths and pushed the door open.

'Ah, there you are, Mary.' The priest's eyes bored into hers. 'I came to hear your mother's confession and give her Communion.' His old fashioned black hat, with its round crown and wide brim, was swinging loosely from his fingers. 'And while I'm here, I may as well take the opportunity of talking to you and Mr Sedgemoor.'

With a sense of foreboding, Mary said quietly, 'We'll wait for you in the back room, Father.'

Ten minutes later the priest found Mary and Harry seated next to each other on the couch. His face stern, he sat facing them. His eyes rested for a second on Harry, then moved to Mary. 'I am deeply shocked and disappointed in you, Mary. I thought your faith in God was strong enough to withstand the temptations of the Devil. But you were weak, and yielded to temptation. You have sinned against the Lord and I hope you have repented and prayed for forgiveness.'

As Mary's head dropped, Harry's arm went round her shoulders as though to protect her. 'Mary is my wife now, Father, and . . .' He was silenced as the fierce eyes turned to him. 'I believe you are a Protestant, and your marriage was one of convenience. You used the Church as a convenience, too!'

When he felt Mary shudder, Harry's temper rose. 'I didn't marry for convenience; I have loved Mary all my life. I didn't lie to Father Murphy, and I won't lie to you. It is true that I only agreed to become a convert because Mary wanted to be married in church. But I intend to live up to it and become a practising Catholic. When Mary goes to church, I'll be with her. But what happens in our life, outside of that, is our own business.'

'And my business,' the priest's eyes bored into his, 'is to make sure that the baby Mary is carrying is brought up in a good Catholic home.'

Mary lifted her head, her eyes clear. 'The baby will be brought up in a good Catholic home, Father; I promise you that.'

The fire left the priest's eyes and his shoulders slumped. Suddenly he felt tired. The war had changed people so much. The Church wasn't important to them any more, and every day he saw God's commandments being broken. He feared for the future. 'These days children are sent to Mass but their parents can't be bothered coming themselves. And little ones need to be set a good example.'

'Our child,' Harry gripped Mary's hand, 'will be set a good example. You can depend on that.'

'Whew!' Harry came back after seeing the priest out. 'I felt like a schoolboy again.'

'He's old fashioned, but a good man.' Martha didn't ask questions. 'How about making the tea, lass, and then we can have a game of cards.'

When ten o'clock came Harry had lost again. 'That's another two pounds you owe me,' Mary laughed as she slipped the cards back in the box. 'I'm off to bed. Goodnight and God bless, Mam.' Without looking at Harry she left the room and ran quickly up the stairs. After undressing hurriedly she slipped into bed and when Harry came in his eyebrows shot up. 'You've been quick!'

'I'm dead tired. It was taking me all me time to keep me eyes open.'

Harry took his pyjamas along to the bathroom to get undressed, and when he came back, his clothes draped over his arm, he said, 'I'll buy a bedside lamp tomorrow, so we won't be breaking our necks in the dark.'

After he'd put the light out, Mary heard him bump into the tallboy and grinned when she heard him swear. Then she felt the bed sag under his weight and her body tensed. She waited for him to reach out for her, but the minutes passed and he made no move. 'Goodnight, Harry.'

As she turned on her side she expected to feel his arm come across and turn her round to face him, but instead he moved away from her. 'Goodnight, Mary.'

When she woke, Mary felt warm and comfortable and snug. Then she realised Harry's arm was wrapped round her waist, holding her tight. He was still asleep and she could feel his breath as it wafted softly in her ear. Gently she lifted his arm and slipped out of bed. She could hear her mother moving around so she made a pot of tea and carried it through to the front room. 'Morning, Mam! It's my turn this morning!'

Martha was quick to note her daughter's happy mood. 'Harry still asleep?'

'Yes! I'm taking him a drink up now.'

Mary stood at the side of the bed looking down on Harry. He was sleeping peacefully so she could look at him without feeling shy. He is very handsome, she thought. It's no wonder all the girls fall for him. As though sensing her presence, his eyes flickered into life and he smiled. 'How long have you been up? I didn't feel you getting out of bed.'

'You were too busy snoring.' Mary waited till he sat up before handing him the steaming cup. 'Don't expect to be waited on every day, you know!' She turned to leave the room but he called her back. 'Stay and talk to me for a few minutes.'

'I've got to make the breakfast.' Mary grinned. 'Don't worry . . . I can make toast without burning it.'

'There's no rush.' Harry patted the side of the bed. 'I'm on holiday, don't forget, so we can take things easy.' His eyes looked into hers. 'Did you sleep all right?'

'Like a log! I must have dropped off as soon as my head touched the pillow because I don't remember a thing!'

Lucky you, Harry thought. He'd lain awake for hours after Mary had fallen asleep. His body ached with desire to touch her, and the only way to control that desire was to lie as far away from her as the bed would allow. Even now, just looking at her, he could feel a stirring in his loins. To halt any further thoughts in that direction, he asked, 'D'you feel like coming to the shops with me to get a bedside lamp?'

'Our wedding present's coming today,' Mary reminded him, 'so someone has to stay in. I'm glad they didn't tell us what it is, aren't you? It's more exciting getting a surprise.' She got up from the bed. 'I'll have to get me mam's breakfast or she'll be starving.'

Harry brooded as he drank his tea. If it weren't for the physical side of marriage, Mary would be quite happy to be friends with him. But, damn it, he didn't want a friend! He wanted a wife!

It was twelve o'clock when Martha shouted that there was a furniture van outside, and Harry went to the door with Mary hot on his heels. She pushed him aside to stand in the pathway watching a small man in brown overalls walk to the back of the van where his mate was waiting. Her face was aglow with anticipation, and when she saw the men carefully remove a sheet from the beautiful rocking chair they'd lowered to the ground, she danced with delight.

'Will you let them bring it in?' Harry laughingly pulled her aside. 'Or d'you want to sit in it in the street?'

Mary ran back into their room and pointed to an empty space at the side of the fireplace. 'Will you put it there, please?'

She was surveying the position of the chair with a critical eye when Harry walked the men to the door. But when he came back she was moving the heavy chair to the other side of the room. 'What the hell d'you think you're doing?' he snapped, rushing to take the chair from her. 'You should have more sense than to lift anything heavy in your condition!'

'I only wanted to see what . . .'

'In future, when you want anything lifting, you ask me.' Harry set the chair down. 'And if I'm not here, then just wait till I am! Have you got that?!'

Mary was about to protest when Martha called, 'Don't keep me in suspense! Let's see it!'

Still shaking his head, Harry grunted. 'Let's bring her in.'

Taking an arm each, they supported Martha through to their room. 'Oh, it's beautiful! Can I try it?'

'You can christen it for us.' Harry grinned as they lowered her down and she began to rock gently back and forth. 'It's very comfortable.'

The chair was made of dark wood, and the spindles in the

back and the legs were carved. 'I'll make some cushions for it.' Mary's eyes were bright with pleasure. 'One for the seat and one for the back.'

'Will you tell this daughter of yours that she's not to lug heavy furniture around?' Harry's face was serious. 'She forgets she hasn't only got herself to worry about.'

While Mary looked uncomfortable, Martha nodded in agreement. 'I'll keep me eye on her, don't worry! I won't let her overdo it.'

When Martha was back in her room, Mary sat in the chair. Stroking the polished arms lovingly, she looked up at Harry who was standing near with a smile on his face. 'I'm made up with it!'

'I can see you spending all your time in it and letting the housework go to pot.'

Mary was indignant. 'I will not!'

'Keep your hair on, I was only joking! It'll be nice for you to rock the baby to sleep in.'

'There's a long time to go before the baby comes.' Mary rocked for a few minutes, deep in thought. Then she asked the question that had been at the back of her mind since Harry had asked her to marry him. 'Don't you mind about the baby?'

'I'd be lying if I said I didn't wish it was mine. But it's not the baby's fault, is it, so I'm looking forward to it. I hope it's a boy.'

'You're in for a disappointment then, because it's definitely a girl!'

'In that case I'll have to wait for a son until we have a baby of our own.' When he saw Mary's face change, Harry went on quickly. 'What are you going to call this daughter of yours?'

'Me mam picked the name, but I like it as well. We're going to call her Emma.'

'But if you're wrong, and it's a boy, what are you going to call it?' Licking her lips, Mary lied, 'I haven't thought of a boy's name.'

Harry looked at his watch. 'We've got twenty minutes to get to the shops before they close for lunch. Come on, get moving!'

Mary felt strange walking down the street with Harry holding on to her arm. She couldn't get used to the idea that she was really married to him. And in the shop when he asked the assistant to show his wife some bedside lamps, Mary felt he was talking about someone else. She chose a small lamp with a dark wooden stand and a white shade, and Harry bought some flex and a plug. They were walking the short distance home when he asked, 'How about going to the flicks tonight? The Carlton's only round the corner and we'd only be out for two hours.'

'But what about me . . .'

Harry was ready for the excuse. 'Your mam will be all right! If we go to the first house we'll be home by eight o'clock. Don't forget I'm on holiday, Mary! I won't get the chance to go anywhere next week!'

As soon as the lights dimmed, Harry put his arm round Mary's shoulder and reached for her hand. She let it lie limply in his until the Pathe News came on, then her fingers curled tightly around his. Her head kept turning away from the screen as pictures of fighting and wounded soldiers flashed in the darkness of the cinema. From the war in the Middle East the scene shifted to the Russian front where the Russian soldiers were battling against a German force far superior and better equipped than themselves. Their casualties were heavy and the sight of wounded soldiers, their uniforms in tatters, being helped along by their comrades, brought a sob from Mary. Hearing it, Harry drew her to him, and her head came to rest on his shoulder, her face nestling under his chin. She didn't move until the news ended, then she moved away and sat up straight.

The big picture was a comedy romance with Clark Gable and Myrna Loy. It was very funny and Mary found herself enjoying it until the cameras moved in for a close-up of the two stars kissing. As their lips met on the screen, Mary felt a tingling sensation running down her spine. It was the feeling she always got when Bob's lips touched hers, and it felt so real she could almost feel the pressure of Bob's mouth on hers.

She could no longer follow the plot of the film. Thinking of Bob reminded her of the conversation she'd had with her mother about Mr and Mrs West. If she didn't tell them about the baby, someone else was bound to and they'd be very hurt. She was still wrestling with her conscience when the lights went up and people began to leave their seats. Making her way up the aisle of the cinema, she told herself she'd have to talk to Harry about it that night.

The new bedside lamp was lit and Mary was sitting up in bed when Harry came back from the bathroom. He sensed

Mary had something on her mind, and as he hung his clothes in the wardrobe, he watched her out of the corner of his eye. She was biting on her bottom lip as she plucked at the bedclothes and he told himself she definitely had something on her mind but didn't know how to tell him. He pulled the bedclothes back but made no move to get into bed. 'Come on, out with it, Mary! What's wrong?'

'Nothing!' Mary's voice came out in a high squeak. 'What could be wrong?'

'That's what I'm asking you! There's something on your mind, so get it over with.'

'I haven't got the nerve.'

Harry climbed into bed and put his arm round her. 'Am I so bad that you're frightened of telling me anything?'

Mary's hair swung across her face. 'No.'

'Then how can I help if you won't tell me what's wrong?' He put a hand under her chin and lifted her face till their eyes were on a level. 'If you don't tell me, the worry will only get worse.'

'It's about Bob's mam and dad.'

'What about them?'

'They're sure to find out about the baby and they'll think I'm terrible for not telling them! I was wondering whether I should write and let them know.'

Harry's arm dropped from her shoulder. 'What good would that do?'

'Harry, Bob was their only son! I was courting him for six years, so don't you think they have a right to know?'

'What about my rights, Mary? Or don't I have any rights? You're my wife, and I'm willing to treat the baby as my own.' Harry's voice was thick with emotion. 'You can't expect me to welcome the Wests to my home when the mother of their grandchild is my wife! And while we're on about it, what about my mam and dad? Are you going to tell the baby that I'm not its real father, and my parents are not its grandparents?'

A sob left Mary's mouth. Harry was right! She'd made a mess of her own life, and now she was trying to make a mess of his. 'I'm sorry,' she gulped. 'I'm no good to anyone!'

Harry moaned as he took her in his arms. 'I love you, Mary, and I'll move heaven and earth to make you happy. But don't expect me to live in Bob's shadow for the rest of my life.'

Hearing the pain in his voice, Mary was filled with pity. 'I could write to tell them, but say I'm married now and can't ask them here.'

Mary never knew whether the tears running down her cheeks were her own or Harry's. He was holding her close, kissing her face, and she cried inwardly. He's so good, why can't I feel anything for him?

When Mary mentioned the Wests' name, Harry felt as though he'd been dealt a body blow. If they came back into her life she'd never forget Bob and his memory would always be between them, a threat to the happiness Harry was hoping for. Given time, he was sure Mary would come to care for him, but not if Bob's memory was kept alive.

Pulling her closer, he vowed that no one would come between them. She was his now, and he wasn't going to share her with anyone . . . not even a memory. 'Come on, love, lie down.' He pressed her back until her head was on the pillow. She was cradled in his arms and the light from the lamp showed her face blotched with tear stains. But this seemed to enhance her beauty and Harry was filled with a fierce jealousy. For years he'd dreamed of Mary from afar, never thinking there was the remotest chance she would one day be his. Now she was, and by God no one was going to part them! 'Go to sleep now, love; we can talk in the morning.' He leaned over and switched the lamp off before tucking the bedclothes in at the side. Then he wrapped both arms tightly round her. 'Goodnight, love.'

Mary dropped off to sleep quickly, like a child, in the warmth and security of his arms. But Harry was too full of emotion to sleep. Lying perfectly still in case he disturbed her, his mind went over what he would say to her in the morning. Should he forbid her to make any contact with the Wests, or should he say she could write, but she must make it plain that they couldn't visit her?

Harry rested a hand on Mary's tummy and felt his heartbeats quicken. There was a baby growing in there, and if she was right, and it was a baby girl, would it be beautiful, like her? He didn't feel any resentment, because if it wasn't for the baby he might never have stood a chance with Mary. He could feel the warmth of her body through the nightdress as his hand moved in a circle over her tummy, and it felt so good. If only she returned his feelings they could be so happy together.

Martha sensed the slight tension between Mary and Harry, and it saddened her. But what could she do? They'd been all right before they'd gone to bed last night, so whatever went wrong between them happened in bed. Sometimes her daughter acted so childishly Martha felt like giving her a good shake. They'd had their lunch and Mary was in her mother's room when Harry popped his head round the door. 'D'you feel like coming to me mam's with me, to thank them for the present? We could call at Vera's, and the Smiths, while we're down there.'

Mary paled at the thought of going back to their old street again. 'I've got some washing to do. You go on your own.'

Harry shrugged his shoulders in a gesture of helplessness. 'OK. I'll see you later.'

Martha waited for the bang of the front door before asking, 'What's the matter, lass? You two had a quarrel?'

'We had a few words over me telling the Wests, that's all!'

'You're being unfair, you know! Harry's doing his best, but you won't even try! Every marriage has its ups and downs, but you've got to pull together and give and take! The trouble is, you won't give!'

'Just leave it, Mam! I don't want to talk about it.'

Eileen called in on her way home from work and she couldn't wait to sit down in Martha's room before reaching into her bag. 'Wait till yer see what I've got for yer.' She passed a small, tissue-wrapped parcel over to Mary with the warning, 'Be careful, they're precious.'

While Martha watched with interest, Mary slowly unfolded the tissue paper.

'A pair of stockings!' The puzzled expression on Mary's

face turned to joy. 'Where did you manage to get these from?'

'Not just a pair of stockings, yer ignorant nit! Pure silk stockings, no less!' Eileen puffed her chest out, then had the grace to look guilty. 'I got them off Jean Simpson.' She held up her hand. 'I know! I'm a polished bugger! I call the woman for everything and now I'm taking things off her! Well I still think she's a stupid cow, but I've got to admit she's not mean. And that Yankee boyfriend of hers comes in handy, I can tell yez! He keeps me kids goin' in chewing gum, and he gave her those stockings for me.'

Mary held up the gossamer-like hose. 'I've never had a pair of pure silk stockings, even before the war. They're beautiful; but I couldn't take them. It's very kind of you, Eileen, but Jean meant you to have them for yourself.'

Eileen's guffaw filled the room. 'Can yer imagine my fat legs in them! And with my nails, they'd be laddered the first time I put them on! No, kid, I want you to have them. You've got the legs for them.'

'I'll save them for special occasions, then.' Mary folded the tissue carefully. 'Have you got time for a cuppa?'

Eileen nodded as she pressed her hands on the couch to lever herself up. 'I want to see the chair, too!' She followed Mary into the back room. 'D'yer like it, kid?'

'It's beautiful!' Mary touched her friend's arm. 'You're very good to us, Eileen; I sometimes wonder what we'd do without you.'

'Oh, go way with yer, kid!' Eileen blushed with embarrassment. 'Anyway, where's the 'appy bridegroom? He hasn't gone home to his mammy already, has he?'

Mary nodded. 'He's gone to thank them for the chair.'

There was a wicked glint in Eileen's eyes. 'I've been expecting him to come knocking on me door, but he must be gettin' all he needs here!'

Mary turned her head without answering, so Eileen persisted. 'How are things on the bedroom front, kid?'

'You'd better ask Harry! I wouldn't know!'

'As he's not here to ask, I'll have to ask you, won't I?'

Mary's head jerked round. 'I told you to ask Harry!'

Eileen pursed her lips. 'Mmmmm! Perhaps he will be knockin' on me door one of these nights.'

'You're welcome!'

'All right, kid! Don't get out of yer pram, I'll pick yer dummy up!' Eileen's smile disappeared. 'I was only kiddin', but you're not, are yer? I don't know what's happened between the two of yez, but I don't think yer should be talking about him like that! The trouble with you is, yer don't know a good feller when yer see one! Yer've built a brick wall between yez, and the sooner yer knock it down the better! Yer might even find yer like what's on the other side.'

'You're right; and me mam's right!' The anger drained from Mary's face. 'I don't know what's wrong with me, but I can't bring myself to like him in that way and I'm getting bad tempered and taking it out on him.'

'If yer don't make an effort, kid, then life's going to be hell for the both of yez! Men aren't like women, yer know; they need sex far more than a woman does. An' as yer've only been married a few days yer can't expect Harry to behave like a flippin' monk!' Eileen gave a loud sigh of exasperation. 'I could understand it if he was a repulsive little sod, but he's a smashing looking feller! Yer don't know how lucky yer are!'

'Is it dangerous to have intercourse when you're expecting a baby?' Mary's question sent Eileen's eyebrows shooting upwards. She suppressed a giggle as she asked herself how any woman of twenty-two could be so ignorant of the facts of life. 'It won't harm the baby, if that's what you mean. When you get to eight months yer tummy might get in the way, but it won't hurt the baby.' She couldn't keep her face straight any longer. 'D'yer know what the height of aggravation is, kid? Well, it's a man tryin' to make love to his eight-month pregnant wife.' She grinned as she patted Mary's arm. 'Or it could be a fat man, trying to make love to someone with a belly as big as mine! We'd both die of frustration!

'Anyway, I'm sorry I can't give yer an excuse for not giving Harry what he wants, but me invitation still stands. He can bang on my door any time he likes.' Playing with a loose button on her coat, she eyed her friend. 'Can I give yer a bit of advice, kid? When Harry comes home, welcome him with a smile on yer face, will yer? When I walked in yer had a right miserable gob on yer, and if he comes home to that, he might just be sorry he didn't stay at his mam's!'

Mary was rocking to and fro in the chair and Eileen thought she'd never seen her looking as lovely. 'Yer startin' to show, yer know, kid, and it suits yer! The chair suits yer, too! Yer'll have the time of yer life feedin' the baby in that!'

They heard the key turn in the lock and seconds later Harry walked in. His face lit up when he saw Eileen. 'I was wondering when we'd see you, to thank you for the present.' He looked across at Mary, and making up his mind quickly, stepped over and planted a kiss on her cheek. 'Hello, love.'

Mary could feel her friend's eyes on her. 'How were your mam and dad?'

'Me dad was at work, but Mam's fine and sends her regards. I saw Vera and Elsie Smith, and they're pleased you like their present.'

'I've just been sayin' she'll look great in that chair when she's feeding the baby.'

'Not the baby, Eileen!' Harry tutted. 'Our Emma!'

'Ooops! Pardon me! I forgot Mary had put her order in.'

Mary stopped rocking. 'Eileen's just given me a nice surprise. A pair of pure silk stockings. Aren't I lucky?'

'I've got another surprise for you. Me mam's making you some cot sheets and blankets, and me dad's making you a cot.' Harry watched Mary's face closely. Her reaction meant a lot to him. It would tell him if she was going to let his parents be part of the baby's life, or was she going to shut everybody out, including himself? When a smile appeared he let his breath out slowly. 'Oh, that's great! I only need a pram now, and I can look around for a good second-hand one.'

'You'll do no such thing!' Harry roared. 'You'll get a new one; and a good one, at that! It'll come in for the next baby.'

Eileen chuckled when she saw the look on Mary's face. 'How many d'yer intend having, Harry? An even dozen?'

Although answering Eileen's question, Harry's eyes

were locked with Mary's as he said, slowly and deter-
minedly, 'As many as it takes to get a son.'

Mary looked so flabbergasted Eileen hugged herself with
silent laughter. Oh, she wouldn't have missed this for
anything. It was time someone gave her friend a kick up the
backside. 'Don't say yer haven't been warned, kid! Now
yer know what yer in for!'

'I might just have something to say about that.' Mary's
voice was quiet, but just as determined as Harry's.

Chapter Twenty-Three

'Hey! Get that thing out of here!' Eileen stood menacingly in front of her two daughters who were stroking a tiny kitten seated between them on the couch. 'If it piddles on that couch I'll 'ave yer guts for garters.'

'Ah, ray, Mam!' Joan cried. 'Our Billy found it in the entry, an' he said it was lost. It's only a baby, Mam!'

'It must belong to someone! An' I've got enough troubles without having a moggy to worry about. Now get it out of here, pronto, before it stinks the house down.'

'Can we play on the step with it!' Edna pleaded. 'We won't let it come in the 'ouse, I promise.' She picked up the little bundle of black and white fur and held it to her cheek. 'It's only a baby, an' it's lovely.'

'Aye, they're all lovely when they're babies . . . just like you two were, and look at yez now! Out with it . . . quick!' The two girls pulled at the kitten, each wanting to hold it. Then they compromised and carried it between them as they flew down the hall. Eileen grinned as she wiped the sweat off her forehead with the back of her hand. She'd been mangling some sheets and turning the handle of the old mangle was hard work. Her dress was sodden with perspiration and she could feel rivulets of it running between her breasts. 'Why wasn't I born rich instead of beautiful?' she asked the mirror on the wall, which had a pre-war snap of Bill stuck in the corner of the wooden frame. 'I could 'ave had maids doin' all me work, while me and me mam sat drinking tea all day. The kids would be at boarding school, of course.' Eileen often held little conversations with herself, and didn't worry if anyone came in and caught her at it. She would say, laughing, 'If I talk to meself, there's no one to answer me back and I win all the arguments. Anyway, I can't think of anyone better to talk to.'

'Whew!' She picked up an old newspaper and fanned her face. 'I don't know whether it's me weight, or the change of life, but that bloody mangle gets harder every week!' Hearing the girls' shrieks of laughter, she made her way down the hall. They were sitting on the pavement dangling a piece of string over the kitten's head and every time the tiny paw shot out to swipe at the string they screamed with delight. Eileen watched them for a while, a smile on her face, then turned her head to look down the street. The debris had been cleared from the site, but the empty space where the three houses had been pulled down after the bombing was a constant reminder of the night Eileen still had nightmares about.

'Ah, well, standin' here won't get the tea made.' She wagged a finger. 'Don't forget, you two ... no cat!'

She walked back into the house and was setting the table

when she heard a woman's voice, loud and shrill. At first she thought it was a couple of the neighbours having a row, but then she heard Edna cry out and she was down the hall like a dose of greased lightning.

'What's goin' on here?' When Eileen saw the woman's hand on Edna's shoulder she nearly fell down the steps. 'Get yer hands off her, Cissie Maddox.' Her push caught the woman by surprise and she stumbled to regain her balance before facing Eileen.

'That's our kitten she's got, Eileen Gillmoss, an' I want it back, right now!' Her face crimson, and nostrils flared, Cissie Maddox glared. 'It's only four weeks old and shouldn't be out of the 'ouse, yet.'

'Then yer shouldn't 'ave let it out of the house, should yer?' Eileen mimicked Cissie's voice. 'Don't come blaming us if yer can't keep yer bloody cat from gettin' out!'

'It didn't get out!' Roughly the same size and age as Eileen, Cissie squared up to her without fear. 'Your Billy came into our 'ouse and took it out!'

'He didn't!' Young Edna cried in protest. 'He found it in the entry.'

'Did he hells bells like! Our Sammy brought him in to show him the litter, an' he walked out with that one as bold as brass.'

Dear God! He's done it again, Eileen sighed. That little bugger will be the death of me. 'OK, Cissie; I'm sorry! Give Mrs Maddox the kitten, Joan.' When the two girls cowered back, the cause of the trouble hidden behind them, Eileen bent down. 'It doesn't belong to us, and yez can't have it.'

She grabbed the struggling kitten by the back of its neck and handed it to Cissie. 'I'll tell him off when he gets in.'

'Fat lot of good that'll do! It's more than a tellin' off he wants, an' I've a good mind to give him a smack meself, for what he's done.'

'If there's any smackin' to be done around here, I'll do it! You lay a finger on our Billy, Cissie Maddox, an' I'll knock yer into the middle of next week.' Eileen's shoulders slumped. 'God strewth, Cissie! Has no one told yer there's a bloody war on?! There's people being killed all over the place, and all you can think about is a bloody moggy! It's a pity yer've nothin' better to worry about!'

The anger was fading from Cissie's face, but she wasn't ready to give in yet. 'Your Billy 'ad no right!'

'I know he didn't, an' I'll give him the back of me hand when he gets in.' Eileen looked down on the two weeping girls. 'It's no good you two bawlin' yer heads off! Yez can't have the kitten, an' that's all there is to it!'

It was the look on the girls' faces that finally melted Cissie's heart. 'If yer like, yer can have it when it's old enough to feed itself.'

The two girls scrambled to their feet, eyes and noses running unchecked, and pulled their mother's skirt. 'Say we can 'ave it, please, mam!'

That's all me mam needs, Eileen groaned inwardly. As though she hasn't got enough to worry about without a cat piddling all over the place. 'I'm . . .' the words died on her lips as she looked into the hopeful eyes pleading with her. She didn't have the heart to disappoint them. But there was a couple of weeks to go yet, and with a bit of luck they would have forgotten about it by then. 'We'll see.' She patted each of them on the head. 'Now go inside, like good girls, and wipe yer dirty noses. I'll be in in a minute to make the tea, but first I want to find our Billy.'

'Let me know if yer want it.' Cissie was anxious now to make friends. 'Most of the litter are spoken for.'

'I don't think we'll be bothering, Cissie.' The folds of flesh started to move upwards to cover Eileen's eyes as she grinned. 'Me mam's got three monkeys to look after as it is, and I don't think she'd appreciate an addition to the menagerie.'

Cissie was looked past Eileen to the man crossing the road. Being short sighted, her eyes screwed up as she tried to see if it was anyone she knew.

'Isn't this Bob West? I haven't seen him round here for ages.'

Eileen whipped round, the smile gone. Oh, God! She'd been dreading this. What was she going to tell him about Mary? And what had other people told him? She watched Bob West draw nearer, then turned to Cissie. She could see curiosity in the woman's eyes and she knew she was hoping for some tit-bit of gossip. Like everyone else in the neighbourhood, she was wondering why Mary Bradshaw had married Harry Sedgemoor so soon after young Bob was killed.

'I'll see yer, Cissie!' Eileen's grip was like steel as she turned the woman to face her own house. 'I won't forget to chastise our Billy.'

* * *

'How are yer, Mr West? And how's Mrs West?'

Bob's dad sat on the couch, his fingers running nervously along the peak of the cap he was twisting round in his hand. He nodded a few times before looking up. 'I called at Mary's, and a strange woman answered the door and said the Bradshaws had moved.' His eyes searched Eileen's face. 'Then I knocked at the Jacksons', and Vera told me Mary was married! It knocked me for six, I can tell you! I couldn't believe me ears!'

'Yeah; it was a surprise to everyone.' Eileen blinked rapidly as she made a play of straightening the oilcloth on the table. 'Yer know Harry Sedgemoor, don't yer?'

'Yes, I know Harry! But what I want to know is, why? How could she do such a thing?'

'She must have had her reasons, Mr West! It's between her and Harry, an' they must know what they're doin'!'

'But she was so crazy about our Bob! How could she change so quickly?!'

'Mary's had a lot of trouble an' I suppose she's had to change, to survive.'

'I can understand that! And I didn't expect her to stay single for the rest of her life! But to marry so soon!' He looked hurt and bewildered. 'I just can't take it in.'

'Look, why don't I put the kettle on, and we can have a cuppa while we're talkin'.' Eileen escaped to the kitchen, her heart beating fifteen to the dozen. She heard the girls playing hopscotch in the yard, and after striking a match under the kettle she opened the kitchen door and warned them to stay out there until she called them. Thank God her mam had gone to a matinee, because she'd never get through this with her mam's knowing eyes on her.

He's going to ask me, I know he is! Eileen's head throbbed as she scooped tea from the old tin caddy. And what do I tell him when he does ask? Dear God, what do I tell him? No matter what I say, someone is going to get hurt.

'Here we are then.' Eileen carried a cup in each hand and passed one over. 'I don't need to ask if yer take sugar, 'cos we've got none.'

Bob watched the tea leaves swirling round on the top of the tea, then looked straight into Eileen's eyes. 'I've got to get it off me chest! There's only one reason why Mary would marry in such a hurry. Is she pregnant?'

Eileen's face turned white as she gasped. She'd been expecting him to probe, but hadn't anticipated him being so blunt. 'Mary pregnant? Oh, I couldn't tell yer that, Mr West! She's been married a few weeks now, so she could be.'

'I still can't believe it! How could she forget our Bob so soon?'

'It's none of my business, but I think Mary got married for practical reasons.' At least she could say that truthfully. 'With her mam the way she is, Mary would never have been able to manage on her own. I think she saw it as a way out of her troubles, an' Harry's been sweet on her for years. He's a good bloke, an' he'll make her a good husband.'

'I know Harry Sedgemoor, and he's the salt of the earth.' Bob shook his head as though it was too much for him to understand. 'But it's not much of a foundation for a happy marriage, is it? It's the last thing I expected to hear when I came today, and I know Lily will be upset.'

'Yer still haven't told me how Mrs West is?'

'She's picking up, but very slowly. We've decided to stay in Preston because there's too many memories for her round here. I've got a decent job, and we've got the chance of a nice little house. That's what I came here for today. To ask Mary if she'd like to come up one day, and see Lily.'

'What are yer goin' to do now, then?'

'I don't know what to do.' The sigh came from deep within him. 'What do you think?'

Eileen folded her arms and hitched her bust up. Her heart was crying for the broken man sitting opposite her, but what could she do? 'It's up to you; but don't you think it would be best to let Mary get on with her new life? Seeing you would bring it all back again, an' it wouldn't be fair on Harry.'

'You're right!' Bob pressed on his knees and stood up. 'Will you tell her you saw me, and wish her all the best?'

Oh, God, I'm going to cry! Eileen pinched hard on the end of her nose to keep the tears back. 'I'll tell 'er, Mr West. And you look after yerself, and Mrs West, d'yer hear?'

Bob pulled the checkered cap down over his eyes. 'I still can't take it in! It's been so sudden! But when me and Lily get used to the idea, we'll probably be glad for Mary. She deserves some happiness.'

The thought flitted through Eileen's head that she was beginning to wonder whether she'd ever see Mary really happy again.

* * *

When Maggie got home from the matinee she found Eileen slumped over the table, her hands covering her face and her shoulders shaking with sobs. Fear shot through Maggie, and she clung to the door frame for support. 'What's wrong? What's happened?'

Eileen raised her stricken face, and the sight of her mother brought forth a fresh flow of tears. Wiping her nose on the back of her hand, she gulped. 'Bob West's been here. He's just gone.'

Relief flooded through Maggie, leaving her weak. 'Thank God! I thought something terrible had happened.'

'And you think that Mr West findin' out about Mary being married isn't terrible? An' me lying me bloody head off to him . . . isn't that terrible?'

Why is it that this daughter of mine gets everyone's troubles? Maggie asked herself wearily as she pulled a chair out and sat down. Because she looks tough, people think she's got no feelings. If only they knew how soft hearted she really is. 'Tell me what happened.'

In between sobs and blowing her nose, Eileen related the whole scene. 'I felt lousy, tellin' him lies! But what else could I do?'

'Nothing!' Maggie said firmly. 'You did the only thing possible. If you'd told the truth, it would have been the end of Mary and Harry's marriage.'

'But he looked so awful,' Eileen sobbed. 'Him and Mrs West have got nothing left in life. Knowin' they had a grandchild would give them something to live for.'

'Martha's told you how Harry feels about bringing the Wests back into Mary's life, and I can't say I blame him. It just wouldn't work out, Eileen, and you must see that for yourself! To tell them they had a grandchild they couldn't see would be cruel. They'd be tormented for the rest of their days.' Maggie patted the dimpled elbow. 'No, love; you did what was best for everyone.'

Eileen sniffed. 'I know that, Mam, but I felt lousy all the same.' She managed a weak grin. 'The trouble with me is, I like everything to have a happy ending.'

'Aye; well life doesn't always work out that way! The picture I've just been to see didn't have a happy ending, either.'

Eileen bent her head to wipe her eyes on the skirt of her dress. 'Yer'd have had more excitement stayin' at home! Me and Cissie Maddox had a stand up fight in the street.'

'You didn't!' Maggie gasped. 'I don't know what's come over you, I really don't. There's nothing so common as two women fighting.' Her tongue clicked loudly as she glared at her daughter. 'In the street, too!'

Her eyes sliding sideways, Eileen looked through half-closed lids. 'I'd given her one black eye, and I'd have given her another, but Mr West came along an' put a stop to it.'

'Oh, my God!' Maggie's head moved like a mechanical toy. 'What must the neighbours be thinking?'

'They were all out in the street, cheering us on.' Eileen's hand covered her nose and mouth, and her voice was muffled. 'Yer'd have enjoyed it, Mam.'

'Enjoyed it!' Maggie was on her high horse, filled with indignation. 'I'll never be able to lift me head up in the street again. We'll be the laughing stock of . . .' she suddenly realised that the tears rolling down Eileen's cheeks were tears of laughter, and as the truth dawned, her body sagged.

'You're pulling me leg!'

The chair creaked under the weight of Eileen's laughter. 'Yer fell for it, Mam! Hook, line and bloody sinker, yer fell for it!'

'I could wring your neck for that! You nearly gave me a heart attack!'

'Go way with yer! Yer've got a heart as strong as an ox.' Eileen pinched at the fat on her arms. 'Anyway, Mam, takin' the mickey out of you has cheered me up.'

'What made you make up a story like that? And why on earth did you pick on Cissie Maddox?'

'I didn't make it all up.' Eileen chuckled. 'I'm not that clever! Me and Cissie did have a few words, but it never came to blows.'

'But what caused the argument?'

'Well, yer see, Mam, there was this little black and white kitten . . .'

Maggie huffed as she pushed her chair back. 'Oh, you're not catching me out again! I've fallen for one of your tall stories, and that's enough for one day.'

'I'm only tryin' to tell you about the kitten.'

'Aye, and you'll be telling me about the man in the moon, next! Try pulling the other one . . . it's got bells on!' Maggie stood up and slipped her coat off. 'Let's get the tea started.'

A cheeky smile crossed Eileen's face as her mother disappeared into the kitchen. Under her breath she whispered, 'Well, in two weeks' time yer still won't believe the story about the man in the moon, but I'll bet yer half-a-crown yer'll believe the one about the little black and white kitten! I'm not sayin' yer'll like it, but yer sure as hell will believe it!'

Chapter Twenty-Four

'We must have been bloody stupid when you come to think of it.' Harry was leaning towards the fire, his hands spread out to the warmth. They couldn't afford to keep two fires going on the small coal ration they got, so he and Mary spent most of their time in Martha's room. 'We knew for years that Hitler was building up his Army and making planes and tanks, but we turned a blind eye. Now we're paying for it. Our lads are being pushed back on all fronts, ill equipped and outnumbered. It makes my blood boil, honest! And the Russians are the same, too! They're fighting with bare hands most of the time. We saw them on the news the other night, fighting in freezing snow and ice, with thin uniforms on and most of them had no soles to their shoes. Many of them were suffering from frost bite.'

'It's terrible.' The only time Martha heard any war news was when Mary was out at the shops and she and Harry could talk freely. Her daughter wouldn't let her listen to the news on the wireless, and she refused point blank to discuss the war at all. 'But at least we're not having air raids every night, like the May blitz.'

'London is! They get a hammering nearly every night!

But I suppose Hitler thinks if he can flatten London, we'll all collapse.' Harry rubbed his hands together then held them out to the flames again. 'Our fighter pilots are holding their own though, thank God! The Germans are losing a lot of planes.'

'We heard planes going over yesterday while you were at work. I never said anything to Mary, but I kept expecting the air-raid siren to go.'

'Oh, I saw them! When we heard the planes, me and one of the foremen ran out to see what was going on. There was one German plane, and it was being chased by two of ours. It was probably only a reconnaissance plane, come to spy out the land, and that's why the sirens didn't go.' The cleft in Harry's chin deepened and his eyes glowed. 'You should have seen those planes of ours; you'd have been proud of them. They dived and they climbed, then they circled the German plane as though they were playing games with it. In fact, there were a group of us watching and we all started clapping. There wasn't one of us who wouldn't have changed places with those pilots so we could have had a go at that German.'

'Your job is just as important! If there was no one to make the munitions, our soldiers would have nothing to fight with.'

'Aye, well, the way things are going the Army might have to start calling men like me up. I'm not a cripple, and I could hold a ruddy gun!' Harry watched the sparks from the fire for a few seconds, his face thoughtful, before turning to Martha. 'If the siren did go, you would get under the stairs right away, wouldn't you?'

'We'd be pushing each other out of the way to get in first, don't worry.'

But Martha knew Harry did worry about them not having an air-raid shelter. Particularly with her being the way she was, and not able to get to a public one. She also knew how guilty he felt about not being in the forces and fighting for his country; and every night she prayed the war would be over before they started calling up men like Harry.

Two days later, on December 7th, Harry was bristling with excitement when he came in off the morning shift. Without taking his coat off or giving Mary her usual kiss, he crossed to the wireless. 'Have you had this on?'

Martha shook her head. 'No, why?'

'Sssh! Listen!'

The commentator's voice filled the room as Harry turned the volume up, telling them that the Japanese fleet had, without warning, attacked Pearl Harbor. The unsuspecting Americans had been caught unawares, and all the ships in the port had been sunk, buildings blown up and hundreds of lives lost.

'Oh, my God!' Martha gasped. 'The Japanese aren't at war with America, are they?'

'That's what makes it so bad.' Harry ground his teeth together. 'They gave no warning at all!'

'What did they do that for, if they're not at war?' Mary asked.

'They will be at war!' Harry unbuttoned his coat. 'The Yanks are not going to take this lying down.'

Harry was right. The next day, reeling from the attack, the Americans declared war on Japan. Three days later, they declared war on Germany and her allies. Britain and the Commonwealth were no longer on their own in the fight against Hitler and his strutting side-kick, Mussolini.

The week before Christmas, Mary opened the door to find Eileen red in the face with exertion, and laden down with bags and parcels. 'Let's get in, kid, before me arms fall off.' She let Mary walk ahead of her, then leaning against the wall for support and balancing on one leg, she kicked the door closed.

'What have you got in there?' Mary watched Eileen dump the parcels on the floor in Martha's room. 'You look as though you've bought Woolies out.'

'Hello, Mrs B.' Eileen flopped down on the chair. 'Am I glad to get rid of those!' She held out her plump hand to show the angry red weals made by the thin handles of the shopping bags. 'I'd rather do a day's work than go through that again. Me arms are six inches longer than they were this morning.'

Mary nodded to the parcels. 'What's in them?'

'I got me Tontine and Christmas club out, so I bought all the kids presents. I wondered if I could leave them here till Christmas eve, 'cos there's nowhere safe in our house. Young Billy knows all me hiding specks.'

Mary clapped her hands like a little girl. 'I'll let you leave them here if you let's see what you've got.'

Eileen tipped one of the bigger bags out on to the floor and passed a couple of boxed games over to Martha. 'It's hard to know what to get to fill their stockings 'cos there's not much in the shops. And kids don't understand when yer tell them there's a war on.'

'You seem to have enough there to fill coal sacks, never mind stockings.' Martha held up a box of Tiddly Winks. 'I remember getting a box of these when I was a kid.'

'And that was only last year, wasn't it?' Eileen laughed as she returned the toys to the bag. 'There'll be another one to buy for next year, won't there?' She eyed Mary up and down. 'You look blooming, kid.'

Mary, in her seventh month of pregnancy, was enormous. But it suited her and she looked lovelier than ever. Patting her swollen tummy, she smiled. 'The size of me, I think I must be having triplets.'

'It'll be lovely next year, won't it?' Martha said. 'A baby in the house makes all the difference at Christmas.'

'It's better for me now than it is at Christmas,' Eileen informed them. 'I can frighten them into doing as they're told, by telling them they won't get anything off Father Christmas if they're naughty. Once they've got their presents I've had it!' The chair creaked ominously before her laughter ricocheted round the room. 'Our Billy told the girls there was no such person as Father Christmas and he had them crying their eyes out. So I said to him, "Well, if yer don't believe in Father Christmas, yer won't be expecting any presents from him, will yer?" Yer should've seen his face! His eyes went all innocent like, and he said he was only pulling their legs. They must be daft, he said, because everybody knows there's a Father Christmas.'

'Poor Billy,' Mary laughed. 'He can't win, can he?'

'Don't you worry about our Billy! There's not many get the better of him, I can tell yer.' Eileen settled back on the chair. 'Mind you, he won't have things all his own way when our Edna gets a bit older. Since she learned to cock her leg over the ball there's no holding her back. The latest craze is singing, "One Two Three, me mother caught a flea, She put it in the tea pot to make a cup of tea, the flea jumped out, me mother gave a shout, and in came a bobby with his shirt hanging out."' Eileen sang in the high squeaky voice of her youngest daughter. 'Yer should see our Billy move when she starts singin' that, cos' every time she comes to the part about the bobby's shirt hanging out, she pulls our Billy's shirt out of his kecks.'

Martha was looking at Eileen with real affection. They had been blessed with having her for a friend. 'It's a wonder you can still laugh.'

'That's not laughter, Mrs B! It's bloody hysterics!' Eileen's nose twitched. 'There's that smell again! I could smell it when I came in . . . it's like carbolic.'

'It is soap you can smell, but it's not all carbolic.' Mary looked pleased with herself. 'Doris next door told me to save all the little bits of soap that get too small to use, and she showed me how to heat them all together in a pan till they melt. When it cools off, you can mould them into big blocks. It doesn't half help, with soap being so scarce.'

Eileen winked at Martha as she jerked her thumb at Mary. 'Gettin' to be a proper little housewife, isn't she?'

'Oh, that's not all!' Martha told her proudly. 'Doris helped her unpick one of her old woollen jumpers, and the two of them are using the old wool to make matinee coats.'

'Yer lucky having the Aldersons for neighbours.'

Mary nodded. 'They're great! Doris calls in every morning to see if I want anything from the shops, and her and Jim come in every Sunday night for a game of cards.'

'I'm glad yer've got someone to turn to if yer ever need any help.' Eileen looked from one to the other. 'Now for my bit of news, then I'll have to be off. First, I've had another letter from Bill. At least it would be a letter if the bloody censors would leave it alone.' She huffed. 'Still, at least I know he's alive and that's better than nothing. Anyway, that's my bit of news, so now on to our Rene. Yez know Alan was fitted with an artificial arm, don't yez?' She waited for their nods. 'Well, they're keeping him in the Army an' he's over the moon. They're giving him a desk job at the Ministry of Defence, and he'll be stationed in Liverpool.' Appreciating the rapt expressions on the faces of her audience, Eileen asked. 'D'yez want to know the best news I've had since the war started? Our Rene's pregnant!'

Simultaneously came the cries. 'Isn't that marvellous' and 'Oh, I'm so glad for them.'

'So that's two extra pressies to buy next year! I'll have to ask your feller for some overtime.' As she stood up, Eileen eyed the bags on the floor. 'Are yer sure they'll be all right here?'

'Positive! Harry can take them up to the little room when he comes in. They won't be in the way, 'cos there's nothing in that room yet.'

'Won't be long now, kid! Wait till our Emma has yez awake all night, crying for a feed.'

'When I put the order in for a girl, I asked for one that didn't cry.' Mary put her thumb to her nose and wriggled her fingers. 'So there!'

'Merry Christmas!'

Mary's eyelids flickered, then lay still, her long black lashes fanning her cheeks. She looked so peaceful Harry felt reluctant to wake her. But Martha was waiting downstairs, eager to open her Christmas present. Leaning over the sleeping figure, Harry whispered, 'Merry Christmas, lazy bones.'

As Mary turned her head her eyes flew open and Harry found himself looking into the vivid blue pools. A familiar thrill ran down his spine and he felt the urge to gather her into his arms. But he knew the response wouldn't match his own for warmth. 'Aren't you going to wish me a Merry Christmas?'

Mary struggled to sit up, her knuckles rubbing the sleep from her eyes. She glanced at the clock which told her it was half past eight. 'I must have been out like a light! What time did you get up?'

'About seven.'

'Is me mam awake?'

'She's like a child down there.' Harry laughed. 'Waiting to see what Santa Claus has brought her. I've made a pot of tea and a plate of toast, so hurry before it gets cold.'

Mary slipped her legs over the side of the bed. 'Just give me two minutes, then I'll be down.' As Harry reached the door, she called, 'You haven't said anything to her, have you?'

'Now as though I'd say anything without you being there!'

Mary was wide awake now. 'I'm dying to see her face.'

'Well, get a move on!'

Harry was waiting at the bottom of the stairs. 'Shall we take it in now,' he whispered, 'or d'you want to open the other presents first?'

'I'll go in, and when I shout, you bring it in.' Mary sniffed. 'What's the smell?'

'I put the turkey in the oven at half past seven, and I've peeled the veg and potatoes. So we've got a couple of hours to spare.' Harry chuckled as he put an arm round her shoulder. 'What are we whispering for?' He raised his voice. 'Me mam and dad aren't coming till two o'clock, so we've plenty of time.'

'You get ready for when I shout.' Mary pushed open the door of her mother's room. 'Merry Christmas, Mam.'

'Merry Christmas, lass!' Martha pointed to the small tree where fairy lights were twinkling. 'Doesn't the tree look lovely?'

'Yes, it looks all Christmassy in here.' Mary's tummy was rumbling with excitement. 'Are you coming in, Harry, so we can open our presents?'

When the door was pushed open, all they could see at first was Harry's back. Then as he got in the room and turned round, Mary's eyes went to her mother's face. 'Merry Christmas, Mam.'

Martha was staring at the rocking chair Harry had placed on the floor. She opened her mouth, but no words would come out. 'Don't you like it, Mam?'

Martha's eyes were brimming with tears. 'I don't know what to say, lass!'

'I can always take it back if you don't like it, Mrs B,' Harry joked. 'Me and Mary didn't know whether to buy you this or a box of hankies.'

Martha was wiping her eyes as she stared at the chair. It was as big as the one in the other room but was made of lighter wood and the carving was different. 'It's beautiful! But you shouldn't have spent so much money on me.'

'Only the best is good enough for the best mother-in-law in the whole wide world. You deserve it.'

'Let me try it.' Martha reached for the crutches leaning against the wall, but Mary held her back. 'Hang on a minute, Mam, till Harry moves your chair out of the way first.'

With cushions at her back, and tears in her eyes, Martha rocked back and forth. 'It's the best Christmas present I've ever had.'

'Can we open our presents now?' Mary went to the tree and picked up the parcels lying beneath it. After picking out the ones for Harry's parents and putting them back, she handed her mother and Harry theirs.

Harry had his head bent as he tore at the wrapping on his present, but he was watching Mary out of the corner of his eye. Eileen had helped him choose her presents, and he hoped she liked them.

'Oh, Mam, look!' Mary held up the blue velvet dressing gown. 'Isn't it gorgeous?' Her face aglow with pleasure, she shrugged off her old dressing gown and slipped into the new one. Stroking the smooth velvet, she moved closer to

Martha's chair. 'Feel it, Mam! Isn't it beautiful?'

'It is, lass! Harry's done us both proud.'

With a shy smile, Mary turned round. 'It's lovely, Harry; thank you.' She noticed the pair of slippers and matching scarf and gloves lying on his knee. 'D'you like your presents?'

'They're just what I wanted.' He smiled into the anxious face. 'Now, while you two are comparing presents, I think I'll go up and get washed and changed.'

Standing in front of the bathroom mirror, shaving, Harry's mind went back over the last few months. To outsiders they were a normal, happy family. Everybody thought he and Mary were like any other young married couple, but when they were in the privacy of their own room, Mary quickly dropped the cloak of pretence. She treated him like a brother she was fond of, but never like a husband. He tried every way he knew to win her love, but it didn't look as though her feelings for him were ever going to change.

As he ran the open razor across his chin, Harry remembered the night, about two months ago, when his hopes had soared and he'd felt certain it was the turning point in their relationship. It was on one of the nights when he couldn't ignore the needs of his body, and Mary was lying passive as he caressed her body. He could read her mind as she lay braced for what was to come, and knew she was hoping it would be over quickly. Then his hand had touched her ripe, full breasts, and he heard a soft cry escape her lips as her body trembled. Hope had surged like a wave, as he prayed that at last Mary's body was responding to his.

371

Deliberately he had taken his time, a hand covering each breast as his thumbs circled the fully extended nipples. Mary's body had squirmed in the bed and his heart had raced as he recognised the signs.

Harry swished the razor in the water in the sink, then went back to his thoughts. He could remember that night, and the sensation, as though it was happening now. It had been dark in the room and he couldn't see Mary's face, but when he whispered, 'All right, love?' he'd felt her nod against his shoulder. He'd run his hand down the length of her body as it arched sensuously, then took her gently on a voyage that was to satisfy both of them.

Harry had expected Mary's feelings for him to change after that night, but he'd been wrong. When he kissed her she didn't turn away but her lips were cold. When he put his arms around her, her own stayed stiffly by her side. And in bed at night there were times when she lay frigid as he satisfied his needs, then she would turn away from him, leaving his body eased but his mind craving. It was the nights when Mary's body disobeyed her mind that Harry lived for. She was no longer a novice at love making, and in the darkness of their bedroom she had learned the art of pleasing. On these nights they were lovers, but the next day, feeling she'd been disloyal to Bob's memory, Mary was too ashamed to look him in the eye.

Harry pulled the plug from the sink and towelled his face. Talking to his reflection in the mirror, he said, 'I've tried everything . . . all I can do now is hope!'

George Sedgemoor undid the top button on his trousers

and breathed out. 'That was a grand dinner, Mary, but I've eaten far too much.'

They were all seated round the fire in Martha's room, and Mary smiled at the father-in-law she'd become very fond of. 'You can thank your son for the dinner. All I did was light the gas.'

'You did set the table.' Harry laughed. 'And you made the gravy.'

'Don't worry, Mary.' Lizzie pulled her jumper down over her ample bust. 'We all have to learn. I couldn't cook when I first got married, either.'

'Aye! And I've got ulcers to prove it.' George fended off a blow from his wife. 'It was years before I got a meal like me mam used to make.'

'I wish I could knit like you, Mrs Sedgemoor.' Mary was holding the knitted pram set that had been her Christmas present from her in-laws. There was a coat, a pair of leggings, a bonnet, and tiny bootees and mittens. 'Eileen gave me a matinee coat, and I've knitted about six meself, so I've got a nice little stock now.'

'I've got all the bedding for your pram and cot.' Lizzie beamed. 'And, I wasn't going to tell you, but in case you go out and buy one, I'm knitting a shawl. But you're definitely not getting them till the baby's born, 'cos it's unlucky.'

'I'm getting really excited about it.' Martha's smile was wistful. 'Mary is embroidering some pillowcases, and considering she's never done it before, she's making a good job of them.'

'They're only made out of flour bags.' Praise always embarrassed Mary. 'Eileen got them for me and told me to bleach them white. They've come up really well, and I'm embroidering some flowers on them.'

'Yeah! She's getting quite domesticated, isn't she, Mrs B?' Harry winked broadly. 'She makes lovely roast potatoes now.'

'I'll never live that down, will I?' Mary aimed a tangerine at his head. 'If you're so clever you can finish the embroidery on the pillowslips.'

Vera and Danny called in for half an hour, bringing Carol. The room was full but nobody seemed to care. There was noise and laughter, and Harry was watching the glow on Mary's face as she took the small doll from the Christmas tree that had been put there for Carol.

Vera had brought nappies for Mary and everyone laughed when Harry pulled a face and complained. 'It's not fair! The baby's getting everything!'

The four months in the Army had done Danny good. He looked healthier and fitter, and at least ten years younger. His laugh came easier too, as he and Vera took turns in kissing the doll Carol kept pushing in their faces. When they'd gone, George voiced the feelings of everyone in the room. 'Being called up was the best thing that could have happened to Danny. It's made a man of him.'

Chapter Twenty-Five

'What time d'you have to be at Oxford Street?'

'The clinic starts at ten, but it takes me ages to walk to the bus stop now, so I don't want to leave it too late.' Mary faced Harry across the table. 'I could be there all morning if it's as crowded as last week.'

'I don't think you should be travelling on buses on your own.' Harry was fiercely protective these days and didn't like her out of his sight for long. 'You're too near your time, and anything could happen. Why don't you knock and ask Doris to go with you?'

'Harry, I've still got another month to go!' She pulled a face. 'Mind you, if I get much bigger I think I'll burst. I feel the size of a house.'

'Being pregnant suits you. You look prettier than ever.'

'I might look all right, but I certainly don't feel it! I don't know what to do with meself sometimes. I can neither sit, stand or lay! I can't even get comfortable in bed because I get cramp if I lay in the same position too long, and I'm frightened to move in case I wake you up.'

'Why the heck didn't you say? I'll sleep on the couch for a

few nights, and you can get a good night's sleep.'

'No! You need your sleep!' A smile spread across Mary's face. 'I don't know how you can sleep though, with the baby kicking the way it does.'

'It's woken me a few times, I have to admit. I'm sure it's going to be a boy because it kicks like a footballer.'

'It better hadn't be! It'll look daft if it is, because everything I've got is in pink.'

'I told you to be on the safe side and stick to white.' Harry grinned. 'I don't want my son to be a cissy.' His smile dropped when he saw Mary's face cloud over, and again he asked himself if she was going to let him be a father to the baby, or was she going to shut him out?

Harry jumped up to open the door when they heard the sound of Martha's crutches. She'd worked hard to become independent and could now move about the downstairs room and make her own way down the yard to the lavatory. Mary waited till her mother was settled in the rocking chair, then took the crutches and stood them against the wall. It grieved her to see her once proud mother dragging her leg behind her, but as sympathy was the last thing Martha wanted, Mary didn't give any. 'You won't be able to sit in that chair when the baby comes, you know! I'll be spending all me time in it nursing her.'

'She's going to be spoilt between the pair of you.' Harry shook his head as he laughed. 'You've got me at it now! I'm starting to say "her".'

'I'd better get a move on.' Mary sighed. 'I don't feel like it, but needs must when the devil drives.'

'It won't be long, lass. In a few weeks it'll all be over, and you'll forget your aches and pains when you've got the baby in your arms.'

'It can't come quick enough for me.' Mary pressed her hands into the small of her back which was aching from the extra weight. 'It'll be lovely to walk again without waddling from side to side like a big gorilla.'

After waving Mary off, Harry took his coat from the hallstand. 'I'm nipping along to me mam's, Mrs B, to ask if I can have me old bed. Mary's not getting any sleep, so I can kip down in the spare room till after the baby comes.' When Martha looked out of the window two hours later, it was to see Harry perched on a coal cart next to Mr Dobson, who was holding the reins of the big black cart horse. The shape of the bed could be seen beneath the sheet Lizzie had lent to keep the coal dust off the bed.

Mr Dobson had been Martha's coal man for years in the old neighbourhood and she would have loved to have chatted to him for a while, but Harry was in a hurry to get the bed upstairs.

It was half past twelve when Martha shouted up to him, 'Harry, if you don't hurry you won't have time for anything to eat before you go to work.'

'Mary can get a good night's sleep now.'

'Does she know?'

'No! I'd have done it before if I'd known she wasn't getting any sleep.'

Martha looked at him with affection. 'You're a good man, Harry!'

'You're not a bad old stick yourself!'

* * *

Harry followed Mary up the stairs that night. 'D'you feel all right? You've been very quiet since I came in.'

Mary was breathless by the time she reached the top stair. 'I just feel a bit sickly, that's all. It's probably with being pushed and prodded at the clinic. I'll be fine in the morning.'

'Call me if you want me, won't you?'

'Don't panic!' Mary didn't like being fussed over. 'Thanks for getting the bed! At least I can stretch out tonight without worrying about kicking you out of bed.'

Careful not to press her tummy, Harry took her by the shoulders and kissed her gently. 'Goodnight and God bless, Mary.' He waited till the door closed on her, then crossed to the room where he'd be sleeping alone.

Mary climbed into bed, relishing the prospect of being able to toss and turn as much as she liked. She lay on her side, but within minutes she was uncomfortable because her tummy was resting on the bed and made her feel sick. The baby must have been uncomfortable too, because it was kicking like mad. Sleep just wouldn't come and as time passed she realised she was missing the warmth of Harry sleeping next to her, and the feel of his arms across her body. I've got used to him now, she told herself, but I'll soon get used to sleeping on me own again.

A week before the baby was due, Mary came back from the clinic looking worn out. 'I haven't got to go back again until the labour pains start.'

Harry should have left for work by this time, but he'd hung on till she got back to make sure everything was all right. 'It must be due soon then, mustn't it?'

'The doctor said it could be any day now.' Mary ran her fingers through her hair. 'It can't come quick enough for me.'

Harry's face was white. 'I'd better stay off.'

'No! I could go for days yet.' Mary tried to sound convincing but she wasn't convinced herself. There were movements in her tummy she hadn't had before.

Harry hovered by the door, reluctant to leave. 'Knock for Jim as soon as the pains start. He's still got that gallon of petrol he's been saving to take you to the hospital.' He walked through the door, then came back again. 'And don't leave it too late, 'cos it's a good way to Oxford Street.'

'Will you stop fussing and go to work! I'll still be here when you get home tonight.'

The first twinge came about nine o'clock, but Mary didn't mention it to her mother because it wasn't really a pain. She had several niggling little twinges after that but nothing she thought bad enough to mention. It was while she was in the kitchen seeing to Harry's supper that the first real pain came, and its intensity had her doubled up in agony. She was like this when Harry walked in. He took one look at her frightened face and asked, 'How long have you been like this?'

'This is the first real pain I've had.' Mary choked back the tears. 'I had a few twinges, but that was hours ago.'

'Get your coat while I knock for Jim.' Harry reached the door and turned. 'Is your case ready?'

Mary attempted a smile. 'It's been ready for weeks.'

Mary was sitting up in bed when Harry strode down the ward beaming. 'How are you?'

'Fine!' Mary's face was white but her eyes were shining with happiness. Harry took her hand and bent to kiss her. 'Congratulations, Mrs Sedgemoor! I'm so relieved and happy I feel like singing!'

'No singing allowed on the wards.' Mary grinned. 'Aren't you going to look at the baby?' She studied Harry's face as he gazed with wonder at the scrap of humanity that had caused him so much worry. It was when the doctor had said 'You've got a lovely little girl, Mrs Sedgemoor', that Mary realised just how much she had to thank Harry for. How ashamed she'd have been if she'd been the only unmarried mother in the ward.

'She's beautiful.' Harry tore his eyes away from the baby for a second. 'But she's got dark hair!' He sounded disappointed. 'I thought she'd be blonde, like you.'

'Give her a chance!' Mary laughed. 'All babies' hair and eyes change colour after a few weeks.'

'How long will you be in?' He sat down on the side of the bed. 'I'm missing you already.'

'If the baby comes on, they'll let me home in a week. I'll have to go to bed for another week, but they send a nurse in each day to see to the baby.'

'Your mam sends her love. She's dying to see the baby.'

'They wouldn't let her in! They only let fathers in!' As

soon as the words left her mouth, Mary realised what she'd said and her face drained of colour.

'I am her father, Mary! I'll always think of her as me own daughter.'

Mary closed her eyes to hide the pain he would surely read in them. During the hours of labour she'd tried to tell herself it was no good thinking of what might have been. But it wasn't easy to forget the man who was the father of the baby lying in the cot at the bottom of her bed.

In the taxi coming back from the hospital, Harry held the baby in his arms. He touched the tiny fingers and his heart lurched as the little fingers curled round one of his. 'She's beautiful! Just like her mother.'

Martha was watching out of the window when the taxi drew up, and she'd have given anything to have been able to rush out and welcome her daughter and granddaughter. When Mary walked through the door she started to cry. All the worries and pent up emotions of the last year were in those tears. 'Oh, lass, it's good to have you home.'

'Hey, what's all this? I bring you a beautiful new granddaughter, and all you can do is cry your eyes out!'

Half laughing, half crying, Martha wiped her eyes. 'It's not every day a woman becomes a grandmother, so I'm entitled to a little weep.'

Harry laid the baby on the bed and went to bring the case in while Mary undid the baby's shawl and blanket. 'There you are, Grandma! Say hello to our Emma.'

'Where shall I put this?' Harry stood inside the door with the case in his hand.

'Just put it in my room, and I'll sort it out later.'

As he ran up the stairs, Mary's words rang in his ears. 'Put it in my room' she'd said. Was it going to be 'your room' and 'my room' from now on?

Lizzie and George Sedgemoor called that night to see the baby, and there was much laughter over what she should call Lizzie and Martha. 'I'd like to be called Grandma, if you don't mind, Lizzie?'

'That's settled then.' Lizzie nodded. 'You're Grandma, and I'll be Nanna.'

'I may as well stick my oar in.' George stuck a thumb in his braces and pulled importantly at the elastic. 'I want to be Grandad.'

Watching them cooing over the baby, Mary thought how marvellously they were taking it. There's not many parents would take it like they have, she told herself.

The Sedgemoors didn't stay long because Harry insisted that Mary go to bed. 'The Sister gave me strict instructions that you were to go straight to bed. So up those stairs with you!'

As soon as Mary walked in the bedroom, she asked, 'Where's the baby's cot?'

'I've put it in the small room. I thought you wanted to start her off in her own room.'

'No! I'll have her in here with me! She needs feeding every three hours, even through the night, so you'd never get any sleep. You'd be better off sleeping in the other room.'

'I can put up with it for a few weeks,' Harry protested. 'It won't be long before she's sleeping through the night.'

'It'll be more than a few weeks.' Mary was determined. 'I'm feeding her meself, so I'll be putting the light on and off and you'd never get a full night's sleep.'

The only time Harry saw the baby that week was through the rails of the cot. A few times he'd gone to pick her up when she'd whimpered but Mary had snapped at him. 'I'm not having her picked up every time she cries! Babies are cute and they soon get to know that if they want nursing all they've got to do is cry.'

'Harry's very good, lass!' Martha said one day. 'He brings in the wood and coal, does the washing and cooking, and even washes the baby's nappies. There's not many men like him around!'

'I know.' Mary sounded off-hand. 'But I'll be up meself in a day or two and I can see to everything then.'

Eileen leaned over the pram where baby Emma had her eyes open and her tiny hands were waving about. 'She's an old fashioned little madam, this one.' Eileen shook the coloured rattle. 'Two weeks old, an' she's all there!'

'She's got a good set of lungs, too!' Harry came to stand beside the pram, smiling at the baby's antics. 'Isn't she beautiful?'

Eileen glanced sideways at him and saw the love shining in his eyes. The more she saw of Harry Sedgemoor the more she liked him. 'Keeps yez awake at night, does she?'

'Well, er, no! Not really!' Harry avoided her eyes as he stammered. 'I'm sleeping in the spare room, so she doesn't disturb me.'

Eileen cocked an eyebrow but kept her thoughts to

herself. There'll be trouble brewing here one of these days unless Mary pulls her socks up. What she needed was a quick kick up the backside!

Mary scooped the baby out of the pram and changed the subject. 'Will you come in me mam's room for a minute, I want to ask you something?' She followed Eileen, waited till she sat down, then stood in front of her, swaying gently from side to side as the baby nestled in the crook of her arm. 'Will you be Emma's godmother?'

'Yer wha'! Me a godmother! Yez must be crazy wanting to lumber the poor mite with me!' But Eileen's eyes were bright with pleasure as she held her arms out. 'Give yer here! A godmother has some rights, doesn't she?'

Mary passed the baby over. 'Well, will you?'

'Of course I will – won't I, sweetheart!' Emma lay comfortably in the wide lap, her head supported by Eileen's hands. 'I'll have to mend me ways, won't I? No more swearin' in front of me goddaughter.' There was mischief in her voice. 'Who's the godfather?'

'Jim, from next door. Him and Doris have been very good to us and we thought it would be nice to ask him.'

Eileen looked up and caught the look of irritation on Mary's face as she dodged away from the arm Harry had slipped across her shoulders. Harry's face paled, and Eileen quickly bent her head so he wouldn't see her witness his humiliation. Oh, dear! He really was going to have to put his foot down with a firm hand! 'If yer'd asked someone a bit younger, I might have been able to click!' Eileen forced a smile for Harry's sake. 'You're a right miserable pair of buggers.' Her mouth puckered as she looked down at the baby. 'Excuse Auntie Eileen for swearin', darling. I'll watch me mouth in future.'

'Father Murphy called to see when we were having Emma christened, and he's going to do it himself, a week on Saturday.' Mary bent to stroke the baby's head. 'We'll have a little tea here afterwards, just for the family and a few friends.'

A blank look crossed Eileen's face before one of her hands travelled slowly down the front of her dress. 'I thought I felt warm all of a sudden! She's wet me right through to me knickers!' She threw back her head and roared with laughter. 'Me an' yer daughter are goin' to have to come to an understanding. I'll watch me mouth, if she'll watch her other end!'

Mary looked at Eileen fondly. What a difference her presence made. It was unusual to hear genuine belly laughter these days, but as soon as the big woman walked in, the house rang with it. God knows where they'd all be today without her. They say everyone has a guardian angel, well Eileen was certainly hers.

Mind you, Mary turned her head to hide a smile, she didn't look much like a guardian angel with her scraggy hair and scruffy clothes. And unless Mary was very much mistaken, there was a faint line of a tide mark on Eileen's neck.

So what, Mary asked herself. I've never read a book that said all angels had to wear white and have a halo!

Chapter Twenty-Six

Martha waved when she saw Eileen's face pressed against the window, and as she reached for her crutches to make the journey down the hall she thanked God that at last she could have a talk to Eileen without Mary or Harry around.

'I had to go on a message so I thought I'd call in and see me goddaughter.' Eileen hadn't tied her turban tightly enough around her head and it had slipped down over one eye giving her the appearance of being drunk. 'I thought I could cadge a cuppa, as well.'

'I can make you a pot of tea, but you'd have to carry it in yourself. I can't manage with these blasted crutches.'

'On yer own are yer? Where's the happy couple?'

'They've taken Emma to the clinic. Harry goes with Mary when he's on mornings.' Martha's face was troubled as she smoothed the front of her pinny. 'Can I talk to you in confidence, Eileen? I've no one else to talk to and I'm out of me mind with worry. It's our Mary. She's not being fair with Harry, and I don't know how much longer he's going to put up with it.'

'She's not still sleeping in her own room, is she?'

Martha's head jerked. 'They think I don't know because I can't get up the stairs. But I'm not blind or stupid. It's got to the state now where Mary barely opens her mouth to him. She's even jealous of him with Emma. He dotes on the baby, and the only time he looks happy is when he's nursing her. But their marriage is a sham. I watched them walking down the road with Harry pushing the pram and Mary walking beside him. Anyone seeing them would think they were a happily married couple. But their marriage is a mockery. She treats him like a lodger, and one of these days he'll pack his bags and walk out. And I wouldn't blame him either, because no man would put up with the way she treats him.' Martha wiped a tear away. 'At least before the baby came she made an effort to be friendly with him, but now she's barely civil. God knows he's tried, but no matter what he does it isn't right and I can see he's losing patience with her. I wonder where she thinks we'd be without him?'

'In the bloody workhouse!' Eileen grunted as she pushed the wayward turban back. 'I had a feeling all was not well. He hasn't been himself lately.' Her fat hand covered Martha's. 'Tell yer what, Mrs B, I'll hang on till they get back and try and have a word with her ladyship. If I can get her on her own in the kitchen, you keep Harry talkin' in here. It's about time she grew up and I think I know just how to do it.'

'Don't say I've said anything, will you?' Martha begged. 'The atmosphere in the house is bad enough now, without me making it worse.' Her head turned quickly and a finger went to her lips. 'Sssh! They're here now!'

'Hi!' Mary's face broadened into a grin when she saw her friend. 'How long have you been here?'

'Long enough to have had a cuppa! Me belly thinks me throat's cut.' As she heaved herself up, Harry came in carrying the baby and Eileen could see the pride on his face. No wonder Martha felt sorry for him. It was a pity he'd been so soft with Mary. What she needed was a smacked backside.

'Yer get prettier every time I see yer.' Eileen tickled Emma's tummy and was rewarded with loud chuckles. The baby was three months old now and the spitting image of Mary. 'Yer might even grow up to be as good looking as yer godmother.'

'God help her!' Mary ducked. 'I'll put the kettle on.'

'I'll give yer a hand.' Eileen winked knowingly at Martha before following Mary into the kitchen. She leaned against the sink watching the cups being set out. 'It's ages since we had a natter, isn't it, kid? How's things going?'

'Fine!' Mary had a feeling she'd been cornered for a reason. 'Everything's great.'

'You an' Harry gettin' on all right?'

'Of course we are! Why?'

'It's just that he doesn't seem himself these days an' I wondered if anything was worryin' him. He doesn't smile much, an' I can't even get him to laugh at me jokes any more.' Eileen was watching every expression on the pretty face. 'Not still sleepin' in yer own room, are yer?'

Mary turned from the prying eyes. 'Yes! But it's only so Harry can get a good night's sleep.'

'Christ, kid, yer as thick as two short planks!' When

Mary spun round, her face flushed with anger, Eileen flung out her arm. 'No! Let me get it off me chest first, then yer can have yer say. But remember, kid, it's me yer talkin' to and not Harry.' She took a deep breath. 'I was the one who encouraged yer to marry him, but I'm sorry I did now! Oh, not for your sake, but for Harry's! You got respectability out of marryin' him. A father for yer baby, a man with a good job, and a man that's crazy about yer. But what did Harry get out of it? Sweet bugger all as far as I can see! A wife who thinks she's done him a favour, instead of the other way round. A wife who doesn't have any feelings for him and won't even sleep in the same bed! And on top of all that, everyone laughin' behind his back.' When Mary's eyes widened, Eileen huffed. 'Oh, yeah, he's had that all right, and more! Everyone knows yer've had a baby, an' they all know it's not Harry's! But he's put up with all that because he loves yer.' Eileen looked down at her feet before meeting Mary's eyes. 'There's a lot of things yer don't know about yer 'usband, kid! I bet yer don't know he takes an hour off work every week to visit Iris Brown in the hossie, do yer?'

'I didn't know Iris was in hospital.'

'No, 'cos yer never asked! Not once have yer bothered to ask what happened to the women in the powder room that day. Iris Brown had half her face blown away, Theresa Corkhill lost three fingers, and Mary Sawyer's scarred for life. That's apart from the other women who were injured. But you've been too busy wallowing in self pity to spare a thought for others that have got more troubles than you've ever dreamed of.'

'I did ask if anyone had been hurt in the explosion!' Mary cried. 'But Harry said things weren't as bad as they first thought. And he never mentioned it again so I believed him.'

'Harry wouldn't tell yer in case yer got upset! And he made sure I didn't tell yer, either! Oh, my goodness me, no! We mustn't say anything that might upset Mary!' Eileen saw Mary's stricken look and realised she was going too far. 'I'm sorry, kid! I shouldn't be shoutin' at yer like this but yer get me so bloody mad! I know life hasn't been a bed of roses for yer, but have yer ever asked yerself where yer'd be today without Harry!? Not only you, but yer mam and Emma? Shall I tell yer where yer'd be, kid? Up the bloody creek without a paddle!' Eileen paused for a while, and when she spoke her voice was softer. 'Harry thinks the sun shines out of yer backside, kid, but he'll only stand for so much. Keep him out of yer bedroom and yer've only yerself to blame if he looks elsewhere for comfort. 'Cos I'll tell yer this for nothin', kid, no one will blame Harry. He's put up with all the sly digs and the taunts, but he won' put up with a frigid wife.'

Mary's head was bowed, her voice barely audible. 'I didn't know they were talking behind Harry's back.'

'Harry wouldn't give a bugger what people said if it was worth it. But is it? Be honest with yerself, kid. The only person you've thought about since the day yer got married, is yerself. Yer couldn't give a monkey's uncle about Harry's feelings.' Eileen let out a deep sigh. 'Yer could make it work if yer wanted to! Bob was yer childhood sweetheart an' he'll always have a special place in yer heart . . . but yer can't love a dream forever, an' that's what you're doing! Bob is a dream, and it's time to let go of that dream and wake up to reality! Christ, Mary, we all have to grow up sometime, so grow up before it's too late.' Eileen moved towards the door. She'd done her best, but was it enough? She had her doubts. 'I'll be on me way. I've worn me welcome out.'

'But you haven't had a cup of tea yet!'

Eileen shook her head. 'I've lost the taste for it now.' She walked through to the front room to say ta-ra to the family and she answered Martha's silent question with a shrug of her shoulders. What would happen now was anyone's guess. And as she waddled her way to the bus stop, Eileen muttered aloud, 'It'll take a miracle to save that marriage, and miracles are in short supply at the moment.'

Martha threw her cards on the table. There was no pleasure in playing with two people who were as lifeless as the dummies in Lewis's window. 'I want to listen to Winston Churchill. He's on the wireless at nine o'clock.'

Mary pushed her chair back. 'Emma's due for her feed. I'll get straight into bed when I've fed her. I'm dead tired.'

Harry listened to her feet climbing the stairs then switched the wireless on. 'She always leaves the room when anyone mentions the war.' He twiddled the knobs to try and clear the crackling on the line. 'How the hell can you ignore a war?'

'I don't know, son!' Martha didn't understand her daughter any more than Harry did. She used to be able to read her like a book, but not any more. They sat in silence, afraid to miss one word Winston Churchill said in that well known, deep gruff voice. The Allies were still having setbacks in the areas of fighting, but they were now starting to have their victories too. Churchill said they must all tighten their belts and pull together to achieve a final victory over the cruel invaders. The Allies had right on their side. They were fighting for freedom for all the people in the countries Hitler had taken by force. And there was never any doubt in the Prime Minister's voice when he said that, in the end, right would prevail. The day after one of his 'state of the war' broadcasts, every person in the country would walk round with their heads held high and a determination to work harder. That was the effect the great man had. His strong voice and his pride and faith in the men and women in the forces, and those at home working behind the lines, made everyone feel ten feet tall.

'We're lucky we've got him.' Harry turned the sound down. 'No one will put anything over on him.'

'No, he's a great man.' Martha sighed. How she wished she was fit and well enough to go out and do her bit to help win the war. 'As you say, we're lucky to have him.'

'Talking about Mary ignoring the war,' Harry looked her in the eyes, 'it's not only the war she ignores, is it? I could go out tomorrow and never come back, and she wouldn't even miss me!'

Martha bit her lip. 'I know, son! You mightn't like what I'm going to tell you, but I'm going to tell you anyway. I had a word with Eileen about our Mary this afternoon. I thought she might be able to knock some sense into her. That's why Eileen followed her into the kitchen. I know she had a talk to her, but it doesn't seem to have made any difference.'

'Mrs B, I've come to the conclusion that nothing is going to make any difference to the way Mary feels about me. I've done everything I know, but it hasn't worked.' Harry ran his fingers through his thick mop of hair, his face pale and serious. 'I've been giving it a lot of thought over the last few weeks, and I really don't see any future for us. I'm twenty-eight years of age, Mrs B, and I need a wife who loves me! It's not too much to ask, is it?'

Martha shook her head and a tear fell on to her hand. Her voice was choked as she cried, 'None of it is your fault, Harry! It's our Mary that's in the wrong.'

Her stricken face pierced Harry's heart and he stood up and ruffled her hair. 'You're still the best mother-in-law in the whole world, no matter what! Now, I'll make us a drink and we can get to bed. It's up early in the morning for me.'

When he carried Martha's drink in, he said, 'I'll take one up to Mary. I don't think she'll be asleep yet.'

Mary had just put the light out when the tap came on the door. It opened slowly to reveal Harry, silhouetted in the glow from the landing light. 'I thought you'd still be awake, so I've brought you a cuppa.' He handed her the cup, then bent over the cot. 'She's fast asleep in the land of nod. No worries in her little world.'

'D'you want to sit and talk for a few minutes?' Mary patted the side of the bed. 'Emma's well away, so we won't disturb her.'

Harry stared down at her with a look of sad bewilderment on his face. She thinks I'm made of stone! I'm supposed to sit on the side of me wife's bed, talk to her as though we're casual acquaintances, then toddle off to me own room like a good little boy! 'Not tonight! I'm too tired and I have to be up early.'

Mary watched the door close then put her cup on the tallboy and slid down between the sheets. She'd made an effort to be friendly and he'd rejected her. She turned on her side, pulling the blankets up to cover her shoulder. If that was the way he wanted it, then it suited her.

At the sound of Emma's high-pitched squeals of laughter, Harry lifted his eyes to look over the top of the newspaper. She was being held aloft by Mary and her face was glowing with pleasure as she waved her arms and legs about. 'Down we come.' Mary's laughter mingled with Emma's as she lowered the smiling face down to her own and kissed the tiny nose. 'And up we go.' Mary's arms stretched upwards. 'Two more, then it's time for your nap.' The smile on Harry's face as he lowered his eyes to the newspaper was tinged with sadness. What a scene of wedded bliss it would look to anyone walking through the door now. A devoted mother playing with a laughing baby while hubby sat contentedly reading the day's news after coming home from working a morning shift. But the happy domestic scene was far from what it appeared.

'OW! You little tinker . . . let go!' Emma had grabbed at the long blonde hair and was pulling hard. 'OW! That hurts!' Mary was trying to disentangle the tiny fingers but Emma held on tight.

Harry put his paper down and moved forward to help. But as his hand reached out, Mary pushed it aside. 'Leave it!' Her voice was sharp, and when she saw Harry wince, she softened her tone. 'I can manage.'

'It strikes me you can always manage! You don't need me for anything, do you, Mary?' Harry was out of the room before Mary could say she was sorry, and she heard his anger in the slam of his bedroom door. Things can't go on as they are, she told herself. It would be better if I came straight out and told him what was making me bad tempered all the time. Better to have a blazing row than carry on as they were, with neither of them happy.

Even if it means losing Harry? Mary posed the question as she nestled the baby's head into her shoulder and rocked her gently from side to side. Is your peace of mind more important to you than your marriage? Mary didn't need to consider the answer because until she'd squared herself with her conscience, and lightened the burden of guilt she carried with her every waking moment, there'd be no marriage. Harry wouldn't put up with her moods forever, and she didn't blame him.

Mary popped her head under the pram hood and gently moved the blankets from her daughter's face. Wide eyes met hers and she tutted. 'You little tinker! You're supposed to be asleep!'

'Put her outside in the fresh air and she'll soon go to sleep,' Martha said, knowingly. 'You're making a rod for your own back by spoiling her the way you do.'

'I'm frightened of a cat jumping on the pram,' Mary said.

'I've heard of a cat sitting on a baby's face and smothering it.'

'It's probably an old wives' tale, lass! If you believed everything you hear you'll never let the child see daylight!'

'I'll take her for a walk after and she'll get some fresh air then.' Mary sat facing her mother, her hands clasped tightly on her lap. 'Mam, I want to talk to you about the Wests.'

'What about them?'

'I'm going to write to them about Emma.' Mary heard the loud gasp and held up her hand. 'Mam, let me finish, please! I can't get them out of my mind because I think it's wicked not to tell them they've got a granddaughter. They've lost so much, I can't live with meself knowing I'm robbing them of Emma, too!'

'You're not the only one who thinks about them, lass,' Martha murmured softly. 'You don't think for one moment that I've forgotten about Bob or his mam and dad, do you? Bob was like a son to me, and many's the night I've cried meself to sleep over him. And I go through the same hurt as you do every time you look at the baby and see Bob in every one of her features. People say she's the spitting image of you, and she may be, but there's plenty of Bob in her too.' Martha picked nervously at her pinny. 'My heart goes out to the Wests, lass, but you know how Harry feels. You've got to consider his feelings.'

'Even if he's in the wrong, Mam? Am I supposed to do as he says even though what we're doing is cruel and deceitful? The Wests have a granddaughter and they don't even know she exists! They lost their only son and I think it's inhuman not to tell them he left behind a beautiful daughter. They'd be so happy if they knew . . . it would give them an incentive to go on living.'

'What do you intend doing, lass?' Martha knew her daughter was right, but she could also understand Harry's reluctance to allow the Wests into their lives.

'I don't know yet,' Mary answered, 'but I've got to do something. Things are getting worse between me and Harry, and I know it's my fault. My nerves are on edge all the time and I'm taking it out on him. If I could only clear my conscience over the Wests, I'm sure Harry and I would get along a lot better.'

'Harry won't have it, lass, and I'm not going to get involved because I can see his side of it, too!'

'Then I won't tell him,' Mary said defiantly. 'I'll write and explain everything to them and at least it will clear my conscience.'

'What good would that do!?' Martha's voice rose, then remembering the sleeping baby, she went on quietly. 'You can't tell them they've got a granddaughter and expect them not to want to see her! Anyway, they probably know all about her! Everyone in the old neighbourhood knows it's Bob's baby so it's bound to have got to them through their niece, Joyce!'

'It's me who should tell them, Mam! They shouldn't have to hear it through gossip.'

'And you're not going to tell Harry?'

Mary shook her head. 'There'd only be a row and he'd talk me out of it. For once in my life I'm going to do something off me own bat. I'll write to them and take it from there.'

'Then leave me out of it, lass. If you're going behind Harry's back, I want no part of it.'

'I won't involve you, Mam, if that's the way you feel. I just want you to know that it's something I've got to do.'

Chapter Twenty-Seven

'Was that the postman I heard before?' Martha pursed her lips when she saw the guilt on Mary's face. 'You've had a letter from the Wests!?'

'Mam, you should read their letter. They sound so happy, I'm glad I wrote.'

'What would you have done if Harry had been home?' Martha wondered if her daughter understood the seriousness of what she was doing, and what it could lead to. 'Remember, lass, one lie leads to another. And a liar has to have a good memory.'

'I haven't told any lies!'

'Acting a lie is just as bad as telling one.' Martha clicked her tongue. 'You've done what you thought you had to, so leave it at that before you get found out.'

'I explained to them about Harry, and they say they understand and won't come near the house. But they want to see Emma, just once.'

'Don't tell me any more, lass, because I might as well tell you straight that I've no intention of covering up for you.'

So Mary didn't say the letter she'd already scribbled to

the Wests was in her pocket ready to post when she took Emma to the shops.

But the following Tuesday, when Harry had left for work on the afternoon shift, Mary could feel her mother's watchful eye on her, and knew her nervous excitement hadn't gone unnoticed. So after wrapping Emma in the big shawl Mrs Sedgemoor had knitted, she popped her head round the door of the front room. 'I'm taking Emma out for an hour, Mam, I'll be back in time for her feed.' And she fled before any questions could be asked.

Martha watched Mary pass the window, the baby cradled in her arms. She didn't need telling her daughter was on her way to meet the Wests. Martha let the curtain fall back into place. Where was it all going to end?

When Mary walked slowly up Moorfields towards Exchange Station where she'd arranged to meet the Wests, her tummy was churning with a mixture of excitement and fear. She knew they were longing to see the baby, but after what had happened would they be glad to see her?

The large station was crowded with servicemen. Some in groups with their kit bags at their feet, others saying goodbye to wives and sweethearts. One young soldier caught Mary's eye. He looked no more than seventeen and was glancing round with embarrassment as an older woman, obviously his mother, clung to his neck, crying. Mary could hear her saying, 'You will look after yerself, won't yer, son? And write to me often, d'yer hear?'

Mary turned away, saddened that someone so young should be sent away to fight in a war.

'Mary!'

At first Mary didn't recognise the elderly couple pushing their way towards her. It was only a year since she'd seen Bob's mam and dad, but they'd aged so much she would have passed them in the street and not known them. They stopped a few feet away from her, unsure of their welcome. But when Mary smiled, they rushed forward to greet her with hugs and kisses. Tears flowed freely as emotions ran high, and it was Mr West who finally broke away to blow his nose. 'I'm sorry, Mary, I couldn't help meself.'

'Can I see the baby?' Lily West held her arms out and Mary passed Emma over. Her eyes moist, she watched the two people who, if it hadn't been for the war, would have been her in-laws. The joy on their faces as they gazed down at their granddaughter dispelled any lingering doubt. This is how it should be, she told herself. It was what Bob would have wanted.

'Shall we get a cup of tea at the cafeteria?' Mr West dragged his eyes from the baby. 'You've got half-an-hour, haven't you?'

Mary nodded. 'As long as I'm home for Emma's feed.'

'I like the name Emma.' Lily West held the baby tight. 'Can I carry her?'

'Of course you can.' Mary took Bob West's arm as they crossed to the busy station cafeteria. 'How's the job going?'

'The job's all right, but I miss all me old mates.' Bob rushed forward to pull out a chair for his wife, who was holding the baby as though she was a fragile piece of precious china.

'It's like holding our Bob again.' Lily looked into her husband's eyes. 'She's the image of him when he was a baby.'

'I know, love. She's beautiful.' Bob put his hand on Mary's arm. 'Thanks for writing to us, and for letting us see her. You've no idea what a difference it's made to Lily. Since your letter came she's been a changed woman.'

'Did you know I'd had a baby?'

When Bob glanced quickly at his wife before lowering his head and answering, 'No,' Mary knew he was lying. He did know, but had kept it secret.

'I should have written to you long ago, but as I told you in my letter, I've got Harry to consider.'

'We understand that, love! And we won't make any trouble for you,' Bob said. 'I've known Harry for a long time and you've got yourself a good husband. He'll be a good father to Emma, too.'

Lily was rocking Emma gently as her fingers traced softly across the silky pink cheeks. 'Bob's right! We won't cause you any trouble, I promise. But d'you think we could just see Emma now and again?' Her eyes were pleading. 'It would mean so much to us.' A tear ran down her cheek. 'She's all that's left of our son.'

'Now, Lily, I warned you before we came that it wouldn't be fair to expect Mary to jeopardise her marriage.' Bob's voice was stern until he saw the despair on his wife's face. 'I'm sorry, love, but I did warn you.'

Mary looked from one to the other. Her head was

telling her one thing and her heart another. Finally her heart won. 'Of course you can see your granddaughter again, Mrs West. I don't know how, but I'll manage it somehow.'

'Be careful, Mary,' Bob warned. 'I wouldn't want us to be the cause of your marriage breaking up. It's only natural for us to want to see the baby, especially Lily, but not at the expense of your happiness.'

'Mr West, my happiness would be for all of us to be friends, and for you to be able to come to our house whenever you wanted to see Emma. But I've got to think of Harry. I can't risk you coming to the house, so we'd have to meet like we have today. That means a long train journey just to spend half an hour on a station platform. It also means you taking time off work because I can only manage it when Harry's on afternoon shift.'

'It would be worth it.' Lily was holding the baby to her breast as though she'd never let go. 'Anything, as long as I can see her for a few minutes.'

Mary found conversation difficult after that. She could think of nothing to say. For the six years she'd courted Bob, the Wests' house had been like a second home to her. Bob had been the link that bound them together, but he was gone now and the link broken. Except for Emma.

When Mary said it was time for her to get home to feed Emma, Lily became tearful. 'Just another five minutes, please!?'

'I'm sorry, Mrs West, but I'll have to go.' Touched by the sadness on the two faces, Mary said quickly, 'We'll meet again soon.'

But that wasn't definite enough for Lily. Ignoring the meaningful look directed at her by her husband, she insisted on knowing when. So it was arranged they would meet again in three weeks. Same time, same place.

When Mary got home Martha never questioned her, and Mary didn't volunteer any information. The less her mother knew the less she would worry. But making her peace with the Wests made Mary feel more content than she'd been for a long time. A picture of their happy faces was imprinted on her mind, telling her she'd been right all along. The Wests had so little left in life, and if seeing their granddaughter brought them such happiness then surely it would be wrong to rob them of it.

Lighthearted, and free from guilt, Mary found it easier to talk to Harry when he got in from work that night. And in the hour before they went to bed the tense atmosphere in the house was eased. But Martha viewed the change in her daughter with apprehension. One of these days the bubble would burst, and God help them all when it did.

'You're early this morning.' Mary walked down the hall in front of Doris. 'I haven't even dressed Emma yet.'

'I want to get to the shops early before they sell out.' Doris grinned down at Emma who was lying on a blanket on the floor, still in her nightie. Little arms and legs waved in the air at the sight of the familiar face, in anticipation of being picked up. But Doris shook her head. 'Not this morning, sunshine! Auntie Doris has got shopping to do.' Turning to Mary, she asked, 'Where were you off to yesterday? I was standing in the queue at the chippy when you passed. It's unusual to see you carrying Emma.'

The question was totally unexpected and for a few seconds Mary was shocked into silence. 'I, er, felt like going for a walk round the shops, and it's a nuisance wheeling the pram round.'

'Shopkeepers are not very happy with prams in their shops, either, are they? Spoils custom for them.' Doris was bending over tickling Emma's tummy and didn't see Mary's discomfort. 'Did you buy anything?'

'I only went window shopping.' Oh, dear God, Mary thought. What if Doris mentions it in front of Harry? He was still in bed but would be down any minute. 'I'd better get Emma dressed before Harry gets up or he'll think I'm a lazy beggar.'

'D'you want anything while I'm out?' Doris asked.

'No, thanks. I'll be going out meself, later.' Mary's head was screaming for her neighbour to go, now! If she could keep Doris from seeing Harry today, she'd have forgotten the incident by tomorrow.

'I'll say "hello" to your mam, then buzz off and let you get on with your work.' While Doris knocked on Martha's door, Mary walked down the hall to open the front door in readiness. She was being rude to someone who'd been very good to them, but she had to get Doris out of the house, quick. And while she waited with bated breath, Mary told herself her mam was right. When you tell one lie, it leads on to others. And Mary had been brought up to always tell the truth. Her mam used to say, 'Tell the truth, lass, and shame the devil'. Now she'd let her mam down. And she'd let Harry down, too! He was bound to find out sooner or later she'd deceived him and he'd be disgusted with her.

When Doris had left, Mary filled a small bowl with lukewarm water and picked up the flannel and soap for Emma's wash. She usually enjoyed the morning ritual, with Emma gurgling and kicking on her knee, but Mary found no pleasure in it this morning. Doris, in her innocence, had made her realise what a dangerous game she'd started.

Mary broke into a cold sweat when she heard Harry's footsteps running down the stairs. And when she handed Emma over to him while she cooked his breakfast, she was too filled with shame to meet his eyes. It was then she knew that in bringing the Wests back into her life, she'd replaced one burden of guilt with another.

As the days went by the turmoil in Mary's head grew. All she'd wanted was to make Bob's mam and dad happy, but she knew now that would be impossible unless she told Harry what was going on. She couldn't live her life telling lies to those who loved and trusted her.

Mary threw herself into cleaning the house from top to bottom. Clothes that weren't dirty were washed, furniture that was already shining was polished vigorously every day, and Emma was taken for long walks. But even tiring herself out to the point of dropping didn't keep her worries at bay. Never once did she regret bringing the Wests back into her life, or consider telling them they couldn't see Emma again. That would be too cruel. But she did regret deceiving Harry and bringing worry to her mam. The only solution was to tell Harry the truth and suffer the consequences.

But knowing what she should do was very different to actually doing it. When he wasn't there she would rehearse over and over how she would sit down with him when he came in and quietly confess everything. But it never happened. For the minute he walked in the door her courage would fly out of the window. She kept telling herself it was ridiculous to be frightened of him. But deep down she knew what it was that kept her tongue silent. It was the fear that when Harry knew she'd gone against his wishes and lied to him, his disgust might be so great he'd pack his bags and leave.

'I'm taking one of my week's holidays next month.' Harry was tightening a loose screw in the kitchen cabinet while Mary was washing a few baby clothes in the sink. 'I'll be able to give this place a lick of paint and distemper the washhouse.' He opened and closed the cabinet door a few times, then grunted in satisfaction. 'That should be all right now.'

Mary didn't look round as she asked, 'What week are you taking off?'

'The third week in August. I think it's four weeks on Saturday.' Harry threw the screwdriver into a drawer. 'And will I be glad! Working seven days a week is no good.'

Mary's brain was turning. 'Wouldn't you be on afternoons that week?'

'Let's see ... what date is it on Saturday?' Harry pressed his fingers to his head and screwed his eyes up in concentration. 'Yep! I would be on afternoons.'

'You'd have been better taking a week off when you were on mornings.' Mary dug her fingers into the palm of her hand. How long was she going to have to go on scheming? She pulled the plug from the sink, and as the soapy water drained away she wished her lies and scheming could be drained away so easily.

'All the other supervisors had booked their holidays ages ago, so I had to take what was left,' Harry told her. 'Eileen's taking next week off. The kids start their summer holidays then.'

'I haven't seen Eileen for ages.' Mary swished the clothes round in the cold water filling the sink. 'I'll take Emma up there next week to see her.'

'She said she'll be up the wall when they're on holiday for six weeks.' The cleft in Harry's chin deepened when he grinned. 'I'll use her words because it wouldn't be funny otherwise.' His voice was a good imitation of the big woman's. 'I'll get no bloody peace at all now! Bloody Jean Simpson in work, and the bloody kids at home! I'd have a quieter life if I was bein' shot at by the bloody Germans!'

Mary's laugh rang out. 'I can just hear her saying that! She's a real case, isn't she? I don't half miss her when I don't see her for a while.' Mary took some pegs from the drawer. 'I want to get this washing out. Will you wake Emma for us? She won't sleep tonight if she's left too long.'

Harry didn't need asking twice. Emma was the brightest

spot in his life. Sometimes he asked himself if he'd still be there if it wasn't for the happiness she brought him. When she was lying in his arms, her blue eyes gazing up at him, he was filled with contentment. And her smile never failed to tug at his heart strings. She was his princess and he idolised her.

Chapter Twenty-Eight

'Hey, missus!'

Maggie rested her hand on the brass fender she was polishing and turned to see her daughter framed in the doorway. She sat back on her heels, rubbing a hand across the sweat glistening on her forehead. 'Well?'

'I've been havin' a natter with Cissie Maddox, an' we're takin' the kids to Southport tomorrer. We're takin' our eats with us . . . sarnies, cakes an' a flask of tea.' Drawing herself up to her full five feet four inches, Eileen squared her shoulders, pushing her enormous bust out. 'Cissie's makin' the sarnies, and guess what she's asked me to make.' Maggie could feel the floor boards tremble beneath her knees as Eileen's body shook with gales of laughter. 'Eighteen bloody fairy cakes!' Chubby, dimpled hands wiped at the tears running down her cheeks. 'An' yer know what my fairy cakes turn out like, don't yer, Mam!? I asked if she wanted rock cakes, but she didn't see the joke! No, she wants fairy cakes 'cos her kids like them!' Eileen clung to the door for support as she doubled up with mirth. 'Eighteen fairy cakes she wants, but eighteen rock cakes is what she'll get! The kids won't be able to eat them, but they can have a bloody good game of rounders with them!'

Maggie pressed at the stitch in her side. 'Stop making me laugh ... I've got a pain now! Anyway, I'll make the cakes. I'm not having the whole street thinking we can't even make cakes.' Maggie turned back to the fender and started to polish vigorously. 'I want to get this grate finished. They said Mr Churchill's speaking on the wireless after, and I want this place looking like a new pin by then.'

'Why? D'yer think he can see it?' Eileen crept forward and lifted her mother's skirt. 'Have yer put clean knickers on for 'im, too?'

'Get away with you! If you want to make yourself useful, go and put the kettle on.' Maggie screwed the top back on the Brasso tin and watched her daughter sway her way to the kitchen. People thought she was as hard as nails, but underneath all the swagger and the swearing, she was as soft as putty.

'Tea up, missus!' Eileen put the steaming cups down then ran a critical eye over the gleaming fireplace. 'Not bad, Mam! I don't think Churchill will have any complaints.'

The sound of high-pitched voices brought Eileen's fist down on the table. 'Shit! Just when yer think yer've got five minutes to yerself, the three bloody Stooges turn up!' She saw her mother's lips tighten in disapproval and groaned. 'I know! Watch me language! But honest to God, Mam, I'll swear those kids of mine can hear me backside hitting a chair from a mile away.' Her two daughters elbowed their way into the room, each determined to get to her first.

Although Edna was two years younger than Joan, she could certainly stick up for herself. 'Ay, Mam, can we go to the pictures tonight?' Edna's eyes were bright with excitement. 'Clark Gable and Myrna Loy are on the Astoria, and Doreen's mam said she'll take . . .' She broke off with a squeal and rubbed her arm. 'Ah, ray, Mam, our Joan just pinched me!'

'Serves yer right!' Joan threw her sister a dark look. 'Yer've always got to be first with everythin'.'

'Watch it, hard clock!' Eileen shook her head. 'In the house two minutes an' fightin' already! If yez don't behave yerselves, there'll be no Southport for yez temorrer.'

There was a stunned silence, then two voices squeaked, 'Southport?!'

'If yez behave yerselves! Mind you, if yer'd rather go to the flicks, it's no skin off my nose! Damned sight cheaper!'

'Oh, no!' the two voices chorused. Southport was definitely one up on going to the pictures. 'Can Doreen come with us?'

'Can she hell's like! I might be a sucker for punishment, but three kids are more than enough for me.'

Edna dug her sister in the ribs. 'Come 'ed, let's tell the gang.' Differences forgotten, the two girls made for the door, only to be brought to a brief halt by their mother's voice. 'Hang on a minute, hard clocks! A lot of mams can't afford to take their kids to Southport, so no swankin', d'yer hear?' Their running footsteps had no sooner faded than they were back again, 'Oh, God, what is it now?!' She glared at the two breathless girls. 'Whatever it is, the answer's no!'

'Mary's comin' up the road, Mam!'

Eileen shot from the chair. 'Mam, will yer clear these two cups away while I go and meet her? Yours 'as no handle on, and mine's more cracked than I am!' Eileen was standing on the step when Mary approached. 'Hiya, kid!' She bent to smile at Emma who was sitting up with a pillow at her back jerking her arms to get to the crowd of noisy children gathered around the gleaming Silver Cross pram.

'Can we walk her up and down, Auntie Mary?' Joan asked, with her arm pushing the other children away in a show of importance. 'We won't go off the side with her.' Seeing Mary's doubtful expression, she wheedled. 'Please? Only to the corner and back, no further.'

Mary eyed the pleading faces and didn't have the heart to object. 'Only to the corner, then.'

There would have been a fight over who was to have first go, but with their mother and Mary watching, Joan and Edna silently agreed to share the honour of pushing the 'posh' pram. Four thin hands curved round the handlebar, and with their friends taking up positions on either side, the procession set off.

'Look at the gobs on my two!' Eileen chuckled. 'Yer'd think butter wouldn't melt in their mouths, but they'll be tearin' each other's hair out later.'

'Let's go in and have a cup of tea.' Mary took her elbow. 'I want to have a talk to you.'

Maggie had already made a pot of tea and had managed to find two cups that not only had matching saucers, but boasted handles as well. She placed them on the table then excused herself. 'I've got some baking to do.'

'Don't yer ever sit down, Mam?' Eileen's chins wobbled. 'I'm sure yer've got a boil on yer backside or summat.'

'It's a pity you haven't got one on your tongue.' Maggie winked at Mary as she passed. 'I'll sit down when I've made the cakes.'

Eileen spread her dimpled elbows on the table. 'How's it goin', kid?'

'It's weeks since you've been to ours,' Mary scolded. 'Me and me mam were beginning to think you'd fallen out with us.'

'I've been busy, kid!' Then Eileen tutted with self disgust. 'What the hell am I lying for!? I haven't been to yours because the last time I was there I opened me mouth too much. An' I've made up me mind to keep out of your affairs.'

'I don't want you to keep out of my affairs!' Mary cried. 'And as for telling lies, you'd have to be good to beat me at that!'

'You tellin' lies, kid? Yer jokin'!'

This is the right time, Mary told herself. She wanted Eileen to hear it from her own lips and not from someone else. 'I've done more than tell lies,' she said softly. 'If I tell you the whole story, will you sit still and say nothing till I've finished?'

Eileen crossed her heart. 'Me lips are sealed.'

Mary laced the fingers of her two hands together and placed them palms down on the table. Her story began on the night of Bob's twenty-four-hour embarkation leave. Her voice was slow and faltering at first, but as she re-lived the last sixteen, unhappy months, the words poured forth, unstoppable. Every feeling she'd kept locked away for so long was now aired with a burning passion.

Eileen sat perfectly still, taking in every word. Her expressionless face hid her inner confusion. The torment on Mary's beautiful face, and in her voice, was having a profound effect as Eileen asked herself how she could have been so blind to Mary's needs.

Mary paused for a while, and the only sound in the room was the ticking of the clock on the mantelpiece. Then she took a deep breath. 'In the bottom of one of the drawers in my dressing table, hidden away so no one can see it, is a beautiful nightdress that Bob's mam must have spent hours embroidering for her granddaughter.' Mary's face looked drained. Everything was out in the open now, she'd left nothing out. 'So now you know.'

Eileen sniffed loudly. 'It's not often I'm stuck for words, kid, but yer've fair knocked the stuffin' out of me.'

'D'you think I've done the right thing, Eileen? I think me mam agrees with me, but she won't say so because of Harry.'

'Don't yer think I've interfered in yer life enough, kid? If I'd minded me own business in the first place, yer wouldn't have married Harry, and yer life might have been different.' Eileen picked up her cup and swirled the dregs of tea leaves around. 'But I still think he's the best thing that ever happened to yer, and I'll never change me mind about that! An' I think if yer tell him, quiet like, what yer've just told me, he'll understand. Yer should have done it ages ago, kid, instead of shuttin' him out like yer have.'

'But d'you think I've done the right thing?'

'Yes, kid, I do! But I wouldn't tell Harry that if I were you. He wouldn't take kindly to yer talkin' to me instead of him.'

Mary blew out a deep breath. 'I feel better now I've been able to get it all off me chest. I haven't known a minute's peace since Emma was born.' A troubled look crossed her face. 'But I'm dreading telling Harry.'

'Do it right away, kid.' Eileen advised. 'Putting trouble off is like the interest at the pawn shop . . . it gets bigger every day.'

Mary had braced herself for an argument, but nothing had prepared her for the rage which followed the mention of the Wests' name. Harry's face was contorted with anger as he pointed an accusing finger at her. 'You know how I feel about them, but you've deliberately gone against me wishes.'

'I've said I'm sorry.' Mary's eyes were wide. 'If you'll give me a chance to explain.'

'Explain! What is there to explain!?' Harry's anger was fuelled by fear. He saw this as the beginning of the end of their marriage. If Mary had any intention of trying to make a go of it, she'd never have done this to him. 'You've done many things to hurt me, Mary, but I never thought when we got married that you'd ever cheat me.'

Mary jumped to her feet. 'It was you who talked me into getting married!' she shouted. 'You and Eileen, and me mam! I didn't want to marry you!' She spun round, away from the stunned, hurt look on his face. Oh, she should never have said that, it was cruel. 'I'm sorry, I didn't mean that.'

'Oh, yes you did! It's probably the only true thing you've said since the day we got married.' Mary turned to face him, and now it was her turn to show anger. 'Ask yourself this! If your mam and dad died, would you be able to push them out of your mind and never mention their name again? Of course you couldn't; it wouldn't be natural! But that's what everyone expected of me! Forget Bob, and forget his mam and dad! They were like my own family, but I'm supposed to forget them! Well, I can't do that!'

'You don't seem to have any trouble forgetting you've got a husband, though do you?' They were facing each other now, and Harry's face loomed nearer. 'It's me that doesn't exist as far as you're concerned!'

'Don't let's shout at each other, please, Harry!' Mary made a move to touch him, but drew back. 'I've come to terms with Bob's death now. But I'll never be settled in my mind until I can mention his name without fear of upsetting someone, and by letting his mam and dad be part of his daughter's life. She's all they've got left of him.' Mary saw the pain her words inflicted, and felt a great sadness. But these things needed to be brought out in the open.'Why can't you understand they wouldn't be a threat to our marriage? You are Emma's daddy, and you always will be. And your parents will always be her nanna and granddad. Nothing will ever change that. All the Wests want is to see Emma for half an hour every few weeks. Is that too much to ask? They have so little, we have so much.'

'What have I got, Mary, apart from your mam and Emma?' Harry's pain was so great he groaned aloud. 'I haven't got a wife, that's for sure! You're not married to me, you're married to a ghost!'

'And that ghost will never be laid to rest until I keep faith with it. Then I'll be able to start a new life.' Mary's quiet voice went on.'Our marriage can survive if I have a clear conscience, Harry, I know it can. So I'm asking you to understand and help me.'

Harry sat down, his anger spent. 'If I couldn't feel any sympathy for the Wests, and all they've gone through, I'd have to be made of stone. And I'm not a hard man, Mary. I have all the sympathy in the world for them, and I understand how they feel about Emma. But I'm frightened that, through them, she might find out I'm not her real daddy. And that would kill me. She means everything to me.'

'That will never happen, Harry, I promise.' Mary was close to tears. 'I know I've given you no reason to trust me, but on this you have my solemn word.'

Harry banged his hand against his forehead. 'I can't see it working out! What are you going to tell Emma when she's older and asks questions about who they are?'

'We'll do it in such a way that no one gets hurt, I'll make sure of that.' Mary held his gaze. 'Just don't deny them the chance of getting to know their own granddaughter. She's all the family they've got now.'

Harry dropped his eyes. 'I won't stop you from taking Emma to see them, Mary. But try and understand things from my point of view. Seeing them with her would be a constant reminder to me that she's not really mine, and I couldn't bear that. So I don't want them ever to come to this house. Will you give me your promise on that?'

'I promise.' Mary closed her eyes and thanked God for answering her prayers.

That night, Mary went to bed first as usual. And when Harry had finished reading the paper he popped his head round Martha's door to say goodnight before climbing the stairs. He saw a glimmer of light from Mary's room and thought Emma must have woken up. But when he reached the landing he found Mary standing in her doorway, silhouetted in the light from her bedside lamp. 'I've brought your pyjamas in here.' Mary spoke softly before walking back into her room.

His heart racing, Harry stood for a moment. Then he followed Mary and closed the door behind him.

The weeks sped by in an atmosphere of pleasant harmony. The guilt she'd carried for so long had gone now, and Mary went out of her way to please Harry and make up for all the pain she'd caused. She was friendly and affectionate with him, but somehow couldn't show the loving she knew he craved. If Doris came in to babysit for them and they went to the pictures, she found it easy and natural to slip her hand into his in the darkness of the cinema. But she could never bring herself to throw her arms round him or kiss him. And no matter how hard she tried to return his kisses with feeling, she could tell by the disappointment in his eyes that that certain something was missing. It was the same in bed. She wanted to be a good wife and willed herself to match the passion in Harry's lovemaking. But no matter how hard she tried, the spark was missing. And although Harry never spoke of it, she knew he was deeply hurt. She kept asking herself why she couldn't love him, but she had no answer. Except, perhaps, that true love only comes along once. And her chance of a lifetime filled with love had died with Bob.

Harry came home from work one day to find Emma had pulled the tablecloth off the table and Mary was on her hands and knees picking up pieces of broken crockery. 'I left her for ten seconds to go out to the bin, and came back to this!' Mary sat back on her heels. 'She's been one little tinker today! You need eyes in the back of your head to keep up with her!'

Harry's eyes went to the high chair where the cause of the trouble was now confined. He found an angel face creased in a welcoming smile, and two arms outstretched to be picked up. 'Just look at her! Who could fall out with a face like that?'

'I hope you feel the same when there's no sugar for your tea.' Mary went back to clearing up the mess. 'The sugar basin was on the table, and that went for a burton, too! A whole week's ration is mixed in with this lot.'

'You're in Mummy's bad books today, princess!' Harry raised the table front of the high chair and lifted Emma out. 'You've been very naughty.'

'You haven't heard the half of it yet,' Mary complained. 'I caught her with my purse this morning, and before I could get to her, she'd put a penny in her mouth! I was worried sick! I had to coax her with a biscuit, to open her mouth. And while I was putting me purse in the cupboard where she couldn't reach it, she was halfway up the stairs!'

'I'll put gates on the top and bottom of the stairs, and that should put a halt to your gallop, young lady.'

'I don't like getting bad tempered with her, but she wears me out!' Mary looked up to see Emma raining kisses on Harry's nose, and her mood softened. He was so good to Emma, and the baby adored him. 'I've tried keeping her in the high chair while I get me work done, but she jerks back and forward on it, and I'm frightened of it tipping over. And I can't leave her in me mam's room, 'cos she's into everything and me mam can't handle her.'

'Get a play pen,' Harry suggested. 'It would solve all your problems. She could play in it to her heart's content while you do your work.'

'That's a good idea! I'll have a look round tomorrow.'

But when Mary went into Emma's room the next morning, all thoughts of a play pen were forgotten. Instead of the usual happy smile, the baby's face was grey and her eyes dull and lifeless. Mary held the little body close, and a shiver of fear ran down her spine when she felt the cold, clammy forehead. She ran down the stairs, crying, 'Mam, there's something wrong with Emma!'

'Give her here, lass.' With Mary supporting the limp form, Martha examined Emma's body for tell-tale signs of measles or chicken pox. She could find no rash or spots, but the dull, glazed eyes told her all was not well. 'She's probably sickening for something.' Martha tried not to sound alarmed. 'It could be the measles, or she could be teething.'

'But she's already got eight teeth, and she wasn't like this when they were coming through.' Mary clutched Emma to her breast and rocked gently from side to side.

'Lass, you don't know you're born with her! Most babies cry all the time when they're teething.'

'Then why isn't she crying now?!' Mary wasn't to be consoled. 'I wouldn't mind if she was crying, but she's so lifeless!'

'Lay her on my bed and go and ask Doris to come in.' Not for the first time Martha cursed her own inability to help. 'See what she thinks.'

Doris was still in her dressing gown, but one look at Mary's distraught face and she was out of the door without a thought how she looked. She stood beside the bed looking down on the still figure. 'I don't know what to think, Mary! Your mam's probably right; she could be sickening for something.'

Mary was kneeling beside the bed, her hand stroking the fevered brow, her eyes watching how laboured her daughter's breathing was. 'Ring for the doctor for us, would you, Doris? I can't sit and watch her like this without doing anything.'

'I'll ring right away, and I'll ask him to come as soon as he can.' Doris turned at the door. 'Don't go worrying now! It's probably nothing!'

Mary looked across at her mother. 'I am worried, Mam! I wish Harry was home. He'd know what to do.'

* * *

Mary was in the hall when Harry opened the door and she flung herself at him, crying, 'Our Emma's sick!'

Harry put his two arms around her while kicking the door closed with his foot. 'There now,' he murmured soothingly. 'Stop crying and tell me what's wrong.'

Mary left the comfort of his arms to raise a tear-streaked face. 'I've had the doctor out to Emma.'

With visions of his beloved princess falling down the stairs, or tipping her high chair over, the initial joy of having Mary rush into his arms turned to fear. But seeing Mary's distress, he tried to speak calmly. 'Don't get yourself upset. Just tell me what's wrong.'

Mary jerked her head. 'Come and see her. She's in me mam's room.'

Harry passed Martha without a glance, dropping his coat on the floor as he went. He bent over the bed first, then dropped to his knees and took a tiny, hot hand in his. 'Hello, my little princess! Daddy's here to make you better.'

Emma turned her head on the pillow, but that was her only response. Her eyes remained closed, as though the effort to open them was too much. Harry felt her forehead, then his eyes met Mary's across the bed. 'What did the doctor say?'

'He said he's not sure. Her temperature's very high, but he said she could be in for chicken pox, 'cos there's a lot of it around.'

'And if it's not chicken pox?'

'I don't know!' Mary's nerves were near breaking point. 'She's been like that all day! I can't even get her to open her eyes!' She sat on the side of the bed and stroked the blonde curls, wet now with perspiration. 'If she's not better tomorrow I'm to call him out again. He's left some medicine, and said she's to be kept in the same temperature. So I'm bringing her cot down here, and I'll sleep in with me mam.'

The night seemed never ending to Mary. She was out of bed every few minutes to make sure Emma was still breathing, and even standing at the side of the cot she could feel the heat from her daughter's body.

'It's always worse at night, lass,' Martha whispered when she felt Mary slipping back into bed. 'She may be a bit brighter in the morning.' But even as she was trying to reassure Mary, Martha was worrying herself sick. She was no doctor, but she thought the baby was too ill to be just sickening for chicken pox.

Harry popped his head round the door at five o'clock. He hadn't been able to sleep, either. 'What sort of night has she had?'

'She hasn't moved! A couple of times I couldn't hear her breathing, and I thought she was dead.' Mary's tearful voice echoed her fear and desperation. 'It's been the longest night of me life.'

Harry crossed to peer over the cot, and an icy hand clutched his heart. His darling princess, usually full of smiles, looked like a china doll. There was no movement from her at all. 'I'll take the day off.'

'No, you mustn't stay off!' Mary would dearly have loved him to stay by her side, because she was so frightened of what the day held in store. But she had to be sensible about it. Other women didn't make their husbands stay off work every time one of their children was sick. 'As soon as I hear them moving around next door, I'll ask Doris to ring for the doctor.'

Harry hovered over the cot. 'I think I should stay off.'

'Harry, if the doctor says it's anything serious, I'll get Doris to ring the factory and you can come home.'

After Harry had left, Mary banked up the fire then made some tea and toast and carried it through to the front room. But the toast tasted like cotton wool in her mouth, and after the one mouthful she could eat no more. But she was thankful for the cup of tea. With her hands curled round the cup, she faced her mother. 'When I've had this, I'll wash and change Emma. It should be about eight o'clock then, and I can knock next door.'

Martha watched with growing concern as Mary laid the still form on her lap and eased off the nightdress, sodden with perspiration. There was no sound from the baby and no resistance. She was like a rag doll. 'I'd nip next door now, if I were you.' Martha spoke calmly so as not to alarm Mary. She could sense her daughter was trying hard to hold back the tears. 'If Doris rings the doctor early enough, she'll catch him before he starts his surgery.'

It was half past eight when the doctor arrived, and after a brief examination of Emma, he turned to Mary, his face serious. 'I'm afraid it's pneumonia, Mrs Sedgemoor.'

'Oh, no!' Mary could feel her legs buckle and she clung to the back of a chair for support. 'Is she going to be all right?'

'I don't think it would be advisable to move her to

hospital.' The doctor ignored Mary's question. 'I'll leave you something to make her more comfortable, and I'll call back this afternoon.'

'She's not going to die, is she?' Mary grabbed his arm and shook it. 'Tell me! I want to know!'

'Mrs Sedgemoor, no doctor can ever say that with any certainty. The next forty-eight hours are critical. If you think you can't cope, then I'll send her to hospital. But I'd rather not move her.'

'I can look after her!' Mary looked to her mother for reassurance. 'Can't I, Mam? Just tell me what to do, and I'll do it!'

'Keep her warm, and make sure there are no draughts. That's probably how she caught pneumonia in the first place. If you drape a sheet around the sides of the cot, it will keep out any cold air that comes in every time you open the door. Wash her down frequently with a soft, damp cloth, and try to get some milk down her.' The doctor snapped his bag shut. 'I'll call back this afternoon, but if you need me before, get your neighbour to ring.'

'My husband asked me to ring his works if it was serious,' Mary said, her hands clasped tightly in front of her. 'Shall I get him to come home?'

The doctor shook his head. 'Let's see how she is this afternoon. And if you have any visitors, don't let them in this room because they'll bring the cold in with them.'

When Doris called later, Mary kept her in the hall while she explained. 'I'm sorry, Doris, but I can't let you see Emma. But you can do me a favour if you're going to the shops. I only need bread today, and this letter posting.'

Mary handed over the letter she'd scribbled to the Wests to say why she wouldn't be able to meet them as arranged. If it wasn't posted today they mightn't get it in time.

Chapter Twenty-Nine

'Go and put your feet up for half an hour, lass, while you've got the chance.' Martha eyed the fatigue on her daughter's face, and the dark circles under her eyes. 'The baby's resting easy now, and she should sleep for a couple of hours.'

'I'll sit here and rest.' Mary yawned as she flopped into the chair and stretched her legs out. 'Every bone in me body is aching.'

'I'm not surprised, going without sleep for four nights! If you're not careful you'll be knocking yourself up! The doctor's just told you the crisis is past, so you could go and lie on the bed for an hour and get a proper rest. I'll call you if Emma wakes up.'

'No, I'd rather stay here. I know the doctor said the worst is over, but she's still poorly.' Mary rubbed the back of her neck. 'I'll have to get Harry to seal the window in her bedroom before she goes back in there.' Mary's lids began to close. 'And block the fireplace up.'

In a matter of seconds Mary was sleeping soundly, and Martha nodded, satisfied. No one could go without sleep for four days, and if Mary didn't watch it she'd be ill herself.

Harry had tried to coax her to go to bed last night while he stayed up with Emma, but Mary wouldn't hear of it. Wild horses couldn't have dragged her from her daughter's side.

Martha picked up a magazine and skimmed through the pages, looking at the pictures. Her mind was too full to concentrate on the words that went with them. Then, through the silence, came the sound of the front knocker. 'Blast!' Martha glanced quickly at Mary, but her daughter was in too deep a sleep to have been woken by the sound. Martha said a silent prayer that whoever was at the door would go away. But seconds later came another knock, louder and more persistent this time.

'Mary! There's someone at the door, lass!'

Mary sat up, startled. Rubbing her eyes, she stumbled to her feet. 'I must have dropped off.' Her legs were so weak she expected them to buckle under her as she made her way down the hall. But when she opened the door and saw who her visitors were, her tiredness vanished. She stared, so surprised she couldn't speak.

'We had to come, love.' It was Bob West who spoke. He had his arm around his wife's waist, as though holding her up. 'We couldn't rest, not knowing how Emma is, could we, Lily?'

Bob's mam and dad looked so forlorn Mary's heart went out to them. 'I'm sorry! I shouldn't keep you standing on the step.' Mary held her hand out. 'Come in.'

'Mary looks terrible.' Harry was standing by Eileen's machine. 'She's absolutely worn out. I tried to talk her into going to bed last night but she wouldn't even consider it.'

'I'd never leave one of mine when they were sick, either!' Eileen pushed the turban up out of her eyes. She could never get the hang of tying the blasted thing so it would stay put. 'An' the doctor said Emma's over the worst did 'e?'

'So he said when he came this morning. She's far from well, and we've got to watch her, but he said the fever had broken and we should start seeing an improvement over the next few days.' Harry leaned his back against the conveyor. 'It hasn't half taken it out of Mary, though. She looked so lousy when I came out, I wanted to take the day off, but she wouldn't hear of it.'

'Yer shouldn't have taken any notice of her.' Eileen moved around him and picked out a shell from the moving belt. 'Why don't yer go an' see Mr Glover now, and ask if yer can go 'ome? He won't mind if yer explain 'ow things are.'

With a picture of Mary's tired face in his mind, it only needed Eileen's words to galvanise Harry into action. 'Right! I'll do it! I never take time off, so he can't complain.'

'Send 'im to me if he does!' Her chins wobbling, Eileen rolled her sleeves over her elbows. Her chubby hands curled into fists, she took up a fighting stance, making Harry grin. 'I'll knock 'im into the middle of next week!'

There was sadness on Martha's face as she watched Lily West bend over the cot and gently stroke Emma's flushed face. It was two years now since Martha had seen the Wests, and those two years of worry and grief had certainly taken their toll. They didn't look like the same two people.

Martha turned her head quickly. She could have sworn she heard the sound of a key in the front door. But she couldn't have. Apart from Mary, the only other person with a key to the front door was Harry, and he was in work. Then she heard the distinct sound of a key being turned then pulled from the lock, and she knew she wasn't imagining things. 'Here's Harry!'

Three faces turned towards Martha, but before her words had time to register the door opened and Harry walked in. There was complete silence as four people, as still as statues, watched Harry's eyes move from one to the other. They saw his initial look of surprise turn briefly to anger, then bewilderment.

Mary broke the silence. Walking towards him, she said softly, 'I didn't know Mr and Mrs West were coming, Harry, it was a surprise.'

'That's true, lad.' Bob West stood up. 'Lily was so worried about the baby she wouldn't let up until I brought her.'

Harry felt as though his head was going to burst. He was floundering in a sea of conflicting emotions, and it showed on his face as he looked from the Wests to Martha, then to Mary, then back again to Lily West.

'Come on, love.' Bob West held his hand out to his wife. 'We'd better be on our way.'

For a second Lily looked defiant. Then her shoulders slumped in surrender. She kissed her finger and placed it on Emma's cheek before walking towards her husband's outstretched hand. Her head was bent as she passed Harry, but it didn't hide the tear trickling slowly down her cheek.

'No, don't go!' His voice broken, Harry touched her arm. 'It's only natural you've been worried about the baby. So stay for a while . . . please!'

When Lily raised her head there was a puzzled expression on her face, as though she didn't trust her hearing. She looked to Mary for reassurance, and when Mary nodded, hope flared in Lily's eyes. 'We'd like to stay, if you're sure you don't mind.'

Harry felt Mary's hand slip through his arm and he squeezed it gently before saying, 'You're welcome.'

Harry was very quiet for the hour the Wests stayed. His eyes kept straying to Lily, and the love and concern written on her face as she gazed down at Emma made him ask himself how he could ever have wanted to keep her away from her son's daughter. It was easy to deny somebody something when you didn't have to see the suffering your selfishness caused, but being faced with it, as he was now, filled him with sadness.

'If you're sure you don't mind us coming on a Sunday, it would save me taking a day off work.' Bob West craned his neck to look up at Mary and Harry who were standing on the top step. 'We wouldn't come till the afternoon, to give you a chance to get your dinner over.' He put his arm across his wife's shoulders. 'Shall we say three o'clock, love?' Lily smiled up at him. They had both grown in stature and confidence over the last hour, and the strain on their faces eased. Life would continue to get better now they had something to live for.

After Mary had closed the door, Harry followed her down the hall and caught her around the waist as she went to turn into Martha's room. 'Can we talk for five minutes?' Without waiting for an answer he propelled her into the back room, and when she went to speak he put a hand gently over her mouth. 'Don't say a word till I've got it all off me chest.' He pushed her down into the rocking chair and sat facing her. 'What a selfish bastard I've been! It's a wonder you don't hate me.'

'I don't hate . . .' Mary's words petered out when Harry lifted his hand.

'Let me finish before you say anything.' Harry studied his nails before going on. 'There's no excuse for the way I've behaved because at the back of me mind I've known all along that what I was doing was wrong. But I wouldn't admit it. You see I didn't want anyone in your life that would remind you of Bob. I thought if I had to compete with him, I'd lose you. Yes, I was even jealous of Bob, Mary! Jealous because he died fighting for his country while I've got a nice, safe, cushy job in civvie street.' Harry pounded a fist on the arm of his chair. 'I knew what I was expecting from you was wrong, but until I saw the Wests with Emma today, I didn't realise how wrong. I don't feel very proud of meself, I can tell you.'

Mary was putting herself in Harry's place, and understanding him as she never had before. A wave of tenderness swept over her, 'We've both made mistakes, Harry.' Mary bent forward to straighten the rug in front of the brass fender to give herself a few seconds to sort things out in her mind. She remembered the icy hand of fear that had clutched her heart when Harry had walked in unexpectedly. Right away she saw the scene from his eyes. How could he be expected to believe the Wests hadn't been invited, especially at a time when he should be at work. It was then Mary realised how much she cared what Harry thought.

Mary straightened up. Today, all her wishes had been granted and her dreams come true. She felt so calm, so at peace with the world. 'We can put all our mistakes behind us, Harry, and start again.' She said softly. 'As me mam always says, "as one door closes, another door opens".'

'Can we start again, Mary?' Harry's dark brown eyes pleaded.

'What you did today has made it possible for me to close the door on one part of me life, Harry! It was the best present you could ever have given me.' Mary stood up, a smile hovering round the corners of her mouth. She crossed the room and sat on his lap. 'I think now is the right time to give you your present.'

Harry quirked an eyebrow as he pulled her closer. 'You bought me a present?'

'Well, it's to share between Emma and me mam, and me of course, but mostly it's yours.' Mary cupped his face between her hands. 'It wasn't bought with money, Harry, it was bought with love.' She brushed his lips with hers before whispering, 'I'm pregnant.'

HOME IS WHERE THE HEART IS

A Heartwarming Liverpool Saga

Joan Jonker

When fun-loving, eighteen-stone Eileen Gillmoss announces that she's expecting a baby, her husband Bill thinks it's another of her jokes. After all, it's twelve years since Edna, their youngest, was born. But when it sinks in that a baby really is on the way, Bill is over the moon and decides the family should move out of their two-up-two-down terraced house in Liverpool to one with more spacious accommodation.

Eileen digs her heels in at first, reluctant to leave the house she loves and friends and neighbours so dear. But a scare in the early stages of her pregnancy strengthens Bill's resolve to provide a more comfortable home for his wife and he finds the answer when a house becomes available in the road where their best friends Mary and Harry Sedgemoor live. Before Eileen knows what's hit her, she's installed in a smart home in a tree-lined road, with posh new neighbours.

Then tragedy strikes and Eileen must come to terms with a loss far greater than leaving her beloved neighbourhood. She tries to put on a brave face, but she can't fool the people who love her, who miss the smile on that round, chubby face and the laughter ringing through her house. They vow to make amends and fate steps in to lend a helping hand.

Packed with sympathetic characters and a wealth of emotions, Joan Jonker's Liverpool sagas, including *When One Door Closes* and *Man Of The House* (also available from Headline), bring to life a close-knit Liverpudlian community in a bygone age.

FICTION / SAGA 0 7472 4861 3

Try a Little Tenderness

Joan Jonker

Jenny and Laura Nightingale are as different as chalk and cheese. Jenny's pretty face and lively sense of humour make her everyone's favourite girl, whereas Laura is spoilt and moody and never out of trouble. Their mother, Mary, loves them both but she's more worried about her father's new wife, Celia, who is about to bring shame on the family . . .

Then Jenny attracts the attention of two young lads in the street who both want to court her. Mick and John have been mates since they were kids but now war is declared and it's every man for himself! Meanwhile, Laura's resentment begins to build and it's only a matter of time before things come to a head. Who will learn that a little tenderness goes a long way?

'A hilarious but touching story of life in Liverpool' *Woman's Realm*

'You can rely on Joan to give her readers hilarity and pathos in equal measure and she's achieved it again in this tale' *Liverpool Echo*

'Packed with lively, sympathetic characters and a wealth of emotions' *Bolton Evening News*

0 7472 6110 5

HEADLINE

Stay as Sweet as You Are

Joan Jonker

With the face of an angel and a sunny nature, Lucy Mellor is a daughter who'd make any parents proud. But her ever ready smile masks a dark secret. For while her friends are kissed and hugged by their mothers, Lucy only knows cruelty from the woman who brought her into the world. Her father, Bob, tries to protect her, but he is no match for a wife who has no love for him or his beloved daughter.

The Walls of their two-up two-down house are thin and Ruby Mellor's angry outbursts can be heard by their neighbours. One day, Irene Pollard, from next door, decides she can no longer stand back, so she and her friends take Lucy under their wing. But sadness remains in Lucy's heart because, despite everything, she still craves a mother's love . . .

'Hilarious but touching' *Woman's Realm*

'You can rely on Joan to give her readers hilarity and pathos in equal measure and she's achieved it again in this tale' *Liverpool Echo*

'Packed with lively, sympathetic characters and a wealth of emotions' *Bolton Evening News*

0 7472 6111 3

HEADLINE

Now you can buy any of these other bestselling books by **Joan Jonker** from your bookshop or *direct from her publisher*.

FREE P&P AND UK DELIVERY
(Overseas and Ireland £3.50 per book)

After the Dance is Over	£5.99
Many a Tear Has to Fall	£5.99
Dream a Little Dream	£5.99
Stay as Sweet as You Are	£5.99
Try a Little Tenderness	£5.99
Walking My Baby Back Home	£5.99
Sadie Was a Lady	£6.99
The Pride of Polly Perkins	£5.99
Sweet Rosie O'Grady	£5.99
Last Tram to Lime Street	£5.99
Stay in Your Own Back Yard	£5.99
Home is Where the Heart is	£5.99
Man of the House	£5.99
When One Door Closes	£5.99

TO ORDER SIMPLY CALL THIS NUMBER

01235 400 414

or e-mail <u>orders@bookpoint.co.uk</u>

Prices and availability subject to change without notice.